Secrets of Alkrose

Alkrose Academy

Book 2

K.M. Moronova

Copyright © 2024 by K. M. Moronova LLC

Cover done by K. M. Moronova LLC

Formatting done by K. M. Moronova LLC

Interior character art done by K. M. Moronova LLC

Stock images licensed through Canvas

All rights reserved.

No part of this book may be reproduced in any form or by any electronic or mechanical means, including information storage and retrieval systems, without written permission from the author, except for the use of brief quotations in a book review.

This is a work of fiction. Names, characters, places, and incidents are the product of the author's imagination or are used fictitiously. Any resemblance to actual events, locales, or persons, living or dead, is purely coincidental.

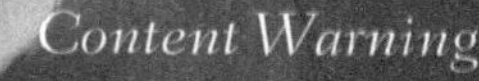

Content Warning

This is an adult dark fantasy/romance book. Some of the content in this book may be triggering for readers. This includes explicit war topics (if you are at all sensitive to war in any shape/form I suggest not reading this book), physical violence, child death, murder, morally gray characters, childhood trauma, and war trauma.

Explicit: War, death, sex, gore.

Fernestia
Alkrose
Grimrose Island
Forbidding Ridge
nnah
Cyprin
Camp
Henniston
Navasik
Fields
Heirah
Barkovah
Whales of Tauh
Tornfret

Playlist

Surrender - IAMX
Casualty - Hidden Citizens
Nocturnal - Elle Vee
Scared of the Dark - Lil Wayne
Love no more - Cody Loaves
2WEI - What a wonderful world
Breathe - Fleurie
Never forget you - Zara Larsson
What could have been - Arcane
Middle of the night - Loveless cover (Ellen Duhe)

Also by K.M. Moronova

Pine Hollow Series (complete)

(Dark Romantasy. Gods/Reincarnation. Why Choose)

A God of Wrath & Lies

A God of Death & Rest

A Goddess of Life & Dawn

Alkrose Academy Series

(Epic Dark Fantasy. Enemies to lovers. Why Choose)

Of Deathless Shadows

Secrets of Alkrose

—

Stand Alones

The Fabric of our Souls (*Contemporary Dark Romance/Thriller*)

For those who enjoy walking the line between the Shadows

1

Terra

The air of Alkrose Academy is thick with power, making the hairs on the back of my neck rise.

I stare at my dear brother. After everything that I've gone through to get here, why am I not relieved to see him? The betrayal of my emotions confuses me.

Neither of us is hasty to speak. Edgar stands prim and proper, wearing black Fernestian tactical gear with a white cloak clasped at his neck, a bright crescent moon emblem at its center. His eyes glow with turquoise lines that weave through the normal green hue, like shattered glass—fissured and broken. The dark circles beneath his eyes make him look paler than I remember.

"Edgar." I say his name in a hushed tone, unintentionally voicing my confusion and sadness. He looks so much older, yet it's only been a matter of a month. It's sickening how much can change when your entire life is ripped out from beneath you.

His glare is accusatory, hostile, filled with hatred. A dreadful sensation sinks into my bones as the air between us ignites with dark energy. So much anger and chaos flickers across his eyes.

His Shadow is a presence my own rejects, pushing against each other like opposing magnets, but the tension feels so much heavier than that. Amser shudders under my skin.

Edgar and I are predators intruding on one another's territory. The two of us stare at each other in horrible, festering silence before Edgar coldly turns away. His light brown hair still curls at the ends just enough to give him the innocent appearance of a boy, but his stride has new purpose, his fists clench tightly at his sides with a million things he's refusing to say.

What is it he thinks I've done?

My fists curl instinctively with the rejection, but that's where my emotions stay. I don't let any of it sink further than that. My Shadow keeps my heart guarded. It's a nice way to avoid the situation.

That's what I'm good at, after all: avoiding shit.

I glance back to the portal we stepped through a mere moment ago, shimmering like black diamonds. Elias emerges last. The portal seizes behind him and dissipates into shadows. I smile hesitantly at him, admiring the way his cold, callous eyes remain impassive to all but me. Once he sees me smiling at him, his features soften momentarily.

I'm comforted that he's here with me. We weathered

the worst of Barkovah together. Though, he *is* the reason it went to shit there to begin with—the beacon for the Void. There's a voice screaming somewhere far beneath the icy veil inside me. My Shadow, Amser, mutes the voice, but I can still hear the faint whispers of my conscience.

He killed everyone. He's responsible. He's the assassin of Fernestia.

I blink to clear my head and let the voice fall into the depths.

It's better this way. *I'm* better this way.

Arthur smiles nostalgically, staring up at the balcony. "It's been a long time since I've been back here." His words lift through the impossibly tall ceilings of the foyer, traces of sun trickling through the enormous windows. The stone walls are immaculate; hardly so much as a crack runs through the gray structure. The fine, glossy floors are marbled and slick. A curved staircase sits on each side of the foyer, joining at the center on the second-floor balcony. Dark shadows cling to the hallways above, drawing my curiosity. I wonder what things this castle hides within its walls.

It's a castle, a really fucking nice one. *Alkrose Academy.* The mysterious and looming name finally has an image. In my head, it seemed black, like a smudge on a map that held only death and illness. A place to die. But it's anything but that in person.

"What exactly is Alkrose's purpose?" I murmur absently as I take in the space around us. Raine looks around with wide eyes as well. He's still completely covered in blood from the fight back in Barkovah. His black hair is wet and slicked to his head. Those blue eyes are bright in contrast though, the crescent Nova moons still glowing around his irises with a turquoise hue.

He seems different. I don't know if it's because of his new Shadow or because of everyone and everything he lost in the city. Or perhaps both. I don't know him very well, seemingly, as we have only known one another for a little more than a week. But there's a distinct change in his mannerism—his air.

I think of the way he pinned me in the stairwell not but ten minutes prior. Destiny... For all I know, he may have lived a thousand lifetimes inside his head in a mere moment. His tired posture, slumped shoulders, and weary frown make me want to hold him and ask him a thousand questions about those possible lifetimes he's already witnessed.

Elias straightens his back and cracks his neck as he walks ahead of us, gesturing to the castle itself in an exaggerated manner. "It is a school for those cursed with Shadows. We break your fucking soul down into powder, add blood, mash you up into clay, then reform you into whatever the fuck the headmaster wants. *The heartless will thrive.*" He recites the latter sarcastically.

Arthur sets his hand on Elias's shoulder. "Let's not give them the entire morbid mantra just yet."

Elias's gray eyes harden at us, ignoring Arthur. "*And the ones with hearts will die.*"

I narrow my eyes and share a concerned look with Raine. His lips press together and a muscle feathers on his jaw, but he remains silent.

"Glad I'm so listened to," Arthur says with a mild grin. He comes off as difficult to piss off. Patience and understanding seem second nature to him. "Anyway, you'll have to excuse Edgar for the time being, Terra. He was restored last night and... well, he isn't taking to it so well, I'm afraid."

Restored? What did they do to him?

Arthur reads my expression and clarifies, "His memories were lost. I gave them back to him and he's having a hard time processing them." He looks back to Elias without skipping a beat, not giving me a chance to press him on it. "I'll show them to the Nova House." The white cloak around Arthur's shoulders lacks any dirt or grime. His beautiful raven-colored hair looks soft and only makes his gray eyes appear more haunting and alluring.

Elias nods to him and looks back at me, want and something else I can't place rimming his eyes. "You will be assigned your own rooms. Arthur will take care of you until I return this evening," he says tepidly.

After all the time we've spent traveling together and all the people he killed so coldly on my behalf, it feels strange to part with him again. We've only just been reunited. My brows pull together tightly but I keep my mouth shut. One thing I've learned with Elias is that it's his way or nothing.

"That's fine with me," I reply, threading my fingers through Raine's and smiling. Arthur's lips quirk into a grin at my remark but Elias lets out a long breath.

"You're insufferable," he growls, his voice low. "Arthur, I'll leave them to you now. I need to speak with Emerai." He shoves his hands into the pockets of his black military pants and walks up the curved staircase. I fight the urge to watch him go.

Arthur smiles and waves for us to follow him. "Sorry

about Elias, he's always been rather arrogant." We follow behind him as he leads us down the corridor beneath the balcony.

"Is he truly the Assassin of Fernestia?" Raine asks as we come out the other end and reach another set of massive stairs. They are straight, made of stone, and much wider than the curved sets in the foyer, facing the outer wall of the castle.

We ascend to the second story and find ourselves in a magnificent hall with high ceilings stretching to the other side of the castle. Maroon banners hang on pillars that frame lancet windows. They emit lovely ambient light, making me and Raine look like heinous murderers.

I focus on how dark the blood is on my hands, trying to place how many people's last drops might be clinging to my skin. Arthur has hardly acknowledged our abhorrent appearances. We stop at two large doors before Arthur turns to look at Raine.

"Yes, he is. And you'd be smart to remember it. Elias is Dr. Cein's right-hand dog and the headmaster's favorite weapon. He's hardly even human anymore. I'd stay far from his bad side." He gives me a pointed look as he says the latter. "Whatever kindness he's shown you up until now will most likely stop. That man has no heart."

No heart. That can't be true. He and I have a connection, one that seeps deeper than just our Shadows, no matter how much I despise it.

"Does he remain here at Alkrose?" I dare ask. I'm not sure whether I'd prefer his presence here or for him to leave and forget about me forever.

"Of course. He goes out on missions occasionally like

he did for this operation, but he's the destruction class instructor. You'll have classes with him weekly."

Raine groans at that but Amser warms in my chest. *Gods.* I can't deny the relief I feel within my own heart as well.

"I believe the other Houses are outside at the moment, so now is a good time for me to show you two around. You'll both be under my guidance here. The other Houses are beneath our Nova status, but you can still mingle with them. Terra, you will be pleased to know that Edgar is in our Shadow House as well," he says with that same mild grin. I'm starting to think Arthur has no other expression than the placid and somber one he wears now.

"What? Really?" I blurt out. Hopefully that means I can speak with him tonight about why he's so angry at me. He's the only family I have left in this cruel world, so we can't leave things as they are, especially when all I want to do is hug him and talk for hours about what's happened.

Arthur leads us through the hallways, a maze of white marble floors and gray stone walls, as he explains the different regiments. Cosmos, Ekko, Polaris, Tauri, and Dvars are on the first and second floors of the main tower. The lofty House homerooms are appropriately labeled with small signs, and emblems hang above the doors.

"As I mentioned, you two are in a higher Shadow House than the rest." Arthur continues to give me long, uncomfortable glances—not in a way that creeps me out. Perhaps it should, but Arthur is so handsome and familiar, someone whose attention you crave. He has a warmth that you've known before. "Terra, you are a Nova. Raine, a Solas. Typically we would have Solases stay in the Cosmos

House, but Raine has been blighted with your Shadow already, so he will remain in the Nova House."

"Wait, what do you mean I've been *blighted*?" Raine stops and glances out one of the lancet windows, gazing down at the grounds in front of Alkrose. Hundreds of people stand in a wide, uneven circle in the snow, a few in the center of it... fighting. The space in the center is marked with fresh, bright splashes of red.

Arthur holds his hands behind his back and looks down from the window next to us. His gray eyes are lifeless and tired. "There's a long, scientific version I could tell you, but I'll keep it basic. Novas are the elite Shadows—gods of the gods. Should you be near one during a moment of uncontrolled hysteria or intentional malice to mark you, you will be blighted. Cursed."

My bones chill. "Cursed in what way?" I ask with bated breath. Raine doesn't look at me, but his jaw is set with tension. His Shadow is fate itself, all-knowing. Is it really a leap to think that it's whispering awful things to him right now?

"Blighted individuals don't live long. Their powers are enhanced briefly, leeched from their Nova counterpart, but blighting is a death sentence no one has survived."

The blood leaves my face and my stomach twists with horror.

Raine looks away and grits his teeth. "You speak from experience, don't you?" His blue eyes are already starting to pale into a gray-navy hue, the crescent moon burning green in comparison—*My blight*, I realize.

Arthur doesn't respond to him, and he doesn't need to. The pain that lingers in his eyes conveys all the answers.

His jaw is tense and his mild grin has faded into a reminiscent frown.

"Did Elias blight someone?" I ask, feeling my suppressed emotions trying to coil inside my chest.

Arthur's jaw tightens at the question. "Yes. And he's since learned to keep from blighting ever again. It's the main reason we keep Novas separate from the others. We would run out of powerful Shadows to observe and mold into power-hungry brutes if we let you blight everyone by accident." He tilts his head at me, his long onyx-colored hair resting just above his shoulders. "Worry not. Elias will teach the Novas how to prevent any further blights from occurring."

Raine looks at me for a long moment, then shrugs. The motion stills my warring mind. "Just part of my story," he mumbles mindlessly, like it doesn't matter that he's been sentenced to die.

The voice hidden beneath my Shadow cries out. I want to let her in, but I know she only promises pain. She's crying and curled up in depths I'm not sure I'll ever pull her out from again. I don't feel anything. I don't want to feel it.

The guilt.

"Right, well, let's get you two to the homeroom so you can rest before the banquet this evening," Arthur says as he resumes his steady stride down the hallway.

We walk for what seems like forever. The castle is going to be a pain in the ass to memorize. On the fourth story we approach large, black double doors that lead outside. They open to a marvelous stone bridge that pillars far above the frozen lakeside. The structure is brilliant—as wide as the walls in Barkovah were and surpassing the view.

I wasn't expecting such wondrous scenery to surround the castle. The steep mountains that border us are capped with white peaks. Mist covers them like a blanket; the tops of the pines are barely visible through the clouds. The lake below is the culprit of the thick air that fills my lungs. Fresh, cold breaths cloud into the winter sky. A smile spreads across my lips.

What a beautiful, slumbering place, hidden away like a cancerous beast.

The three of us cross the bridge to another enormous part of the castle. I glance back to the circle of people standing before the main doors. Raine's eyes are trained on them too. They're all circled around two individuals.

"What are they doing down there?" I tentatively look ahead at Arthur. He walks in a slow, steady stride, his hands tucked into the pockets of his dark military jacket.

"Hm? Oh, they are participating in the Culling Assessment. We can't take in too many students at a time. It's horrible, but what hasn't been awful in this war? Most of them are Tauris or Dvars anyway. Many don't even make it to the doors of Alkrose; they are either euthanized or sent to the front lines as bait." He says each word heavily. He hates what Fernestia is doing as much as we do.

"Why not just send them to battlefront then? Why do all of... *this*?" Raine asks coldly.

Arthur nods thoughtfully. "Would you send potential experiments to the battlefront without assessing them first? Everything here is closely observed and documented. Also, we can't have strays causing problems on the front lines. If you were sent, you'd surely run away, wouldn't you? That leaves a good chunk of soldiers who need to be babysat. The purpose of this is quite simply *power*—destruction of all the Shadowless. Dr. Cein is particular about his vision for Fernestia, a perfect world of only strong individuals in whom he sees purpose," Arthur mutters with a calm voice. He tilts his head at Raine. "Does that answer your question?" he asks, not unkindly.

I butt in before Raine can respond. "Why are *you* doing all of this if you clearly don't approve?"

Arthur's shoulders tense. "What makes you say that?" He shifts, those gray eyes giving nothing away. "I suppose I'm just tired, is all. You mistake my boredom for disapproval, I'm afraid." My brows pinch with skepticism but I decide he's not going to tell me even if I press him about it, so I let my eyes fall to the hundreds of students once more.

Raine watches the fighting below, wincing when one student slices another's head clean off. The spray of red is easy to see against the bright snow backdrop.

My eyes trail, indifferent, to the next section of the castle. The Nova House is its own separate structure. It looks like a cathedral, cold and lonely against the harsh, biting winds. It boasts extravagant two-story lancet windows that reflect the world behind us like mirrors. Twin ebony doors arched into a point open seamlessly as Arthur pulls the handle. As we step inside, it's as if we pass through a veil of magic keeping the heat inside from escaping.

My eyes widen and Raine's do too. Arthur grins as he catches our surprise. "Nifty little trick we've come up with.

Sealing veils are rather complex; I'm afraid you won't learn those until your second year."

I press my hand through the doorway to feel the odd invisible veil once more. It's like slipping my fingers through water, only breaking the surface to find the emptiness of air on the other side. "How long are we supposed to stay at Alkrose?"

"It is like any other academy—four years. Each is broken up into two semesters, at the beginning of which we hold an exam."

Raine shifts on his feet uncomfortably at my side as he asks, "Like the *Culling*?"

Arthur smiles but it doesn't quite reach his eyes. "Yes. Precisely. The first-semester exam always starts, unfairly, the day after the first-year students arrive. Shall we continue?" He turns and lifts his arm sweepingly to show us the room.

I interject, "Why aren't we down there then?" Not that I want to be, of course, but it seems wrong that we get to skip it while the others... Well, the others are slaughtering each other.

"Novas don't need to be culled. It's mainly to gauge the other students, specifically Polaris, Ekko, and Cosmos," Arthur says plainly. Raine shifts uncomfortably beside me and I remember we're still covered in dried blood. When neither of us says anything else, Arthur returns to his gesture of the grand room.

Everything is adorned in black: the walls, tiles, furniture, and drapes. The only source of light is the massive fireplace. A roaring blue fire licks into the air ferociously. I've never seen such an alluring flame, cobalt colored and obviously filled with magic. An enormous coffee table sits in the middle of the homeroom, four long couches surrounding it. Ebony fur blankets and pillows are neatly placed on the corners.

It looks like no one has ever lived here. Everything is untouched .

Did Elias live alone here all this time?

"This is the Nova House homeroom." Arthur makes eye contact with me again and I quickly look away. Elias would be pissed if he knew my cheeks warmed under Arthur's heavy stare. It's not fair that he's unnaturally beautiful and reserved—he doesn't flash haughty smirks that drip with lust like Raine and Elias do. "We will hold meetings here, but it is also your new home, so please do make yourself comfortable. The other House students will likely congregate here so you can all get to know one another."

Raine steps forward and brushes his fingers along the spine of the black sofa. "Do you reside here in Nova House?" he asks Arthur.

Arthur nods. "Yes, my quarters are across the hall from Terra's room. My study is in the east tower." He tilts his head to an ascending staircase on the right side of the homeroom. Another staircase leads upstairs on the left, which I'm assuming is where our rooms are located.

My brows knit together. "Was it just you and Elias here until now?" There's a coldness here. Perhaps it's the dark colors, or the emptiness. The lonely look in Arthur's eyes makes more sense now that I'm breathing the stagnant air of his home.

"Yes, for quite some time. But I spend most of my time

at Za'Afiel now. There's more laughter there and the children don't fight for their lives like the adults do here. They don't even know where they are, they just know they're content. I dread the day that Dr. Cein approves them for further... studies."

Raine *tsks* and gnashes his teeth. "How could they be content? Their entire families have been slaughtered. And what the fuck do you mean by *studies*?"

Arthur dips his head momentarily, and when he lifts it again, his face is somber. "I take their memories and keep them locked away until they're ready to join us at Alkrose. Za'Afiel is the only peaceful place left in the world. Laughter and ignorant bliss fill the halls."

"So, what, you just sit in a dark study all day, alone, and listen to the last cheerful voices before they're eventually extinguished?" Raine snaps at him, but anger doesn't take Arthur's emotions. He nods and firms his lips.

I can't help but feel bad for him. "You hold onto all their memories? How does that work?"

Arthur lifts his shoulders and drops them softly. "Some might think I've lived many lifetimes through this power of mine. But really I'm just a cataloger, holding onto terrible things that are best left forgotten."

My breath stills inside my lungs. "Is that what happened to Edgar?" He looked so disheveled and lost within himself. I have no doubt he's spoken with his Shadow, a Nova; his fractured eyes told me the moment I saw him.

"Yes. Edgar didn't take too well to his restoration," Arthur mutters as he slowly slides his hands back into his pockets. "He blighted his friend too, which he will not take well. He's in a fragile state of mind."

"Why was he so—" I clench my hand over my chest, small ebbs of pain burning there from deep within. My Shadow snuffs it out and I'm left hollow. "Why was he so angry with me?"

Arthur opens his mouth but seems to think better of it. He pauses. "I'm sure you two will figure it out."

Raine looks at me, the color of his pale skin showing beneath the cracks of dried blood.

"Go on, head upstairs. Your rooms are at the end. Edgar might be in his. I have matters to attend to but will fetch you both when the Culling is complete. Try to rest until then." Arthur leaves us standing in the black, dreary room.

Raine gives me a sideways glance, tired but comforting. "Shower with me?"

I nod slowly. "Can we talk to Edgar first?"

2

Edgar

A stillness hangs heavily in my room. I sit at the edge of my bed, hunched over with my hands clasped, my chin resting against them. My thoughts are burdened with blood and hatred. A darkness has moved into the chambers of my heart. My mother's emerald necklace hangs ominously from my neck, slightly twirling and reflecting light onto the glossy black tiles.

A small knock sounds from my door. Then a small hollow voice. "Edgar? Are you okay?"

Lucina.

I narrow my eyes at the floor and remain silent. Never in my life have I craved to be alone, but now it's an insatiable urge. I want to be alone, I *need* to be alone.

I much prefer silence since arriving. No one has

anything to say that can take my pain away. A part of me wishes I never got my memories back. If I had thrown myself off the cliff and remained foolish, then at least I would be dead and not plagued with the horrid truth.

The terrors I crave to unleash upon Fernestia and all who helped them.

Oh, how I wish I remained ignorant.

The ghost of myself that haunted me at Za'Afiel Sanctum, Sully, tells me to feed on the pain. To let it fester and rot because pain turns into power. Is this how villains are made? How monsters' hands craft other monsters? I'm what's left—a molded piece of discarded art.

I'm hopeless, angry. What can one man like me do anyway? My power isn't strong enough for what I want to do... Is it?

"I'm coming in," Lucina says against the door. I forgot she was there.

She cracks the door open and peeks in. I don't bother meeting her gaze.

I can't.

Lucina makes her way through my gloomy room and opens the long, burgundy curtains that I left shut. Light floods in and I wince. She lets out a sigh. "I never got to apologize for what happened back at the manor." Her fingers nervously fiddle with the ends of her sleeves. "I'm sorry I tried to help Arthur. I didn't know what all this was until he gave me my memories back. I know it's not enough, but I really am sorry."

I look up at her and she holds my gaze. When I don't respond, she firms her lower lip and nods. Her blue eyes dance with pain.

"After Ash was taken from the manor, we all lost a lot of hope... I didn't want to lose you too. So I was desperate to do anything to keep you with us." Her voice is faint and filled with sadness. I manage to nod. I know Lucina's heart is pure.

She looks disappointed that I have nothing to say, and she mutters, "There's someone here to see you." She turns back toward the door. Her white hair is smooth and clean, fresh from a shower and comb. Dressed in her black tactical clothes, she looks like a warrior, someone fit to kill when told to.

She may be beautiful, but she is a mindless fool, jumping when others tell her to.

"I don't want to talk to anyone right now," I snap at her.

Lucina turns back at me and frowns. "Well, they're here whether you like it or not," she mutters. The sounds of her steps grow distant and are replaced with two sets of others.

I'm reluctant to look up. I know Terra is here and I can't bear to speak with her.

"Edgar." Her voice is placid and smooth.

My eyes lift to meet hers and I clench the sheets beneath me. *Why is she here?* She looks so accepting. I couldn't stand her fucking face when she walked through the portal, her eyes filled with awe and affection for the men accompanying her. One of them is with her now and it makes my stomach churn with bile.

A large lump forms in the back of my throat, one I'm not sure I can swallow. She is covered in dried blood. Her partner is too. Does she even know what she's bathed in?

This is not the sister I remember. Sully whispers from beneath my skin, *She left you to die with your parents. She knew.* Is that true? I have no reason to believe that Sully tells the truth, and yet my heart falters.

"What's become of you? You're a shell of the sister I knew," I say in a raspy, hateful voice, my glare burning through her emerald eyes.

Terra's expression wanes, her eyes widening in disbelief. "Edgar, it's me."

I stand and cross my arms as I circle her and her companion. I sneer at the sight of them. "You betrayed us. Mom and Dad are dead because of you."

The male bares his teeth and takes a daunting step toward me. "What the fuck did you just say to her?" His eyes are royal blue and turquoise crescent moons rounds each iris.

I hold my ground. "I said *it's her fucking fault.* She betrayed us." My fury surprises her. She stumbles to find the words to say, so I beat her to it. "Just leave. I wish to be alone." I sit back down on the bed. Terra's companion clenches his teeth so tightly it makes my own hurt.

No one speaks or moves.

"I didn't betray you, Edgar. Never," she finally says quietly. We stare at one another until my pain is so overwhelming that I bite my cheek to keep the tears from welling in my eyes. "Never you, never our family."

After a moment of silence, she leaves. Her companion shoots me another glare before following her out. I let out a sigh and fall backward on my bed.

I believe her... so why am I still so angry?

I close my eyes. Terra had the warmest smile of anyone

I've ever known. She wouldn't smile like she does now. There's something crooked about her.

Something *crooked*. I ponder the thought.

Like Sully. She must have one too—a Shadow.

And Sully despises it. The weight that pulled away from her was intense and I only noticed its absence once she left.

Pain changes you, Edgar, remember? She needs to be disposed of. That's not your sister, not anymore, Sully whispers inside my head.

I ponder that too.

3

Terra

Raine comes with me to shower. I don't think he has any interest in seeing his own quarters at the moment. I must admit, I only let my weary eyes skirt my dark room before I'm walking straight to the bathroom. A bed, desk, and lancet window with a reading seat. Dust curls in the one stream of light that beams into my room. A stack of books that I'll nosedive into later perhaps, but the only thing I want right now is to get all of this blood off my skin.

The octagonal white tiles make the bathroom practically shine. There's not a spot of grime or dirt in here. Raine moves to the shower—only a wall of glass separates it from the rest of the bathroom—and turns on the water.

He doesn't bother stepping out of the shower as he

strips his matted jacket from his skin and unties his combat boots. I watch soundlessly as Raine's muscles flex beautifully under the stream of water. The dried blood rehydrates like water paint, returning to its intoxicating color as it spills from his body and down the drain.

His pants are the last to go, sliding slowly down his legs, freeing his half-hard cock. My throat is dry and heat pools in my core as I watch my handsome, broken man tilt his head back in the hot water, parting his lips just enough to look serene.

I unzip my jacket and shed my ruined clothes, stepping out of my pants languidly and drawing Raine's eyes back to me. Red streams of water glide down his face. He raises his hand for me and smiles. "Come here."

He steps aside for me to submerge myself. I hiss as the heat stings my skin but it quickly becomes soothing and I let out a long breath. Raine stands at my back, his hands softly touching my skin and helping wash away the blood.

I could lose myself here and pretend I'm back at home. Pretend my life isn't some far-fetched tale. The thought of Finn being as different as Edgar makes my stomach curl with dread. I lower my head and let the water run over my face.

Raine grips the base of my neck with one hand as his other smooths down my waist and cups my ass. He brings his lips close to my ear and takes a deep breath before whispering, "Want me to entertain you, babe? I know your head's probably all fucked right now with the nasty things your brother said." He pauses. I lift my head and meet his gaze. He sets both hands on my hips and guides me back until we're both under the water. "Let me try to take it away?" he says sadly.

I stare at his weary blue eyes and let my gaze lower to his soft lips. "Raine, I know you're hurting from everything that happened in Barkovah. Don't hide your grief," I murmur against his lips as he presses his forehead to mine. It's then that I notice his tears, almost impossible to see.

"I let them all down; I let Bennie die." The anguish in his eyes tugs on the emotions locked behind my Shadow. I don't dare reach and find them. I can see, clear as day, how much he hurts, and I never want to feel that pain again.

"What happened at the hotel, Raine?" I ask in a soft voice.

His eyes well with emotion and he sets his head on my shoulder as a trembling sob leaves his chest. "One second everything was normal and then people starting fucking exploding. The ones that didn't started to panic. There were so many fucking dark smoke figures." He wheezes a heart-wrenching breath. "Everyone was confused and scared so they opened fire. Bennie—he was... He was right in front of me and took so many fucking bullets."

I never thought hearing a grown man sob would be so sad. His shoulders tremble and all I can do is wrap my arms around him. "It wasn't your fault."

He stops shaking and stills, pulling away and looking down at me with realization in his eyes. "No, it wasn't, it was Elias's. I should've killed him when I had the chance."

I shake my head. "I don't think you ever had that chance, Raine. He was letting you torture him."

He bites his lower lip, dropping his shoulders in defeat. I trace the scar on his neck and jawline. He returns the gesture, wrapping his thumb and forefinger around my chin and pulling me close. His breath is warm against my lips before he presses into me for a long kiss.

Raine deepens the kiss, urging my lips open with his tongue as he lets his hands explore my body. The evidence of his arousal is nestled between my thighs and he thrusts his hips softly into them.

I smile and whisper, "We have a million other things to do right now."

He chuckles and kisses me fervently, biting and pulling my lower lip until I squirm in his hold. "Well, I was just sentenced to death, remember? So I don't really care."

My breath leaves my lungs and I jerk back, clenching my jaw. "Don't say that."

Raine arches a brow. "Why not? I don't think that instructor was lying; I don't think he's even capable of it," he says indifferently as he turns the shower off and grabs two folded towels perched on the edge of the sink.

He hands me one but I don't unfold it. "There has to be a way around it. A loophole or something." Inside my chest, the emotions are battling against Amser, trying to rise, but my Shadow prevails.

The way Raine watches me so carefully with his blue eyes knots my throat. His voice is raspy and low as he replies, "You don't feel anything bad after you shut it off, do you? Did your Shadow truly steal all the emotions from your heart?"

I'm not sure what to say. I don't want to hurt him, so I settle with: "I don't want you to go anywhere, Raine."

He smiles bleakly at that and nods with a small scoff. As he leaves me behind and shuts the door behind him, I'm consumed with an odd sense of emptiness. The longer I protect myself from my emotions, the more I dislike the lack of them.

My eyes lift to the foggy mirror. The girl I see, no longer stained by blood, is one I don't recognize.

4

Elias

I'm going on three days of no sleep. That underground torture chamber left me restless. An average human being would be suffering greatly by now, but Velis keeps me fueled with enough energy to stay awake for months at a time. Well, as long as I'm killing and it gets the life force it needs to feed my body.

Thankfully, I've only had to do that once.

Three days is nothing, but I'm still fucking tired. Worrying about Terra is more draining than I thought it'd be. Then again, I never imagined I'd find my Shadow Mate. A rarity among Shadows.

Of all people, I deserve one the least.

I take a long breath as I head to my quarters. It's been a long, long time since I've returned here. The corridors are the same, the stones a dreadful gray, and the death that hangs in the air is as tantalizing as ever. Each new recruitment cycle brings Shadows we've never seen before, but if what Arthur spoke of is true, then we've finally found the one we've been searching for—the one Cein has been searching for.

Edgar Eldridge.

His eyes are already fractured and filled with hate that will only continue to grow; Alkrose will make sure of that. But I still have my doubts about him... If it truly is the Shadow we seek, then I'm not sure why Emerai thinks he can control it this time around. My spine constricts with the memories of the last time I came face to face with *that* Shadow.

I enter the eastern tower to the right of the Nova House and ascend the spiral stone stairs all the way to the top. The scent of dust and clay mix in the air, a smell I particularly dislike. The dark oak door to my study is locked and looks untouched.

Good. Nekane and Kallos haven't been invading my space again.

Velis wisps out from my fingertips as dark smoke and unlocks the door. I step in and take a deep breath of my room, the only place I've ever really known as home.

It smells like a cabin, the firewood giving off a piney and smoky scent. My bed is a mattress on the floor with black blankets pooling off the edges. There are no photos on the walls or silly sentiments that some of the others like to keep. There isn't a point, not for me. Candles and papers are strewn about my desk, old books still piled up against walls by my reading window where I left them.

Everything is the same except me.

Somehow I've changed and that thought unsettles me.

I quickly shower off and get dressed in clean clothes, all too aware that I'm late and Headmaster Emerai will lose his temper if I'm not present at the Culling Assessment. I dress in a clean set of black tactical gear, complete with my black gloves and vest, before clasping on my white cloak, a crescent moon brooch at the center of the cowl.

Foregoing looking in the mirror, I leave my room in haste. I stopped looking at my reflection a long time ago. I can't remember the color my eyes used to be, only that it wasn't this distilled gray that I despise.

A shout echoes through the valley as I exit the Nova House. I glance at the mass of people huddled in front of Alkrose. The Culling Assessment. Oh, how I love this day. The weak get tossed out, some interesting gems come to light, and then the fun really begins. Better yet, I don't have to worry about Terra. She's fortunate to avoid the first-semester exam, or I suppose the other Houses are lucky that the Nova students do not have to participate in it.

The scent of iron prickles my nose and goosebumps shudder up my arms. I crack my neck. Velis is craving bloodshed, and I'd be lying if I said the scent of blood didn't make me primal. I once dreaded the unwanted hunger—but I find the Shadow's craving for death to be a fitting exchange.

I've been awake for three days. Velis needs to kill again soon.

I step off the side of the bridge and let my body feel the air around me, whistling and filling my lungs with shards of cold pain. The fall is greater than the Shadowless can survive—four stories. I land on my feet and the ground reverberates beneath me. Velis hums eagerly, deep in my chest. He can always sense my excitement for the Culling.

The lake is completely frozen over this time of year. I walk straight across it and get to the gathering quickly, approaching hundreds of students. Not a single head turns my way—a little surprising, but I'll take the reprieve. I spot Kallos and Nekane standing close to one another on the other side, their arms crossed, with grim expressions on their faces.

Always so serious. They never took to the Culling very well. Velis and I seem to be the only two having any sort of fun anymore.

Headmaster Emerai shouts above the murmuring students, "Cosmos and Ekko are next. Send forth your students."

I grin. Making an unexpected entrance is always my game. Emerai enjoys the thrill too, so I know I'm not at risk of getting in trouble with Dr. Cein. I'd love to fight a Cosmos—they're the strongest we have around here typically and they still die so easily. But who knows, maybe I'll get some amusement out of this one.

I break the circle and face the Cosmos House student, a dark-haired young man with despair on his face. I know a broken toy when I see one; he is a shattered mess. The students gasp and start to whisper amongst themselves. "*That's not a student. Who is that?*" My eyes flick over to Kallos and Nekane, who remain impassive. They know the way this goes; the destruction instructor gets to show off.

But I don't miss the grimace that flickers briefly across Kallos's face.

Pity. I wanted to have fun, but it seems he's taken a liking to this one.

I smile and crack my knuckles. My tongue glides across my teeth as I prepare to turn this boy into red dust.

5

Finn

My black cloak whips viciously in the winter wind. The sting of Martin's death is fresh; it's bitter in my mouth. His blood soaks the snow beneath my feet, a dark, disturbing red.

I clench my teeth. I pity the poor bastard from the Ekko House who will face me; I'm in a really fucking bad mood.

Corvus already fought, and so did Kai. Both were successful in their battles, thank gods. Fistfights mainly, beating their opponents into bloody messes, but not killing them. No one exerted as much cruelness and power as Frederick did against Martin. And I'll remember that when I'm tearing his head clean off his shoulders.

I see a flicker of white. I glance up at my opponent and my eyes widen. A brilliant white cloak dances with the wind. A sharp young man, maybe a handful of years older than me, wears it like a warrior sent from the gods themselves. His hair is as white as Kai's. His eyes are gray. A Fernestian? Why is he the only one wearing a white cloak?

There's something dark in his soul, making my Shadow, Laphia, curl inside my veins.

"He's not a student from Ekko House," one of the Ekko students says.

A roar of agreement rallies around them, but Emerai raises his hand to silence them. Smiling, he shouts, "It would seem that our destruction instructor, Elias, has finally arrived. He will have his fill. Proceed."

Elias smirks, making my blood chill. My brows pull inward and I can't keep the terror from pooling inside my chest. The circle hushes as everyone holds their breath.

"What are you waiting for?" Elias says in a low tone. "It's not fun if you don't struggle a little first."

I grit my teeth and change my stance, firm against the uneven snow. Taking a sharp breath, I try to focus on my inner magic, picturing the bird made of flames I summoned in the Cosmos homeroom. Martin appears in my mind. In his hand is a long, fiery blade. A buck-toothed smile passes over Martin's face and then the darkness whisks him away.

When I open my eyes, there's power flowing through my veins, burning hot like the phoenix's flames, collecting in the palm of my right hand. A blinding flare whirls through the air, lashing out at everyone standing in the inner circle to the right of me.

Elias takes a step backward, his eyes flickering with fire and excitement.

I grasp the flame in my palm and it solidifies into a blazing sword of fire, like hot steel just pulled from the forge. Licks of embers spew from the blade. I can't help the manic grin that curls my lips. There is darkness inside me and I want to kill this man more than anything. He's not some student in the same boat as me, he's Fernestian and a professor at this heinous academy.

Elias doesn't waste time; he charges me and lunges at my left side. I spin hastily on my heel and swing the fire blade down with a heavy thrust. My bloodlust is peaking inside of me, Laphia urging me on.

Elias throws his head up and evades a slice to his throat. My blade digs deep into the snow, farther even, into the frozen earth beneath. I wince from the hold the ground has on my sword and look up in horror. He's already on top of me, throwing me to the ground and away from the weapon with ease. Elias follows up with a bone-shattering kick to my ribs.

This guy is lethal. He's strong.

My lungs instantly ignite with pain and I cough violently, curling in on myself. I gasp for air and try to push myself to my knees but Elias is already in my face, smiling wickedly, bloodlust gleaming in his eyes. A starved demon.

The evil within this man is unlike the rest of the Fernestians I've encountered. He truly enjoys what he's doing.

It makes my skin crawl.

"Get out of my fucking face!" I shout. Elias cocks his head, smiling, looking almost bored with me.

Fine, you want to play games? I grab Elias's forearm and set fire loose in my palms. Flames burst from my skin and the instructor's eyes flash with surprise. He groans in pain as he jerks away from me. His flesh melts down to the bones. His tendons are crisped, but still function, making a grotesque crunching sound as he lifts his arm to inspect it. I look down at my fingers; burned flesh clings to me like meat stuck to a skewer. I gag at the sight and the rancid smell of it, shaking my hand to try and get rid of the muck.

A manic, too-long smile crests over Elias's face. His gray eyes shift with a white crescent moon of light. It reminds me of Kallos's eyes when he used his powers. Something is about to happen. What power does Elias hold? A surge of malicious magic thickens in the air, and Elias's Shadow spills from behind his body like a shroud of black mist. A few gasps shrill from students. They feel it too.

He is an unholy god in the flesh.

Sweat drips down my face. What the fuck *is* he? Elias smiles and raises his destroyed arm. The smell of his burnt flesh nauseates me.

"You were fun. Nothing special though, unfortunately," Elias says nonchalantly as his arm rebuilds itself. His skin is the last to restore; it forms like cloth pulled from thin air and wraps around his arm.

What the fuck has Fernestia done to us?

"Bye, asshole." Elias's voice is resentful, as if he knows me. How could he possibly know me? He raises his hand to deliver his final blow.

"Elias!" An angry feminine voice rises from the crowd. A woman in a brilliant white cloak steps in front of Elias.

Her brown hair wisps beautifully in the breeze. My eyes widen slowly. *It can't be her.*

"You can't intervene in the fight," Emerai shouts from his place at the head of the circle.

Elias's expression shifts from bloodthirsty to something warm and affectionate within the span of a millisecond as he looks at the woman.

No, that's not her. Why is that monster looking at her like that?

Elias reaches his hand up and brushes her face softly. Fernestians showing any sort of affection is laughable. Fury swirls within the chambers of my heart. This fight isn't over yet. I'll fight both of them if I have to. I pull my fire blade from the ground and slash it toward the two. Embers spray over them and Elias's face hardens once more.

"Oh, you're still here, are you?" Elias hisses at me. Then he speaks to the woman beside him. I still can't see her face. "He clearly doesn't value his life, Terra. Let me kill him."

My chest twists and the air is suddenly colder.

Terra.

The woman turns to face me, her cheeks rosy and emerald eyes gleaming like the gems I once adored more than life itself.

"Terra?" My voice quivers.

She stares at me for a few seconds before a flicker of regret crosses her face. Her gaze isn't what I remember. Her eyes are dancing with Elias's. Who is he to her? Worst of all, she doesn't look at me the way she once did. The warmth is gone. She looks like Terra, but she's so different.

"Finn," Terra murmurs like this moment is as bittersweet as ripping a bandage from your skin. "It's been a while, huh?"

6

Terra

Finn's anguished amber eyes hollow out my chest. His ebony hair whips furiously in the wind, catching embers off the sword he wields encased in scorching flames.

He always had perfect golden eyes. It isn't fair, the despair nestled in his gaze. I recognize the hurt flickering across his eyes, the same pain that I felt the night he abandoned me. Strange, I've been so eager to see him again—yet my heart is callous. Only icy rage burns from the deepest chambers of my heart.

He stands with his arms lax, looking lost but not helpless as he clutches that impressive inferno in his right hand. This must be his power. Amser coils inside my consciousness, curious about Finn but also wary. It whispers to me, *Laphia: The Eternal Flame. The Phoenix.*

My eyes widen.

"He was never worth your tears," Elias retorts under his breath, only loud enough for me to hear. It surprises me that he recognizes Finn just from our brief conversations about him. I knew he was listening intently, even when his face disguised it.

I glance over to my assassin. His white hair is messy from the fight, strands hanging over his forehead. "No, he wasn't," I mutter. I stare blankly at Finn. "How did you know it was him?"

Elias grunts. "I'm Fernestia's top assassin. I can find anyone by their description alone. You misjudge my perceptiveness and attention to detail."

Finn realizes the fight is as good as over and drops his blade into the snow; it sizzles as the fire extinguishes. He reaches his hand out to me desperately as he finally finds words. "*Terra*. Terra, you're okay... You—" He examines me with weary eyes. "You're alive."

An easy grin spreads across my lips. "No thanks to you."

He visibly flinches and his brows pull together with fierce torment.

I don't let him have a moment of reprieve. "You know, I was hunted down in the forest after we went our separate ways. I was stabbed by an assassin, only saved by the Shadow in my veins and a fickle thing called *fate*. I died that night, Finn. The Terra you knew is dead."

His mouth opens and closes a few times in an attempt to say anything that could matter, but of course, he can't.

Nothing matters anymore. Our ties are severed. I just needed to see him one last time to realize that.

"Terra." Raine's voice startles me and I turn to meet him. "Let's go back." He holds his hand out for me and I take it. Elias's brows lower into his usual scowl as I step into Raine's arms.

Finn watches us, unblinking. His rugged beauty is as haunting as ever, and I struggle to pull my eyes away from his amber gaze.

"Give me someone else," Elias demands and the headmaster responds to him but I'm already too far away to make it out. Raine escorts me back to the front doors of Alkrose but the scent of fresh blood draws my eyes back to the fighting.

I turn in time to watch a spray of blood pulse from some girl's neck. Her eyes are wide; I see so much of myself in them. Elias killed her without a second thought. It could've been me if not for my Shadow being Elias's fated mate.

Raine and I silently watch from afar.

Arthur breaks away from the circle and walks toward us. Was this the *matter* he was talking about attending to? I hadn't noticed him until now, but then again there are too many people in the crowd to pick apart.

"What are you two doing down here? I told you I would come and get you." He rubs his face, dark circles evident under his eyes. Despite his scolding, he perks up when he looks at me. "Terra, you look brilliant in your new cloak. Glad to see you've cleaned up."

I offer him a short nod. I hadn't noticed Raine was dressed in his new clothing until Arthur mentioned it. He looks so much better. His dark hair is wet from our shower, black tactical gear tight against his muscles and the beautiful white cloak clasped around his shoulders. Raine notices me taking him in and smiles.

"It doesn't feel like our entire world just ended, does it?" he says grimly. "Playing academy in the woods feels like an easy getaway. Do you think we're children who will just forget the past?" Raine pins Arthur with a cold, steely glare.

Arthur considers Raine before cracking open the journal he's holding. He flips through a few pages and stops, takes in what the page offers, and then closes it. "Of course I don't. You are hosting power that far exceeds anything you could possibly fathom. We simply aim to show you the world that can exist once the Shadowless are eradicated. Unfortunately, your options are to die with them or become one of us. But we both know your time is limited, Raine."

Raine gnashes his teeth but doesn't respond. Arthur said the words so matter-of-factly, his gray eyes devoid of emotion.

"Now, please return to the Nova House until I retrieve you for the banquet. Unless, of course, you'd prefer to get on the headmaster's bad side." Arthur crosses his arms and stares at us expectantly. I share a look with Raine before we both retreat toward Alkrose's main doors.

We don't talk until we reach the Nova House common room. Raine startles me when he finally speaks, his voice raspy and deep.

"So that was the guy from your village, I'm guessing?"

I look up at him and find soft curiosity in his eyes.

"Yeah. I thought I'd be—" I pause, struggling to find the words to convey the emptiness inside me.

"Relieved?"

I shift on my feet, looking down at the dark tiles. "Yeah. Something other than what I'm experiencing now." My fingers tangle in my cloak over my heart.

Raine watches me from beneath dark lashes. "Arthur is right. We aren't who we were before the Shadows. So it makes sense that you don't feel the same. I've only just merged with mine and I already feel so... altered." He touches his forehead delicately, wincing at the brush of his own fingers against his skin.

"Does it hurt?" I ask carefully.

Raine's different. His Shadow is vicious within him—he said so himself on the stairwell in Barkovah.

His eyes meet mine and he nods slowly. "Yeah. So much, babe."

My chest sinks and my gut twists. "What does it feel like for you?" I smooth my hand across his and he lets it remain only momentarily before he pulls away like he always does, so reluctant to accept any sort of affection.

"Like I've read every novel there is for each person I meet. Like I've experienced each death and beginning over and over, small differences, but ultimately the same story." His eyes flick up to mine and falter as confusion pulls my lips into a forlorn frown. "I've watched you die so many times already. It's been a matter of hours here in the real world, but in my head, I've been gone for so long. Things are getting mixed up." He presses his hands to his head and looks off distantly as if he's seeing another vision as we speak.

I want to help. More than anything, I want this to stop for him.

Amser hears my plea and responds, *There's no helping him. Destiny has always been confused and melancholic, only ever able to focus on the ending of each story rather than the middle.*

"I'm sorry," I say. I'm not sure there's much else that can be said.

"It's fine. It's better than thinking of my own fate, I suppose." He chuckles sadly before straightening his back and trying to give me his best grin, even though it's broken and crooked. "But I'll remain by your side until the end." He can't keep his voice from cracking. Before I can say anything or comfort him, he stands and presses a kiss to my forehead. He leaves the common room, walking up the stairs.

And for the first time since Finn left me in Navasik, I feel completely and utterly alone.

I wait a few minutes before I make my way up to my room. It's right next to Raine's but seems so far away. For the last four weeks, I haven't slept alone—or been alone, for that matter. If my Shadow counts, I guess I'll never really be alone again, but Amser doesn't feel like a person or something comforting. It's like a tumor that speaks once in a while, only really sparking to life when I'm near men of interest to it.

My door closes soundlessly behind me as I press my back against it and slide down until I'm sitting on the floor. My eyes wander to the pile of bloody clothes on the floor of the bathroom. I'm sure someone will be stopping by to collect it eventually.

My room is like a dome of the universe, circular, with black panes that make the walls appear to be windows. Almost like an ebony greenhouse. The paintings on the ceiling are of purple and blue aurora lights with stars twinkling in the distance. It looks so real. As I stare at it, I swear I see the lights moving and deduce that it's not a normal painting.

I lower my gaze to the furniture. There's a quaint study corner made up of an old oak desk, a chair, and ancient books stacked in piles of fifteen to twenty tomes. A lamp hangs from the ceiling above the desk, casting a warm ambient light. A white rug in the shape of a crescent moon lies in the center of the room, matching the enormous bed adorned in white blankets that tumble over the edge. It faces the only window in my room, an arched lancet one with beautiful stonework framing it and a reading nook at its base.

My new prison is a beautiful one, but all I can ponder is how lonely I'll be here.

I'm nose-deep in one of the books on my desk. It's academic, filled with Shadow definitions and techniques for users to learn in order to harness certain powers. I'm quite enjoying learning about the Shadows. It's the first time I've had a chance to read on my own and get a sense of them without someone else telling me.

A sharp knock comes at my door.

I turn as Arthur steps in, well-mannered and completely impassive. But I don't miss the glint of adoration in his eyes for me, the look of a wanting man, though he hides it well. I find that I like his restraint, but I also wonder how far it will stretch.

His eyes trail down to the book in my hands and he smiles faintly. "Studying already I see," he mutters politely, hands placed behind his back to keep his posture straight.

I shrug. "There's nothing else to do."

His head tilts and he looks around the room. "Where is Raine?"

"I think he's resting—his Shadow weighs heavier on his mind than most I think." I pin Arthur with a distrustful stare. I know Raine's predicament isn't his fault, but I can be angry with him for Edgar's memories. If they were truly so heinous, why couldn't he just not return them?

Arthur doesn't even flinch. "Yes, it seems that way, but don't fret. Raine has a strong mind. He'll be fine."

I glower and fold my arms over my chest. "Remind me how you know me?"

He grins and gestures toward my bed. "May I sit?"

I nod and watch him as he walks over and sits gracefully at the edge of the white sheets. He's easily the same height as Elias, but his sharp cheeks and dark hair make him appear more foreboding. A sort of handsome that piques your interest and makes you desperate to touch the planes of his skin, to feel the muscles and bones that hide beneath all that beauty.

"It was a long time ago. We were young. I'm not surprised you don't remember me. I'm not much for the memory," he says playfully. I scrunch my brows to let him know I'm not impressed with the pun and he laughs; it's lovely and deep, tugging all the right places inside my chest, making me wonder if I do in some way remember him. "I'm afraid I wasn't very kind either, so do forgive me. But enough about the past, tell me about you. Do you like your room?"

I let him change the subject. He's guarded about the past.

"It's nice... Do I have to sleep alone though? There aren't rules against that, are there?" I ask meekly.

Arthur seems to find enjoyment in that. His smile grows. "You may sleep wherever you wish," he murmurs and raises his hand for me as he stands. "Come now, the first-semester banquet starts soon. The Nova House is to enter last, with grandeur."

"Really?" I scowl incredulously at him.

"Really," he echoes as he leaves the room.

I trail behind him. His scent is crisp and earthy, like crushed autumn leaves or old tomes on a rainy day. Warmth spreads through my veins and my Shadow hums quietly in my soul, something sad and longing.

"How long have you been here?" I ask as we walk down the dim hallway.

He keeps his stride steady, hands clasped respectfully behind his back. "Hmm, since I was eighteen, so six years."

I lower my head with dread. "That's a long time."

He turns to look back at me. Light from the common room illuminates him. His gray eyes soften. "Yes, I suppose it can seem like a long time, can't it?" He speaks with melancholic weight. How does one describe the heaviness that others imbue into their words? It cannot be done; it is felt through your marrow and veins.

Arthur continues his steady walk down the stairs and I'm left sorting through the thoughts in my head. There's way too much to take on at once. I can't think of how Edgar stared at me like a stranger. I refuse to think of Finn and the betrayal that gleamed in his eyes as I threw away our past. And gods, I cannot think of Raine and his death sentence.

So instead, I focus on the soft half grin Arthur gives me as we reach the bottom of the stairs. I want to touch his lips and feel how soft and aching they are. My Shadow pulls closer to him but I remain at a distance.

Some things are better left yearning.

We're the first back to the common room, so I sit on one of the couches and wait. A few minutes pass before Raine circles the couch and sits beside me. His warmth bleeds through his shirt as he presses up against me. I tuck stray hairs from his forehead behind his ear and he gives me a sleepy smile. I'm relieved he seems to be feeling better after some rest.

Voices echo from down the hall as more people arrive. I've never seen them before, besides the white-haired girl who let us in Edgar's room earlier. They all look around eighteen. Arthur motions for them to sit and they take the couch across the large coffee table. They look at me with the same curiosity that I do them.

Another young man takes a seat on the empty sofa adjacent to us, and by the way the others stare at him, I'm guessing he's a sight to behold. Everyone's eyes are filled with shock but they don't dare utter a word. His eyes are gray; he's the youngest person I've seen whose eyes are completely turned like Elias's and Arthur's are. His hair is dark gray, like soot, and he's dressed as we all are in our Nova uniforms, black tactical gear and white cloaks. Battle ready every second of the day.

Edgar is the last to join us. He remains standing. The blue flames of the fireplace flicker across his emerald eyes as he glances at me. He holds my stare long enough for me to feel uncomfortable, then looks away.

Everyone I knew before the Skyfell is now a stranger.

"Right then. This is our Nova House—as you can see there aren't many of us so we'll stay tight-knit. Terra is Edgar's sister." Arthur gestures and everyone looks at me. I nod with acknowledgment. "She came to Alkrose with Raine. Edgar and his group come from Za'Afiel: Alani, Lucina, Tamaris, Rowan, Aervin, and Vinnie."

I observe each of them as Arthur introduces them. They are focused on the last member of our Nova House, not me.

"And this is Ash."

The silence that follows is unsettling.

"You've been here... all this time?" Aervin is the first to speak, his voice trembling with emotion as he stares at Ash. "We thought you were dead."

Ash keeps his icy gaze on the fire, unfazed. Edgar eyes him curiously. He seems not to know him either.

Arthur clears his throat. "You'll have plenty of time to catch up after the banquet. Now, when we arrive I expect you to remain silent unless spoken to by myself or another professor. I'm the reasonable one, so don't believe you'll get away with bad manners because of your status. You aren't stronger than the professors, and you certainly are not stronger than the headmaster. Am I clear?" He eyes each of us until we're all nodding.

As the others follow Arthur out, I catch Lucina's gaze. She stares at me meekly. She's beautiful—hair as white and iridescent as Elias's but eyes as blue as Raine's once were. A fracture of turquoise breaks through her irises like shattered glass.

She's been blighted—by Edgar, I'm assuming, since his eyes hold the same fractures. Beside me, Raine notices her eyes as well. Lucina flinches and turns to follow the others, leaving me and Raine as the last two in the common room.

"If she's the only blighted one from Edgar's group, then why are the others with him?" he grumbles, crossing his arms tightly across his chest.

Something unsettling tugs at my heart. It takes me a second to realize it's my Shadow that feels so discomposed. "I don't know, but it can't be good."

We leave the Nova House and walk slowly behind the others. Our cloaks wave in the wind behind us like sails caught at sea, the frigid air stinging my cheeks as I glance up at the grim sky.

I wonder what Elias is doing right now.

7

Elias

Breaths roll in the air as I let out a long sigh. I only killed two of them, two that would never survive the second-semester exam anyway. The message was clear though: I don't have a problem killing students.

Blood drips from the tips of my fingers and Velis purrs inside my chest with satiated glee. The remaining students stare at me with wide, frightened eyes—except for Finn. That defiance in his gaze makes me want to take him apart piece by piece, slowly, until he begs for death only I can grant him.

Velis coils against my thoughts and mutters, *Leave the boy alone. Amser will retaliate if you hurt him.*

I roll my eyes. Terra's Shadow is the cause of so much unwarranted trouble. I wait beside Nekane as the headmaster releases the Houses and directs them to meet in the mess hall for the banquet. I need to inform him of my unfortunate circumstances with Terra.

Nekane pulls the purple hood of his cloak up as snow starts to fall and the wind picks up. He narrows his red eyes at me as he whispers, "Trouble getting here on time? I heard from Kallos that you took down Barkovah last night. What was the holdup? Emerai and Dr. Cein nearly sent reinforcements."

I keep my expression impassive as I straighten, ignoring the blood on my white cloak. "I ran into *complications*."

Nekane raises a brow at me, his red eyes searching for information.

"*Two* complications," I clarify. Terra and her fucking dog.

"Elias, I've known you for six years and this is the first I'm hearing of the Assassin of Fernestia having godsdamn *complications*." Nekane crosses his arms and glowers at me. I am not forgetful of our history. Six years of unrelenting torture, training, and brainwashing, yet our friendship still stands in some fucked-up, contorted way.

I shrug, trying to keep my temper reeled in the best I can. "Well, I wasn't expecting to find my Shadow Mate in that shithole, Navasik."

That gets his attention. Nekane grabs my arm. "Your *what*? You're joking, right?"

I grimace at his grip. "Have I *ever* made a joke?"

His face pales and he looks up as Emerai struts toward us. "No—I suppose you haven't." He releases my arm and shakes his head. "How is that even possible?"

"I don't know. I'm hoping to speak with Dr. Cein regarding it and how he would like to proceed." Nekane nods thoughtfully but doesn't bother responding as Emerai stops before us. We both give him a curt bow.

"Headmaster."

Emerai grabs a fistful of my hair and lifts my head. "What the fuck were you doing out there, Elias? Do you have any idea how exasperated Dr. Cein is about your delay? You were given *direct* orders and your delay alone practically threw off the entire operation."

I stare into Emerai's eyes indifferently.

"He had *complications*." Nekane laughs beside me. He always was Emerai's favorite, probably because of how sadistic they both are.

"Explain," Emerai mutters, his eyes narrowing. He looks shockingly similar to Nekane. If I hadn't been at Phase One with them when they were initially captured, I'd think they were brothers. Their dark hair is the exact same shade and length. Their only significant difference is their eyes: Nekane's are haunting red, while Emerai's are dark blue.

"I found my Shadow Mate, sir. I brought her with me; she's in the Nova House as we speak."

He looks at me, calculating what to say. "Was she the woman that stopped you from killing Kallos's new brat?"

Nekane scoffs. "I was hoping you'd kill him anyway. Cocky little fucker, that one is."

You and me both. "Yes—she is the Time Nova. The other Crescent Shadow we've been searching for."

Emerai doesn't give away what his thoughts hold, only looks at me with cold eyes. "I'll contact Dr. Cein and let him know the circumstances. Keep her close, I don't want her Shadow getting too attached to anything else for the time being." He releases the vice grip he has on my hair and straightens his golden cloak. The sun brooch at the center gleams with his power funneling through it. I surpass Emerai in strength, but Cein recognized my inability to show better judgment when it comes to holding order. Emerai is his perfect puppet master, pulling all the strings while the doctor is away.

"Yes, sir."

He turns to head to Alkrose for the banquet, but he stops and glances back at me. "You haven't bred her already, have you?"

My pulse spikes and I have to school my expression into indifference. *Yeah, I watched Raine fuck her on her knees while I was tied up like an animal.* The very thought makes my teeth grind. "No, but her *blighted* has. She's on herbs, so we don't need to worry about that."

Emerai barks out a harsh laugh as he resumes his stride. "Well, at least he'll be dead before long."

Nekane looks at me with a borderline concerned expression. "Let me guess, she wouldn't let you kill him either."

I level him an annoyed look because he can already see the way she's ruining my reputation as the heartless one. "No—I most certainly *did* kill him. She reversed time and undid it."

My old friend laughs as he grabs my shoulder roughly. "I like her already."

The mess hall is a loud, expansive room. The arched glass ceilings above allow natural light to flutter in, but the sconces add a warm glow to the ambiance. Walls made of stone as gray and cold as my heart hold all the students of Alkrose within them. It's a room that contains many grim memories, a place I despise yet also call home.

How long has it been now... Nekane said six years, but somehow it feels much longer than that. My memories are blurry and drenched with blood. It's hard to pick everything apart and lay it out exactly as it should be.

But I remember enough.

Six long tables extend through the massive room, one for each class. Technically there are seven strains, but due to the shortage of Solas Shadows, the few we do have room with Cosmos. The Nova table has been empty since myself and my comrades used it. My eyes linger where we shared many meals and conversations.

There used to be so many more people by my side. We all learned the hard way why it is important to let the Shadows take hold. To seal away the pain.

I take my seat at the head of the room next to Kallos; Nekane sits on his other side. Headmaster Emerai sits in the center, watching as the students filter in. Long ribbons of cloth lie across the ridiculously long tables, white with gold slivers of thread that dance into intricate thorns and vines placed as centerpieces.

The scent of roasted meats and bread fills my nostrils. The Culling Assessment is always followed by a great feast. Cruelness followed with generous accommodations for the survivors. Step one in brain-fucking these idiots.

"You look like shit."

I tilt my head to look at Kallos; he watches me with that calm, sardonic expression he always has. So nonchalant and carefree.

"I've been up for three days. Of course I look like shit." I close my eyes and try to think if I'll sleep tonight or not. There are reports to file and it's difficult to rest when Cein is upset. I consider myself a man to fear, but Cein is far more... *creative* than I am when it involves punishment.

"Care for a drink? I can whip you up a potion that can help with the looking-like-shit part," Kallos offers dryly. Nekane nudges him to let him know he wants one too.

"Sure," I mumble. I sense Arthur's grim presence enter the room and slowly open my eyes to see the Nova House students filtering in.

The room hushes as the other students take notice of the sixth House they've yet to meet. Arthur walks like liquid smoke down the center aisle. To his left is the Cosmos House, and to his right is the empty table for the Nova House.

I straighten as I watch them walk in, looking a bit too eagerly for one in particular. I quickly disregard anyone who isn't *her*.

My heart clenches the moment I find her.

She's wearing her black tactical gear and a magnificent white cloak, the same as I wear. Her dark brown hair is pulled back into a tight ponytail, still reaching halfway down her back in beautiful rich waves. Her eyes flicker with awe as she takes in the mess hall, then her gaze lands on me and I steel my face to not give anything away.

I'm experiencing that strange, fluttering feeling in my chest when she looks at me again. It's different than before and a bit painful. Do I miss her? Fuck, I need to stop thinking so much.

I glance away casually, looking for her brother, who callously greeted her in the foyer this morning. My search stops the second I see his sinister green eyes boring holes into mine. His power seethes from his skin like a mist evaporating off a lake, invisible to most, but well-trained soldiers like me can see it. Kallos stiffens next to me and Nekane utters a curse beneath his breath.

"What the fuck is that?" Kallos says in a low, dangerous tone.

"My mate's brother."

They both lean over to look at me, but I keep staring at Edgar. The evil inside that young man makes Velis coil uncomfortably inside my spine. I know then that Arthur's suspicions were right. This is the Shadow we've been searching for.

Sully.

A girl with white hair pulls Edgar's attention away and all the tendrils of hate in the atmosphere dissipate.

"We'll need to have that one contained quickly." Nekane leans back in his chair. "Possibly your mate too, if she's his sister. Sibling Novas are—"

"Volatile," I finish for him. Both he and Kallos grunt their agreement. "I'm sure Arthur is already twisting his little strings of memories to keep him in check."

Arthur makes his way through the tables and sits next to me. Emerai starts his speech but I'm much more interested in all the things I've missed during my time away.

Arthur seems to pick up on my heavy stare and looks over at me. His eyes are dull and he looks tired, but there's a light within him that I haven't seen since... well, since before they were captured in Fernestia all those years ago.

"Arthur, that boy—" I start, but he lifts his hand calmly.

"I know. Trust me, *I know*. I held his tainted memories for weeks." He looks down at his table of Novas, small in number, but the power in the few is far superior to the rest. "He has darkness inside his heart as well as his Shadow."

I study Arthur's expression. He's always been the emotional one out of us all, but his eyes are betraying far too much today. Has Edgar gotten under his skin somehow?

"Is he going to be a problem? I'll move the blight class to tomorrow morning." I write down a note to give to Emerai after the banquet. The report on my excursion will have to wait.

Arthur doesn't answer my question. He only presses his lips into a firm line as he carefully observes the students. "He isn't talking to Terra. That's odd," he says more to himself than to me. He pulls out his journal and jots some notes down. I've learned that note-taking is the only way Arthur retains things. Perhaps the Shadow within him devours little pieces of him so he has trouble remembering. I've always wondered why he's so attached to his little notebooks.

I lean back in my chair and glance over to the Nova

table again. Terra looks weary and doesn't talk with anyone besides Raine.

Perhaps some of her emotions are returning to her. I think she'd be better off leaving them muted, but no one listens to me anyway, so I'll just let things play out. "She's fine. She turned off her emotions."

Arthur grins somberly. "I know, and yet she still suffers."

I don't have time to delve into how he could possibly know that.

"You need to brief me after this so I'm up to speed with everything," I mutter and let my eyes trail unwillingly back to Terra.

8

Terra

The headmaster congratulates the students who survived the Culling. Based on the red snow that I saw from the bridge to the Nova House, several died or were severely wounded. Then the headmaster moves on to the classes and how we are expected to behave.

The only thing that results in execution or punishment is trying to escape the grounds or directly assaulting an instructor. Students are permitted to fight and it's essentially lawless, so I'm relieved to be in the separated Nova House. At least until I look around and see all the glares and sneers we are getting from the other tables.

Emerai makes it clear that we are the elites here.

"You'd think they'd be more afraid of us," Edgar snarls

as he crushes a hard piece of bread in his fist. Crumbs roll across the table and Vinnie looks sharply at him, cursing under his breath with fear flickering across his eyes.

"*Edgar*," I snipe at him but he only throws that unfamiliar, hate-filled gaze my way.

Ash pokes at his food and doesn't bother adding his thoughts into the mix. Everyone else listens intently to the headmaster. One thing is apparent: everyone at *our* table is certainly afraid of the Novas. The threat of blight is enough to seal the deal for anyone who doesn't want a death sentence. Lucina and Raine's eyes bear the mark and I don't miss Rowan and Tamaris's glances at them.

Raine takes notice too and lowers his chin, staring down at his empty plate. I want to urge him to eat, but I feel the emptiness inside my heart too. How are we supposed to function after everything the last twenty-four hours have brought? My eyes linger over everyone's plates; hardly anyone is eating.

Emerai closes his speech with a well-rehearsed statement. "Remember, the Culling Assessment was just the beginning of your time here at Alkrose. The second-semester exam is eleven weeks from today and half of you will not survive it." His voice rolls through the silent dread around us. I dare glance over the crowd and see fear in everyone's eyes. A few mouths drop open. "But your sacrifice will not be in vain. The strong Shadows will learn and shine amidst the horror. Be brave. Face death boldly."

The headmaster bows and leaves us to eat and have the night to ourselves in preparation for the classes tomorrow, but how can anyone have an appetite after that? I swallow hard and glance up at the professor's table. Elias's eyes are homed in on me and it makes my skin prickle. A sigh escapes me as I quickly advert my gaze.

Try to focus on something else, I tell myself. *Classes, think about the classes.* Studying and training just became a top priority for me. Our schedules are in our journals, already placed in our rooms. I make a mental note to look mine over when I get back to my desk tonight.

Edgar's companions talk quietly amongst themselves. Edgar eats in silence, sharing words with Lucina. Raine has a distant look in his eyes. He's probably thinking of Bennie. Of his own inevitable demise or even mine.

I lift my eyes across the table and find Ash staring at me. His gray eyes are filled with more shadows and grief than I myself have. A small smile pulls at my lips. I can relate to that. "Hey."

Ash sharply looks away. "What?" he mutters.

I consider him for a moment. He purposefully sat away from his old friends even though they keep peeking over at him, obviously eager to speak with him. "Are you okay?"

He glances up with surprise and a bit of hostility. "Why wouldn't I be?" He's so thin, with sunken cheeks that tell me he hasn't been eating as he should or maybe has been exerting too much of his Shadow.

"You just look like you could use someone to talk to." I reach my hand out and set it on top of his.

His eyes light up and fury flickers across his face. "Don't fucking touch me!" Ash snarls. Raine stiffens beside me and a low growl rolls from his throat.

Ash glares at us both and shoves out of his seat, storming out of the mess hall. The others watch him with confusion pulling at their brows. Guilt ebbs in my stomach; he didn't even eat. He's so thin... I stuff a few rolls and fruits in my pocket to bring back and leave at his door.

I force myself to eat a few bites of the roasted meat and mashed potatoes on my plate before I call it. No one spoke to Raine or me over dinner, so I don't bother saying anything as I stand to leave. Raine silently follows. I'm thankful I at least have him, a constant in all this chaos.

The only thing I want right now is to lie down and sleep, curled in his arms. Elias's too. I look up at where the instructors are seated and can't help the longing I feel when our eyes connect.

Elias's stare is heavy and lingering as I look away, still very much aware of his gaze. I wonder if he'll steal me away in the night. Gods know I want him too.

We're halfway down the great foyer before footsteps echo in the hall behind us.

"*Terra.*" Finn's voice is firm and desperate.

Raine and I both turn to face him. I reach for Raine's arm, but he flinches away. I wince. It still stings when he does that, but I understand he has his own demons.

"You can head back. I'll be fine," I tell Raine. If Finn really wants to hash this out now, then so be it.

Raine doesn't move for a few seconds but eventually recedes, giving me one last look before walking down the long hall alone.

Finn waits until we can no longer hear Raine's footsteps before leading me outside. The cold night air takes the breath from my lungs and burns with icy dryness; it's a sensation of existence and quite frankly, in this moment, it's very much welcome. This has all but felt like a dream since everything went to shit in Barkovah.

Armed soldiers man the entrance, reminding me that this is very much a prison and not a typical academy. The tactical gear they wear is black from head to toe: vests, jackets, pants, and headwear. Only their eyes are visible; their mouths are covered with black masks. Assault rifles hang loosely in their hands, the muzzles dangling at their feet. I've pieced together that most of the lower-ranked soldiers have guns and use them primarily over their powers. Is this the fate of Dvars, Tauri, and Polaris Shadows? At least they're alive and not fed to the wolves.

I notice more walking the grounds in the distance, tracing a path that appears to circle the castle.

Finn steadily leads us up to the lakeside. The ice is thick and glistens with moonlight. It's not that late, but the winter sun cycle has the evenings starting early, and the peaks of the mountains make daylight hours appear even shorter than they already are.

Finn stops along the edge of the lake. Neither of us looks at the other. It's awkward; the tension is palpable between us.

"How, uh, are you?" he asks, rubbing the back of his head.

I repress a cruel laugh. That's really how he wants to start our conversation? How very like him. "I'm alive. How are you?" I say, annoyed.

Finn leans down and picks up a skipping rock from the shore. He spins it a few times as he mutters, "Not great. Martin... He died this morning." He throws the rock and it skirts over the ice of the lake, making an odd sound that reverberates through the air.

Martin is dead. For some reason, I find it hard to

compare his death to the rest of our village. So I say coldly, "Our entire town is dead, Finn."

"Mm," he grunts his acknowledgement.

We stand in silence for a few more moments before he speaks again.

"I'm sorry for leaving you in Navasik."

Amser curiously ventures closer to the surface of my skin, beckoning for his Shadow. I'm sure he feels the pull within himself too. It's proof that we are not the same people we once were and there's nothing in this world that can change that.

When I don't respond, he turns his head and I can't fight the urge to look at him any longer. My eyes lift to his and all my walls threaten to come crumbling down. Finn's amber eyes are a sea of burnished sap, orange and hot like a sunset on fire. His jaw is sharp and tense; strands of his lovely ebony hair flutter softly in the light breeze.

He tentatively reaches his hand out and brushes my cheekbone. The warmth of his fingers seeps into me, making me grit my teeth.

"I don't think *sorry* will ever fix this, Finn." I clench my fists at my sides. His brows pull tightly together as anguish fills his expression. Amser brushes against his Shadow where his hand rests on me and it hums with delight. Our Shadows seem to like one another, but I have to draw the line there.

I take a step back and his hand falls back to his side. "What you did can't be undone."

"Terra, I thought I was keeping you safe. I was afraid my father would come after us and you know how he was...

I didn't know all this would happen. I couldn't have known." He looks down at the ground.

It's all too easy to feel pity for a beautiful man saying he's sorry and he wishes things were different.

"Of course you couldn't have known, but I was ready to take a chance with you, Finn. The two of us against the unknown world, remember? Instead, you broke my heart." My hand rests over my chest. "You didn't even look back."

His eyes lift back to mine. "I didn't, did I?" he says as if he can't believe it.

I shake my head. "No, you didn't."

I'm already shifting to head back to my room when Finn steps in front of me. His voice is firm with conviction as he says, "It can't be undone, but I won't give up, Terra. Never again. I won't give up on us." He grabs my hands. I never thought I'd see the day Finnick Rott would beg for anything, let alone for me. "I promise you, I'll fix this. All of it."

A cruel smile forms on my lips. "It's sad that you think any of it can be fixed, Finn, and especially sad that you think I can be the girl I was. There is no *us*. Good night." I pull my hands away. The cold breeze chills me to my core, but I've been frozen inside since the night we said our final goodbye. And just the same as that night, I don't look back at him as I leave him standing alone at the lakeside.

9

Edgar

Aervin and Lucina walk with me back to the Nova House. From the expansive bridge overlooking the lake, I spot Terra standing with Finn down at the edge of it. I stop to watch. The air is cold, the sky cloudless and filled with stars.

Aervin stops at my side. "So that's your sister, huh? She seems—"

"Off," Lucina interjects as she slows next to us.

"Yeah—she seems off." Aervin smooths his hand over the back of his head, his brows pulling down in concern. "You seem *off* too, Edgar."

I look away from my sister and Finn, feeling more certain that none of this is a coincidence. What's the likelihood that all three of us would survive and end up in the same place? Sully lurks beneath my skin and whispers dark things that twist and turn in my mind, making me more certain by the second that my doubts are valid.

I grin callously. "Off? Does your Shadow not tug on your insides and twist you into something more sinister, Aervin?" I tilt my head in his direction and he flinches.

"Um... No, it doesn't," he mutters hesitantly. Lucina's brows pull closer together as she firms her lips.

Their Shadows don't have the power I do. Sully's voice curls into my spine and wraps around my bones. *They will die, all of them.*

My eyes widen at that. "Shut up. Shut up." My hands shoot up to my scalp and I fist my hair. Lucina gives Aervin a worried look.

Aervin sets his heavy hand on my shoulder and pulls me in for a tight hug. His blonde hair brushes against my cheek as he mutters, "Don't let it take you away from us, Edgar. We need you... and I hope you need us too." He pulls back but keeps his hand planted on my shoulder. "Don't let the Shadows drag you into the dark. We're all still here, aren't we? We'll be okay as long as we stick together."

I stare into his green eyes for a few moments before firming my jaw. "We're going to end up like Ash." My voice is raspy and low.

Lucina steps closer, her eyes calm but determined, as they always are. "We won't." Her smile is bright, and the white cloak clasped around her shoulders brings out her luminescent features.

Aervin grins and sets his arms over our shoulders as he guides us back toward the Nova House. "Let's get the others and meet in the homeroom; we need a proper reunion with Ash. I have so many things I want to ask him." Aervin's voice deepens with pain.

I'm still uncertain what I think of him. Maybe if I met him back at the manor, I'd welcome him with open arms, but after remembering everything, I don't think I'm capable of letting other people in anymore.

Lucina and Aervin decide we'll meet in an hour, so I shower and get dressed in the evening attire provided. It's inconvenient that Nova's color is white, my least favorite color of all. I frown at my reflection in the mirror as I assess my lounging clothes, an ivory shirt and pants. At least they're comfortable.

A familiar form peeks behind me, making my skin rise with goosebumps.

"Sully." I stare at him in the mirror. He looks exactly like me but paler, more dead and sinister. He no longer presents himself as a ghastly boy but as a near-perfect reflection of myself. "Why do you hide in mirrors and in visions only I can see?"

Sully smiles, the edges of its lips curled but its eyes stony and lifeless.

It's just how I am. Each of us is different in our own ways. I prefer to shadow my vessel's subconscious. Trust me, you don't want to meet the real me.

I narrow my eyes and turn to look over my shoulder but there's nothing there. When I return my eyes to the mirror, it is closer, just against my back. I inhale sharply at the cold air that rolls off its fingertips.

"My subconscious?"

It laughs. The sound echoes as if we are in a cave. *Yes,*

before you received your memories, you saw a shattered boy, traumatized and trapped in your mind. Now you are whole, somewhat, and I reflect that.

I shudder and shut my eyes at the memories of my parents, liquified and steaming into piles of mush and bone.

The homeroom is already filled with all my friends by the time I enter. Ash stands by the fireplace, indifferent. His eyes are gray, and I wonder if it's from the Shadows. A lot of the instructors have gray eyes. It's as if the Shadows are stealing something vital from us.

I take a seat next to Aervin, feeling a bit out of place. Ash was their friend and not mine. There's a pained silence that floats in the air around us, making me somber.

Aervin threads his fingers together and grits his teeth. "I'm so relieved to see you, Ash. You're... *alive.*"

Lucina shrinks back farther into the couch with her brows knitted. Her relief that he's okay is evident, but there's a deep confusion there too.

Vinnie adjusts his circular glasses and leans forward; he's closest to Ash and speaks lower. "Are you truly okay?"

Ash stares at him for a moment, slowly blinking and looking distantly at the fire. "I am... I'm sorry you all worried on my behalf."

Tamaris stands abruptly, angry and fueled with her usual spite. "*Well,* care to explain what happened?"

Ash closes his eyes and lets the silence hang in the room for an uncomfortable few minutes. "There's not really anything to explain. Surely, you went through the medical exam the same way I did. Arthur brought me here after they confirmed I was Nova, and they forced me to use my abilities for Fernestia." His voice shakes as he says the latter.

Rowan tousles his auburn hair in frustration and frowns. "Wait... you've been helping them? What exactly is your Shadow capable of?"

Aervin shifts beside me. His despair is palpable. It's evident he really cares about Ash and now his view of his friend seems to be hanging in the balance. Ash doesn't seem excited to see his friends or sad for the time apart. It's odd. He's cold, so unlike how they described him to me.

Ash's eyes open and find Rowan's. "Yes, I have. My Shadow can warp space."

We're all confused for a moment, but then it clicks in my head. My veins turn hot and I'm on my feet in a second, fists clenched at my sides. My emotions get the better of me. "Wait, *you* made the portals?" My tone is sharp and resentful.

To his credit, Ash doesn't shy away from my lethal glare. His dull gray eyes linger on me with little interest. "I did."

He made all of this possible for the Fernestians. Without the portals, they wouldn't have been able to travel like they had. My gut sinks and twists painfully.

"It was to protect all of you," he says softer, but my rage cannot be quelled.

"This—*all of this*—is your fault," I say with venom. Aervin's head snaps toward me; anguish and rage twist his features, but he remains silent as I continue, voice drawn low and deadly. "My parents are dead—"

Ash takes four long strides toward me. My eyes widen with his icy confidence. His Shadow spills from the tips of his fingers in dark wisps, chilling my bones. "All of our parents are dead, dickhead. The only thing I did was speed up this shitty situation in order to save my friends." His eyes flick to Lucina. "And it looks like you've already blighted one of them. As far as I'm concerned, *you* are the one killing the only people I care about left in the world."

Vinnie and Alani share a concerned look before Tamaris glares at me and snaps, "What the fuck is he talking about?"

Blighted? What *is* he talking about? Lucina's blue eyes have the fractures that my Nova Shadow imprinted on her —is that what he means?

I clear my throat. "I haven't killed anyone." It comes out more uncertain than I'd like.

Ash's eyes remain cold and steadfast as he mutters, "She'll die before the school year is done, and it'll be your fault."

My eyes widen and words escape me. *No.*

Vinnie pushes his glasses up and looks closely at Lucina's eyes. "Is that what the fractures in her eyes are?" Ash nods and the rest of my friends look over at me slowly, judgment and disbelief replacing their former faith in me.

"How do we get rid of it?" Rowan asks in a voice that threatens to break my heart. I don't want any of them to die, let alone Lucina.

"It can't be removed," Ash says plainly, looking at me with cold eyes.

The room quiets and Lucina just smiles bleakly at me. She must see the despair on my face, so why is she just sitting there looking at me like all of this is fine?

"It's okay, Edgar," she says softly and I know she means

it. The dark circles beneath her eyes reveal her weary heart and it makes me sick.

"It's not." I shake my head.

A terrible pause follows until Aervin speaks up, his voice low in case anyone is nearby. "I don't want to do things for Fernestia like you, Ash. I want to fight against them. Edgar and Lucina do too. That's why I called all of us together."

Rowan shifts uncomfortably in his seat but Tamaris and Alani look interested. Vinnie just stares at the coffee table, lost deep in thought.

Alani speaks up first. "I don't want to help them either." Tamaris nods beside her. Vinnie and Rowan seem on the fence about it.

"You're just going to get yourselves killed," Ash says vehemently.

"So you're going to keep helping them?" Aervin says as his face twists in disgust. Ash nods, his face impassive. That seems to get the rest on board.

Vinnie clenches his teeth and mumbles, "It's all the same either way. I'd rather die fighting for my country and what's right."

It's difficult to watch them fall apart over this. I know Ash's memory was something they all cherished, but now it seems like he was nothing more than a farce. So easily swayed by the illusion of safety, or perhaps it's the power.

Ash takes notice of the shift in his friends and shakes his head. "You'll all die. Don't say I didn't warn you." He stands and heads up to his room, leaving the rest of us in silence with nothing more than the fire crackling.

10

Terra

At least the view isn't terrible.

I take deep breaths of night air as I sit at the edge of the bridge, my legs pulled up to my chest. I'm right outside the door to the Nova House. Edgar and his group were having a meeting in the homeroom and I didn't feel like conversation tonight, so I settled for the silence of the mountains and stars.

I lean over to look through the window and see that the homeroom has cleared out. They all looked so serious and angry earlier; I wonder what they were discussing. Thoughts mingle in my head as I take another deep breath and watch it curl in the cold air. It feels nice out here, so I decide to enjoy it a little longer. I shut my eyes and let my thoughts take me somewhere less awful.

"What are you doing?"

My back stiffens at Elias's voice. I look up and find him staring down at me with displeasure. Blinking the drowsiness from my eyes, I try to feign a smile. "I wasn't quite ready to go inside."

He stares at me before silently offering me his hand. I look from his hand up to his face. His brow rises just a bit. There's warmth in his gaze. Why do I cherish that so much? The way he looks only at me with that vulnerability ignites flames inside my heart.

I take his hand and he pulls me to my feet.

"Let's go inside," he murmurs as he presses his mouth to the back of my head. He sounds as tired as I feel. I'm very aware of the weight of his hand against my waist, pulling me in close to him and sending heat through my limbs.

He guides me toward my room and I wonder if perhaps he'll stay with me tonight. I hate to admit how reliant I've become on his presence.

My room is cold and dark. Elias steps inside, making his way over to the far wall and kneeling at the fireplace. He tosses a match on the strange black wood, which instantly ignites. He looks back up at me and for a moment, he looks anything but a Fernestian assassin, on one knee and warming my room for me.

I smile wearily and mutter, "Thank you."

He nods, keeping that straight expression of his. "This is Shadowed Wood. You don't need to replace it and it will burn steady for as long as it is needed. It's imbued with power like the veil out front," he says quietly as he stands and moves back toward my door.

I sink my teeth into my lower lip before grabbing his forearm to keep him from leaving.

Elias stops and glances down at me expectantly, quietly.

"Please, stay," I whisper.

His eyes are rimmed in red. Fatigue pulls at his grin. "Are you begging me?"

My brows pinch together but I'm too tired to argue with him. "*Please?*"

He tilts his head to the side and lets out a lovely laugh. "Where is your pet? You don't want him?" Elias taunts me, lifting his hand to my face and brushing my hair to the side. I lean my cheek into his palm.

"No, I want you," I murmur into his hand and his other tightens on my hip.

"Since when?"

I try to pull my head away so he won't see me scowl but he grips my jaw so I can't move.

"Since *when*, sweetheart?" He brings his lips to mine, the closeness of him sending chills up my spine.

I swallow hard and stare into his hollow gray eyes. "I don't know when it happened, maybe when I saw you tied up in the basement and bleeding for me. But... I want to be close to you." The words are like bullets to the chest. I'm a traitor to my nation for feeling this way for Elias. For wanting all the sin and darkness inside him.

There's no point in denying it anymore.

Elias growls—a deep and low vibration that rolls from his throat like a wild beast. He flips the lock on my door and cocks my head back, driving his mouth down onto mine. His kisses are feverish and hungry, consuming me with each push as he guides me back to my bed.

He nudges me back and I fall onto the sheets with a small gasp, my hair a halo around my head. I don't have a moment's reprieve before his lips are back against mine. His hands slide up my wrists and pull them over my head.

I tilt my chin up and moan. Elias presses kisses down my throat, nipping and sucking as he gets to my collarbone. He's in his full tactical gear, straps, pockets, and the tough fabric rubbing on my arms, but I want his skin against mine.

Elias leans back and raises one of his dark brows as I start to unzip his jacket and pull at the sleeves. "You look tired," he says in a low, seductive voice as he shrugs off his shirt. His stomach is tight, muscles forming dips and valleys on his sun-kissed skin. Scars trail up his torso; I can't help but let my fingers glide across them.

"So do you," I say slowly.

"*You* are the sole source of my weariness. I can't stop thinking about you. The way you bite your lower lip and suck in breaths when I'm too near. It drives me absolutely crazy." He unclasps my brooch and tosses my cloak to the ground, my jacket soon after.

I arch my back as his cold hands smooth across my sides. He grips my flesh hard and possessively pulls my chest into him. His skin is soft and he smells of crisp pines and smoke. I whimper when his mouth finds my lips again, his tongue greedily entangling with mine.

His Shadow pulls Amser where our stomachs are pressed together, sending heat and urgency to my core. I tighten my thighs together but Elias doesn't allow me to hide the evidence of my arousal. He buries his hand between my legs and starts rubbing my clit through my pants.

I cry out and he groans into my mouth. My hands fumble with my zipper but Elias swats them away. He takes over, moving slow and purposefully. A breath gets caught in my lungs as he brutishly pulls my pants down. He then yanks his past his knees, freeing his erect cock.

My eyes immediately flash down to it and I swallow hard. Last time we couldn't even do foreplay without me biting his dick and him slapping my pussy with his cock.

His lip kicks up in a savage smirk. "Are you going to be a good girl this time?"

I give him an innocent smile and nod slowly beneath lust-drunk eyes.

He laughs and lowers the head of his dick to my entrance, rubbing my sensitive flesh with his soft tip and earning a sharp inhale that turns into a moan. His hair falls over his forehead and his eyes are focused where he flicks his dick on my clit.

"Show me how much you want it, sweetheart. I don't fuck girls who bite my dick without a little bit of penance."

I can't help but squirm beneath him as he toys with me. "What do you want me to do?" I rasp between breaths. I jut my hips up in an effort to get more friction from him but he pulls away.

"*Show me* how badly you want it," he says cruelly, sitting back on his haunches and fisting his massive cock as he waits. His abdominal muscles are tight and on display. My eyes trail over all the grooves of his skin.

This is why I should've just fucked Raine again. He doesn't play around like this.

Yet, somehow this is much more satisfying.

I swallow my pride and lower my hands to my pussy, spreading myself wide for him to see every inch of me. I watch as lust fills his eyes and darkness settles over his features. *Oh my fucking gods.*

"That much?" He lowers his lips to my center and drags his hot tongue over my slit like a starved man, groaning and gripping my thighs tightly.

I throw my head back against the sheets and muffle my cry, keeping my lips gnashed together in an effort to keep quiet.

Elias crawls over me languidly, licking and kissing as he makes his way back up. I only lower my chin to look at him when I feel his cock pressing inside just enough to make me squirm.

His white hair falls beautifully over his forehead and those gray eyes hollow my soul as he stares down at my face with desire.

"What is it about you that drives me absolutely *mad*?" he whispers, drawing out his words as he slowly pushes his hips into me, filling me with his dick so entirely that I stop breathing altogether until he's up against the hilt.

I can't respond because his mouth is already back over mine. He grinds his hips into me brutally, drawing out muffled moans between our kisses. His Shadow pulls against mine where we're joined and it's unlike anything I've ever experienced. The sensual sounds that leave Elias's throat make my mind empty of anything beyond this moment.

He pulls back and starts to pump into me, pulling all the way out and then pushing back in again in savage thrusts, pinning my arms down against the sheets and devouring me.

Our pants and soft moans fill the room, the crackling of the fireplace making me forget for a moment where I am. Elias's thrusts become sharper and more powerful as he reaches his limit. I'm clinging to his strong shoulders and digging my teeth into his flesh as he takes me over the edge. I cry out and his entire body flexes as he pumps into me one last time, holding himself tightly against me as his dick pulses and throbs inside me.

He presses one final kiss to my lips before pulling away and blinking down at me, looking exceptionally like a normal man and not at all like an assassin.

"I told you the bad guys get the girl." He grins and withdraws from me, lying down next to me and pulling my body in tightly against his chest.

I shut my eyes and let myself enjoy this moment for what it is. I'm not sure when I'll have a reprieve like this again. Especially with Elias. My Shadow curls comfortably against his chest and I've never felt so complete in my entire life.

"Do you have to be bad?" I whisper against his collarbone, smoothing my thumb over his neck and letting my fingers get lost in his sea of white hair.

He chuckles at that. "I tried once to be a hero. Do you want to know what it got me?" He threads his hands through my hair and combs gently. His breaths are slower, calming. I nod reluctantly. "It got me a bunch of dead friends and more blood than I could ever wash from my hands. It's easier to be the obedient villain. The sexy guy that gets to kill people," he says with a laugh, but I think he's trying to cover up his pain beneath it.

I push away enough to look up at him. "Is that true?"

"Well, look at me, I'm sexy and—"

"Not *that* part." I shove him and his expression falls into a weary, uncertain frown.

"Yeah, it's true. So, yes... I do have to be bad." His throat bobs as he swallows nervously. I can tell he really doesn't want to discuss it so I decide I'll bring it up another time.

I nuzzle back into the crook of his neck and he wraps his arms around me. As sleep starts to take me, a horrible thought surfaces.

I'll have to choose eventually—between what is right and *him*.

11

Finn

I stare at the ceiling, listening to Kai toss and turn in his bunk below me. I've hardly slept more than fifteen minutes at a time before waking up. I give up the idea of a good night's rest.

Terra is heavy on my mind. She's really fucking mad at me and I don't blame her. The look on her face was enough to make me want to crawl under a rock and die. I groan and press my palms against my eyes.

Eventually I get up and look through my textbooks. We'll be starting classes today and I'm determined to learn as much as I can. I want to be strong like I should have been for Martin.

Now that we've had a taste of what the exams are like, I'm committed to doing everything in my power to not let any more tragedies befall us. The only problem is we have no clue what the next exam entails. I highly doubt it will be something as simple as one-on-one combat again.

"Oh, come on." Kai nudges his elbow into my side. I didn't hear him get up—I was too lost in my thoughts, apparently. "What are you moping about *now*?" He glowers at me and I can't help but smile at his cheap attempt to make me feel better.

He knows what I'm depressed about; we talked about it all fucking night.

A message writes itself in the air in front of our door, scorching the space with bright, gilded words.

All students are to report to the mess hall immediately. Classes are to follow.

Kai shares a shocked look with me before shrugging like it's just another day.

Everyone is weary after yesterday. To say that the Culling Assessment was draining is an understatement.

There is a sinister aura that hangs heavy in the air, coating my skin with its stickiness. The long tables are filled with students from each House. The Nova House has arrived but Terra, Raine, and Edgar are absent—possibly one of the others I didn't recognize yesterday too. My eyes lift to the platform where the professors eat, and I notice the destruction professor is gone as well. My stomach twists with rage. I don't want him anywhere near her, but there's nothing I can do.

I feel entirely helpless.

Meats of all kinds are displayed on beautiful plates, drenched with sauces and seasonings. There's bread and coffee distributed liberally as well. Kai scowls at the coffee but takes big gulps regardless. I do too, even though it tastes like shit without cream. I don't think I can make it through the day without it.

We brought our heavy leather books with us. Each is the color of the student's house, the Cosmos color being black. A map of Alkrose takes up the first few pages. My first class is anatomy, taught by Nekane. I blow out a breath and glance at Kai's book; at least we have the same class.

"What the hell are we going to learn in *anatomy*?" he mutters between bites of his breakfast.

I shake my head. "I don't even want to know."

Kai sticks with me after we finish breakfast. The map in the book doesn't help as much as I was hoping it would, but we eventually find our way to the third floor and locate the long, well-lit hallway crowded with students.

"Corvus!" Kai shouts and his hand shoots up into the air. My eyes find our friend a moment later. His dark hair is pulled back into a short ponytail. Corvus nods at us and makes his way over.

"Cool, now the four of us can—" Kai stops himself. There are no longer four of us. Martin's lifeless eyes spring back into my mind and I have to swallow a few times before I can speak.

"It's okay." I lower my eyes so he can't see the pain flickering there.

Kai wraps his arm around my shoulder. "It's not, and it never will be. Sorry for the slipup," he whispers and my jaw clenches with grief. Corvus raises a brow at us as he stops a breath away.

"What's wrong?" Corvus asks, looking at Kai.

I glance up at him and mumble, "Everything."

We stand in silence until the doors start to open. The instructors stand behind them. My stomach tightens as my eyes land on the anatomy class's instructor, Nekane. This guy has it out for me for some reason, just for being a Solas classed Shadow, it seems.

His red eyes meet mine and I shrink in my cloak a bit, trying to avoid his gaze. Corvus and Kai trail behind me as we walk through his door. Our eyes instantly flash with surprise as we step into a massive catacomb-like library. The walls are made of stone, gray and slick with slime. The air is heavy with moisture and my tongue curls at the acidic sting. The lighting is dim—hundreds of candles burn on the floors and shelves that extend high above. Skulls rest on the rows amongst the books and tomes. Black liquid, long dried, stains the stones beneath them.

"Gods, what the fuck is this place?" Kai hisses unsteadily under his breath.

Corvus takes a few steps closer to the walls and inspects the stones and books. He takes a sharp breath. "I think we are in the Library of the Dead."

Kai narrows his eyes and grimaces. "I don't know what the fuck that is, but I'm not interested in finding out."

"It's the historical library that resides on the northern isle of Cyprin. They must've taken over the catacombs when they invaded a few years ago. We've just passed through another portal." Corvus looks grimly up at the dripping rocks above us.

I've never heard of this place, but it emanates dark magic—the sensation hurts my bones.

Nekane shuts the door as the last student steps

through. He makes his way to a raised podium in the center of the room. Black mist drips from his right hand and his pale fingers curl around it as it forms into a cane.

"Anatomy of the Shadows." The instructor's voice sends chills up my spine. "Today, we will learn the inner paths of summoning and how they can travel through us."

Nekane raises his cane. I wouldn't know it was a part of his Shadow had I not just witnessed it spill from his fingertips.

"Watch as I recall it back into me," Nekane instructs and the cane disperses into smoky wisps and flows back into his skin. It enters through his palm and spreads through his veins like poison. Then, for a split second, his forearm bones become visible beneath his flesh as the black poison seeps back into them.

The room is eerily silent as we take in what we've just witnessed. My eyes trail down to my palms and I ponder on what my own Shadow is capable of.

Nekane opens his black tome and flips a few pages in. He clears his throat and says, "Shadows are nothing but the aura of the gods they once were. They can flow within and out of you at their will. Once you enter the nether levels of unity, you will be able to control their dispersal as I do."

Kai raises his hand and we all give him a sour look. "What do you mean by nether levels?"

Nekane considers him momentarily before grinning and walking over to a chalkboard hidden behind a stone pillar. The candlelight flickers as we follow him around the bend.

He draws a diagram of a human body and then

proceeds to tick off lines that lead to the skin, flesh, and bone, then deeper into the chest: ribs, heart, and spine. Nekane sets down the chalk and waves for Kai to come to him.

Kai gives me an uncertain look before swallowing and moving to stand next to the instructor.

Nekane's cloak, like Corvus's, is a rich purple, making Kai's black one look drab in comparison. He grabs Kai's arm and I watch as my friend visibly jolts beneath Nekane's pale hand.

"Kaidel, you haven't let your Shadow seep past your surface level yet. This is perfect—why don't you let it sink into your flesh for demonstration," Nekane says nonchalantly and steps aside, placing his hands neatly behind his back and watching expectantly for Kai to do as he said.

Kai lowers his arm as his brows pinch together. "Um, I don't know how."

Nekane laughs. "You don't feel it beckoning to go deeper? Let it in."

After a few minutes of nothing happening, Kai slumps his shoulders. "It's no use, I don't feel anything." Nekane's eyes slide to me and his too-calm demeanor sends chills up my spine.

"Finnick, let's try you instead. Come now." Nekane steps back up to the chalkboard. I pass Kai as he returns to stand next to Corvus. The instructor presses his cold hand to my shoulder and I instantly feel what Kai must have.

Icy veins spread through the surface of my skin; it calls to my Shadow, which pools along the area to combat the chill. Fire burns inside my flesh and banishes the cold in a mere second. I flinch as Nekane takes one sweeping step back, his eyes widening on me and his jaw flexing.

"Finnick, you're already near the nether levels—impressive. I'm assuming you let it in during the assessment exam when your friend was *eaten*, yes?" I scowl at him and he nods thoughtfully. "I want you all to call out to the Shadows inside you and ask them for their names. Let them sink into you as far as you can."

Corvus raises his hand and Nekane nods at him.

"What if we don't want to?"

"Then you will be slaughtered in the second-semester exam. You can't expect to compete with those who've achieved the nether levels." Nekane smiles and draws a circle around the chest of the diagram. "Unless you can reach this point with your Shadow, you will certainly die."

I think about his words for the rest of the class, sitting disheartened in a chair as I observe Corvus and Kai trying to speak with their Shadows. What does the second-semester exam entail exactly? It looms over my conscience, drawing in my anxiety and despair like a magnet.

Kai gives up and sits next to me as Corvus continues to whisper to himself.

"Done already?" I glance over at him and frown at his deflated expression.

"Yeah, it's no use. I just don't hear anything. I'll try more later in our dorm. Maybe I just need a peaceful environment away from the others." His eyes flick over to Frederick and a lump forms in my throat at the sight of him.

His mouth has scarred where his face tore. No one else's Shadow has transformed the host itself. So why his? Beyond Frederick is one of the strangers I saw sitting at the

Nova table. His gaze snaps up to mine and I flinch. His eyes are green and his hair is a soft, light brown, almost blond. He offers me a hesitant smile. He's by himself and I don't see the harm in welcoming him over with us, so I nod and return the grin.

He walks over and nervously greets us. "Hey, I'm Aervin. Mind if I join?"

Kai waves his hand carelessly, still leaning back in defeat. "Yeah, yeah. Join the band of losers while you still can, our numbers are growing," he says sarcastically. Aervin laughs and sits beside me.

"I'm Finn, this is Kai, and that's Corvus," I mutter, nodding at the two friends I have left. Aervin nods and looks at the ground in silence. "So you're a Nova?" I pry—why not, I figure.

Aervin hesitates. "I'm not actually a Nova, but I'm in the House because of Edgar. We met at Za'Afiel. It's a manor on Grimrose Island."

Kai's brows pull together with curiosity. "Why did they have you all out there? Please don't tell me they pampered you." Aervin's brows knit innocently and he doesn't have to say more. "Godsdamn it," Kai huffs.

Corvus finally joins us, looking annoyed with himself. "Shit. At this rate, we're all going to die." I give him a leveled look but he shrugs. "If you think Frederick is the strongest thing we need to overcome here, you're a dumbass. We have to get stronger. Do you guys want to meet up after classes later and practice in the courtyard?" Corvus notices Aervin and raises a brow.

"Aervin, Edgar's friend in the Nova House," I explain and Corvus nods like he doesn't really care.

"Anyone is welcome to join."

Aervin smiles with gratitude. "I could use the practice."

Kai and I both nod and return to watching Frederick and his group of aggressive friends. Their Shadows radiate power—it makes my skin curl.

We're definitely fucked.

12

Terra

Raine is silent all morning. We had to wake up earlier than the rest, so today's already off to a shitty start. I woke up in bed alone. Raine knows I was fucked senseless last night because my thighs are sore and when we showered together this morning, he could see all the hickeys and bite marks on my skin. Hence the silent treatment.

Apparently, blight classes need to be taught far away from the academy. We wait in the homeroom in silence. When Edgar and Ash join us, the air becomes suffocating with tension. I hate this so much. Maybe Edgar is willing to talk to me today though.

"Edgar, I—"

Elias steps down from his staircase and cuts me off

with a long sigh. We all look at him and shrink in our seats a bit. His eyes snag on me and my veins twist at the darkness I find in his cold, gray gaze. Back to the distant charade. All the vulnerability I saw in his eyes last night has vanished.

"Let's go," Elias says curtly and the four of us follow him outside.

The cold winter wind is brutal against my skin. We make our way across the bridge and down to the courtyard. The forest walls off the back of the usable area. A small path cuts through the trees and stretches far away up the slope of the mountain. Snow crunches beneath our feet as we march across the courtyard and up the path. I give up on the idea of warming my feet anytime soon.

We walk for the better part of twenty minutes. I'm surrounded by three men I have issues with and one stranger.

At least one is my blood and can't really evade me.

"Can we please talk?" I slow down a bit and walk beside him. Raine and Ash don't give us a second glance as they walk ahead.

Edgar doesn't reply, but his expression is much softer than it was yesterday, so I'm praying that he will be willing to hear me out.

"I don't know what you think happened in Navasik, but I didn't know what would happen. If I did... I would have stayed and convinced Mom and Dad to run with us. I would never leave you intentionally, Edgar." I stare at him and the tendrils of pain deep inside me fester, begging to be released.

He looks at me with eyes carrying the weight of the

world. "Deep down, I know you wouldn't... I don't know why I was so convinced. There's something dark inside me now, Terra. It won't stop telling me things I know aren't true. I—I feel so mixed up." Edgar's eyes meet mine and he looks so fucking exhausted. There are scars in his gaze that weren't there before, but now they're evident, looming and cold. His eyes are rimmed with red. He just looks tired.

"Did you see what happened to them?" I ask, biting the insides of my cheeks. I only saw the aftermath, and that was awful enough. I can't fathom what he's seen.

Edgar lowers his chin and mumbles, "Yeah, I did. Heirah soldiers were there too, Terra. We never stood a fucking chance."

My feet stop moving. "What are you talking about?"

He glances back at me, looking so much older than he is. The dark circles beneath his eyes make his skin appear paler than it should be. "I saw it—they helped Fernestia infiltrate our country. I'm certain that Finn's father was a part of it. His men were there to clean up the aftermath," he says with venom.

My chest sinks. "No, that can't be." I search his eyes for any doubt but find none. "I was in Barkovah, and there was no sign of any military force. Raine was leading the city when I arrived. Finn's father couldn't have been involved. They fled to Whales of Tauh."

Edgar lets out a small grunt. "I know what I saw."

As we resume walking I let my thoughts run rampant. Is Heirah working with Fernestia? But why?

Elias turns his head and looks at me briefly. My stomach curls with heat and I have to shake my head to keep from thinking about last night. "Barkovah was taken. I was there when everything fell apart. He's the beacon for the Skyfell." I nod toward Elias and lower my eyes to the snow. He's the reason my family is dead and I should hate him more than anything, and yet I can't.

Edgar's deadly glare slowly returns to his eyes. "And you've been by his side this entire time?" There's judgment in his stare. Of course there is. Why wouldn't there be? But it doesn't stop it from stinging all the same.

"Not by choice... My Shadow has a thing for his," I say quietly.

Edgar narrows his eyes, but before he asks me to elaborate, we nearly walk straight into Raine and Ash.

Elias gives Edgar an assessing look and mutters, "Let's start with Ash since he's already received blight-training from Arthur."

Ash walks to the center of the small clearing and shuts his eyes. When they reopen, circles line his pupils like doorways. Elias stands next to him and as he blinks, the crescent moons from the other night return to his eyes.

"Novas have a distinguished power, one that is visible in our eyes. As a defense mechanism, if we are not in tune with our powers, we cast out a blight in times of distress." Elias holds his hand out toward the clearing and darkness blasts from his palm, scorching the snow and trees into black smudges.

I raise a brow in confusion. I've seen him kill without so much as a trace of Velis before. His gaze catches mine as he speaks. "Uncontrolled power like this will blight those around you who are not Novas or in full unity with their Shadows. While if you are in control—" Elias performs the same attack, but this time, there is no dark smoke. A pine tree snaps in half and falls without a trace of him having anything to do with it. "No evidence of your power will be left behind."

Elias nods to Ash and he performs the same attack. He slices a lone tree in half with no evidence of magic.

"Until you can do it perfectly like that, we'll be here every morning practicing," Elias states and looks from me to Edgar expectantly.

I swallow tightly. Raine stands tall beside me, his eyes unmoving and cold.

Elias grins at him as he points to Raine's chest. "Terra has already blighted Raine, so he makes the perfect test dummy." Elias's hand clamps down on Raine's shoulder and his fingers dig into his flesh. Raine's brows twitch but he shows no fear.

"Why not just practice on the trees?" I scowl at Elias.

He shrugs as he mutters, "Higher stakes and whatnot by using a live target."

Asshole.

I try to intervene but one hard look from Elias stops me. His gray eyes burn into me, making me believe that he very much has an issue with me being so close to Raine.

"Edgar, I want you to try to decapitate him from twenty feet away. Keep your Shadow in check. You won't stop until I think you're stable enough to join classes. Raine, try to keep him from taking your head clean off," Elias says with an eerie grin.

"That's insane!" I interject, but Raine dismisses me with a low grunt as he takes his position twenty feet away as instructed. Edgar fists his hands at his sides and looks at Raine with determination.

Elias grabs my wrist and drags me to the side of the clearing so we can watch.

"This is fucked up. If Raine gets hurt—"

"You'll *what*?" Elias snaps, his jaw set and eyes trained carefully ahead. "We aren't playing games anymore, Terra." My stomach curls and I want to lash out at him but I think better of it. He's been tolerant of my outbursts so far, but with his peers around, I'm not so sure how far that tolerance will stretch.

The snow crunches behind us and I turn my head to find Arthur walking up the path from the forest. His gray eyes calmly meet mine as he stops beside me. "Sorry I'm late. I had to attend to a few matters at Za'Afiel. Cein will be arriving this evening to discuss your mission delay, Elias."

I look between them. Elias's permanent glare is set in stone, while Arthur has a light air about him. I've heard this man's name tossed around a handful of times. Who exactly is Cein? From what I've gathered, he seems like someone in high standing, maybe even higher up than the headmaster.

My assassin offers him no reply so we watch Edgar in silence. Ash stands alone on the opposite side of the clearing, his hands tucked into his white cloak, almost blending in completely with the white trees surrounding him.

My breath seizes as Edgar raises his hand.

An explosion of power bursts from his palm and the gravity around us instantly intensifies. My feet dig heavily into the earth and panic rushes me as Raine's eyes widen, his hands barely lifting in time to shield himself from the black wave of power that crashes into him.

"Control," Elias barks out to Edgar and my brother lowers his hand, breathing heavily and shock glazing his eyes at his own strength.

My body urges me forward to protect Raine but Arthur's hand lands on my shoulder. "He's okay," he mutters softly. I only believe him once the smoke clears and I see Raine standing completely unscathed. "Well done, Raine. You are a natural at blocking frontal attacks." Raine gives Arthur a hesitant glance but seems reassured by his praise.

Edgar shakes his head and tries again. His attack this time is much smaller, and the gravity of it doesn't pull at my feet as immensely. Raine deflects it better, casting the remnants of the black smoke to his side and staining the snow with the aftermath.

Elias makes Edgar perform the same attack over and over until his legs are visibly shaking and he falls to one knee. His control has tightened significantly since he started but Elias still isn't impressed. It's already past noon and my stomach is twisting with hunger. My legs are sore from standing in one spot all day in the cold.

"Head back to the castle, Edgar. You'll be here tomorrow morning again until you can be in complete control." Elias dismisses him with little regard. Ash helps Edgar to his feet and they head back together.

Raine falls to his knees next from exhaustion and Elias sighs, looking at Arthur with an expectant glance.

"I will take his place for your training, Terra." Arthur smiles warmly at me and my Shadow coils inside my chest. I hope he didn't hear me and Elias last night; his room is right across the hall, for gods' sakes.

"Are we going to be here until nightfall?" I ask with a deep sigh.

Arthur leans down and helps Raine up from the ground. His gray eyes are somber and deep with secrets long left behind. "I'm afraid so, at this rate," he says simply. Raine can hardly keep his eyes open as he heads back to Alkrose.

I stand where Edgar had and position my legs as he did. Elias circles me slowly and nudges my lower back so I straighten it. His scent seeps into me and I fight off the urge to lean into him.

"Same as your brother, try to decapitate him," Elias mutters a little too close to my ear. Chills crawl up my spine and I shudder as he steps away.

Okay, I can do this.

Arthur's white cloak waves in the wind, the gray sky cloudy above him. His shoulder-length ebony hair sways softly and his gray eyes stay on me. Cheeks rosy and jaw tight. His presence is that of a lonely wolf caught in a snowstorm.

I swallow hard. How can I even imagine decapitating such a beautiful creature? My veins hum as I focus on his throat, narrowing my eyes and remembering to stay in control. I don't want to blight anyone else ever again. I've already sentenced Raine to death and that thought makes me sick.

I raise my hand and a black shard shoots from my fingertips, slicing through the air silently, and my throat seizes as blood trickles down Arthur's neck.

13

Terra

Arthur's eyes are wide, his hands trembling as he brings them to his neck.

I look from him to Elias in shock, worried I'll be in trouble for hurting a professor.

"I'm so sorry!" I start to trudge toward Arthur but he raises his hand and flashes me a reassuring look.

"I'm fine, just took me by surprise, is all." He chuckles and the slight smile that pulls at his lips is reassuring enough that I stop.

Elias turns to me. "That was really good." His voice is light for once. "How did you even blight Raine with that much control over Amser already?"

My eyes fall to my hands. "If I had known what my emotional outburst would've done to Raine, maybe I could've prevented it." Flashbacks from the hotel and all the bodies and blood linger ominously in my mind.

Elias and Arthur share a look before Elias urges me to continue with training.

I perform the same attack until the sun starts to lower in the sky and the shadows of the trees stretch across the snow.

"Let's call it. I need to be in my study before Cein gets here, and you've impressed me today," Elias mutters as he offers me a hand.

I'm panting and kneeling in the snow like Edgar. My exhaustion far exceeds what I thought possible. It feels like staying awake for two days straight, that dizziness and sick feeling that envelops your entire body. My muscles are drained of power and energy alike. Even the hum of my Shadow feels dulled.

Elias leaves in a hurry to get to his meeting so Arthur and I take our time heading back.

"I hope I didn't miss too much in classes today," I say. The trail is narrow but we walk side by side. His tactical jacket brushes against mine and I find that I really enjoy Arthur's presence. It's quiet and patient, never rushed or forced. He has that calm, intriguing air of someone who waits for things they crave the most.

"You must be hungry after being out here all day," Arthur says awkwardly and I can't help but raise a brow at him. He laughs and rubs the back of his head. "Sorry, I'm not great at conversation."

I like that about him too.

I shake my head and grin. "I don't think it's that. You're just being really careful for some reason. Are you shy around girls or something? Aren't you a little too old for that?" I tease him.

He shoots me an offended look but we both crack a smile. "I'm not shy; I've always just been careful." He looks ahead, seeming deep in thought. "And I'm only twenty-four, though some would say I have an old soul." His eyes flick back down to me, waiting to see my expression.

"Well, you look tired for your age." He glowers at me and I laugh. "But I *am* starving. Is dinner already over?" I look at the darkening sky and frown at the stars that are peeking through.

"I'm afraid so. I can sneak you into the kitchen though."

I narrow my eyes at him and he chuckles again, finding my skepticism funny. My stomach growls loudly and my cheeks warm.

"Right, I'll take you straight there then." He covers his mouth and I know the grin he's hiding is lovely.

We reach the bottom of the slope and the courtyard stretches out before us. The amber lights from Alkrose are bright against the snow. Students are training in the open area; amongst them are Aervin and the two I noticed keeping close to Finn yesterday.

Finn's too distracted and doesn't see me, but his white-haired friend looks up at us and studies me with curious blue eyes. He looks like a younger version of Elias, less built and rugged but similar enough to make me think they hail from the same nation. My bet is Cyprin. Most white-haired individuals with beautiful blue eyes are from the eastern part of the world.

I quickly look away and stick close to Arthur's side as

he leads us to the mess hall. It's an odd room to be in when it's empty. The space seems triple the size without the crowd of people to fill it.

We walk to a door off the back side and enter a massive kitchen. White tiles, metal sinks, and countertops make up pretty much the entire area. It's immaculately clean and there's no food in sight.

My stomach growls again and Arthur just grins, giving me a sympathetic look as he opens one of the large fridges. He snags a few pieces of bread and a slice of meat, handing me the plate and grabbing a cup of water while I wolf down my sad little dinner. He frowns as he hands me the cup. "I'm sorry we made you practice so long. Elias is very stern in his blight classes."

I swallow and take a long drink before replying, "It's okay, I'd rather be a little hungry than blight someone else." I look down at my hands and think of Raine. "I don't know what I'll do with myself when Raine—" I stop, unable to finish that thought.

Arthur takes my empty plate and cup, setting them in the sink, facing away from me as he says in a low voice, "You might be able to find something in the library that can help."

My heart jumps at the small trace of hope.

"Like something that might keep the blight from killing him?" I stare at Arthur as he slowly turns to look back at me. There's a somber light in his eyes, but he nods. My brows pinch. I'm hesitant to let the hope in. It tangles with my Shadow's ability to reign in my emotional turmoil. "Why would you tell me this?"

Arthur walks over and leans over me, pressing his

palms to the counter I'm sitting on. I inhale sharply as his face lowers to mine. His nose is a mere breath away.

"I'm not unsympathetic, Terra. Why wouldn't I try to help?" He pins me with his steady stare.

"You're not at all what I expected," I whisper. The air is dense around us, thick with tension.

"That makes two of us," he says in that low raspy voice, letting his eyes fall to my lips before glancing back up to my eyes and pulling away. "You should head back to the Nova House and get some rest."

I take a deep breath and fight the desire to look back as I leave the kitchen.

My room is filled with lavish things, but it feels oddly empty. I sit at my desk and exhale slowly, lowering my head to my arms. I'm exhausted from training but I want to study or at least read through some of the books for my classes. I've already lost an entire day compared to everyone else and I need to search the library as well. There are a million things encircling my mind and that only makes me wearier.

A soft knock on the door wakes me.

Did I fall asleep? *Godsdamn it.*

I open the door expecting Elias, but it's Raine. My heart lurches all the same.

His blue eyes study me carefully. "You weren't at the mess hall for dinner, so I got worried." The scar that carves the side of his jaw is hardly visible in the dim light.

I don't give him a chance to retreat—he grunts as I grab his wrist and pull him into my room.

"Miss me?" He laughs, brows knitting tight with exhaustion.

"Please don't be mad at me," I say sadly. He opens his mouth to argue but I cut him off. "You literally fucked me on your torture room floor in front of him, so I don't want to hear it," I say dryly, crossing my arms. My Shadow doesn't want to be tied down and quite frankly, neither do I.

Raine's eyes soften and he sighs with defeat. "Fine. I can't help but feel greedy with you though."

I press my hand against his chest and when he doesn't push me away, I pull him in and hug him tightly. His arms wrap around me just as surely, and his breath is warm on my neck.

"Gods, I fucking missed you," he whispers as his fingers thread through my hair.

I nuzzle into his embrace. "Then don't go." He pulls back, his gaze filled with hurt, but he nods.

I decide not to tell him about what Arthur said. It's hard enough having hope myself. I don't want to give him hope and then take it away.

We go over our class schedules for the week. It looks like we have three together and that's a big win for me. Shadow sex ed, Shadow riding, and blighting.

"*Shadow sex ed*?" Raine's smirk pulls at my smile as well.

We're sprawled out on my bed and already dressed in

our night attire. I forgot how fun "sleepovers" are. Finn used to sneak into my room all the time back in Navasik and we'd fuck and laugh and talk until the sun rose. Those were blissful days.

"Do *we* get to pick our partners?" Raine says in a low, voluptuous tone.

I nudge him playfully, unable to keep the heat from pooling in my core. "I don't think it's like *that.*"

His mouth twists as he laughs. "I think it's going to be worse than we think it is. Let's hope Finn isn't in our class."

My smile immediately fades. "Don't even joke about that." I roll and pull my pillow over my head. Raine follows me into the sheets, grinning handsomely and pressing his nose against mine. His black hair is tousled, the pillow pressing down on his head.

"Don't pout, babe. It doesn't suit you," he taunts, staring into my eyes. I'm distinctly aware of his hands brushing up my side and sliding beneath my shirt.

I run my hand over his cheek and he leans into it, pressing a kiss to my palm. The sheets are soft between us and his lips smooth over my skin, drawing a breath from my lungs. "I know I shouldn't feel content here, but I do. Does that make me a monster?" I ask just above a whisper.

Raine hums in thought. "Maybe a little bit, but I don't think it's fair to blame yourself. Our Shadows have suppressed a lot of the emotions we'd normally be experiencing. I woke up this morning and hardly even remembered anything about Barkovah or the people under my care." His eyes are sullen and he looks away from me.

He doesn't remember them?

"You remember Bennie, don't you?" I search his face

but his expression remains impassive. A small gasp rolls from my lips. "How could you forget?"

He keeps his gaze elsewhere as he mumbles, "I only see the future, so many futures and paths. The past has all been lost to me. My Shadow tells me that we'll all lose more and more of them as the days draw on. Slowly digesting our memories until we're mere shells of what we once were. Like carcasses left to rot with disease."

"Gods, are you serious?" I sit up and his eyes finally snap back to me.

Raine nods and lays his head across my stomach. "Try to remember Bennie for as long as you can for me," he says with melancholy in his voice, making me think he hasn't completely forgotten the child yet, but it still pulls at my heart.

My fingers thread through his hair and I lie back down, staring at the ceiling of my room where stars and planets are painted intricately. One bright star in the center of the room looks like it's exploding; light stretches out farther from it than the others—a nova. I'm curious if the other Houses have symbols like this similar to their marks.

As I'm lost in thought, Raine's hands push up under my shirt. The pads of his fingers are callused and raise goosebumps across my skin as he reaches the underside of my breasts.

"Will you forget me?" he asks between hot kisses against my stomach, trailing up to my sternum. I writhe beneath him and bite my lower lip to keep from moaning as he cups my tits and squeezes them. "Will you forget me when I'm dead?"

I look down at him. His blue eyes pierce through mine.

"I'll never forget you, Raine. *Never*. How could you even think that I would?"

He lets out a few low chuckles and murmurs over my breast, "Let's put it to the test then. I'll leave a note in one of your books, and if you forget me, maybe you'll remember me when you find it. Even if it's just for a moment."

I shove him back and he grins like this is funny. "Stop it. We're going to figure out a way to stop the blight." I say the latter with trailing eyes, wondering how much I believe in my own words.

Raine rolls over on his back and lets out a long breath. "It's okay. I always knew I wouldn't live a long life, not with how I grew up, and especially when things went to shit in Barkovah." His eyes flick back to me, so calm, yet I feel anything but. "You'll be okay. Just keep your heart muted and I'm sure you'll forget me before long."

I open my mouth to argue with him that I still remember everyone, but when I think of my parents and family, I come up blank. I know I had them, but their faces are empty now—like mannequins. Faceless and absent of any life. The motions we went through, the places are still the same, but everything that makes them *them* is gone.

The thought of being muted to my emotions forever is distasteful. My Shadow shifts inside me, letting its hold on my emotions loosen, and I'm enveloped in them.

"Raine." I fist the sheets as a well of tears brim my eyes. His brows raise and he quickly sits up, wiping away tears as they fall. "I don't want you to go."

"Hey, I'm not going anywhere right now. We still have time. But it's nice to see you letting your humanity back in for my sake." His lip kicks up and my heart sinks a bit further into the depths.

"How do you know that?" I ask, still feverishly wiping away tears.

Raine pulls me into his chest and strokes my head, brushing my hair to the side and pressing kisses along my temple. "Because I've already watched it many times. I wish we'd gone in the stairwell together. But I'm happy you'll have more time than me," he whispers ominously. I want him to explain it all to me, but I recall that he is unable.

He holds me until I stop crying, and once our minds are a bit less weary, we whisper about what we think the sex ed class will entail until we fall asleep.

I wake up to Elias's white hair and cold steel eyes staring down at me. He doesn't say anything but nods toward the door. I carefully get up from the bed. Raine's soft breaths tell me he's still fast asleep. Thank gods, the last thing I want to deal with is them bickering.

Elias shuts the door behind us and doesn't bother looking at me as he starts toward the Nova homeroom. I wait until we're at the bottom of the staircase before I dare speak.

"What time is it?" I yawn and try to shake the grogginess that pulls at my mind.

He ignores me as if I hadn't spoken. I deflate and

follow him silently across the homeroom and up the eastern stairwell that leads to his quarters. He has a bit of a limp that he didn't have earlier. I figure he'll ignore me if I ask, so I don't. The stairs spiral up a pillar for two floors before passing an ebony door. When he doesn't stop and enter, I figure it must be Arthur's study.

We continue up another story before reaching the top of the staircase and a white door. Elias shifts to his side and finally looks at me.

"Why was he in your room, Terra?" He levels a glare and I give it right back.

"Fuck you."

He bares his teeth and shakes his head before opening his door and motioning for me to enter. My eyes take a moment to adjust to the dark. He turns on a small lamp sitting at the corner of an old desk and his entire room becomes visible. An impressive shelf of books lines the far wall, a reading nook is tucked in the center of it. A lancet window overlooks the back side of Alkrose and the forest beyond. His bed rests on the ground, draped in black sheets, unmade. The floor is strewn with papers and half-burned candles sit in puddles of black wax atop his desk. He's as messy as I am.

Elias lights his fireplace. It burns evenly just like the one in my room.

"Is this really *your* room? I pictured you being an uptight clean freak." I smile at him.

Elias collects some of the notes on his desk and piles them carelessly. "Unfortunately," he mutters and takes a seat. He removes his cloak and drapes it over the back of his chair. "You're much better at control than your brother.

I'm concerned his Shadow might be a problem." I still; if Elias is worried that can't be good.

"Why?" I sit in the window nook, facing him, and grab one of the dusty books on the cushion. Amser pulls in my veins to be close to him. It's unbearable to refuse it, but I manage.

Elias leans against his hand, legs crossed and disheveled strands of hair falling over his forehead. He looks like a god. "His Shadow is malicious and ill-willed. Don't get me wrong, a lot of Shadows are a little aggressive and bloodthirsty, but his is different."

My brows pull together and I set the book down. "He mentioned earlier to me that it was whispering terrible things to him. He looked really confused and lost in himself." I recall his weary eyes and my heart sinks a little more. "Is that why you brought me here?"

He nods. "My meeting with Cein didn't go well." His gaze remains pinned on the floor. I quirk a brow with concern. "He's furious with the delay I caused. Apparently I was summoned to escort Edgar myself at Za'Afiel, but obviously I was locked in a bunker worrying about you." I shrink a bit, feeling guilty, but at the same time not—Elias is the bad guy here, not Raine. "Edgar's restoration went poorly because of my absence so I need to get him back on track. He needs to be controlled."

I stare at Elias for a few seconds. "You want *my* help?"

He nods.

"Elias, I'm not going to—"

"It's in everyone's best interest. If we don't get him tamed, I'll have no choice but to—" He cuts himself off and gnashes his teeth, looking away sharply.

"You'll have to what?" I say quietly, dread building in my chest.

"I'll have to execute him."

I stand and fist my hands at my sides. "No."

He unfolds his legs and leans forward in his chair, resting his arms on his thighs and clasping his hands together between them. He looks up at me beneath dark lashes. "If we can't get him tamed, then I promise you, I will."

My lower lip trembles and my eyes flick to his right ankle as blood catches my attention. It trickles down the small stretch of skin visible at his ankle. He follows my gaze and shifts so his black pant leg covers it back up. He's hurt. Why hasn't it healed already?

"I'll help you then... I just got Edgar back. I can't lose him again." I shut my eyes and think of how different he looks now, so damaged and cold. The world has ruined him.

And that's not his fault. It's not his fault that the darkness swallowed him whole and infected his mind like poison. Even now, I know he fights the demon inside of him with everything he has, but how long can a soul fight before it tires? The Shadows don't grow weary. They consume at a constant rate.

Elias grins, pain ebbing in his gaze. "Good. Now, you should get some sleep." He shifts in his chair and starts organizing his papers and books again.

He's hiding the wound from me. My eyes drift back to the floor where his boot was and I stare at the blood smeared over the tile. Why does he always pretend to be fine? The mask he wears can't hide everything.

I walk to his bed, curious to find out if his sheets smell like him. Grabbing a book off the black nightstand next to his bed, I settle in the center and pull the sheets up to my stomach.

He looks back at me but I keep my focus on the book, touching the pages and smiling at the scribblings of notes. It's written in Fernestian, so I can't read it, but it's humanizing to see his handwriting, to know he's not just a heartless killing machine. His penmanship is good. The curls at the ends of some of the letters make the corners of my mouth turn up.

Elias watches me for a while before deciding to call it a night and shuts off his lamp. He strips his military jacket off and leaves his tight black undershirt on. His pants hit the floor and I finally glance up to see if he's still bleeding.

His knee has a thick black wound, as if someone stabbed a blade straight through his kneecap. Blood oozes from it, but he doesn't even bat an eye as he grabs some medical tape, wraps it, and uses a white towel to wipe his blood away.

When he's finished, he crawls into the bed like nothing happened. I give him a concerned look.

"It's nothing," he says, crawling closer to me and pulling me against his chest.

"Why haven't you healed? Did Dr. Cein do this to you? Who is he exactly?" I say as he wraps his arms around me securely, my face buried in the crook of his neck. His bed indeed smells like him, but with his arms wrapped around me, I inhale his intoxicating ashy scent straight from the source.

He nuzzles his face into my neck and takes a long,

deep breath. My hand spreads across his shoulder and I grip his shirt tightly. It hurts that he'd rather suffer alone. It's been beaten out of him to know anything else.

"Go to sleep," he whispers. The dim, flickering light of the fire casts a warm glow around his white hair.

"Are you... okay?" I ask softly, trying to push away from him so I can see his expression, but he holds on tight and doesn't let me move. I take that as his silent *no*.

It's different than it was before. Our Shadows don't jump across our skin together with excitement and lust, feverish for the connection—instead, they circle from deeper within. Like a somber dance, courting and looking further into one another, not just seeking power.

Elias makes a choked sound and pulls away, his brows pinched together tightly. Anguish and resentment flash across his gaze. "I don't like this."

I lean back and let my eyes linger on his collarbone. "Don't like what?"

He reaches up and tugs on his shirt where his heart lies beneath. "Whenever I look at you pain spreads inside my chest. I hate it." His eyes are distrustful and wary.

"Don't tell me you care about me," I say with a light, joking tone, but Elias's face only grows more severe. It's sad to think he never learned how to understand his heart. "Tell me who Cein is, Elias. I want to help you."

Elias stiffens but reluctantly murmurs, "He is the founder of the Shadows. In a way, he raised me." His voice is devoid of nostalgia; it holds only disdain.

My eyes widen and I find myself clinging to him desperately. "He was the one that put a Shadow inside you as a child?" A lump forms in my throat and air evades me.

A somber grin pulls at my assassin's soft lips. "I was the first one. He found me when I was living on the streets in Cyprin and gave me a home. Though it came at a price." His eyes grow distant with memory. "But enough questions, training resumes tomorrow and you'll be expected to attend classes, so we'll be up before the sun rises."

I fight the urge to wrap around him and let my chest connect with his. Raine would be upset if I ditched him all night. I should head back. I stare at Elias for a moment before shifting off him and standing from his bed, heading toward the door with the somber thoughts of a young Elias, alone and tormented by the man named Cein.

"Good night," I say softly. Elias grunts in reply, not pleased that I'm leaving him to go back to Raine, I'm sure.

The door clicks shut behind me and I think I hear Elias press against it before I start down the stairs. When I reenter my room, Raine is still tangled in the sheets, deep in sleep. I crawl into bed and curl up next to him, threading my fingers through his dark locks of hair and thinking of every possible way we can keep him alive.

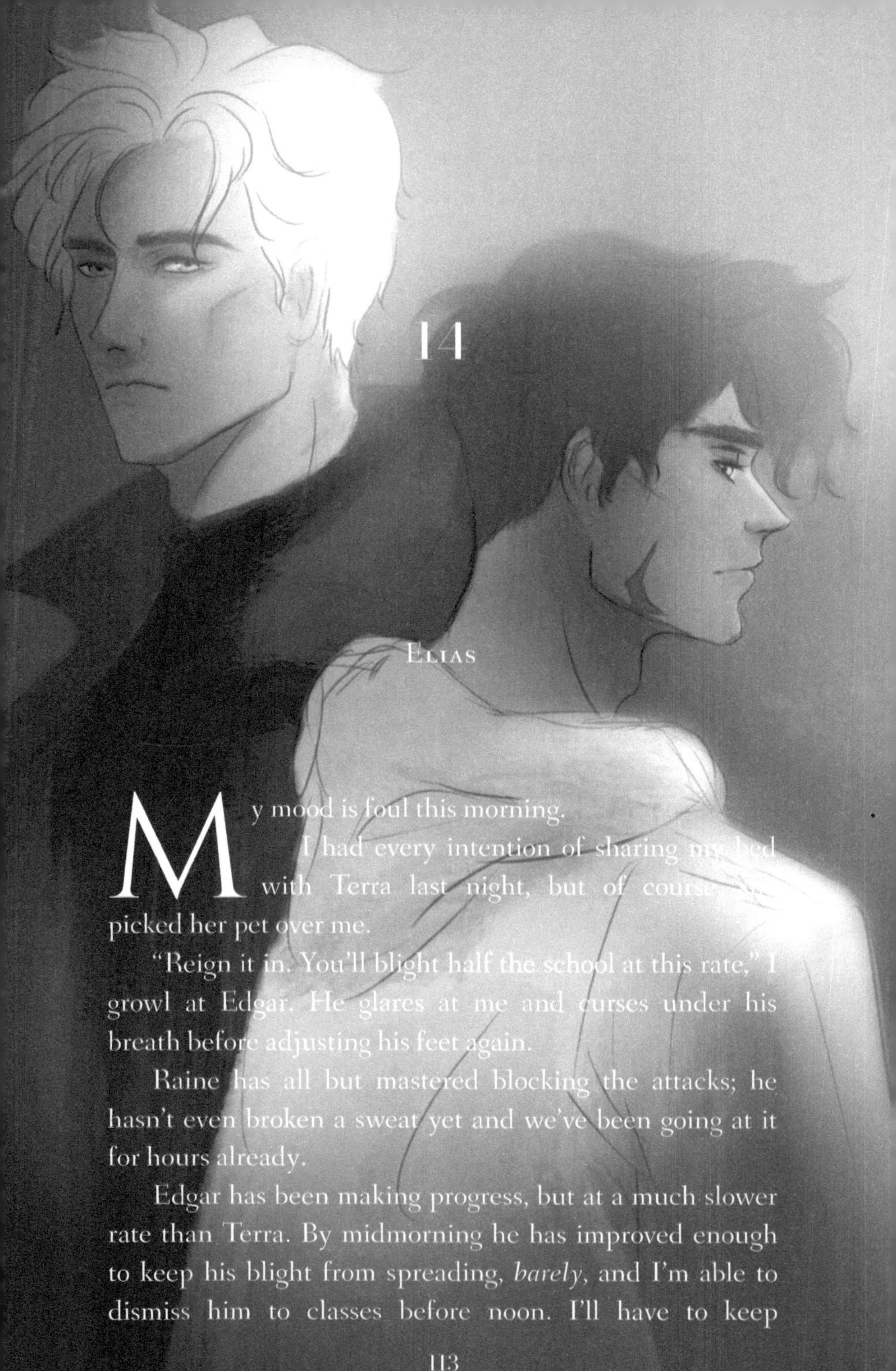

14

Elias

My mood is foul this morning.

I had every intention of sharing my bed with Terra last night, but of course, she picked her pet over me.

"Reign it in. You'll blight half the school at this rate," I growl at Edgar. He glares at me and curses under his breath before adjusting his feet again.

Raine has all but mastered blocking the attacks; he hasn't even broken a sweat yet and we've been going at it for hours already.

Edgar has been making progress, but at a much slower rate than Terra. By midmorning he has improved enough to keep his blight from spreading, *barely*, and I'm able to dismiss him to classes before noon. I'll have to keep working with him in the mornings, but as long as he isn't attacking anything, which I tell him specifically not to, he should be okay.

Terra and Raine look tired from their late night, but neither of them complains.

I nod for Terra to take her place for practice while Raine switches out with Arthur. I'm mildly surprised when he comes to stand by me. I glance over at him.

"Why did I need to switch with Arthur?" he asks as he shoves his hands into his jacket pockets, tilting his head back and breathing in deeply. He's almost my height and carries much of the same heaviness on his broad shoulders. Perhaps our similar emotional damage is what Terra likes so much. I peg her as the type of woman who wants to *fix* things. It's the light in her eyes that gives her away. She wants to tend to us, make us less broken.

"Just watch and you'll see why," I mutter under my breath, silently sending a prayer to the gods that Arthur doesn't slip up like yesterday. He was a millisecond from having his head sliced clean off. We may have our differences, but he's one of my only remaining friends.

Terra takes a long breath before shifting her stance and letting Amser pulse from her as if she was born with it. The line of power that bursts from her hand intends to decapitate; it cuts through the air faster than the eye can trace.

Arthur bends backward in a flash, his cloak flowing over the snow like a fresh white blanket. He straightens just as swiftly, a cocky grin spreading across his lips.

Raine gasps at my side and I glance at him. His eyes are filled with awe at how magnificent our little Nova is.

Though it's early, I trust that she can keep herself from blighting if she tries hard enough. Her resolve is impressive. As is her desire to remain pure and untainted.

"Well, at least I know she'll be okay when I'm gone," Raine says low enough for only me to hear. Arthur walks over to Terra to tell her how well she's doing. They're completely oblivious to us standing on the sidelines. "I'm really going to die, aren't I?"

I don't enjoy Raine's presence, especially since I let him be my torturer for the entirety of last week. But one thing I admire about him is the loyalty he seems to feel toward Terra. If he's worth anything, it's as a shield for my mate.

At least until his dying breath.

"Yes, you've been blighted. I've yet to meet someone who has survived it." I watch as the light dims in his eyes. My skin prickles with the strength teeming beneath his. He houses the Destiny Shadow. I met it long ago. Why do I see so much of my old friend in Raine? The thought is too heavy, so I let it sink back into the depths of Velis's grasp.

I clear my throat. "But, should anyone have the right circumstances to *possibly* overcome the blight, I think you might have a small, insignificant chance."

I meant for it only to lift his spirits a little so he wasn't so gloomy, but he looks at me sharply, his jaw set and eyes brimming with torment. "Really?" he asks.

"It's not a good way to die, Raine. And even though I utterly despise you, I'd rather see you cut in half instead of dying the way the blight takes you," I mutter as I watch Terra try a few more attacks on Arthur, mildly aware of Raine's lingering eyes on me.

"Is that your way of confessing you don't hate me?"

"No, I very much don't like you."

Raine cocks his head back and laughs. Terra's eyes flash over to us and she grins at the sight of us not skinning one another.

"I do believe there is a way. So don't give up hope," I say with an even tone, then subsequently a deep pit sinks inside my chest. *Since when do I tell people to* have *hope?* It's usually the other way around.

"Why are you being kind to me? I fucking tortured you." Raine seems genuinely curious as to why I care.

Him and me both.

This guy is annoying, Velis growls, the sound ringing through my ears until it slowly subdues.

I was once as ruined as Raine. Did he really think I was unconscious during my torture? No, I was very much awake. Very aware of his tears crashing to the floor as he cut into my skin because deep down he hated what he was doing. Perhaps I see myself in him. Someone doing something heinous and against their morals to keep those they care about safe. By the end of my torture, he was practically begging me just to give him the information about Fernestia so he didn't have to continue.

I think of the boy I saw cradled in his arms after the Skyfell. The way Raine's mind broke and he ripped the brains out of anyone who was in his way. Perhaps that's why... I don't wish for him to die. He reminds me so much of—

Stop, Velis hisses. *I can't keep your heart suppressed forever if you tug on the emotions.*

That gives me pause and I redirect.

"I just hate seeing Terra worry about you," I say with impassive eyes. Raine narrows his own at me; I don't think he buys it, but he doesn't say anything in return. Instead, a somber smile pulls at his lips. "Try the library, the old books on the third floor up near the back windows."

That's where *we* used to study. I shut my eyes and I can see all of us again. Strange how they still feel so close even though five years have passed.

Raine looks at me like he can't quite figure me out. "Thank you, Elias."

I inwardly groan at him thanking me. "Don't mention it to Terra. Just do your research and keep quiet about it, got it?" If Cein or Empress Raven find out I'm trying to unblight another student they'll punish me again.

My knee throbs painfully and I shift my weight to my other leg.

Raine nods and we don't speak for the remainder of the session.

When Arthur calls it, I nod my silent agreement: Terra is ready to join the rest of the students—her control is outstanding. Edgar, on the other hand, I'm uncertain about. His hold on his Shadow is erratic.

Terra smiles at me as she and Raine take their leave and head back to Alkrose in time for lunch. Arthur and I walk slowly back toward the castle.

"Her muscle memory is brilliant," Arthur says thoughtfully. He jots down more notes in his journal as we walk. Such a nerd, always carrying that book around.

"Uh-huh," I say mindlessly as I try to remember what I usually start with for the first-year students in the destruction class. They'll be learning their riding forms with

Arthur today, so I'll try to make them use that knowledge somehow in tomorrow's training. "Let me know what Raine's form is after their class today, will you?" I pull my hood up over my head when I feel eyes on me from the center tower. I always notice Emerai's heavy gaze.

Arthur pulls his hood up as well. One of Emerai's most irritable traits is his ability to read lips, even from great distances. He is the perfect war tool for recon.

"Sure, if I even get to see it," Arthur mumbles and looks at me. His eyes are rimmed with red; sleepless nights, I'm guessing. "I like this group the most. They have so much promise and life still. It reminds me of us, back when we arrived." He laughs but his smile soon fades into a nostalgic frown.

I lower my eyes to the lake as we descend the final hill. The mist has fallen low in the valley this morning, the sun's rays warming the top layer of ice to an amber hue.

"They remind me so much of them. Which is why we can't fuck up again." I can't keep the ice out of my tone.

Arthur nudges me. "The past is the past, Elias. No amount of trying to help these students will bring back our friends."

Something cold pierces the inside of my heart, a pain I thought I'd long forgotten, but there it is, festering inside me still.

"You expect me to believe you aren't helping them?" I banish all the faces from my past with one sharp breath.

Arthur lets out a low sigh and a short laugh, returning to writing in his journal. "You know I do what I can." He nods at my knee. "Cein?"

I sweep my cloak over my shoulders so he can't see my

limp. "Yeah, he's not happy at all about the delay. You try lying to him about why you let some punk skin you alive for a week."

"Not possible, Cein cannot be lied to," he says, knowing damn well that I already know this.

"Exactly."

Arthur levels me a concerned expression. "Why *did* you let Raine keep you so long?"

"Well, when I woke up down in the bunker, my first thoughts were to kill them all and get to the surface. But then I realized that my Shadow beacon wouldn't read at that depth in the cement tomb. Terra was looking for her brother and that Solas boy, and I wanted to give her a chance to find them."

I lift my gaze to Alkrose, sleepy and drab in the cold, gray and black mountain terrain. Clouds huddle low today, clinging to the stone walls and crisping the air with their cold, wet sting.

"And surely you didn't think that would take a week?" Arthur eggs me on. I don't look at him though, I keep my gaze on the dreary view.

"After a few days, I came to the conclusion that I didn't want to go back up. That brat Raine would tell me how much Terra was enjoying the city and how she fawned over him." I let out a half laugh, running my hand down my face. "And I wanted her to enjoy that for as long as she could, because I knew what would come next. What I didn't account for was her Nova and mine together in the bunker creating a stronger beacon."

Arthur tuts. "Ah. *That's* how they found you." He flips his journal open again and jots down more notes.

I nod. My knee throbs and a shudder crawls through my spine at the memory of Cein sawing into my leg with his Shadow, a sharp serrated blade, as he threatened to make Terra the next beacon at Whales of Tauh. I will never allow that to happen.

No one can hold the weight of that much death and guilt except me.

15

Finn

Kai throws rocks over the icy lake as we wait for the Shadow riding class to begin. It makes strange sounds, like thin metal waving swiftly and making the air itch at your ears.

"Stop that," Corvus hisses at him.

"What else am I supposed to do?" Kai drops the rocks and blows warm air over his reddened fingers.

I raise a brow at him. "Wait like the rest of us."

He gives me a firm, annoyed look before his blue eyes catch on someone behind me. I turn as Terra and Raine join the class. My cheeks heat and my gut twists.

"Hey—over here, you two!" Kai shouts and waves at them. My eyes couldn't be wider and the *what-the-fuck-*

are-you-doing stare I'm leveling Kai with couldn't be clearer.

Corvus grins and I stiffen my legs to keep them from giving out on me as Terra and Raine walk over to us.

Raine has the same dark hair I do, but his eyes are a piercing blue. His jaw is sharp and the scar across it only makes him look more frightening. A few truckloads of students came in from Barkovah this morning, and from what I heard, Raine was their callous leader after the Skyfell in Navasik.

"I don't think we've been properly introduced yet. I'm Kaidel; this is Corvus," Kai says like we're meeting at a picnic party. Corvus nods cordially but gives me a sidelong glance. "I've heard a lot about you, Terra, and who is your friend?" He already knows who he is, but I let Kai be his courteous self and ask them anyway.

Terra assesses him for a second before smiling and linking arms with Raine. My stomach sinks further. I swear she's doing it on purpose to get at me.

"This is Raine." She touches his arm gently. I yearn for her to hold onto my arm like that again. I swallow my pride and nod at him with a weak grin.

Kai and Corvus engage in light conversation with them while I stare at the snow. After a few minutes, Edgar sulks over with Arthur trailing him. According to my book, Arthur's our professor for Shadow riding. He's elusive to all but the Novas, it seems; I suppose it makes sense since they're all holed away in the eastern tower away from everyone else.

Edgar stands next to his sister. The air is heavier when he's around, like he's barely containing his power. A girl with white hair tied back into a long braid notices him and eagerly joins us too.

"Lucina, I didn't know you were in this class." Edgar perks up a bit and the tense energy rolling off his shoulders subsides. Terra greets her cheerfully aswell and Lucina smiles widely at them both.

"I'm just relieved to see familiar faces," Lucina says shyly. She looks at Edgar the same way Raine looks at Terra.

Watching them together makes the weight of the exam and the lingering death seem not so heavy. But my small reprieve fades as my eyes shift to the Darkflies standing by the entrance of the castle, switching shifts with the morning soldiers. Their fingers are always on their guns, ready to kill.

I wonder which moves faster: a bullet or a Shadow.

Arthur holds up his journal and it vanishes into a shroud of black mist. He takes his place at the shoreline of the frozen lake, all of us pausing our chatter to await his instruction.

His gray eyes find Terra and soften as he speaks. "Good morning—I hope you are ready to embrace your Shadows and let them walk freely by your sides today. If not, don't fret. It may take some of you a while to coax them out." Arthur spreads his arms out and his Shadow shimmers into physical form beside him.

It's shrouded in black, but it's much clearer and much more *real* than I ever thought possible. His Shadow looks like a wolf and stands as tall as Arthur. The face is that of a canine's skull and the bones that peek out from the mist forming its neck and ribs make my throat dry. Its legs are long and too thin for any normal animal. Antlers spread from its head, making it look like a mythical creature in a storybook. The tail is long and wispy, evaporating into the air like licks of flames.

"This is my Shadow's physical form. Shadows are vicious in combat and can travel at fast speeds, an obvious necessity in times of war. Now, I want you all to try and summon your Shadows. Don't be afraid to ask for help. If you wish to survive, you'll master this by the second-semester exam. If you are unable to summon your Shadow, you are easily slain. On the other hand, should you be able to summon but your performance is subpar, the spectators of the exam will mark you off to be sent to the front lines."

Every hair on my spine prickles and I swallow hard. The front lines? To fight against our own nation? I want to think it's just a scare tactic, but nothing else here has made any sense so I'm not holding my breath.

We break into groups. Raine, Terra, Corvus, Edgar, Lucina, and Kai remain around me and we try to summon our Shadows out.

Terra's Shadow comes out first, easily, in a slow, elegant strut. It's a feline of some sort, big enough to ride. It resembles Arthur's wolf in that its face is a skull and the spine and ribs are the only real shape that hold the mass of black smoke together. Its eyes are two bright dots in the center of the eye sockets, chilling my bones as it looks at me.

"Holy shit, how did you do that?" Kai's eyes grow wide and he walks up to the feline Shadow, pressing his hands against the smoke until his fingers touch something firm beneath. "It really does have a physical presence. I can't push my hand through it," he says mindlessly as he examines the creature.

Corvus steps beside him, his eyes dancing with the same mystified look. "Amazing."

A small smile crests Edgar's glum face and he tries to approach the Shadow too, offering his hand warily. It growls at him and he glances back at Terra.

"It doesn't like your Shadow... Sorry." She deflates as if the thought of their Shadows being enemies upsets her greatly. Lucina pets the creature's long snout and smiles, giggling and looking at Edgar to make sure that he sees.

Edgar just shrugs and mumbles, "It's fine."

Terra turns her attention to me and grins. "What about yours?"

My fingers curl at my sides. I don't know if I can call my Shadow out—I know only its name. *Laphia.*

Corvus gasps as his body releases the same black mist. It forms a creature of feathers and bone. A crow the size of a man, but with four wings and eyes as red as rubies. Bones prick from the wings and the chest plate.

What dark gods sent these creatures to us? They're sinister and appalling.

Kai backs into me, taking us both to the ground. "What the fuck, Corvus," he sputters. I'm as speechless as Kai is.

Arthur notices our group's advancement and approaches us. "Great job over here. Terra and Corvus are already well on their way to preparing for the exam." The professor leans in and looks closely at both the Shadows. The creatures remain still, as if there are no thoughts going through their heads, which I know isn't the case. They clearly speak and think just as we do. They seem oddly calm and relaxed with Arthur.

Raine doesn't bother even trying to free his Shadow, just keeps his arms crossed and observes Corvus miserably failing to mount his crow for flight.

Kai and I exhaust every avenue we can think of to tempt ours out. Laphia has been silent since Martin's death. That may prove to be a problem. Does it only wake up in dire moments? I might have to ask Kallos for some pointers later.

Edgar stares hollowly at the frozen lake. His lips move slightly, as if he's speaking with himself—or worse yet, to his Shadow. Chills crawl up my spine as I watch him sit slumped over a rock like a shell.

Lucina steps beside me and crosses her arms in concern. Her hands grip her upper arms as if she's cold. "He's been like this since he was restored," she says grimly. As I glance her way she shuts her eyes somberly.

I whisper, "Do you think he'll come out of it?"

She draws in a long breath before opening her eyes and muttering, "No. I miss him so much already. We all do. But if this is the new him, we have to accept that." Lucina offers me a sad smile before she walks to Edgar's side and sits silently. He continues to whisper to himself.

I consider talking to him to see how he's doing with all of this. I know he was at a different location and underwent an alternative process. As my feet start to move toward Edgar and Lucina, Laphia speaks loudly, the scratchy voice curling around the base of my neck like steel. *Stay away from Sully. It is poison. It is rot.*

I freeze and goosebumps rise across my arms like I've

been dropped into a cold bath. Laphia may be cryptic but its message is clear—Edgar is dangerous.

A frown pulls at my lips as I look at him, sitting alone with his demons, unaware that those who care for him surround him. Lucina lets her head rest on Edgar's shoulder, and he finally notices her and flinches—not even noticing she was there.

Kai sprawls out over the couch in the Cosmos homeroom and exhales loudly. I lie back on the couch across from him, hissing in pain as my sore muscles relax.

"You'd think we'd be in better shape after the trip across the country to get here," Kai complains.

I reply, "You'd think that we wouldn't have to go through impossible classes and then exercise like we're in the military for three hours after lunch. We don't have another class today, do we? I was hoping to catch Kallos this afternoon." I lift my hand and stare at the mark of the cosmos and stars on my palm. The ceiling is lit with purple and blue clouds of astral lights, stars twinkling intermittently.

"Hmm, I think we have one more—a night class." Kai lazily pulls his book up from the floor and flips to our schedule. When he slams the book shut, I nearly have a heart attack.

"Gods, what class?" I sit up and shoot him a glare.

Kai's covering his face with both palms. There's only

one class that would make any of us cover our faces like that.

"Sex ed," we say simultaneously and with the same dreadful tone.

"There's a silver lining," Kai says sarcastically.

I frown hard at him. "*What*?"

"Kallos is the professor."

I press my palms into my face. "Godsdamn it."

16

Terra

I've asked myself "why" a billion times already and still come up short of an answer, so I just accept that this is happening even though the majority of us are already adults and have vast knowledge of intimacy.

Sex ed is on the first floor, past the indoor gardens that line the west side of the castle. I let my eyes browse the enormous windows and the plants that thrive inside. I would say it's beautiful, but every single plant is a shade of red. The vines are a deep maroon crawling up the panes like veins. There are leaves of softer reds and bright roses, poppies, and smaller flowers I don't recognize.

Raine glances over as we pass the gardens and leans in close to whisper, "Morbid fucking Fernestians." I find myself nodding and pulling my gaze away from the blood-red room.

The classroom is filled with people I don't recognize, all dressed in the same tactical gear we wear but with different colored cloaks. Raine and I are the only ones to bear white. The rest are beige, purple, red, and blue.

I let out a breath of relief that no one I know is here. This is going to be so difficult to sit through. I take a desk in the back and slump in the chair with my hood pulled up. Raine takes the seat to my right. Light murmurs fill the room as we wait for the professor.

The empty seats to either side of me pull out just as the professor walks in. I eye him carefully as he struts confidently across the room, long golden hair tied back in a ponytail, golden eyes. He has three black bars on either side of his mouth, almost like stitches. Even though his mouth is firm and flat, it gives the illusion that he's smiling.

I recognize him as the head of House Cosmos. His cloak is gilded, unpatching of the Cosmos House color, black. His face is composed of sharp features and he has a beauty that most men don't. A golden god of a man. Where Nekane and Elias are rugged, he has a soft, angelic appearance. He's lovely to look at. I wonder why his eyes aren't gray like most of the Fernestians'.

He takes a seat at the head of the class and his eyes land on the person next to me. I'm curious enough to look.

My stomach twists when I find Finn's amber eyes and high cheekbones. He glances at me and our cheeks turn rosy in unison.

No, oh gods, not him.

Kai is sitting on his other side making a face that reveals how funny he thinks it is.

Someone else takes a seat in front of me. I am utterly aghast to find Edgar is in this class too.

"Welcome to Sex ed." Kallos flicks his fingers in the air and light etches words into the empty space above his head, blurry and not quite readable yet. Kallos mutters, "You can have sex with anyone except a Shadow Mate. We are going to learn how to practice safe sex when you have an aggressive Shadow inside you."

My jaw is hanging loose from my head. Raine shifts uncomfortably in his seat and Kai is hardly holding himself together, both his hands pressed to his mouth to keep his hysterical laughter in. Edgar sinks in his chair and refuses to acknowledge any of us behind him. I'm grateful for that.

"Basically, you can fuck whomever you'd like since the chances of you finding a mate are slim to none. I believe we only have a few couplings in the entire academy, so it shouldn't be difficult." Kallos stands and flicks his fingers in the air again, making the words in the space above him legible.

They read: "*Consensual Violent Sex*."

Everyone groans simultaneously and I'm tempted to get up and run out of here. Kallos's eyes linger on me for a moment before he continues with the class and I can't help but wonder if he already knows about my situation with Elias.

But does he know that we're actively fucking? And Raine, too... *Oh gods*.

I half listen as Kallos explains the ins and outs of our Shadows' lust and their call to others' powers. He shows us a few concoctions of birth control potions, which the men take. (Wow, smart, world-shattering. Who would have thought the Fernestians would be the first to say "The men are the reasonable things to use contraceptives on"?)

"Okay, now I will show you the savage pull Shadows can have and correct ways to proceed when courting a female," he says casually. Meanwhile, almost everyone's head is buried in their arms or their hands are pressed against their faces.

Kai bursts out laughing. "Are you seriously going to *show* us?!" Finn curses under his breath and smacks Kai on the arm.

Kallos doesn't seem one bit bothered by his Cosmos student's comment. "How else can you grasp how vicious it can be?" the professor says with a light grin. His eyes flick back to me and he raises his hand like a gentleman. "Terra, care to help me?"

My soul exits my body.

I'm stunned. Every single face turns back and stares at me. Fuck this. No. Kai starts laughing again and I glare at him. Finn's eyes are rounded like this is the worst thing he's ever been subjected to and my stomach curls with horror. Even Edgar looks back at me, but instead of the despair I was sure I'd see in his eyes, he's on the verge of laughing too.

Kallos lets out a soft chuckle and draws my attention back to him. "I promise, nothing with our clothes off."

Is that supposed to make this less awkward?!

My jaw drops again but the seriousness of Kallos's expression and his lax beauty settles the fear in my chest.

There's a pull deep in my bones; Amser is drawn to him and urges me forward.

This fucking Shadow is going to be the end of me.

Kallos keeps his hand raised for me as I slowly stand and make my way to the front of the classroom. His golden cloak graces his broad shoulders. Up close, the six bars on his face look less like stitches and more like ebony staples embedded into his perfect bright skin.

I let my hand slide into his and the thrum of our Shadows connecting sends a shudder down my spine. Amser immediately takes to him and a carnal throb floods through my entire body.

Kallos winces at the sensation and a frightening look of pure lust flickers across his eyes. Does every male crave a female Nova that badly?

My Shadow answers me even though I didn't directly ask it. *Yes.*

The professor wraps his hand around mine. The smooth surface of his skin is unlike Elias's or Raine's. His hands aren't callous or cold; they are entirely warm and kind like Arthur's. My curiosity piques.

His power is immense, I can sense it just from our connection, and as I look out across the classroom, I realize they must be able to feel it too. Everyone's eyes are wide.

Finn and Raine have lovely blushes across their cheeks and it makes my heart beat faster. Edgar is already looking anywhere but at the two of us. I quickly look back at Kallos, which doesn't calm my nerves at all.

"That wave of power you all sensed is the greeting of two Shadows who deem each other worthy. When this happens, a strong urge to devour one another will fall over you," Kallos says through gritted teeth. His jaw is flexed and he tightens his grasp on my wrist. I swallow dryly as I stare into his practically starved eyes.

He said *devour,* right?

Kallos pulls me closer, letting our chests press together. The low growl that rolls from deep in his throat sends heat through my core, making me press my thighs together to quell my traitorous body's outrageous urge.

"Everything inside you is heightened now. You have to fight the bad instincts. Alkrose rules are that anything you and your partner agree to do is permissible, but if there is no mutual consent, then that is where permission ends. For example: Terra, I want to kiss you. She's going to say—"

"*Yes,*" I blurt out—I don't know what just came over me, but my heart hammers inside my chest at the embarrassment that follows. Kallos sucks a breath in and his Adam's apple bobs as he stares down at me. There's so much restraint behind his well-trained impassive expression.

His eyes drop to my lips as he says with a raspy voice, "If they agree, then it is permissible." He clears his throat, looking away from my lips and back at the class. Sweat starts to bead down the side of his neck and I can't help but grin wickedly at how diligently he's controlling himself right now. "Now, let's say you're already tangled and embracing them closely, but you decide you don't like where things are headed and your partner can't stop. Here is a trick to instantly snap the Shadows' connection and bring you to your senses."

Oh my gods, I can't.

Kallos pulls me against his chest. I genuinely don't

think he knew what he was signing up for. My Shadow pulls his in so viciously that he audibly loses his breath. I'm as consumed by him as he is by me and my knees falter. Kallos is in no better shape and he ends up leaning my limp body over his desk as his legs give in.

The classroom lights up with gasps and the only one laughing his ass off is Kai. I can only stare into Kallos's golden eyes. His expression of shock quickly fades and his lips pull up into a handsome smile. He looks into my eyes with curiosity.

"No wonder Elias is so possessive of you. Your Shadow has quite the *appetite*," he whispers in a deep, tempting voice. I bury my teeth into my bottom lip—his erection is pressed against my lower abdomen. "Elias might know how to please you, but I doubt those boys do. Tell me, are you satisfied?"

Raine and Finn? Is he really going there right now?

Kallos's lips are close to mine. He has a lovely scent, musky, with a bitterness like metal.

I can only stare at him and imagine what filthy things he really wants to say. His attention snags back on the class, who are all wide-eyed and silently watching our professor as he pins me to the desk beneath his sculpted body.

Kallos clears his throat and returns to the lesson. "To snap the connection you need to have control over your Shadow. Firmly tell it to let go and it will."

I wait for Kallos to cut the connection but he doesn't. My brows raise and horror flashes through his gaze for a moment. My mouth pinches into a tight grin.

"Do you need me to do it?" I whisper, enjoying this

entirely too much, even as his knee slowly nudges mine apart. If we weren't in front of like fifty other people, I wonder where this would go.

He lets out a short, deep laugh and nods. He's the complete opposite of Arthur. Bright, lively, and full of humor. I find myself drawn to them both in different ways.

I scold my Shadow for having wandering eyes and demand it release him.

Kallos winks at me as thanks and straightens his posture, helping me up and letting his fingers linger around my arm for a second too long before jerking his head for me to take my seat.

Raine and Finn have concerned expressions but I can only smile at Kai's inability to keep his laughter contained. My brother has both palms covering his face and I can't help but die a little inside.

"I thought he was going to fuck you on the desk," Kai sputters and Finn shoots him a death glare.

I sink into my seat and groan. Great, I'm sure rumors will run rampant about this.

Kallos talks for a few more minutes before dismissing us with advice to "prepare" for the next class because it will be more in-depth. I'm not entirely sure what to do with that information, so I try as best I can not to think about the professor's erect cock and how perfect it felt against me.

Finn stops me when class is dismissed and everyone else funnels out of the room. Kai lingers but gives us space to talk. Raine rolls his eyes but stands close to Kai. I want to do anything but stand here and talk to Finn, but honestly, after sex ed, I'm feeling surprisingly relaxed.

"Yes?" I ask halfheartedly as I collect my books and level him with a disinterested stare.

"Want to come train with us tonight? We're going to meet in the courtyard after dinner and I'd really like it if you joined us." His smile is nervous but he asks sincerely.

It wouldn't be the worst thing to try to mend our friendship, would it? A night training with him... it sounds nice.

"Yeah, I'd like that," I say in a friendly tone. His amber eyes soften on me and I'm relieved that this feels so natural.

"See you tonight then." He grins and nods at Kai; the two of them walk to the front of the room to speak with Kallos.

I'm tempted to eavesdrop but decide against it. I'm eager to get to the library and search for anything that I can find on blights. Hope is something I think we could all use a bit of right now.

17

Terra

I'm surprised to find Raine on the third floor of the library.

His white cloak contrasts brightly against the dark rafters and aisles. The rows are long and tall, filled to the brim with books, candles, skulls, and bottles filled with an assortment of things. The ceilings are tall and drafty, and the distinct scent of old pages gives me an odd sort of comfort.

Candles flicker with a warm glow and give off enough light to read without straining the eyes. It's a magical little dark corner he's found, and I wonder how he knew exactly where to look to find this section. I've been in here for hours, burning the midnight oil, trying to find anything remotely close to Shadows and blights with no luck.

Raine perks up as he hears my footsteps. "Hey," he says with more life than I've heard in his tone all day. "What are you doing in here?"

I narrow my eyes at him because he's anything but the reading type. "What are *you* doing here?"

"Just trying to learn more about this place, I guess." He nods to the table and I take a seat next to him. The red rug beneath us looks old and worn. Two cups of tea are set on the table.

I raise a brow at him. "You drink tea?" He winks at me and I let out a short laugh.

He smiles and those beautiful teeth shine brightly as he mutters back, "Of course I drink tea. I expect you do as well, right? Two sugar cubes and a dash of milk?"

"Yeah, but how do you know that? You knew I was coming?" I ask. I take a sip of the tea and hum with delight as the warm liquid glides down my throat.

Raine shrugs. "I'm *all-knowing* now, remember?" he says with a cocky grin.

I nudge him with my elbow. "Since when did you get fun?"

He laughs and it draws one from my lips as well.

"I guess having the weight of Barkovah off my shoulders and my imminent death has made me want to enjoy what time I have left," he says sadly.

"What are you really doing here, Raine?" I ask more seriously and pull my brows together with concern. He's probably here trying to find answers, just as I am.

"I'm actually here because someone told me I might find something to lift the blight."

Did Arthur tell him? It couldn't have been Elias.

"That's actually why I'm here too," I admit and he flashes me a thankful grin. I set my cup down and press my hand over his. He flinches at my touch and pulls his hand away, jaw clenching.

"Why do you always do that?" I ask in a soft, somber voice. He's so reluctant to be touched and loved. It hurts to watch him pull away from affection. "It's okay if you don't want to tell me."

He stares at my hand on the table and shakes his head. When he speaks, he draws out each word. I can hear the grief in every one of them. "I... don't have a great past."

"I think you'd be surprised at how many of us don't," I offer with a sad smile. It's odd, isn't it? Smiling when you're hurting so deeply. I wonder if it is a coping mechanism.

Raine looks up at me and analyzes my face. "I think if we look for information about breaking curses, we'll be able to try a few things." He hands me a book and I take it, dropping the matter as easily as he did. I refuse to make him say what haunts him. He'll tell me when he's ready.

"There's nothing specifically on the Shadows though, is there?" I ask, already sure I know the answer.

Raine's eyes fall to the book in his hands as he mutters, "No, there isn't. Not for the blights and Novas anyway. Anything on Shadow anatomy, casting, and forms is already in our class texts." He turns a page and skims through it.

It's weird to see him so still, reading, and not looking entirely drained. I think of Barkovah and the small boy who used to follow us around. My chest seizes and my lower lip trembles; I suck it in, biting down on the fat part of it.

I don't remember who that child was. What was his name?

I'm forgetting, just like Raine said I would. The thought weighs on me as I flip through the book, searching desperately for anything that might lead to us breaking the blight. Because I won't forget Raine—he can't die.

After an hour of reading and skimming, I come across a handwritten note stuffed into the crease of the book. It's hard to read, so I scoot closer to the lamp on the edge of the table and hold the slip of paper at an angle to read.

Elias accidentally blighted them, all of our friends, but I think I found a way to stop it. Our squad cannot lose another... Our hearts cannot bear it, especially Elias. He won't recover from this. I just hope I'm not too late.

My eyes widen and I hold up the tattered note. Raine glances up at me.

"Someone left this here. They know how to stop the blight." My voice is shaky with hope. Raine doesn't smile, but he nods with determination.

"Let's start there then. Does it say who wrote it?" He carefully takes the note from my hand and looks it over.

I shake my head. "No, but the handwriting might help us determine that. Where do we start though? The professors, castle staff, soldiers... I don't know how we're going to narrow it down. Assuming whoever wrote it is still alive." I sullen and look back at the book the note was hidden in. Could it have been Arthur? He did send me to the library to find something; maybe he wanted me to find it and ask him.

"'Our squad.' Whoever wrote this was Elias's friend," Raine says as he narrows his eyes at the note. He has a point; the way the writer speaks of Elias is knowing. "How many of the Fernestians look like they've been here as long as Elias?"

I nod. Only the professors, really. The Darkfly soldiers are far beneath the Bleeding Suns and I haven't seen Elias so much as acknowledge them in passing. "Yeah, you're right. So we'll start with them. We shouldn't keep our sights too narrow, but if we notice anyone who's been here for six years, they are worth looking into."

Raine grins and somehow this castle filled with dread and malice feels less burdensome.

"Hey, Raine."

"Yeah?"

"Once we get rid of your blight, we should try to escape this place, all of us. I think we could do it—I can talk Elias into it too. He acts tough and brutish, but I don't think he really wants to be."

Raine hands the note back to me and firms his lips into a thin line. "Don't get your hopes up for either of those things. I don't see a fate in which I survive—and Elias will never turn against Fernestia. His hands are too red."

There's truth in that. How does one turn back when they've already done so much damage? There's nothing left to salvage. The debts are far too great.

We put the books back and head out of the library.

I consider how we're going to check the professors' handwriting. They each have studies like Elias's, I'm sure, so we can sneak into them and compare when I find an opening. Arthur is the only one I think I can just ask. I'm not sure how I feel about the others and where their loyalties lie. Nekane is going to be the hardest one, and I can't even think about Kallos right now without feeling his chest and erection.

I close my eyes and think about who to start with as Raine and I eat quietly in the mess hall. The other House tables are filled, chatter roaring into the arched ceilings, but the Nova table is empty for the most part. Edgar and his friends are nowhere to be seen, besides Tamaris and Alani. Ash sits close to them, making me wonder if they've gotten over their quarrels. Ash has been keeping to himself these past few days. He's prickly and guarded, spending most of his time alone in his room or whisked away for portals. He is one of Fernestia's main assets, that's for sure. The Portal Nova.

Tamaris nudges Alani. "Your Shadow is worthless for riding."

Alani slumps her shoulders and nods reluctantly. "Yeah. Of course I get stuck with the stupid Shadow." She drops her fork and crosses her arms. Her hair is pulled up into a high ponytail with a pink bow at the band.

I tilt my head with amusement and ask, "Dare I ask what the form is?"

She glowers and shakes her head. Tamaris spits it out for her. "It's a fucking salamander."

Raine chokes on his drink and Ash cracks a grin. Alani looks mortified and pulls Tamaris's long, black hair. Her head jerks to the side and the two instantly start bickering. Ash, Raine, and I laugh at the exchange. I know her riding form is important and can affect her performance in the second semester, but at least she can summon it. That was one of the requirements to avoid being sent to the frontlines, wasn't it? Small win.

The doors to the mess hall swing open as a group of new students enter. These must be more from Barkovah—they've been coming in waves through the portals. I wonder why. Perhaps it takes a toll on Ash and he can only process a certain amount of people at a time.

Raine looks at the new students as well, his eyes cold and uncaring. "I don't recognize any of them."

Ash leans on his arm, palm pressed to his chin. "They've been moving people from Cyprin as well, so I'm not surprised you don't recognize them."

"You can tell where they're coming from?" I ask.

He nods and looks without interest at the frightened students as they filter through the room. "My Shadow scans anybody that passes through."

I give him a sympathetic frown. "Isn't that tiring?"

Ash's eyes flick over to me like he doesn't believe my compassion. "Yeah, it is," he says coldly.

The dense silence draws over our table as Tamaris and Alani take their arguing elsewhere.

I let my eyes trail up to the professors' table at the head of the room. I think of the note we found as I look at each instructor. Raine can check Moss and Flick. I will check Kallos, Nekane, and Arthur's studies. Hopefully we won't have to wait too long for the opportunities to arise, but I might be able to recruit help.

I glance at the Cosmos table and quickly find Finn and Kai. They're talking with their books strewn out in front of them, preparing to train after dinner. I think the easiest way to get into Kallos's study would be having them distract him. Kai seems good at that kind of thing and Finn is so eager to be on good terms again I think he'll do anything I ask of him.

Perfect. I'll ask them tonight.

The courtyard stretches alongside the entirety of the lake. At the other end lies a smaller building that looks more like a structure I'd find in Barkovah. It's single-story and bunker-like. Now that I think about it, it's not on our maps.

I let my curiosity fade as Raine and I approach Finn and Kai.

Side by side, they raise their right hands into the air and continuously try conjuring their Shadows. Finn's brows are pulled tightly together, irritated that he can't seem to summon his.

"Terra!" Kai beams and Finn stiffens at the sound of my name, looking up meekly and giving me that same nervous smile.

"Hey, still no luck?" I say as I walk over and stand before them.

Finn shakes his head and Kai throws up his hands dramatically and says, "We're utterly hopeless."

"Speak for yourselves," Aervin mutters as he turns to greet us. I didn't see him standing next to them; his Shadow is tall and has wings that curtain him from view. It turns its head completely around without moving its body and my stomach twists with the ferocity in those cold, soulless eyes. It looks like an owl, but longer, the head stretched long and slim, similar to Corvus's crow.

"Shut up, show-off," Kai growls, but that friendly grin is still on his face. Aervin shrugs and smiles, obviously proud of himself. "As if we aren't stressed enough that we won't be able to summon them."

"Hmm," I hum and press my hand to my lips, thinking of the circumstances in which I was able to let Amser flow from my body. "Well, when my Shadow first came out it was under duress and I had let it sink further into my consciousness." What I don't tell them is that I shut off my emotions completely in that moment, letting the darkness inside and giving Amser my woes.

Finn doesn't look pleased to hear that, but Kai nods eagerly. His cheeky attitude is starting to grow on me. At least one person is keeping the hope alive inside us all.

"So, maybe if I attack you it will pull them out?" I say uncertainly. Raine shifts on his feet and grunts, obviously disagreeing, but he doesn't bother saying it.

"Fine, let's give it a try. What's the worst that could happen?" Finn rolls his shoulders back and flexes his hands; his arms are veiny. He's put on quite a bit of muscle mass in the past month. Not huge, bulging muscles, but lean and sharp. The kind that feel comforting wrapped around you.

I force myself to look away and clear my mind. *This will be good practice for me too*, I tell myself as I try to focus on letting my Shadow out.

Black dust spills onto the snow and takes the form of the small cat. I frown. I was hoping for the larger feline form Amser took earlier. It looks up at me, seeming to read my mind, and shifts, growing in size to the same height that Velis was in his riding form.

Amser's presence is calmer than Velis's. Not as greedy and starved. The sun has long since set, and yet it remains in control and not feral, as Velis becomes at night. Its skull is gray and the ribs and spine jut out prominently. The legs are black, only bright, sharp claws are visible, digging into the ground as Amser stretches. Cold black smoke rolls off my Shadow's body and curls against the ground before wisping out.

Elias and I may be the Crescent Novas, but the differences between our Shadows are great. Mine seems to want to give—its body, power, everything—while his only takes.

Kai takes a sharp breath while Finn remains impassive. His eyes flicker with fire at my Shadow.

Amser waits for me to nod before it attacks Finn, knocking him ferociously to the ground. He hisses out in pain, sprawled out on his back with his knees up. "That didn't fucking work, not even a little," he croaks as he pushes himself back up and brushes the snow from his pants. Kai and Aervin laugh together while Raine watches with a scowl, his arms crossed.

Finn's heated amber eyes stare through me, warming my chest as he gives me that same old smirk he's been giving me since we were kids.

I crave his attention, but I want him to earn mine.

Amser knocks Finn over repeatedly until he can hardly stand back up. He bleeds from deep cuts on his arms, earned from blocking the hard blows, but there's still no sign of his Shadow coming out. After a moment, the cuts heal and he wipes the excess blood off with his sleeves. Good thing we've got several sets of tactical clothing.

"Come on, Finn. You're stronger than this," I taunt him. He struggles to his feet and spits out blood off to his side.

"It's not working; Laphia isn't convinced that it is needed." He shakes his head and a few strands of his lovely black hair fall over his forehead. He slicks them back with sweat.

Convinced it is needed... That ignites an idea in my head.

"Well, what if *I* was in danger?" I ask, looking around the courtyard for another student to spar with, one that Amser is unfamiliar with. I spot a well-built man training on a practice dummy and trot toward him.

Finn's eyes grow wide. "Wait, Terra, not him!" he whisper-shouts after me, but he's too late. I'm already approaching the man and he turns slightly to look at me. His eyes are feral, bloodshot and itching for something to stimulate his mind. His lips are reddened with what looks like blood and his grin spreads all the way to his ears, sending chills down my spine. He's literally a snake.

I fist my hands at my sides and force a smile. "Care to practice with us?"

He observes me for a minute, watching me as if he can see straight through my skin to the Shadow within me. Maybe he can? I've seen weirder things.

Finn catches up and stops at my side, stepping slightly in front of me and drawing the man's eyes to him.

"Finnick. What a surprise—I didn't know you were friends with one of the Novas. How did you manage to catch this girl's eye, hmm?" The man's voice is sharp and deep, matching how he looks. His short blonde hair is slicked back. Even his dull eyes are reptilian.

"She's an old friend from my hometown. Terra, this is Frederick," Finn mutters without looking at me, keeping his amber gaze planted firmly on Frederick.

There's obviously bad air between them. Maybe I made the wrong call, but this might actually be beneficial to getting Finn's Shadow to come out.

"Frederick killed Martin in cold blood during the Culling Assessment."

Finn's words hollow out my chest. Pain tears at his voice and sinks into me in kind.

"Finn... I'm so sorry. I didn't know—"

"It's fine. But I'm not training with *him*." Finn turns his back to Frederick and as he does, bloodlust laces the air.

Blood spurts from the corners of Frederick's mouth and it rips open like a snake's. The skin tears and hangs loosely like uneven cloth. His teeth are razor sharp.

He lunges for Finn. It happens so fast that I'm not sure what else to do other than shove Finn out of the way, so that's what I do.

Frederick narrows his eyes and lets out a loud growl of frustration as he closes his mouth and crashes into me. Was he really intending to bite Finn?!

Cold snow stings my back but I'm otherwise unharmed.

Finn shouts as Frederick grabs me by the arm, dragging me up in a bruising grip. Amser perks up from where Kai, Aervin, and Raine are standing. My Shadow charges straight toward us and fear slips into my veins. For once I wish that we weren't separated.

"What the fuck is wrong with you?" I tear my arm from Frederick's grasp but he doubles down by fisting my hair. I cry out as he shoves me down to my knees. He's strong—*really* fucking strong.

"Let her go. Right. Now." Finn's words are heavy in the air and his eyes burn brighter than a moment ago. I was right—fire, actual fire, burns through his gaze and steam spreads in the air around him as if his skin is hot to the touch.

"Make me, you little bitch," Frederick says coolly, his breath coiling in the air as his elongated tongue slides down my cheek. I shiver and try to fight him off but his grip is too tight; my scalp burns the more I struggle.

Kai, Aervin, and Raine run to us, just behind my Shadow. I'm not sure what Amser is going to do to Frederick but it won't be good. Before they can reach us, Finn shuts his eyes and something magical happens.

Unlike the rest, Finn's erupts from his chest. It's not dark and smoky like the other Shadows. No, as Laphia emerges from beneath his cloak, it casts a warm, blinding light, chasing away the shadows of the trees and the night around us. The snow turns a lovely shade of orange, like a sunrise, or fire that scorches the earth.

Finn's eyes flash with flames as enormous wings spread before him. I have to shield my face from the heat that sheds off the creature. Frederick releases me as he does the same. I fall to the ground and look up between my fingers, gasping as I fully take Laphia in.

It's an enormous bird made of brilliant fire, wings

long and thin with orange and yellows lashing together. Its tail is drawn out, beautiful and whimsical, flowing through the air like an iridescent ribbon twirling in the night sky.

His Shadow is a phoenix.

But that is no Shadow—it's anything but. How is this possible? I watch in awe as Finn's lips draw up into a malicious smile. His intent to kill spills from him and places a heavy weight inside me.

There he is. Finn. My heart aches as old emotions resurface inside me.

Amser grows increasingly curious and prowls toward him. I'm sure my Shadow can feel the ache in my soul yearning for him.

Frederick cowers on the ground before the phoenix and pisses his pants as the flames of the bird's wings lick at his feet.

Finn's going to kill him.

Kai shakes Finn's shoulders but to no avail—he's in a trance of sorts, or maybe this is him giving into his Shadow. Or perhaps it's what he truly wants. For some reason, I can only hear Raine's words about Elias earlier: *"His hands are too red."* If Finn does this I'm not sure he'll be able to forgive himself.

The fire crashes down around Frederick and the screaming that ensues is bone-chilling. Raine leaves my side and snaps his fingers in Finn's face. Instantly, Finn twitches and looks at me with horror. His phoenix stops the assault and releases Frederick.

The smell of burning flesh surrounds us. I shiver as Frederick gets to his feet and flees, completely covered in burns. His tactical gear is almost completely seared off. I can't help but wonder how long those will take to heal.

Aervin chases after Frederick, cursing at him. Finn takes a step to pursue them, but Raine blocks his way.

The phoenix flies high into the air, circling the lake and drawing people inside Alkrose to the windows. They gather and stare in awe at the great creature.

Finn trudges over to me and thoroughly inspects me, gently tilting my chin to either side with his soft hands.

"I'm okay," I reassure him, and he stops searching me.

His eyes soften and vulnerability flickers across his face. "I was so scared he was going to kill you like he did Martin... Godsdamn it, I'm glad he didn't," he chokes out and slowly sets his head down on my shoulder. I brush my hand through his hair and pull him in close. "No more of us are going to die. I can't take it," he whispers. It's evident, all the death he's seen thus far. All the heartache that I'm without.

"Then will you help me save Raine from his blight?" I say weakly, too ashamed to give it any more voice. Guilt tries to seep up from within, but my Shadow guards it well.

Finn pulls back and looks down at me. "What do you mean, his *blight*?"

18

Terra

Raine turns in for the night, but Finn and Kai stay with me. We sit on the bridge that leads to the Nova House as we watch Finn's phoenix circle above the lake. It's so bright that it almost seems like daylight. I fill Finn and Kai in on Novas' ability to blight if they are out of control. Their expressions are grave.

"So Raine's going to... die?" Kai's grief sounds sincere.

I nod. "Unless we can find a way to reverse it. I found a note in the library that I think gives us a lead, but we'll need to compare it to the instructors' handwriting."

Finn sets his hand over mine and I don't pull away. It actually feels really nice to have his reassurance and comfort—he's always made it easy to love him.

"We'll help any way we can," Finn says and Kai grunts

his agreement. Relief floods me and I lean over to hug Finn. His arms wrap around me hesitantly at first before he grips me tightly, as if he'll never let go.

"Thank you."

Kai stands and stretches. "I think I can find a way to get Kallos away from his study for a bit while you compare the notes. Or you can seduce him like you did in class. I'm one hundred percent certain he'd fuck your brains out and tell you whatever you wanted to know."

Finn chokes on a breath and I let out a sharp laugh.

"I'm going to let my phoenix burn you alive," Finn growls and Kai raises his hands innocently.

"Oh, I was just kidding," Kai says but I don't believe him for a second. "Too soon?" He looks between us. I know Finn's filled him in on our past. There's a light that shines in his eyes whenever he sees us together.

We both say *yes* at the same time.

"Can you give us a second, Kai? I'll meet you back in our room."

Kai's smile grows suspicious and he nods happily before heading back to the castle, leaving Finn and me out here alone. I don't dread it like I did the first night—being alone with him.

Finn looks up toward the stars and smiles bleakly. "Isn't it weird that no matter what changes down here, the realms above us seem to always be in rhythm? It's reassuring—always constant. I only pray that the gods haven't forsaken us."

I stare up at the same sky, pondering his words. Finn's thoughts are as dark as my own and as consuming as the night.

"They must have forsaken us, Finn. How else would all this chaos be unfolding? They've turned their backs on us and we're completely and utterly alone, plunged in hell," I mutter, squeezing my knees to my chest and resting my head on them, watching Finn as he looks over at me with a smirk.

"Ever the negative, bleak girl I see," Finn muses.

I chuckle at that. "Even more so now, I'm afraid."

He reaches over and brushes my hair back from my face. "Once we get rid of Raine's blight, I think I know how we can escape Alkrose," Finn whispers as he studies my face. His eyes always fill with warmth when he focuses on my eyes. He's always loved the emerald color of them.

"Really? How?"

He shifts to face me and I do the same, lowering my legs and sitting up straight. "*Portals.* We found one that leads to a far-off beach. I suspect it's somewhere south—Lamnah, or even Tornfret. We can find someplace safe and start a new life."

My smile fades. "They know those portals exist. Ash made them *for* Fernestia. I'm certain it won't be that easy. Plus, I'm Elias's... Shadow Mate. He'll never let me escape. Even if we find a way off the grounds, he'll hunt me down. I can never escape him, Finn."

Finn's eyes harden. "What?" He seems to have only heard the *mate* part.

I look away and shrug. "It sucks, but there's nothing I can do about it." He looks at me like he's been betrayed, but wasn't he the one who let me down when I needed him? It's not my fault my Shadow is tethered to Elias. It takes all my strength to keep those spiteful words in my mouth.

"You know, I don't want to sound like the jealous ex, but I can't believe how fast you moved on, Terra," he says weakly, hitting me where it hurts.

I stand abruptly and level him with a hard glare. "Finn, you're the one that left me. What were you expecting?"

His eyes narrow with pain and he slowly stands. "I was keeping you safe from my father," he says tightly. His black hair is disheveled in the wind, only he can make anguished eyes look so beautiful.

We stand in silence for a moment. I shut my eyes and change where this discussion is headed for the sake of what we've managed to salvage of our friendship.

"At least you figured out how to cast your Shadow in its form. Try to help Kai in the meantime. We should get some rest now, though, okay?"

Finn lowers his chin. "Okay... Can we forget this part of tonight? I don't want to fight like this."

I give him a tight smile. "Yeah—we can do that. Goodnight, Finn."

He watches me turn to walk away. "Goodnight, Terra."

Finn calls Laphia back to him just before I reach the Nova House door, the exhaustion of the day pulling at me. Without Laphia, darkness falls generously again.

Ash and Edgar's friends are sitting around the fireplace, talking in low voices. Aervin is safely seated next to Rowan. I don't spot Edgar amongst them and concern pulls at my conscience.

They hush when they notice me.

"Have you seen Edgar?" I ask, hopeful that he's in his

room and I can check on him. But they all shake their heads. "Okay, thanks anyway," I mutter before walking back up the flight of stairs to my room.

I flop on my bed and stare at the ceiling. *Where has he been? He's been so absent and far away in his mind. I hope he's okay*. I laugh a bit at that thought because it's certainly not funny.

Of course he isn't all right—none of us are.

19

Edgar

I simmer in my thoughts during lunch. It's been over a week since we came to Alkrose. Everyone acts like this is the new normal. Is that truly what they all want? Even Terra seems content here; she seems to have made up with Finn already too. I stare at my cup of tea, somewhere else entirely in my mind.

Lucina startles me by grasping my hand. I flinch and look up at her; those bright blue eyes are filled with worry.

"I'm fine," I mutter, already knowing she's going to ask me what's wrong. What isn't wrong? So much is wrong that it's beginning to feel right. I've discussed this with Vinnie many times over already. He feels it too, the acclimation to the horror.

Lucina lets out a sigh. "Can we at least be civil again?

You've all but shut us out this week and I don't think keeping yourself locked away with your Shadow is helping you." Her hand trembles beneath mine. "Please?"

She draws out the last wisps of kindness in my dying heart. I don't want to be alone, does anyone? Not with my ghosts, at least... I grip her hand tightly and she lights up with hope.

"I'm *trying*," I manage to say convincingly. No. No, I haven't been trying, but maybe I can. Maybe it isn't too late to try to patch things up. To weave my friends and sister back into my heart.

Lucina smiles, those bright blue eyes so distant with the turquoise Nova blight covering them. "Okay, good," she says softly before pouring us more tea.

Rowan and Vinnie swap anatomy notes across the table since Rowan's been struggling. Not to be morbid, but I doubt Rowan will survive the second-semester exam. He hasn't been able to summon his Shadow or speak with it, not to mention grasp any of the subject matter in our studies. We all heard what went down during the Culling Assessment, and the parameters of the next exam have yet to be released. All I can hope for is that we get to be on teams.

The days still go on, though, content and quiet for the most part. Everyone will be satiated until it's them on death row. We're slowly being consumed and digested by this castle filled with dark, promising magic.

As we enter the study hall on the third floor, the long-haired blond professor, Kallos, dips his head to each of us. I level him with a scowl to let him know I still don't trust a lick of what he's trying to impose on us. His golden eyes narrow with a smile as he studies me closely. I know the professors have an agenda for each Nova as they do Ash—their prized ponies, each to serve a purpose.

I've yet to discover what my purpose is to them. Terra's is a bit clearer. Being a time wielder, she holds great power. I wonder if, as she unlocks more of her powers, she'll be able to control more time, reverse more than just one's injuries.

Kallos has six bars on his face—three on each side of his mouth as if someone's stitched him up, making his smile haunting and eerie. He looks god-like. A shimmering and precious jewel of Alkrose.

"Still angry about your predicament, Eldridge?"

I roll my eyes and clench my jaw at the professor. "Of course I am. Aren't you?"

"No—you'll find it's much harder to keep the fire burning inside yourself than to just let it simmer out," Kallos mutters indifferently. I don't like that answer, but what am I supposed to do about it?

The classrooms in Alkrose aren't as lavish and shiny as the rest of the castle. There are five rows of desks with simple chairs tucked neatly under them. Dark shadows shoot to the farthest corners of the walls as Kallos raises his hand and the shades on the immense windows open, a trick he's performed daily. It still awes me.

He is an emissary of light itself.

Kallos lets his golden cloak swirl in his wake as he approaches the board up front. He presses his palm to the blackboard. Scrolls of beautiful gold writing etch along as his mind compels them. Everyone watches in silence as the words finish with a silent wisp.

Name Retrieval: Demand the Shadow's Name

A deep dread overcomes me as the memories of the boy with the skull enter my mind. Is that truly what my Shadow looks like or is it an illusion? I wish I didn't know its name, but I already do.

Sully.

"Now, we already went over the basics last week regarding the sensation of the Shadows and how to interact with them. If you've been successful in the Shadow riding class and have seen your Shadow's form, or even a semblance of it, please raise your hand." Kallos's golden eyes flick over the heads of the students.

The majority of the class raises their hands, with the exception of a few of those in beige cloaks. The Dvars students are much lower on the power totem, so it makes sense. They nervously scan the room and probably feel outcast compared to the rest of us. Vinnie, seated to my left, adjusts his glasses as he surveys the room too.

"Good. Now, if you have actually *spoken* with your Shadow, keep your hand raised." All the hands go down, every single one—except mine. I swallow thickly. A thrum of power surges through me with all the eyes burning my skin.

Lucina and Vinnie stare at me from the seats beside mine. Lucina was there when I first properly met Sully; her blight proves it. But I haven't spoken about the encounter with her or any of my friends from Za'Afiel.

Kallos's gaze rests on me. "Good. Do you know its name?" I lie and shake my head. "All right—it's still a good start. I will demonstrate first, then."

The odd black-haired friend of Finn's sits in front of me. I believe his name is Corvus. I study him and consider whether he is a potential traitor like Finn.

"Can I help you?" Corvus says flatly without looking at me. I don't know how he can tell I'm staring holes into the back of his head, but he can. His purple cloak tucked to his side contrasts well against the black tactical gear.

"What do you make of Finn?" I ask evenly, deciding not to avoid him.

That gets his attention. Corvus turns to look at me and his eyes narrow with suspicion. "What's your relation to him?"

I smile bleakly. "He's my sister's ex."

Corvus doesn't offer me a response. He just assesses me with his black eyes. I can sense his bright mind from the analytical thrums his fingers are making on the desk.

Okay. How about this then. "I think he's a traitor to our country and a fox in the hen coop. I'll ask you once more. What do you make of him?"

He hesitates and mutters a little too quietly, "I met him at the encampment site. Finn isn't... He wouldn't do that. Why would you even consider that he would?" He says the words but I can tell he isn't entirely sure of them himself.

I lean forward and rest my chin against my palm. "He wouldn't? It seems strange to me that he asked my sister to run away with him the morning of the attack. Seems *odd* that his father is the general of Barkovah, and yet, where is he?" My voice is a whisper, but Lucina and a few students around us turn to watch. Vinnie sets his hand on my arm but I ignore him. "It seems too convenient that he would be here—perfectly untouched and cared for. Like someone important. Don't you think?" I tap my finger against the desk in the same fashion Corvus does, and he takes notice, looking down at my fingers then back at my eyes.

At the front of the room, Kallos crosses his arms and lets out a weary sigh.

"Edgar, it seems you're keen on being the center of attention today. Why don't you come up here? You can be the first to demand the name of your Shadow," Kallos says unenthusiastically. His golden gaze lazily hovers over me.

My blood is hot inside my veins and I can sense Sully coiling and twisting with hatred deep in my chest. This isn't me. I try to take a soothing breath before moving.

I obey and absently walk to the front of the class.

"All right. Now close your eyes, and since you have seen your Shadow already, picture it. Think about every detail you can remember. Demand it to appear before you and share its name," Kallos says calmly.

"You sure about that?"

"Yes." Kallos side-eyes me, suspicious.

I bite down on my lip. *Don't be afraid. Don't be afraid.*

Taking a deep breath and closing my eyes, I let myself picture Sully. At first, I just see myself, or rather, an image of who I was before becoming the young man watching as his father's blood dripped from the window pane... *No. Don't think of that.* I quickly shake the thoughts.

I wince and strain my mind to focus. The Shadow appears so dull in my mind. The skull isn't as horrifying as it was at the sanctum. The eyes of the Shadow are red. They flick up to me and there's nothing—a horrible and empty nothingness inside those eyes. Something sharp twists inside my chest.

A simultaneous gasp rolls from the students in the classroom. Echoing. Swirling. Dancing at the base of my ears. Ringing, louder and louder until I hear that horrible phone ringing in my conscience as I did when my father splattered across the window. Ringing and ringing and *ringing*.

Until.

"*Edgar*!"

Kallos's voice drowns out all the others. My eyes fling open and I take a steadying breath. Lucina, Vinnie, and Corvus are gawking at me with fear burning their eyes. Disgust and terror morph their frowns into expressions reserved for monsters.

Before me stands Sully, a boy with a skull in his hand, and blood is smeared across those beautiful windows that Kallos opened, painting the room red. There's tension in the air, deep and dark and awful, yet no one dares to breathe or move a muscle.

My breath catches in my chest as I realize everyone can finally see it as I do. Sully smiles, grins so widely that its dry lips split and bright, fresh blood sheens. Iron fills my senses. If fear has a scent, this is it.

"Kallos—what do I do now?" I whisper it so quietly I'm unsure if he hears me.

The professor's golden eyes are wide with shock. "You lied to me, Edgar. You know this Shadow's name as well as I do."

Sully's decrepit smile fades as its eyes widen. All of a sudden it's no longer a boy. Its eyes spread off in each direction slowly as if it's being pulled apart. The skull drops to the ground and it splashes, flicking black liquid at my white cloak.

Kallos is in front of me before anything else can happen. In a blur, he washes me with a veil of golden light.

"Sully," Kallos whispers at my Shadow with gritted teeth.

How did he know its name? *Sully*. The name thrums against my inner walls. I can feel the room spinning. The Shadow lets out a cackling laugh that seeps into the marrow of my bones. I can almost see the form it's taking behind Kallos's golden cloak, but I can't quite make it out.

"Sully, leave," I shout and shut my eyes fiercely.

The blinds shut all at once as screams and golden light burst through the classroom. Darkness moves like black sand, weaving and snuffing out the glittering wisps of Kallos's light.

I can't see anything.

Feathers tickle the back of my neck and whirl around me like a tornado. I'm breathless. Before my mind can settle on any of the rushing thoughts, it stops. It all just stops, and silence ensues.

A moment later the room returns to normal. The blinds open and natural, un-reddened light filters in and dapples the desks. Kallos's hair is mussed and the students are out of their desks, pressed to the floor, scattered and hiding.

I look at Kallos. He takes a long, relaxing breath as he runs his hand over his head. "All right... Who would like to try next?" I tremble as I stare at him, waiting for him to address what just happened, but he only whispers, "I need to see you after class," looks at me briefly, then nods for me to head back to my seat.

The rest of the class is a blur to me. Only thoughts of my Shadow and how terrifying it is trickle through my mind. How does Kallos know its name? He speaks as if he's encountered it before. Is that possible?

I remain in my seat as the others gather their things and leave the room. Vinnie and Lucina spare me a look before I wave them off. "I need to speak with the professor," I mumble.

Vinnie's eyes narrow. "Are you all right, Edgar?" I raise my shoulders and drop them. He nods in understanding. Lucina smooths her hand over my shoulder wordlessly and the two of them leave. Corvus lingers after everyone else is gone.

Kallos approaches and sits on the desk before me. The sun emblem brooch at the center of his gold cloak is bright. "Edgar, Arthur has told me much about you and your Nova sibling, Terra. However, he forgot to mention that your Shadow is Sully." He looks at Corvus and studies him for a moment before nodding. "Thank you for cutting in when you did. I was a bit too surprised to handle that situation as well as I should've."

Was Corvus responsible for the feathers?

I struggle to meet Kallos's eyes. I'm not even sure what to say.

Kallos goes on: "Sully is a Shadow I met a long time ago. I'm not sure we're taking the right precautions with it. I'm sorry, Edgar, but I will have to place a cast on you to keep it in control until you're ready to handle such power."

My pulse thrums loudly in my ears and my heart

clenches tightly as if Sully is squeezing it with rage. I choke out a breath. Kallos seems to know already that my Shadow is rejecting his words; he raises his hand and golden light emanates from his palm.

Sully speaks low in my head, its voice scratchy and eerie. *Let him cast the power that I give you. See what it costs, boy.* My muscles twitch involuntarily.

By the time the light fades. Sully feels like a small tumor, balled up and contained like a heavy lump of coal in my chest. Its power is locked away and out of my reach. A trickle of blood flows from each of my eyes, dripping onto my desk and painting the surface red.

"Gods, what did you do?" Corvus says with a shaky voice and comes to my side to inspect me.

Kallos cradles his hand as if placing the *cast* on Sully physically hurt him. "Help me get him to the infirmary and then head to your next class, Corvus. Not a word of this to anyone. I'm only trying to help."

Corvus gives Kallos a wary look, but seems to trust him enough to give a firm nod. I groan as they lift me from the desk and guide me out into the hall and down to the second story.

Kallos tries to keep me conscious as my head bobs from left to right with each step we take. "How old are you now, Edgar?" he asks.

I try to remember. It takes a few moments. "Seventeen, turning eighteen next week." The words come out in a slur.

"Good. And what's your House name?"

I try to say it, but everything fades to black.

20

Finn

I know where I'll likely find Terra at any point in the day. Not because I'm stalking her or keeping a close eye, but because I know her so entirely. Her habits here aren't so different from her routines and desires in Navasik.

In the mornings, she enjoys her tea, normally sipping it as she reads and brushes up on the day's subject matter. During the short breaks between classes, she walks with Raine through the gardens on the first floor. I'm envious of the way he holds her, though I'm relieved she isn't alone.

At night she usually sits on the bridge leading to the Nova House, legs dangling off the side as she stares up at the stars.

But it's early, no later than ten, and she's already in the

gardens today, without her usual companion and looking distant and weary as she stares at the peculiar red flowers and vines.

I consider going inside to speak with her. There's nothing more I crave than to be close to her, to wrap my arms around her waist and breathe in her lovely scent of cold mountain air.

Terra's eyes lift and I sip in a breath and hold it, watching her carefully as if she'll stir should I move. Her emerald gaze flickers with warmth and she gives me a small but alluring smile before turning her back to me and disappearing behind a wall of red ferns.

My sweet little thing. She wants me to give chase just as I would in the forest. Who am I to deprive her of a thrill?

I slip inside the garden room, a terrarium truly, with walls of glass two stories high. The aroma of the plants is a comfort that reaches inside my chest. Should I shut my eyes, I would find myself somewhere beneath the warm sun.

My tomes are heavy in my hands. I set them down on an old stool, the legs uneven and tilting with the weight of my books. The garden is much bigger than I could've imagined; the glass panes stretch far off to the west side of the castle. It's easily the size of a ballroom but filled with pathways, plants, and foliage in every shade of red.

I silently walk through the path, brushing my fingers against some leaves as I pass the long tables. She's always been better at this game of chase than me, but now with Laphia, I think the tides may have turned in my favor.

She's there. Dead ahead, Laphia purrs inside my head

and heat floods through my bones. The fire within me desires her as if she's oxygen itself.

The corner of my lip kicks up and I lower into a crouch as I approach a shelf of maroon ferns. They're as tall as I am, leaves drooping down all the way to the tiles. Terra lets out a small breath as if she's holding in a laugh with both her hands pressed over her lips.

My smile grows and I turn the corner swiftly. Terra's eyes widen and she lets out a quiet gasp followed by the sweetest squeal as I grab her around the waist and pull her close to my chest. She laughs and clings to me, her fingers brushing my collarbones before they find the vest.

Her laugh is entirely contagious and I let a deep chuckle slip from my lips too. Although we're different, we still have remnants of ourselves somewhere deep down.

I smooth my thumb over her cheek and pull her back to look into her eyes. Terra looks up at me and for a moment we're still, unmoving as our souls and Shadows dance between the breath of air we share.

"What are you doing here alone?" I ask in a mere whisper as I trace my finger across her jaw, stopping at her soft lips and dragging my thumb slowly over the bottom one, pulling it down a bit.

She takes a deep breath and shuts her eyes before mumbling, "Raine wasn't feeling well so I thought I'd see the flowers alone today before class."

He isn't feeling well? Shit, I hope the blight isn't already taking hold of his health. It's only been a little over a week. My face must reflect my somber thoughts because Terra's brows pinch together and she frowns.

"Is there any way we can search Kallos's study

tonight?" she asks, sounding tired. I know she's been losing sleep over this. Her guilt shows no matter how hard she tries to hide it.

"Of course. Come by after nine, that's usually when Kallos goes for his evening meetings." I let my eyes drop behind her and see a stone bench, the edges carved to look like branches, two cushions cover the seat. I guide us over and sit down, pulling Terra to sit over me so I can stare into her eyes.

It's the first time she's allowed me to be so close and intimate. It makes my heart wrench. I yearn to press kisses against her skin. "Terra?"

"Yeah?" She lets her body relax around mine and her legs ease to either side of my hips. Her hand presses against my chest and she stares into my soul, unblinking.

I swallow dryly. "You know you can always come to me if you need to talk, right? Anything and everything, I'll listen for hours if you need me to. Just don't isolate yourself. I'm here—I will never leave you again."

She gives me a sympathetic smile and nods slowly. "Thank you, Finn."

My cheeks warm as her eyes drop to my lips. I'm hesitant, gods know I want to kiss her, but I don't want to push this. "I think we should—"

Her mouth presses against mine, making my heart stutter and a sea of emotions flood through my veins. It's a light and endearing kiss, one of forgiveness and hope. She pulls back and smiles at me before standing.

"I'll see you at nine." She winks and I'm so fucking tempted to follow her as she walks away, letting her fingers brush over the tops of leaves as I did, but I'm a patient man.

Kai covers his mouth as Nekane smacks Frederick's back, hard. The long metal stick he uses to point out the vertebrae sends chills down my spine. However, I find Frederick's protruding spinal bones and ability to flex them even more disturbing.

"Who knew anatomy class could be so hilarious," Kai says. He buries his smile in his sleeves, but I don't think he'd fool anyone who looks our way.

"Hilarious? It's fucking gross. Just make sure you're taking notes today; I'm tired of lending you my notebook," I mutter as I write in my journal, circling that Frederick's bones are flexible and he can contort them at will. All this information is pertinent to the second-semester exam. As much as I hate to think about it, I'll need to know how to kill fast and efficiently. Each day that passes only shows how dangerous the other students are becoming. Distrust between the Houses has flared and more students are sticking to their own Houses as a result.

"Here, copy mine. You're already so far behind," Aervin mutters and rolls his eyes at Kai. Our white-haired friend sheepishly grins and jots down all the notes from Aervin's book.

Nekane turns Frederick to face the class. "Open your jaw," he instructs, and Frederick obeys, letting his mouth fall open.

His skin parts to his ears. It's gruesome to watch but

seems painless for Frederick, who's not even wincing, although his jaw hangs loosely at the hinges. His teeth are sharp like a viper's and his eyes fade into a subtle red as if the blood vessels have burst from the effort.

Nekane grins and points at the hinge of Frederick's jaw as he goes on. "Some Shadows prefer to give you their strength directly rather than forming outside of you. Frederick here has a Serpent Shadow. They aren't common, even less so for one to morph its host. Though it does give him a rather nasty bite, doesn't it?" Nekane laughs at his own joke, but none of us do. "Just because a Shadow bearer has a shifting ability does not mean they can't summon them. Don't let your guard down around these ones."

My fists tighten against my desk. If I get the chance to kill Frederick during the second exam I'm taking it.

Nekane goes on about more of the Shadow anatomy and has us practice letting our Shadows further in for the remainder of the class. Kai, Corvus, and I just sit and chat since we're not exactly keen on letting our Shadows dig too far within our souls just yet. We'll try to resist as long as possible. At least, that's our unspoken agreement. Aervin seems willing to try, but his continuous curses tell me he's not having much luck.

Corvus has been oddly silent for most of the class, so I press him. "Is something wrong?" I flip through a few pages in my tome, not expecting him to say much.

His black eyes narrow and he looks up at me from beneath his dark hair. "Has Terra made up with Edgar yet?" I raise a brow at him and my eyes instinctively dart to Kai's. Aervin stops what he's doing and turns to look at us too. He has the same questioning look I do. Why would that matter? "I had my morning class with him and... he's different from the rest. There's something off about him, something *wrong*."

Kai leans in closer. "Well, *I* could've told you that. Haven't you seen him talking to himself in the courtyard and the hallways?"

"Edgar told me his Shadow whispers bad things to him," Aervin says grimly, staring at the ground in thought.

I look between the three of them. Why haven't I noticed? I only noticed by the lake during the first Shadow riding class when he talked to himself oddly. "I *guess* he's different, but you weren't in Navasik when the Skyfell... I think he watched his parents—"

"We all watched our parents melt, Finn," Corvus snaps and my mouth closes with guilt. "But haven't you felt that emotion and pain fade? Like it never happened? Do you even remember what they look like? Because I fucking don't."

Kai's brows pull together. "Of course, I—wait. No, I can't remember." His eyes widen and he looks at me. Aervin shakes his head slowly. Him too?

I think of my mom, and as awful as it makes me feel, I don't remember her face at all. I shake my head in disbelief. "What the fuck," I say with a shaky breath. My father's face comes to mind no problem though. Of all the people I wish to forget, of course I'd remember him. Can we only forget the dead? The trauma they bring us?

Corvus nods. "Each day, things are taken from within us. Specifically bad things, people we've lost. I've been keeping track. For us, the progression is slow, but constant. I don't think that's the case for Edgar."

Aervin grunts. "Of course you've been keeping track. You and Vinnie would get along great. Bright minds and all that." His tone is sarcastic but there's no doubt Corvus is brilliant.

"Why do you think that it's different for Edgar?" Kai asks quietly as Nekane glides by us, giving us questioning looks as we continue with our low conversation.

"He accused Finn of being a traitor to Heirah. You should've seen the hatred in his eyes. The raw fury that he was holding onto. The pain was fresh, like he could see everything and remember clearly, unlike us." Corvus pauses and his eyes grow distant with thought. "And then he brought out his Shadow and... it was something else. It wasn't like any of the others." The fear in his voice is so distinct that the hairs on the back of my neck start to rise.

My throat feels dry with worry, but still, I ask, "What did it look like?"

Corvus glances up at us as a bead of sweat trickles down the side of his face. "It was a puppet of a really realistic-looking boy—mimicking Edgar. A dark mass stood behind it, holding up the puppet, making it move and look like a real person... but I saw it. Its eyes were two hollow holes with red in the center and it was using Edgar's trauma like a toy. I've never been so afraid and keenly aware of anything in my entire life." Corvus swallows hard and his hands tremble as he sets them on his knees for stability. "There's something terribly wrong with him."

I look to Kai and Aervin, then back to Corvus. "Terra is meeting us at nine p.m. in the Cosmos House. You should come too. We can talk to her. She's trying to find a way to un-blight Raine, but I think she should know about this too."

Corvus hesitates but nods. "I just hope we know what we're getting into."

21

Terra

The expansive corridor leading to the library is challenging to walk through as students shuffle by one another to get to their next classes. I barely manage to weave my way through and slip inside the silent library.

I exhale a long breath and take in the scent of old, torn pages and ink.

There are a few young women sitting on the first floor, studying and talking in hushed voices. I make my way up to the third story, heading toward the back wall where it's secluded.

I'm relieved when I find the section empty and quickly set my books down on the desk and turn the lamp on. It's already dark outside; I don't have much time before I need to fetch Raine and get to the Cosmos House.

Candles burn at the center of the table, on the bookshelves, and in windowsills. I wonder who lights them. They never seem to burn out, so they must be like the fireplaces at Alkrose, undying and constant.

Whispers rise from a few rows ahead of me and I lift my chin, brown hair curling over my shoulder as I slowly stand to investigate.

The voices sound male, but I'm too far away to distinguish them. The bookshelves are tall and wide, packed with tomes and artifacts. I take the row on the other side of the voices and stop in the center, kneeling down and quietly pulling a few books from their place.

I peek through the slits between tomes and can make out two white cloaks. My chest instantly tightens as their voices become clear. *Elias and Arthur.* I can barely make out Arthur's lovely black hair. What are they doing talking up here in secret?

"We shouldn't be speaking here, you know Emerai may very well have ears throughout the castle," Elias says in a hushed tone, his usual irritation coming through.

"This is urgent, otherwise I wouldn't have risked it," Arthur whispers as he looks around to make sure no one is listening.

It feels criminal to eavesdrop on them, but I remain crouched and still.

"The second exam has been decided. Blood Crowns." Arthur's voice cracks as he says the latter and Elias lets out a small sound that I've never heard him make. I wish I could see his face; he sounds completely taken aback.

"Decided by *who*? Emerai cannot put them through the Blood Crowns yet. They are first-year students, for gods' sakes." The fear in Elias's voice sends a shudder down my spine and sweat rolls down my temple.

Arthur sighs. He takes a moment to respond. "The Empress herself and Cein decided. They want to push this group to their breaking points quickly. They've found the Novas, Elias. All the pieces of their board game are aligned and they're ready to take the leap. They have no interest in training this group as they did the rest." He pauses and I can hear him swallow. "There are only a few individuals that they have their eyes on this time."

Elias growls and slams his fist into the bookshelf, sending a handful of heavy books toppling over my head. I smother my mouth with my hands, holding back the surprised grunt that almost escapes from my throat.

I remain still, ignoring the throbbing on the top of my head. Arthur lets out a long sigh and mutters, "Calm down, Elias. We will figure something out. Let's talk more about this elsewhere."

Their footsteps start down the aisle in a steady stride. I panic and rise to my feet quickly, heading around the opposite way and tiptoeing back to the desk I was studying at as if I never heard a thing.

Arthur appears first at the end of the aisle and his eyes instantly lock on mine. "Terra, I didn't expect you to be up here this late," he says carefully, fishing to see if I'll be surprised to see him up here as well or if I perhaps over-head things I shouldn't have.

Elias appears casually behind him. His expression is

calm. If I hadn't overheard their conversation I'd think nothing of it.

"You weren't eavesdropping, were you?" Arthur asks innocently enough, smiling in that calm and handsome way he always does. He takes a seat across from me and Elias sits to my side.

I raise a brow like I have no clue what he's talking about. "Do I even want to know what you're referring to?" I say meekly. Arthur's shoulders relax; he buys my charade. Elias takes a deep breath of relief too. This Blood Crown exam must be pretty ominous if both of them are this uptight about it. There's a twisting sensation in my stomach.

An easy smile spreads over Arthur's lips as he says, "No, just teasing you. Where's Raine?" He quickly changes the subject and my heart sinks instantly.

"He's not feeling well," I mutter, thinking again of how pale his skin was this morning. He writhed in pain for an entire hour and insisted I leave for the day without him.

Elias and Arthur share a look, one that lets me know this is only the beginning of the blight's effect.

"I can help you study today, if you'd like. I would hate for our Nova to be left to her own devices." Arthur smiles and grabs one of my books to see what I'm brushing up on.

Elias shoots him an annoyed expression before crossing his arms. He looks like he'd rather be anywhere than here.

"You don't have to stay," I tell him.

"Maybe I *want* to stay," Elias says quietly in his deep, antagonized tone.

I look over at him with an arched brow. He holds his

scowl firmly. His white hair is mussed today, windblown, unlike its usual careful style.

Arthur covers his mouth and stifles a laugh at our exchange.

"Are all the textbooks and education really going to help me for the exams?" I ask honestly. It's a fair question, since most of us are studying our asses off for something we have no clue about.

"Yes. You will need every bit of information, because you never know what you'll come up against during an exam. The physical fighting is just as important as the mental game. Elias was at the top of our class, and his brains saved a lot of lower-ranked students during trying times. I have no doubt you can do the same if you put your mind to it, Terra."

My eyes widen and I look at Elias. His face is impassive and hard, but there are so many emotions behind those gray eyes. I see a lake of misery.

"*Don't,*" Elias warns Arthur and crosses his arms over his chest. His black tactical vest can't keep his heart hidden —nor can his Shadow.

"You saved people?" I ask incredulously. There's a softness to the question; the realization that the man I know him as now, the heartless Assassin of Fernestia, perhaps wasn't always so cold and cruel. Not at first.

Elias's jaw flexes and he grimaces, looking away from me and down at his intertwined fingers. How can he hold so much pain inside himself so flawlessly?

Arthur clears his throat and says, "Dark days are ahead of us at Alkrose, Terra. I think it'd be best if I started tutoring you in the evenings. One-on-one."

One-on-one? My throat dries but I manage to nod slowly.

Elias leans forward and rests his elbows on the table and adds: "I'll help Raine. He still hasn't summoned his Shadow and he's hopeless without it."

"That's awfully *generous* of you," Arthur says with a taunting grin.

"Not as generous as you privately tutoring Terra." They stare hard at each other, having an unspoken conversation with just their eyes.

I wrap my arms around myself at the chill that settles inside me. The Blood Crowns exam... What is it? What's the test? They won't tell me, but I'm determined to find out more about it.

I look up and meet Arthur's gray eyes. "When do we begin the sessions?" I ask with the new motivation.

His sharp, alluring cheekbones catch the candlelight as he grins. "Tomorrow evening."

22

Edgar

The infirmary is simple. Enormous, with vaulted stone ceilings and large arched windows that pillar it, but *simple* nonetheless, empty of life. Dusk has fallen by the time the nurse finishes her scan on my head. Apparently, some Shadows can analyze damage to bodies. A gift, she told me, belonging primarily to lower-class Shadows, but that ability seems more than priceless to me. Every army needs medical personnel, no matter how invincible they may seem.

I sit up in the metal-framed bed, taking a second to recall everything that led to this moment. Kallos placed some sort of containment on me—I can feel some of his Shadow curled around mine, keeping it closed off and away from my mind.

Everything seems a bit clearer now without Sully looming over my every thought. I'm hoping it stays away.

I let out a long sigh and rub my temples to ease the pounding headache I've been left with. I've never felt so worn down in my entire life. It's as if I've been awake for weeks, not resting even though my eyes are closed.

Kallos finishes speaking with the nurse at the far end of the room and walks back over to me, taking a seat on the stool next to me.

"How do you feel?" he asks sincerely, but I can only focus on the stabilizer bars on his face, making it look like he's smiling. He notices and says, "Finn was curious about them too."

"Why are yours the only ones on your face like that? It looks like you're always smiling," I say with a monotone voice.

He folds his hands over his knee and looks over at the entrance to the infirmary as another person enters through the double doors. "It was punishment for my defiance when I was a student like you; a reminder of my actions."

I don't show him any emotion. "Why make you a professor then if you're *so* defiant?" I ask, spotting Corvus walking toward us.

"Because I still have much to lose," he whispers sadly before straightening and smiling at Corvus.

I study Kallos with new eyes. *Does he still have much to lose? Like what... or who?*

Corvus takes the stool on my other side and dips his head to Kallos. "I wanted to check in on him. I hope it's okay."

Kallos waves his hand dismissively at him. "I have no arguments about the matter," he says with a mild grin.

"Why do you care?" I ask Corvus, staring at him with assessing eyes. I haven't said more than ten words to him.

"I'd never seen such a malevolent creature before. I like learning and studying things. My apologies if that's a bit callous, but I think you're someone who prefers the truth." Corvus's dark eyes are as calculating as mine and there's something my Shadow likes about his presence. I do enjoy brilliant individuals—Vinnie would probably be interested in picking his brain as well.

I give him a short grunt as a reply and a small grin pulls at the corner of his lips. The door opens again and the three of us raise our heads to see Arthur approaching. He doesn't seem concerned, just in a hurry.

Kallos keeps his golden gaze even, balancing his emotions calmly as usual. "*Sully*." Kallos whispers my Shadow's name and Arthur's eyes narrow at the sound of it. "We knew we would meet it again." Kallos looks at Arthur with scrutiny burning through his gaze. "Do you care to explain to me why I was not made aware that *this* Shadow was in the castle?"

Arthur flinches under the weight of Kallos's tone. "Apologies, Kallos. I should have informed you." He sets his hand on Kallos's shoulder. "I was hoping Edgar wouldn't reveal Sully until after the second exam. I thought it might be safer for everyone—"

"I placed a cast on him," Kallos interrupts sharply and Arthur's eyes widen with horror.

"You did *what*?" Arthur asks but it doesn't seem like a question, more of an accusation. His gray eyes shift to me and I feel like he can see through me. Every fiber of my flesh and bones. Right down to the Shadow inside my veins.

Kallos stands—he and Arthur are eye to eye. The golden-cloaked professor explains, "Sully cannot be left uncontained—"

Arthur's jaw slackens and he lets out a deep, chilling chuckle. Is the cast really that bad? He's acting like it's the worst of his problems.

"Kallos, did you even think about how Edgar will be able to fight in the second-semester exam with a Shadow cast placed on him? He's a lamb to the slaughter now," Arthur says hopelessly and looks at me like I've lost all purpose.

Kallos looks from me to his colleague and flexes his jaw. "*Shit.* It didn't even cross my mind." Corvus shoots me a worried glance and I can't help but feel damned. How am I supposed to have hope of saving what's left of my nation if I'm dead after the second exam?

Arthur takes Kallos's place on the stool and threads his fingers through his dark hair as he stares at the ground. "It's fine—I'll figure something out. We cannot lose any of the Novas." He doesn't sound like it's going to be fine. The distraught way he's acting leaves me with a heavy and unsettling weight in my chest.

It dawns on me that I've yet to thank Corvus for stopping my Shadow's outburst. The thought of what could've happened if Sully hadn't been stopped curdles my stomach. I look at Corvus. "Thanks for helping me back in class."

Corvus's eyes widen with my admittance, but he

remains stoic. "I couldn't just do nothing." He stares at the white sheets in front of him. He seems worried about something.

Everything was chaos in that room. Kallos couldn't hold back Sully's sudden appearance. Does he have a weakness against my Shadow? I mean, he's a *professor.* That would explain his anger at Arthur's nondisclosure.

A shudder ripples down my back at the thought of my classmates seeing Sully. They all looked so terrified of... well, me.

It's a terrible feeling, to be exiled just from a look. But I know deep in my bones that none of them will walk close to me in the halls again. Fear keeps people away, furthering the loneliness I've found myself in.

"How did you do that anyway?" I run my hand down the side of my face in an effort to calm the storm that's building behind my eyes.

Corvus studies his hands closely for a few moments before replying, "I just... It was like instinct. I was actually hoping you could explain how I was able to do it, Kallos." Both our eyes sweep back to the professors.

Arthur is still in doom mode with his face in his hands, but Kallos has been paying attention. His golden eyes narrow. "You were able to summon your Shadow in an extreme situation. Your rank is Ekko, isn't it? Your Shadow is no doubt a bit shy compared to higher-ranked Shadows like Cosmos and Nova, but when it senses danger it can take the reins, so to speak, to protect you." Kallos lifts his hand and flicks his wrist. Gold dust wisps in the air and forms a nearly translucent leaf.

My eyes widen at the display of gilded sand. Kallos's

magic is so... beautiful and steady. No signs of darkness or sinister intentions steep beneath the flow of it—much like Finn's.

It hurts a bit, to think that I was not gifted with a beautiful power. Instead, I received a Shadow feared even among the professors. Something so malicious that I fear it beneath my veins. Am I that rotted? I once thought I had a strong heart, one that could persevere through anything no matter how awful.

But I can see it clearly now—I don't have the heart of a hero. I have the heart of a weak man. One that craves revenge because it feels better. It soothes that gaping and starved darkness that only desires for others to suffer as I have suffered.

I was never meant to have a bright, beautiful god inside my bones. Only the darkest, most greedy deity would call my soul to its own.

"See this?" Kallos says. "My Shadow is ranked as Solas. It is a gentle one, but filled with immense power. It was shy too at first—it only appeared when my life was in danger."

Arthur lifts his head and looks at Kallos's hand, then to me, watching my reactions closely like he's anticipating something.

Corvus nods his head. "So mine is shy?" He stares at his hands for a few moments. "I can summon it easily in the riding class, but other than that it is quiet and powerless."

"Well, as I'm sure you've been learning in your other classes, you need a name to let it sink to a deep enough level inside your soul," Kallos adds.

"How am I supposed to do anything with this cast on my power? It's as if it's... muted and out of reach," I ask, teeth gnashing together with frustration as Kallos looks away with guilt.

Arthur stands and shakes his head. "I'm sorry, Edgar, you won't be able to summon Sully until the cast wears off. Until then, you'll need to study harder than anyone else here. The next exam involves you going through a portal, and unless you can break free of your cast—"

"Arthur," Kallos hisses, and Arthur shakes his head. What more was he going to say?

"Gods, this is a mess. Forget what I just said." Arthur shoulders Kallos aside as he stalks back toward the doors. "Just... don't do anything stupid until then, Edgar," he says with dread. The doors swing closed behind him and silence falls over the three of us.

Kallos walks towards the infirmary door after a moment. "I will see you two in class tomorrow." He leaves with that, and I'm left with terrible thoughts, fearing what all of this means for me.

"Come on, I'll help you back to the Nova House." Corvus helps me from the medical bed. Once standing, I shake Corvus off me. I'm still a little dizzy but I can manage just fine.

"I can go on my own," I snap. I don't need his kindness. It's better to keep everyone as far as possible. I only need Terra and my friends from Za'Afiel.

Corvus gives me a sympathetic look. "You know, you don't have to fight your demons alone." He raises a hand to his chest. "We have all been mortally wounded inside. We can try to heal together. You don't have to—"

"Shut up!" I shout, teeth bared and hands tightly clenched at my sides. "I don't need to fight my pain. I don't need to *heal.* I don't want to heal." I face Corvus with rage burning inside me. "I want to make them pay for what they've done."

Corvus's jaw flexes but he doesn't say anything as I turn away and leave without another word. My white cloak flutters in my wake as I walk down the dark halls back to the bridge over the lakeside, only swaying a few times from the dizziness that still tugs on my body. I make my way back into my entirely too-large, empty room and stare at myself in the mirror. At Sully.

It stands there behind me, observing me in silence with the same shattered eyes I have—turquoise lines that etch over my irises.

It's quieter after Kallos placed that cast on me, but Sully still whispers all the same. Fuck. I was hoping it was gone.

One cast cannot get rid of me. In fact, let's put it to the test, shall we? Sully says as it grins.

23

Terra

Raine leans against the wall around the corner of the Cosmos House. His body is taut, muscles beautifully stretched as he cranes to check if the coast is clear. The marbled walls are cold and keep the hallway's air brisk. Raine levels me a sly smirk as I peek over his shoulder to see if Kai and Finn have shown up yet to let us in their homeroom.

I was able to cross Elias off the list pretty quickly as his room isn't difficult for me to get into. I'm not sure who else we can trust here besides Arthur, so we've been cautious about comparing the notes to professors.

Raine cleared the lower House professors, Flik and Moss, off the list too, so it's either Kallos, Nekane, or Arthur. After them, we need to find any other potential members of Elias's original group that may still be alive. One pops into mind: Emerai. I mentally add him to the list.

"How are you feeling?" I ask, straightening beside Raine and lifting my hand to his cheek with affection. His skin is warm and he shuts his eyes, leaning his weary head into my palm and letting his hand slide up the back of my hand.

"Better now. I just needed some sleep."

"Are you sure?" I ask, letting my brows pull together with concern.

He nods and smiles brightly. "Yeah, don't worry about it, babe."

I think about what Elias said about tutoring Raine. My chest warms that my assassin seems to be lightening up about him. "Have you been able to conjure your Shadow yet?" I ask, keeping my eyes on the Cosmos entrance. It's not like we aren't allowed in there or anything, but on the off chance that Kallos is still inside, I'd rather not risk him growing curious about us. I already have more than enough of his attention in sex ed.

Raine rubs the back of his head and stalls. "Uh, well, not exactly. No."

I focus on him, drawing my brows tightly together. "Elias said he's going to tutor you in preparation for the exam." Raine rolls his eyes, which irks me. "He's not so bad; I think he genuinely wants you to succeed. Even if he just wants you to be able to protect me in the exam."

He lets out a short breath and mutters, "At least we have a common interest. I guess it won't be so bad. I can't argue with a man who wants me to be useful before I die."

He brushes my chin with the tip of his thumb and gives me that cruel grin of his.

"Raine, don't say that." The hurt is evident in my voice, but I'm okay with being vulnerable around Raine. "We're going to find a way."

He raises his shoulders and lets them drop dramatically. "We'll see."

I'm about to give him a lecture about being morbid, but I catch a flash of white hair in my peripheral.

"It's Kai! Let's go," I whisper-shout and Raine follows close behind me as we slink down the hallway. The sun has long since set, which helps with our cover.

I'm not surprised to find the Cosmos House commons empty. It's late and most of the students are out in the courtyard training or already in bed.

The Cosmos homeroom is much different than ours. The ceilings aren't vaulted and the theme is pretty plain, cream-colored walls with dark blue furniture and an average-looking fireplace.

"This place is rather mundane," I say, and Raine nods thoughtfully.

Kai laughs and holds up his hand; the back has a mark that looks like a cloud of stars. *Cosmos.*

"You have to have this to see the cosmos of stars and lights on the ceilings," Kai mutters as he walks across the large space to a door on the other side. Finn cracks the door open and waves us into the study.

Raine goes first and I follow behind him. Kai winks at me and stands guard at the door lest Kallos return.

Kallos's study is what I would consider organized chaos. It's stuffed with loose pages and notes, piles of wax-sealed letters, and books stacked high on the floor near his desk. Old framed photos fill the entire length of the walls. The scent is musky, mixed with freshly blown-out candles and sage.

Finn smiles at me, eyes dipping down to my lips briefly before he catches himself and clears his throat. My cheeks warm and Raine looks between us, seeming to notice a change in the air. "There are plenty of notes in here to compare. Kallos is on the messy side though, so you might want to check his desk first," Finn says.

Raine gives him a quick once-over before nodding and looking for something he can compare on Kallos's desk.

"Have you been in here before?" I ask Finn as I step closer to the photos on the wall. I'm drawn to the images of people; they look sad and hopeless, yet small smiles crest each of their faces. That's when I catch the cloaks they're wearing. They are the same style and colors we're wearing now.

Finn moves to stand beside me and his scent of crisp pines warms my senses. I've missed his presence. I've missed him. The kiss we shared in the gardens reminded me how utterly hopeless I truly am in his hands.

"I have actually—on my first night here."

I raise a brow. "Get in trouble?"

He laughs and his amber eyes find mine. "Something like that."

"I wonder what it was like for them back then." I trace my finger over the photo of the group of friends. I quickly recognize Arthur and Kallos. One person looks like Nekane and... is that Elias? My eyes widen. This is the group of friends we're looking for. I trace each one with my eyes and memorize their features. Unfortunately, I don't recognize most of them. I lower my hand and am surprised when Finn threads his finger through mine gently. "Do you think we'll survive the exam?"

Our eyes meet and he grins weakly. "Honestly, I'm scared, Terra. I don't think this gets easier; they're training us for war." His gaze hollows as he looks back at the photo. Kallos had so much life still in his eyes. Arthur too.

Finn's father has been training him for war since he was a fucking kid. That monster's face surfaces in my mind, cruel and hardened by his callous life.

"Do you think your father is in Whales of Tauh? Preparing for Fernestia's next assault?" I say as I walk down the row of photos. Near the end of the wall I stop and stare at a small, unframed picture tacked to the wall. It's crumpled and depicts a boy in black and white. But I'd know that face anywhere. My fingers brush along the tattered picture and my lungs clench.

Elias. He already looks broken, frowning, eyes cold as he stares into the camera. Why does it make my soul ache to the bitter center? Did he ever have a chance to find his heart in this cruel world?

I doubt it.

"I don't know." Finn's voice startles me and I slip the loose photo into one of my pockets to look at again later. It wasn't even framed, so I pray Kallos will not notice its absence. "My father was supposed to be in Navasik that day, but the Skyfell happened before I could get home." He says the words with deep dread and the pain of that day flickers across his eyes.

"I'm sorry, Finn," I say, setting my hand on his arm.

He offers me a sad smile and an insignificant raise of his shoulder. "I'm just glad you weren't there. I can... still hear them screaming."

A shudder rolls through me at the thought of it. Barkovah will forever haunt me, and I'm grateful my Shadow keeps most of the phantoms at bay.

Muffled voices speak on the other side of the door.

Raine stuffs some samples into his pocket and the three of us quickly exit the study, finding Kai and Corvus waiting for us with grim expressions.

I let out a relieved breath. For gods' sakes, I thought it was Kallos.

Finn nods at his friend like he was expecting him. Raine shares an uncertain look with me.

Corvus looks like he has a million things he needs to say, but he chooses one I didn't expect. "I was just with Edgar in the infirmary."

My stomach drops. "What? What happened to him? Is he okay?" My feet are already carrying me to the exit. Corvus steps in front of me, earning him a low grunt from Raine as a warning.

"He's fine—he's already back in the Nova House," Corvus says as he nervously looks at his friends. "But Kallos placed a cast on his Shadow, which is going to make the second exam difficult for him to pass. Arthur said—" He quickly stops talking and shakes his head. "If he can't break the cast before the exam, he doesn't have a chance." Corvus's dark eyes hold secrets. I study Finn's features; he must sense it too.

"What the fuck is a *cast*?" Kai sits on one of the couches and we all awkwardly follow suit. Raine doesn't lean back in comfort though; he remains sitting straight and ready to leave at any moment.

Corvus holds out his palm and a small black feather appears, floating just an inch above his skin. We all lean in, awed, as Corvus whispers, "Kallos said Edgar's power was too dangerous unchecked, so he placed a sort of containment blanket over it with his own. This will keep Edgar from being able to harness his power." Corvus trembles as he waves his other hand over the feather. A thin layer of black dust tops the feather like a cloth draping over it.

I'm impressed with his ability to control it so delicately —obviously, he's been paying close attention in Nekane's class.

Finn's brows pinch together and he leans back on the couch. "So, Edgar can't use his powers at all?"

Corvus shakes his head. "In theory, no. But I can still sense it lingering just beneath his skin. Honestly, he's dangerous. I think Kallos made a good decision, but I don't think it's going to hold his Shadow as long as they were hoping." Corvus looks at me with sympathy and regret. "Terra, I saw what his Shadow can do with minimal effort and it's fucking horrifying."

Raine side glances at me before firming his lips. "So? What do you want us to do about it?" he says indifferently. Corvus holds Raine's cold stare. I can't fight the chill of his harsh words. That's my brother.

"There's something wrong with him. I think you should try to talk to him and convince him to not let his Shadow further into his soul. I have a really bad feeling about it. I think there's a way we can help him in the next exam without using his powers."

I process that information silently. Based on what I overheard Arthur and Elias talking about—the Blood Crowns exam—I doubt he stands any fucking chance without his powers. Even if his Shadow is malevolent, he needs it to survive. We all do.

I stand. Raine is at my side in a moment and I nod at Corvus. "Thank you for letting me know. I'll see what I can do." My throat is rough from the emotions I'm keeping back. Finn looks at me with silent concern. I smile at him. "Thanks for helping us tonight. I'll let you know what we find tomorrow."

The three of them look adrift as we leave. If what Corvus said is true, not only do I need to talk to Edgar about his Shadow, but I need to figure out how he's going to survive the exams as well.

Fuck. Everything just keeps piling up higher and higher.

Raine waits until we're crossing the icy bridge before he says anything. "It's not a match."

"Huh?" I look up at him, confused. He smiles at my knack for getting lost in thought. The only nice thing that's happened tonight is that Raine is feeling better.

"The notes, they don't match. So who's left?"

"Arthur and Nekane—oh, and I think we should check the headmaster too. It has to be one of them," I say with little hope. We could just be chasing ghosts here. What if the person who wrote that note died a long time ago? "I saw an old picture in Kallos's office. A group of students. We can pick up from there if we don't find a match."

Raine shrugs. "Good recon work. If we ever get out of here I'll make you my lieutenant." His voice is cheerful and light but I can't find the energy to be jovial. I lean into him and he wraps his arm around me. "You're awfully mopey tonight."

"No shit." I laugh because it's not funny at all.

My brother is losing his mind, my ex-boyfriend is helping me save someone I cherish dearly from his death sentence, and my Shadow Mate, who is very much the enemy, has my heart twisted tightly in his grasp. Now toss in the mystery of what the Blood Crowns are.

I sigh, letting my brain shed some of the stress.

Before we reach the doors to the Nova House, they swing open and Edgar comes stalking out.

Something's wrong with him.

24

Terra

Raine freezes and flashes me a surprised look as Edgar stalks by as if he doesn't even see us.

I hold my hand up to Raine to let him know I'll handle it and chase after Edgar. He's fast but I reach him before he gets to the halfway point on the bridge. I place my hand on his shoulder and he turns on me with surprising speed. His eyes are practically glowing turquoise in the moonlight.

My legs instinctively carry me a few steps back. His skin is pale, eyes wider than they should be, and his teeth are grit together hard. There's a vicious light in his gaze, one I don't recognize at all.

"What?" he says cruelly.

"Edgar... what's going on with you?" I try to shake the

fear that's rising inside me and replace it with calm and care for him. My Shadow isn't helping; it thrashes uncomfortably inside my chest as if he's a threat. A darkness rolls over my skin in his presence. The cast was supposed to keep his power contained, but he feels like a caged animal trying desperately to escape. Perhaps he is dangerous. He certainly looks it with his light brown hair lashing wildly in the breeze, those glowing eyes bore holes into my soul.

Edgar observes me for a second before smiling unpleasantly. It's ominous and cold—something I've seen cross Elias's face when he's going berserk. "Nothing, I'm perfectly fine." His voice is scratchy and crooked.

"Really? Because you don't look *fine*, Edgar," I say with worry eroding my voice. "Have you been speaking with your Shadow? I think you need to stop, you look... You look —" My eyes trail him up and down, taking in his frail state.

"I look *what*?" he says slowly in a monotone voice.

I stiffen my resolve. "You look like you're losing your fucking mind."

He dramatically looks down at his body and back up at me. My entire spine chills with the sinister energy in his eyes. "You think *I'm* losing my mind?" he says with that fucking eerie smile. "How about I help you find yours, Terra."

I clench my fists. "Knock it off. Do you even hear yourself? What do you think our parents would think of you right now?"

That strikes a chord in his conscience—his entire face falls into shock, then hatred, and deep, painful rage. Tears fall from his reddened eyes and I instantly regret what I said.

"Fuck you," he says through gnashed teeth. Edgar drops his head. I slowly approach him, but when I hear his maniacal laugh growing, my very marrow curdles inside me. He throws his head back, tears and snot falling down his chin as he laughs hysterically. "You know what our parents would think? They'd think you're a fucking whore, Terra. Living your best fucking life while everything is anything but fine. So you tell me. Who's lost their mind?"

Edgar lowers his chin and his glare burns into my skin as I choke out a few tears. A knot twists in my throat; I can't swallow it. It's too fucking raw.

"You should've died with them," he says venomously, his laugh instantly dying. He stares at me like he's not even present. Then he lunges at me.

I raise my arms in time as he collides with me. One moment we're glaring at each other with our teeth bared, tears crashing as we struggle on the bridge; the next, we're falling over the edge. Raine shouts but my focus is entirely on my brother's hateful expression. His power is out of control right now, wisping from the seams of his very soul. If anyone gets too close to him, they'll surely be blighted.

Edgar clasps his hands around my throat and squeezes. I'm in survival mode and can't spare a single moment to acknowledge the weight of what he's trying to do. All my mind can process are his cold, bony fingers caging around my windpipe and strangling the air from me.

I grip his brown hair and yank his head to the side. The momentum shifts our fall so that he's below me. Air leaves my lungs as I see the rapidly approaching ice of the lake. Everything is white and gray, everything except Edgar's furious green eyes.

What have we become?

Our bodies slam into the ice. The pain and gravity steal the breath from my lungs. Instinct takes over and I inhale sharply before we fall through the shattered ice. My entire body convulses with the freezing water burning every inch of my skin. The frigid water stings my eyes but I can't shut them. Fear keeps them open against the agony.

The moon shines bright enough to illuminate the ice cap above. The light blue water almost glows. In any other situation, it would be beautiful. A plume of bright red blood blooms like a terrible, morbid storm cloud beneath the ice. I lose my breath and bubbles escape around me as I spot Edgar's limp body slowly sinking into the depths of the lake.

For a moment, I'm worried he's dead, but his eyes open and the horrible turquoise glow pierces my soul. He opens his mouth like he's screaming at me and darkness answers his call. It gathers throughout the lake, moving like an enormous snake in languid, spine-chilling motions. It's unlike anything I've ever seen.

Fear solidifies inside my veins and I try desperately to swim for the surface. Amser tugs sharply along my spine in warning, and I turn my head in time to see Edgar swimming after me with a manic smile, blood trailing in the water behind him.

I want to vomit. I can't fucking hold my breath any longer.

Amser, help me! I call to my Shadow and it responds in kind. Angry and vengeful.

The ice above me explodes. Soft green and blue lights like an aurora in the night sky dance across the ice wall as I gasp for air. My breaths burn the inside of my lungs with each shuddering inhale I take.

Raine's on the shore screaming at me. Armed Darkfly soldiers line the edge of the lake but no one dares to interfere. Raine is far away but I can sense his fear from here. He takes off running across the lake to get to me. I start sliding across the ice toward him; the sheet cracks beneath my feet and my heart bursts with adrenaline inside my chest.

An audience is forming on the bridge and behind Raine. Fuck, what if someone gets blighted? The Darkflies are useless; they stand and watch fearfully. Where are the professors? The headmaster?

Where is Elias?

Elias. The thought of him comforts me.

Amser disperses from my body as black dust and forms quickly into a large feline, bones on the exterior with shadows teeming beneath as the mass. I jump onto its back and Amser dashes across the ice, seemly not at all concerned about it giving way beneath our weight. We're a hundred feet away from the shoreline and almost to Raine when I see a massive black creature under the ice, coiling and festering as I would imagine a trapped serpent trying to escape a tank it has outgrown would.

This is his power suppressed? If anything, the cast Kallos placed only made it angry. It's beyond formidable. I cannot fathom how Edgar has even managed to keep it inside himself.

My lips are dry and my heartbeats pound so loudly in my head that I can't hear anything else. Faster, we need to go faster.

The ice shatters in front of us and I'm thrown off Amser's back, skidding across the ice and screaming as my skin burns on the cold sheen.

Edgar stands before me, holding his hand to me as if he's trying to help me up. Blood pools beneath his feet and steam rolls into the air as the heat from his blood meets cold ice. "Face death boldly," he says with wide eyes, like he's absent, not even truly here.

"Edgar!" I scream at him. His eyes twitch and before either of us can do anything else, four figures appear on the ice in the blink of an eye. As fast as a lightning strike but as silent as snowfall.

Arthur, Nekane, Kallos, and Elias.

Elias's back faces me. He turns to look down at me, cold gray eyes flickering for a moment with concern for my wounds, even though he knows Amser will heal them. Then his jaw sets with fury and he cracks his neck. "Arthur, take Terra to the shoreline. We can handle this." His low voice has the same absence I heard in Edgar's. Is it the Shadows?

I remember the field and the boy with hazel eyes who lay before me with every joint in his body severed, his eyes staring far away into death.

"Elias, don't kill him!" I scream as Arthur scoops me up with one arm and practically teleports us to the shoreline. He grabs Raine with his other arm like we're both weightless. Our feet are on the ground before I can even finish speaking.

"Don't worry, he won't," Arthur says soothingly. He sets us both down and Raine crashes into me, taking my shoulders in his broad hands and holding me an arm's length away to inspect me from head to toe.

"I'm going to fucking kill that little—"

I cut Raine off with a hard glare. "It's not Edgar. There's something wrong with him." My voice quivers as my entire body trembles.

"Yeah, he's almost not even human anymore, Terra." Raine unzips his coat and presses me into his chest, hugging me tightly and rubbing his hands on my back to try to warm me. I tremble mindlessly as I watch the three instructors circle Edgar like he's a wild beast.

"He's still my brother."

25

Elias

This little fucking prick.

If he weren't a Nova, I'd pull his bones from his flesh one by one until he begged me to kill him. I know Emerai and Dr. Cein have been waiting for Sully to find another suitable vessel after what happened six years ago, but I thought they'd learned that this one is different.

It cannot be tamed.

Nekane's eyes fall to the ice below us as he mutters, "You guys seeing this?"

Kallos and I look down as well.

The lake is coiling with black scales, and large oval-shaped eyes the size of a full-grown human stare up at us.

Sully is a serpent this time around? I suppose it's better than its prior form.

"It's just a snake, Nekane," I say with little interest and step toward Edgar.

Nekane scoffs and Kallos only stares down with a perplexed expression.

Edgar turns on me and lashes out, his power precise and lethal. Almost as perfect as when Terra nearly took Arthur's head clean off.

I raise my arm and block his attack with the back of my hand, leaning forward as he leaves himself vulnerable. I grab his neck with one hand, squeezing the little fucker's throat until tears spill from his eyes and I see the fight go out of him like a light.

"Listen, Edgar, and listen well. If you try to kill your sister again, I will gut you so slowly, so agonizingly, that you'll beg me to take you apart joint by joint." My words draw a deep fear into his eyes, but I'm not sure he's got the message yet. I drop him and he gasps for air. My foot comes down on his head and he screams as I press my boot against his ear, crushing the other side into the ice. "Do. You. Understand?"

He cries and gasps for air. "Yes! Yes!" He squirms beneath my boot and sobs as blood spills beneath his head.

Kallos crosses his arms at my choice of treatment, but I seem to be the only one who remembers how vicious Sully truly is. How twisted and cruel. I lift my boot and glare at Edgar as he clutches his head.

Nekane laughs as Edgar stands, tears and blood staining his cheeks. *Okay, maybe Nekane remembers too.*

"Get him out of my sight," I say to Kallos before stalking back to the shore.

"Elias, the four of us need to speak tonight. Meet us after midnight at the Broken Rock," Kallos says with a grim tone. I don't turn to look at him, but I nod. Edgar lets out small grunts of pain as Kallos helps him walk back to the courtyard.

What a fucking mess. We haven't gone to Broken Rock since the night before the first Blood Crowns exam. The memory sets my teeth on edge and I shudder it away.

As I approach the shore, students move to the side, watching curiously as I approach Arthur and Terra. She looks up at me with deeply pained eyes. Raine is curled around her like a blanket, but for some reason, it doesn't bother me like it did before. Even Velis accepts his Shadow, lingering close to the edge of my skin curiously.

I'll have to sort that out another time.

"Is Edgar okay?" Terra asks innocently.

I won't lie to her. "I doubt it."

She shakes her head and lets tears stream down her cheeks. What's with all the crying? She shouldn't have turned her emotions back on. I sigh and open my arms to her. Her eyes widen, but she only hesitates a moment before releasing her hold on Raine and molding herself to my chest. I secure my arms around her.

Raine levels me a look, not angry or jealous, but curious. I just smirk back at him.

She'll always choose me when it comes down to it.

"Let's get you cleaned up, sweetheart," I whisper to her softly and she nods into my chest.

My room is cold, but after I light the fireplace and stoke the flames, the temperature quickly rises. Terra stands in the center of my room, staring at the floor, her mind somewhere distant.

I brush her hair back. Her clothes are soaked and freezing. My fingers trail softly down the skin of her neck and goosebumps rise over her arms. I've never wanted to be so gentle yet brutal with someone in my entire life.

"You need to get out of these clothes or you'll freeze," I murmur, watching her eyes lift to mine and brimming with tears once more. She nods. I have no clue what to say regarding her brother. What do *I* know about comforting people? I usually just kill them. Comfort is complex and foreign to me.

I slowly unzip her tactical jacket and slide it off her shoulders. It falls heavily to the floor. Steam rolls from her bare skin. I swallow hard—of course, she's not wearing a bra. I force myself to look away and grab a spare blanket to drape over her shoulders before I remove her pants.

She holds the blanket firmly over herself and presses her lips into the soft fabric. I have her sit on the edge of my bed as I find a towel to dry her hair with. Then I settle behind her and rub the towel over her wet strands. She startles me when she finally breaks the silence.

"He was really trying to kill me, wasn't he?"

My hands stop moving and I lean forward, resting my

chin on her shoulder. Her skin is hot and smells of cypress. I shut my eyes and murmur, "Yes, he was."

She reaches her hand up to my hair and threads her fingers through the white strands, stroking them back and leaning her head against mine.

"What do I do now? Everything is falling apart." Her voice cracks. The sound presses deep into my chest.

I turn her around so she's facing me, her soft legs intertwined with mine. Her rosy cheeks and pleading eyes are making me uncomfortable. That weight I hate so much settles back over my heart. As her eyes dip down to my lips, I have to wrestle the Shadow's hunger inside myself.

"Do you want me to kill him?" Her jaw drops and she's about to yell at me before I crack a grin. "I'm kidding."

Terra's face shifts from shocked to relieved and she starts laughing. I wasn't kidding, Sully needs to be dealt with, but it's nice that she finds me funny. At least humor seems to be helping her mood.

"He hardly even looked like himself. His eyes are different, and I don't mean the fractures. I mean *inside.* There was something bad. Evil." She tucks her knees into her chest and rests her chin on them. The blanket is draped over her back but her front is open to me.

I smooth my thumb over her cheek. "His Shadow has corrupted him, Terra. He doesn't have long before it takes him completely, especially if he keeps letting it sink further into his soul. Either the headmaster will have his heart or Sully will. I doubt there is an in-between for him."

Her eyes flash up to me. "What do you mean the headmaster will have his heart?"

Fuck, I shouldn't have said that, but I guess she

would've found out sooner or later anyway. "Haven't you been curious why our eyes are gray?" I tap the side of my head and she stares into my soul, nodding. "Headmaster Emerai has the Shadow that Keeps. It collects the hearts that have been replaced by the Shadows, and once it has, you're basically enslaved to it. Fernestia controls you so long as Emerai has you."

Terra sits up more, jaw trembling, nails digging into her knees with anger. "Why didn't you tell me this sooner? Raine's eyes are already starting to fade and—"

"Why would I? Look at my eyes, sweetheart. You give in or you die like lambs. It's better that the students don't know. Trust me, it's just... easier this way." My throat tightens as the images of my fallen comrades flash through my mind. Terra catches the falter in my voice.

Her face softens and she leans in closer, the blanket slipping off her shoulders and pooling around her waist. "Arthur told me you've blighted people before." My eyes widen at her admittance and unwelcome pain spreads through my chest. "Who did you have to kill, Elias? Sometimes I can't tell if you genuinely are a psychopath or if you're just doing what you're told."

She wants to be cruel? I like this side of her.

"I killed them all, Terra. Just as I did the people in the field. Just like I would have killed *you* if it weren't for us being mates." My hands rope around her throat, but there's no fear or disdain in her eyes. A dark and lustful grin pulls up at her lips.

"You can't hide the pain in your eyes, Elias. You're not as heartless as you try to be," she whispers against my lips as she stares into my hollow soul. I swallow hard from both the aching wound in my heart and her closeness. "They were all your friends, weren't they? The ones you blighted."

A crooked, weak smile spreads across my lips, my eyes dry. "The only ones I ever had." For a moment Terra just looks at me with so much sympathy and understanding, I hate it. I desperately need to escape those pitying eyes.

But she won't let me run away—she leans in and presses her lips against mine. I want to push her away. My chest aches and the emotions are drowning me, but her soft lips are a comforting place to fall.

I don't do *vulnerable*, and yet the moment her mouth opens for me, our tongues feverishly seek one another.

She unzips my jacket and lifts my undershirt up, pressing her bare breasts against my chest, making me groan with every soft slip of her skin on mine. I wrap my arms around her waist and pull her close. She's still cold from the lake.

My lips pull away from hers and she gives me a confused look. "Don't try to fix me—some things are meant to be broken." I pull the blanket back up over her shoulders and lift her up off the bed, carrying her to the fireplace and sitting with her in my lap for the warmth of the flames to reach our faces.

I'm meant to be broken. I stare emptily at the fire as old friends greet me in my conscience. They never leave—not for long. Arthur keeps them fresh in my mind, as punishment, I think.

"Help me save Edgar, please," Terra pleads with a hushed voice.

Gods, I'm getting too soft.

"Okay," I mumble as I press a kiss on her shoulder, fully intending to break that promise.

I carry Terra back to her room after she falls asleep in my arms. She's had a really fucking hard day and all I can think about is crushing her brother's head beneath my foot again.

Raine lifts his head from her pillow and watches me carefully as I set her down next to him. He opens the sheets and draws her in close to his chest, keeping her warm in my stead.

"We're starting private tutoring tomorrow. Dawn, at the blight training grounds," I whisper to him and he just nods drowsily before nuzzling his lips into the crook of Terra's neck. Her soft brown hair hides her face, but I bet she's smiling in her dreams.

I hope she isn't too ruined when Raine's clock runs out.

The door closes soundlessly behind me. I take my time walking down the east bridge, down the steps of Alkrose, and out past the courtyard, farther still into the forest beyond the blight training grounds.

The wind often whispers to me when I'm alone in this forest. I know not if it has a name or lore, I only know that the pines reach for me. They beckon to my soul and bring dreary reminders of a life I've long since left behind.

Why now? Of all times... Why does being around Terra make me so nostalgic? It is as if she's warming that dead part of me and bringing it back to life. Even Raine gives me dark, haunting glimpses of the past.

My thoughts escape me as I stop before a wall of jagged rock. The minerals are so ebony that you'd hardly be able to find it on a moonless night. I lift my hand and let my fingertips brush along the edges as I walk around the broken rock.

Kallos and Arthur both look up at me as I turn the corner to the dip in the boulder. It makes a peak above, but below, it's similar to the mouth of a cave. Funny, now that I'm older, our meeting spot looks much smaller than it once was.

Nekane leans against the far wall of the rock and smirks. If I close my eyes, I can see the three of them as hopeful young idiots. But I see the four ghosts of us that linger in the dark, wondering why we left them behind.

"You're late," Kallos quips as they all gather around a firepit in the center of the cave. The flames are blue and undying. No foliage or snow reaches this dark place.

"I was doing damage control," I retort coldly. Arthur raises a brow at me and smiles like he knows all my secrets. I'm certain he does.

Nekane wraps his arm around my shoulder and lets out a chuckle. "You were going to crush that Nova brat's head in, weren't you?"

Kallos's glower only grows more impatient as he mutters, "We only have an hour before the headmaster returns to the grounds."

We silently sit on the old stone seats, looking attentively at Kallos. He was the one who initially found this spot for us to share all of our secrets and freedom plans.

Being here now, I feel some of that hope returning. Perhaps we can still someday be free.

"I placed a cast on Edgar's Shadow today in class. The power with which he fought his sister was a mere sliver of what he's hiding beneath the surface and I fear that he will break the cast quickly. He shouldn't have been able to use any of the Shadow's power at all," Kallos says dryly.

Chills crawl up my spine. "*That* was with a cast in place?" I say incredulously. Nekane looks as surprised as I am but Arthur firms his mouth into a flat line. He shares a look with me and I raise my shoulders.

"Arthur already knew?" Nekane's brows pinch together and he sits up straighter with interest.

Kallos nods. "One of the other students knows too, Corvus. I wasn't thinking rationally at the moment I placed it, given that Edgar will need his Shadow during the exam... but after witnessing Sully mere moments from breaking free of the cast, I'm more concerned about the other students."

"I never expected him to attack his own sister like that," Arthur mumbles absently, writing notes in that journal of his. "I doubt he'll be able to break it as easily as you're assuming, Kallos, but maybe we should each place one over Sully?" Arthur's eyes grow distant and he frowns.

Nekane shrugs. "I don't care what we do with that boy, but if we can't keep him contained the headmaster might order an execution like last time."

The three of them nod in agreement.

"I think we should kill him," I say remorselessly.

Kallos levels me with a dark stare. "You know we can't."

"Why not? We have the Space Nova and the two Crescents; we are enough. They don't need him," I challenge Kallos and he stands, his golden eyes flickering with the light from the blue flames.

"He's a human being, Elias. You may not remember what weight a life holds, but I do. I haven't lost my heart."

My teeth grit together and I clench my hands over my knees before standing as well. "Fine. If you want to try to save him, be my guest. But I hope you remember who is sent to slaughter the lamb when you're finished with him. I want *you* to remember who has to fucking look the tortured remains in the eye and kiss them goodnight. Me. And when that time comes, and come it shall, I hope you remember who it was that had a heart, Kallos. Because I wanted to end it for him before he became like Midas."

Arthur and Nekane share a grim look. Kallos shakes his head furiously at me and turns his back. "Just go, Elias. We'll finish this discussion without you. I'd forgotten how insensible you are."

Low blow.

I leave without another word, not letting Kallos's cruel words sink too far into my chest.

Only, I don't walk back to Alkrose just yet. There are four gravestones around the far edge of the broken rock. I bend a knee next to them, letting my fingers brush across the hand-engraved names and stare hollowly at them.

Midas. Camil. Acadi. Serina.

"Hello, old friends."

26

Terra

A cold breeze draws in from the headmaster's study.

I shiver and make a face at Raine. He smirks at me and nudges my shoulder with his. "No backing out now, babe. We need to see what he's hiding in here," he murmurs softly as he lets his Shadow slowly seep from his fingertips and unlocks the third door we've had to get through in order to get this far.

This is why I shouldn't have told him about the headmaster stealing hearts. Raine is too curious and reckless just to ignore these sorts of things.

"I didn't think we'd actually go looking for the hearts. It's probably more metaphorical, anyway. I doubt there are literal hearts in jars in there," I whisper as I glance uneasily over my shoulder for the hundredth time.

The lock clicks and Raine shoves the door open. I glare at him for being so loud but all that earns me is a silent laugh from him. I do appreciate him trying to cheer me up though; Edgar has been weighing heavily on my mind since he attacked me a few days ago. Arthur pushed our private lesson to today so I had time to recollect my mind.

"Let's see," Raine murmurs as he steps through. I follow behind him and shut the door quietly behind us.

The headmaster's study is dimly lit with black candles that have almost completely burned out. A long desk takes up the space in the center of the room. Old papers, candles, pens, and books lie scattered. He and Elias share that habit.

Raine searches the wall of books while I take to searching Emerai's desk, pulling out the heavy drawers, not entirely sure what we're looking for when it comes to the hearts. I find a few notes to compare to the one we found in the library and quickly cross him off the list.

"Hey, come here," Raine whispers after several minutes have passed.

I close the last drawer and walk to his side. "What'd you find?"

The shelves are dusty and the oak is warped from moisture. The books are arranged neatly in comparison to the mess on the headmaster's desk. Raine points to a gap between the tops of the books and the shelf above where an inch of space is visible.

"What?" I ask again.

"Look closely." Raine moves over so I can stand where he is. I narrow my eyes at the space. It's dark, but there's a glint of something in the next room. "A secret room behind a shelf? That seems too obvious," I say hesitantly.

Raine smiles and shrugs. "Tacky or not, we should check it out."

We each take up a side of the bookshelf and move it out far enough so we can slip inside. The room is cold, the kind that feels drafty and ominous.

It's too dark to see anything besides glinting from glass or something reflective across the room.

"I don't like this," I whisper.

Raine ignores me. He leans down and inspects something close. I watch him so intently that when hands softly land on my shoulders, I yelp.

"Terra, it's only me," Arthur says lightly.

Raine stands quickly, his eyes wide with fear.

"It's okay, it's Arthur," I tell him and he settles a bit, keeping his stern glare on his face. My beautiful Raine is so untrusting.

Arthur flicks his fingers and lights turn on above us. It's still rather dim; they only illuminate the center of the room, leaving the shelves and walls in the dark.

"What are you two doing here, might I ask?" Arthur says in his calm, level voice. My eyes linger over his sharp jaw and I look away when amusement flashes across his gaze.

Raine answers, "You'll have to torture it out of me, *Fernestian.*"

Arthur chuckles, which only fuels Raine's hate fire more. I intervene. "Elias said something curious about the headmaster collecting hea—"

The light around us darkens in the blink of an eye and Arthur presses his warm palm softly against my lips.

"Don't say it here," Arthur says with dread permeating his expression. His dark hair falls over his forehead and touches my nose. My heartrate rises; his lips are mere inches from mine.

"Why?" I ask with bated breath.

Arthur smooths his hand gently over my throat and down to my collarbone. His gray eyes linger on my lips as he slowly shakes his head. "Many ears in Alkrose lend themselves to the headmaster."

Raine's face sullens and he uncrosses his arms. "Where does the headmaster keep them?"

The air is heavy and thick as Arthur regards us in silence. "The headmaster consumes them. There is nothing to find," he says matter-of-factly and lowers his chin. "Now, let us leave before Emerai returns."

I stare at Arthur's empty expression. I don't quite believe him, but we follow him as he guides us quietly out of the headmaster's study. We stop at the bottom of the stairs on the second floor and I look at Raine.

"You go ahead. I have a tutoring session with Arthur," I say with a weak smile.

Raine furrows his brows and looks from me to the instructor before dipping his head. "Fine. Don't forget to meet us in the courtyard after supper though. Finn, Aervin, and Kai will be expecting us."

I follow Arthur as he saunters to one of the classrooms down the hall. He waves me in first and shuts the door behind us, then selects one of the window seats that line the south wall of the class and pats the space next to him with a bleak grin. Warm orange sunlight drips over him, welcoming all the hollow parts of his cheeks. I yearn to touch his handsome face, to draw lines with my fingers over every valley where his flesh meets bone.

I curl myself into the arched space and pull my legs close to my chest. He watches me and cocks his head to the side. His soft lips draw up into a smile. Being this close to him beckons a desire from so deep within that I'm not sure if it is mine or my Shadow's.

"What is it that runs rampant through your mind, Terra?"

I study his gaze and all I find is kind endearment. I hesitate, but say slowly, "Edgar... He's never been a violent person, but I don't know how we can ever face one another again."

Arthur's expression remains blank. "He has certainly created a rift between you, hasn't he?"

I grit my teeth and bury my face in my knees. "I don't know what to do."

He leans forward, pulling his knees up to his chest as well and resting his head on his forearms. "I'm remorseful to say I'm at a loss as well. I would tell you if I knew how to stop Sully. I promise you that." He speaks properly but his gaze is anything but.

I stare down at the academy towers beneath us. The courtyard is out of view from here, but the lake stretches almost out of eyesight along with the fog that lingers around the grounds today.

"Terra."

I break my thoughts and look up at Arthur. "Hm?"

"The technique I plan on teaching you today might get a bit... involved. I've heard you aren't foreign to it since you've been in Kallos's class."

A light laugh rolls easily from my lips. "I won't lie and say I didn't expect something of the sort. Close contact with other strong Shadows makes Amser... intense."

He laughs with me, a joyous and simple sound that could easily live in my head forever.

Arthur is in his mid-twenties. Looking at him, sitting with his knees up and so lax, he looks nothing more than a young man who wishes to study, read, and be at peace. I've always thought he looked tired, but staring at him now, eyes dreary with maroon blush that paints his lower eyelids, I'd say he's been tired since long before we met. I wish I could take that away from him.

"What?" he asks with a warm smile that breaks my heart. He looks at me like he can wait centuries and longer if need be. Patience and understanding flicker across his old soul.

"I was just admiring your devotion to whatever it is that keeps you awake at night—do you not sleep well?" I ask with a sympathetic grin.

He perks his head up a little as if he's surprised I noticed. Then he looks away, staring longingly into the dim room, at ghosts perhaps. He doesn't respond as he shifts and stands. I watch him curiously as he walks to the center of the room, turns, straightens into a polite posture with one hand behind his back, and offers me the other. His black hair falls beautifully around his shoulders and my heart aches to run my fingers through it.

I oblige and meet him in the middle of the classroom,

slipping my hand over his. "What are we doing?" For a moment, a rather silly one, I let myself think he's going to dance with me.

Arthur grins and closes his hand around mine. "I'm going to teach you a useful technique for the exam, remember?" A dark flicker flashes across his eyes and I swallow hard as his Shadow tugs viciously at mine. I sink my teeth into my lower lip to keep from moaning at the divinity of it. Stronger than Kallos's, softer than Elias's. Arthur's lips twitch at the sensation, but he remains expressionless. "This is called Shadow leeching. It is the act of borrowing another's strength by leeching parts of their Shadow."

A dizzy spell falls over me as his Shadow siphons mine like a glass of water and I fall forward. It feels as if his Shadow has sucked the life from my veins. Arthur catches me, his hand still clasped tightly over mine. He lowers us to the floor in one fluid motion.

"I just leeched some of your time magic," he says in a low tone. My blood chills. I feel so helpless like this. Amser doesn't answer my call, as if it's muted inside me. "Now, I want you to take some of mine. Draw it in, and once you can feel it building inside you, cut it off from the rest of me."

I stare at him incredulously. "I have no idea how to even begin to do that."

He chuckles and helps me stand back up. "Just think of it like sucking in water from a straw."

My brows crease and I can't help but smile. "A straw, huh?"

Arthur looks confused for a second before his eyes

narrow at me. "You've been spending too much time with Elias, I see," he says with an eye roll. "Go on, then, give it a try."

I shut my eyes and focus on the sensation of our Shadows, trying to draw his into me but finding no luck. Letting out a sigh, I release his hand. "It's not working."

He stares at me in thought and then steps closer, pressing our chests together and leaning me back over a desk until I'm lying flat over the surface. The wood groans against the tile as he lets his weight burden me. Every fiber of my being lights up and I'm hyper aware of every inch where his body is against mine.

I study his beautiful face gazing down at mine. He tries to mask it with indifference, but a well of kindness and warmth he'll never allow anyone to know peeks through.

"Try again. Focus, Terra. There will be worse things to distract you in the exam than me," he murmurs against my neck. His lips are warm and a shudder spreads throughout my body.

Somehow I fucking doubt that. What is more distracting than your professor pushing you back on top of a desk in an empty classroom? My Shadow's presence grows stronger with my increased heartrate and I take shallow breaths as Arthur's warm ones heat my skin.

I try again, focusing on his Shadow and where it dallies around mine. It slowly draws closer and when I feel it entering my bones, I gasp, losing my hold on it.

Arthur straightens himself, quirking his mouth in disappointment. "I was sure that would work." He presses his hand to his mouth in thought.

I lie back on the desk, staring at the ceiling as I relish in that sensation. It wasn't like anything I've felt with Elias or Raine, nor Kallos or Finn.

How can something hurt yet contain so much subtle pleasure? All-consuming and not all simultaneously.

"Arthur, what was that feeling? Did you feel it too when you took my Shadow?" I lift my head when he doesn't respond.

His eyes flick to me like he's only now hearing me. "Hm? Oh, yes, I did."

That's not enough. I press him. "What was it? You're not my mate and yet, every time you touch me, I feel... lonely."

His eyes drift to the floor. "Lonely, huh? That's not how I would—"

"Not lonely in the moment we're together, but all those that follow. In the seconds you touch me, I'm filled with longing and so much sorrow... but after we part, I'm utterly lonely. Is that how you feel too?" I ask, desperate to know I'm not the only one.

His weary eyes meet mine again and he nods.

"I told you, time and memory are old friends. Never together, never apart. Always lonely," he mutters sorrowfully.

I sit up and take his hand. "That's dreadfully sad. Who says that's how they have to be? Why can't they be in harmony?"

His eyes turn cold and distant, his lips paler than they were a moment ago. He mutters softly, "I say so."

"That's quite cruel, don't you think? Who are you to

force this tragic feeling upon us?" My voice is husky with the emotions building inside me. I can't stand to be this close to him for this long. The desire to consume him claws at my soul. His presence alone is familiar.

Every inch of this man cries out to be touched—felt and kissed. It's unbearable to breathe the same air as he does. I turn, needing to put distance between us before I do something stupid.

As I turn my head he catches my neck, hand sprawled out over my jaw as he pulls my attention back to him. His fingers dig into my skin and splay across my throat in a tight hold.

My heart skips a beat and I hold my breath, eyes widening. Before I can make much sense of what's happening, Arthur's lips are against mine. His scent of old pages and comforting tea spills into me. I whimper as he pulls me in closer, loosening his grip around my neck and sliding his hand into my hair. He kisses me as if he's been thinking of my lips for a very long time—kisses me as if he has before.

Such a starved, carnal man. Lovely and lonesome.

He's made my heart realize what loneliness is too. And I consume his demanding kisses just as viciously.

His other hand wraps around my waist and he lifts me up, carrying me toward the front of the classroom. I pull away from his lips as he sets me down on top of the long desk. My lips part to say how insane this is but his mouth is back on mine and he lowers his frame over me.

Elias might have to make room for another man in my life.

Our Shadows tangle hopelessly and my heart yearns for Arthur.

He deepens the kiss, parting my lips with his tongue. I wrap my arms around his chest and let my fingers explore his toned back, every curve where his muscles dip into the bones beneath and sculpt his perfect form. He lets out a low moan as my hands come back around his waist and I trace his hip bones with my fingertips.

Arthur breaks our kiss and inhales deeply. "We should stop."

"You started it," I murmur against his lips and he sets his forehead against the desk with a groan. "Best we don't get caught though. I'm not sure what Elias will think."

Arthur lifts his head back up and looks at me. This close, his eyes don't look quite gray. They almost have an ashy-green hue to them. "Elias doesn't own you. Don't let him be delusional enough to think that he does. You're more than all of us, Terra." He pauses, looking down at my lips, swollen from our brutal kisses. "Now, do you want to learn the technique or not? Take part of my Shadow." Arthur lowers his lips back to mine and I try to focus on the Shadows inside us and not the hard bulge in his pants pressing against my core.

I thread my fingers through his hair and focus on how wispy and dark it is. Slowly, I draw his Shadow within me once more. This time I'm ready for the odd sensation that assaults my marrow and blends into my body. Amser circles around it, leaving a wide berth for it to fill.

Abruptly, all the focus I have vanishes. Arthur's lips are trailing down my neck. He slowly unzips my jacket, pulling my shirt up and revealing my breasts. He looks up at me momentarily and murmurs against my nipple, "You're going to lose it again if you don't focus."

His Shadow slips away from my hold and I'm honestly finding it hard to care right now. Arthur's tongue is hot and wet as he strokes my tender skin over and over. I squirm beneath him and fist his hair.

He stops and I'm tempted to let him know I've bitten Elias's dick for playing this very same game.

"I won't continue unless you can learn this, Terra. It's important that you know it for the exam," he says in a perfectly annoying professor's tone.

Somehow that turns me on more.

I manage to messily sever a part of his Shadow that I still have a hold on, and the moment I do, his tongue resumes and my back arches up into him. A breath that is not my own coils inside my lungs.

"Good, now your reward," Arthur mumbles, lips gliding down my stomach. His fingers are warm and he easily unbuttons my pants, sliding them down and pulling my underwear with them.

I swallow hard. Is this really happening?

His gray eyes lift to mine before he dips down and starts stroking my core with his tongue. My head instantly drops back and I curl my fingers into the desk as I stifle an urgent moan.

Students are in the hallway walking past the door as Arthur devours me, lapping at my center like an impoverished soul. He yearns for me; I can feel it in the way he grips my hips greedily, demanding more. His strokes slow and he pushes two fingers inside me, pumping into me over and over until my eyes are rolling to the back of my skull and I'm squeezing his head between my knees.

"A-Arthur," I cry softly.

He lifts his eyes and watches me as I moan his name and whimper beneath his hand and tongue. He nips lightly on my clit and this time I can't keep quiet. I cry out and moan as I ride out the orgasm, grinding into his face as the last waves of the high settle and come crashing down.

Arthur presses a kiss on my inner thigh and stands, looking satisfied with the mess he's made of me. He licks his lips and smooths out his hair while I pull my pants back up.

My cheeks are warm. There's a blush across his too.

I think we just crossed a line that we can't come back from.

"Shall we go practice in the forest now?" he says academically, completely dismissing the relations we just shared. I quirk a brow. "You took some of my Shadow, and I ought to show you how to use it, shouldn't I?" He grins and offers me his hand like a gentleman. I take it and he helps me off the desk. Before letting my hand go he presses a kiss to the back of it. "You truly are a delight, Terra."

I chuckle and look into his eyes. This close, I'm certain there's a bit of green to them. Does he still have some sliver of his heart? "Arthur, what color were your eyes before they turned gray?"

He seems taken aback, pausing to think for a moment as if he's forgotten.

"Green. Not emerald like your own, but a sage green. Dull but pleasant." Arthur grins nostalgically.

"I have no doubt they were lovely. Your gray eyes are

beautiful too, you know," I say as I nudge him. He laughs and I find I'm taken with that as well.

"Let's hurry. You still have to meet Raine and the others this evening."

I find myself staring at the back of his head the entire way to the blight grounds, wondering what Arthur would be like if not for Alkrose.

27

Terra

"Terra. Wake up."

I wake from a dreamless sleep and meet Raine's soft blue eyes.

"Raine? What are you doing?" I sit up and rub my eyes, groggy. It's still dark out and feels much too early for class. Four weeks at Alkrose is enough to get a schedule computed into your system.

He tosses my white cloak at me and I barely catch it before he mutters, "Arthur's study is next. Do you have the note?"

I yawn and try to shake the tendrils of drowsiness that tug at my mind. "Yeah, give me a second." Arthur would likely have told me if he was the one who wrote the note, and I doubt it's him since he's the one who sent me looking in the library. Unless this is all some game to him and he's a sadistic bastard, but I really doubt that's the case.

I clasp my moon brooch to secure the cloak around my shoulders and turn on my desk lamp as I rummage through the top drawer. The note is tucked between my anatomy and Shadow riding books.

Raine smiles when I hand it to him and we sneak out into the hallway as quietly as we can. The entire tower is silent. The crackling, flickering light of the eternal blue fireplace gives us barely enough luminance to see.

I'm pretty sure Arthur's study is the first door I passed when Elias took me to his room. We silently make quick work of the staircase, stopping at the first door we reach. Raine presses his head to the wood and listens for a few agonizing minutes.

I'm so tired—between private tutoring with Arthur, classes, finally breaking into the Ekko House and crossing Nekane off the list, and practicing after dinner each night with the boys, I could sleep for an entire year. Not to mention rebuilding my relationship with Finn, avoiding Edgar, and messing around with Elias and, apparently, Arthur. But above all is the stress and lingering dread that each passing day brings us as we inch closer to the second-semester exam.

Ugh.

"There's no one in there," Raine whispers and tries the doorknob. To our surprise, the door opens. He glances at me and I nod. We're already committed to doing this, so we'd better do it quickly.

We slip inside and quietly shut the door behind us. It's pitch black and I feel around the room until I stub my foot on something and muffle the *ow* that instinctively comes out of my mouth. My hands fumble upon a lamp a moment later and a dim light illuminates the room.

"Well, this isn't what I expected," Raine says a little louder than a whisper.

The room is completely empty, with the exception of the oak desk and a meager lamp in the corner. The room is devoid of dust but there's nothing in here that would lead me to believe it's Arthur's study or that he even uses it.

"I guess he has another office where he keeps his things," I mumble as I check the two drawers on the desk, both empty. I try not to think too much about the professor and what he and I did together. My cheeks are already warming at the mere mention of his name.

Raine groans and slides his hand over his head as a troubled look spreads across his face. "Sorry I woke you up for this." He looks at me with weary eyes. He never tells me if he's in pain. I know he doesn't want me to worry, but still.

I shake my head. "It's fine. I was hoping you'd stay with me tonight anyway, so let's go back. And maybe we can use this room for something since it's empty, you know?" I try to see the positive side to the situation since I'm still mildly annoyed with Finn for saying I'm a negative person.

Raine tilts his head and looks around at the four blank walls. "Yeah, I guess you're right. In Barkovah, I had a room that I used for all the operations and to keep things straight with the lookout swaps." His eyes are heavy and dark underneath. I slowly lift my hand to his cheek, waiting for him to pull away, but he doesn't this time. My palm presses against the cold hollow of his cheek and he shuts his eyes. "Every time we try to find information, we take ten steps back," he says in a defeated tone.

"We'll find something soon. We can't give up. Are you okay?" I gently try to get him to open up to me. The torment behind his eyes hurts deep inside my chest.

He considers me for a moment. "It's nothing—let's get back to your room."

I don't take that as an answer, maybe because I'm tired or even because I think he'll feel much better if he just says it. Holding darkness inside only allows it to fester and infect parts of you that aren't yet broken.

He steps toward the door, but when I don't follow him, he glances back at me, his brows pulling together in question.

"Stop icing me out, Raine. You don't let anyone in. Doesn't it hurt? Aren't you tired of protecting the things that infect your mind so feverishly?" I ask with bated breath. He stares at me like an empty man, offended and scared of the feelings he's buried within himself. "Let me in."

Raine takes a significant step toward me. I take a couple back until my legs bump into the desk. He leans over me, setting a hand on each side of my body and bringing his face close to mine. Our noses touch and I inhale his crisp scent, a cold, damp storm.

"You want in? The dark isn't for pretty little things like you, babe." His lips coast mine softly, sending goosebumps up my arms.

"I'm adept in the dark—you aren't the first man to take me for a walk through it." My lips curl into a soft grin.

Raine raises a seductive brow as his fingers gently glide up my stomach and back over my ribs. My skin comes alive with every brush of his fingertips. Heat coils inside my core and I swallow eagerly as he chuckles, pressing his lips to mine.

His hands maneuver under my thighs and he lifts me up, setting my ass on the edge of the desk and moving closer until his torso is pressed against mine. Our kisses are starved, each of us demanding more with each nip, suck, and coax of our lips together. My fingers glide over the scar on his lower jaw and he groans as my tongue urges his lips to part.

"I'll let you in, but don't say I didn't warn you. I trust you, Terra," he says in a low, raspy voice as he scoops me up and carries me to the stairwell. Our lips crash together as he takes me to the homeroom. "Don't be sad when I'm gone. Promise me," he whispers as he lays me down on one of the sofas and kneels above me, his forehead pressed against mine.

"I won't," I lie.

Raine laughs quietly and presses back down into me. His kisses hold weight now. In Barkovah they had a loose, careless feeling behind them; these are covetous.

I sip in a short breath as one of his hands dips beneath my pant line. He caresses my inner thighs in a teasing motion, breaking our kiss and pressing his lips down my neck, collarbones, and sternum until my shirt won't allow him to kiss any lower.

"Does your Shadow burn where we touch? Like the second we connect, we'll ignite and never part again completely?" His voice is raspy and hushed. I try to focus on his words, but he's lifting my shirt and swirling my breast with his tongue, squeezing my thigh once more before his fingers find my clit and stroke me gently.

"Yes. It yearns for you so fiercely," I whisper as I press my lips to the top of his head. He smells like the forest. If I shut my eyes, it's just us, far away from everything else in this life. In a different time.

He groans when he finds how soaked I am. A breath gets caught in my throat and I stifle a moan as he pushes his fingers inside me.

"Raine," I whisper to the shell of his ear and he lifts his head. Those blue eyes melt my soul. He kisses me again and I try to reach for his belt before I recall how *in control* he needs to be when we're intimate. My hands stop midair and I bring them back to his chest.

"It's okay," he mutters, looking at me with trusting eyes, and somehow that hurts because I don't feel like I deserve it.

I smile weakly and gently remove his belt and unbutton his pants. He pulls down mine as well, sliding his wet fingers up and down my slit and making me writhe beneath him. His cock is already hard—I run my hand over his shaft a few times in rhythm with his fingers.

Raine groans and kisses up along my neck, showing his affection with those soft, desperate touches. He moves in closer and rubs his dick along my core. The sensation makes my entire body jerk and I can't help but wiggle my hips eagerly for him.

He presses his tip into me slowly, spreading me open at a tortuous pace and filling me completely. He presses his forehead against mine and lets out a groan that reverberates through my chest.

"What is the dark to you? The dark for me... was Mara. She was one of the leaders in our misfit group," he murmurs with his forearms pressed to the cushions around my head. "She was two years older than I was and she was a vicious woman. Cruel and greedy."

I stare up into his beautiful eyes. They're filled with vulnerability and pain.

"She took a liking to me and would beat me relentlessly. As we got older, she also took other things." He stops and I know. He doesn't need to say it. He lets his body fall into mine and he hides his face as he whispers, "She gave me the scar on my jaw when I finally told her no. I was so angry and blind with rage—I took that blade she always cut me with, and I stuck it right into her fucking skull."

I inhale sharply at the gore, picturing how hard he must've swung to pierce her skull.

"She didn't even cry. She knew how sinister people like her were bound to die," Raine says darkly. I'm disturbed that he still has an erection after talking about it, but then again, Raine enjoys the morbid things. He looks down at me with a small smirk. "I told you that you wouldn't like the dark—the wicked things of the past."

I hold him tightly, afraid to let go. His broad shoulders are so tense and strong beneath my hands, yet he trembles, his soul weak. "I'm... so sorry, Raine." What else can one say?

He nods. "She took everything from me, but that didn't mean I had to take it out on the world. I'm sorry for my cruelness, Terra. You've shown me that kindness, warmth, and trust can exist in my heart again." Raine kisses me dearly, pressing into me slowly.

Raine, Elias, Finn, Arthur. They're already finding their chambers inside my heart, locking themselves in. I'm not sure there's anything I can do to remove them.

Amser and Raine's Shadow merge in our chests and it feels as if his blood has entered my veins. We're never to be separated again.

Our kisses are silent. An amber flicker of light catches my eye. I glance to the side of the homeroom and notice a figure on the couch across from us. It's hard to make out who it is in the dim light and the ecstasy of Raine inside me; the Shadows mingling so fervently makes my vision blurry.

Raine's thrusts are long and deep, pumping into me and drawing short breaths from my lungs. His hands smooth over my body and wrap around my lower back as he ruts into me harder and faster.

"Oh fuck, Raine," I whisper, wrapping my hand around my mouth to keep in the moans. His brows pull together and the veins in his neck protrude as he grinds into my pussy a few more times before spilling inside me and groaning. His teeth clench and his hips softly pump into me.

I ride out the end of the orgasm with him, completely taken with how different sex is with two Shadows. It adds an entirely new sense to the experience.

Raine pulls out of me and helps me slide my pants back up before he fixes his own. Then he looks over to the couch across from us and levels a calm look at the person sitting there. I'd almost forgotten. Passion like ours makes everything around us insignificant.

I blink a few times to clear my vision and am mildly surprised to find that it's Elias. Of course it's Elias. I'm astounded he didn't intervene; he's not even chained up this time. I think Raine really is growing on him.

His cold gray eyes don't let any emotion slide past them.

Raine and I watch silently as Elias slowly stands up, walks to his stairway, and ascends without a word.

I look at Raine and he shrugs. A slight grin pulls at his lips. "Let's get to bed. I don't think we'll get another weird pass like that again." He laughs as he helps me up. We sneak back into my room and crawl close to each other in bed. Raine finds rest quickly, but I stare at the lit-up novas and stars on my ceiling as I think about Elias.

Since when does he pass up a chance to say something snarky? I wonder what's distracting him.

28

Terra

Elias's class is my least favorite. Not only because I have to watch him kick everyone's ass in an effort to teach combat, but also because his movements and attacks are documented so carefully beneath his tight black shirt.

I'm not used to seeing him without his vest and cloak. He's been so busy these last few weeks that I've hardly seen him, spare the night he watched Raine fuck me.

I watch intently as my assassin easily throws another male student over his shoulder, his stomach muscles flexing and recoiling as he straightens. Elias hasn't even broken a sweat yet. It's a fearsome thing to think about; even the second-year students can't land a hit on him.

My eyes linger over the senior class as I think about

their time here. There's only a handful of them left, all ranked Polaris, Ekko, and Cosmos; the lower ones must've been all wiped out. All their eyes are gray.

That thought unsettles me and I think of the Blood Crowns exam swiftly approaching.

"*Terra.*"

My name leaving Elias's lips startles me and I straighten my back as I meet his gaze.

"It's your turn," he says as indifferently as he does with the other students. I hesitantly make my way up to the front of the group. My breaths thicken the air with white plumes. He kicks my ass every single time.

A fresh blanket of snow arrived last night and training in the courtyard has been wearing us all down. It's freezing out here; Elias's three-hour class is hell.

I stand awkwardly, trying my hardest not to look at Elias with the longing I feel deep in my core. He raises his hands into the familiar fighting stance and lunges at me with frightening speed.

I fall back on my ass to duck from his assault. He lands on the ground behind me and snaps at me, "Again. Don't avoid the attack, *block it*."

Standing and wiping my pants, I let out a sharp breath. "I can't. I've tried to block you, but you're too brutish."

He leans in close and pulls me in by the collar of my cloak until our noses are a breath apart. For gods' sakes, why is he so provocative when he's being mean? "You *will*. Or you'll die in the second exam. You'll *all* fucking die if I don't start seeing some improvement." His voice is raspy and cruel as he says the latter, looking at all the students behind me, specifically the Dvars and the Tauri. "You think this is a game or just some silly training, but your survival depends on this. Every decision you make is life or death."

Elias stalks over and grabs one of the smaller Dvars students, a boy from Lamnah with dark hair and very frightened eyes. My stomach curls as Elias places the student before me.

"I'm going to attack with the intent to kill this boy, and unless you can stop me, he will die." Elias turns callously and walks twenty feet away to resume his attack stance.

My heart drops. "Wait. No, Elias, stop!" I scream but it falls on deaf ears. His face is stone; it's obvious he's made up his mind.

The sound of my teeth gnashing together makes my throat constrict. I fist the boy's tan cloak and throw him down to the ground behind me as I step over him. My arms lift instinctively and a veil of darkness clouds over him as Elias crashes into me with a frontal attack. Dark strands of my hair whip furiously into the air with the force of his strike.

A sharp grin lights Elias's face and he lifts his hand to attack with his Shadow this time. My eyes flick down to the boy with horror; I know what happens when Elias uses Velis.

Hot, sticky liquid spatters across my back and soaks my hair. My legs tremble and I turn in time to see the skeleton of the boy still sitting, flesh and skin ripped away from the white bones as if stripped by acid. All the organs and vital components still lie beneath unharmed.

Before his blood can trickle like rain around us, something cracks inside me, desperation or fury, I'm unsure.

Seeing the heart inside the boy's skeleton is still intact, I press my hand to the skull within a fraction of a second.

I'll need to go deeper in your soul to reverse time on this one, Amser mutters indifferently as if it sits upon a throne inside my spirit and dully watches my life like it's some disturbing opera.

I close my eyes and open the doors inside myself, feeling as Amser sinks further inside and an enormous surge of power befalls my heart.

Time is my power and I'll use each second as carefully as I can.

The crimson snow around Elias and me pulses like a living beast and then reanimates into threads of veins and flesh, muscles weaving back into themselves and connecting back onto the bones. The boy's skin returns like an unwrapped present being glued back together in perfect pieces within the blink of an eye.

Just as swiftly as Elias dismantled him, he's whole again.

The Dvars boy blinks and falls to his knees, piss yellowing the snow at his pant legs. The class is silent. I'm not sure there are words to say after such terrible atrocities.

Elias tilts his head back and laughs. "Good, not exactly what I was trying to teach you, but I suppose in a way you succeeded at the task," Elias mutters, tilting his head to the side and giving me a damning grin. He smacks the Dvars student on the back of the head and the man lets out a small gasp before looking at me with wide, brown eyes and dipping his chin.

"Thank you for saving me," he says through trembling teeth before he gets up and staggers back to his group.

Elias ends the class after a few more rounds with other students, but wraps his arm around my shoulder so I don't leave. I try not to think about what Edgar is doing while he's skipping classes. He hasn't shown up since the night on the bridge.

"I want to show you something today," Elias says quietly, keeping his eyes on Alkrose. I look to the third floor where he's staring and find Emerai watching us like a statue. His face is impassive, calculating.

Somehow, I manage to break the headmaster's dreadful gaze and glance back toward the lake. "Show me what?"

Elias throws his white hood on and starts walking back to the castle. He extends his hand to his side for me without looking back and I can't help but smile as I trot to catch up to him. I weave my fingers through his and look up at his sculpted jawline. His gray eyes flick down to me.

"I really shouldn't be showing you this, but consider me a fool."

A fool he is.

"Elias—"

"Shh," he silences me as we come out the end of a portal. It's dark and the air stings my nose with sulfur and ash. My eyes burn and my throat itches.

Where the hell did he bring us?

Amser is on high alert inside my veins, making the

hairs on the back of my neck rise. Elias remains tense and quiet for a few minutes as he scans the area before he visibly relaxes and kneels beside me.

"This is the battlefront in our pursuit to win Whales of Tauh," he says coldly. His eyes are red from the sting the air brings but it doesn't seem to bother him. White strands of his hair get swept up in a gust of wind and his hood flies back.

"*What*? Why would you bring me here?" I ask, fear trickling through me like poison. Explosions rumble in the distance but the dust and dark keep visibility low.

Elias looks at me with dread. "I want to show you first-hand what is happening while we are at Alkrose. You see that wall?" He points south and I follow with my gaze.

Above the dark, cloudy dust is a wall ten times the size of Barkovah's. The sky is auburn, muddied and dim with smoke and death. People are standing on the top of the wall, so far up they're nothing more than specks moving about.

Elias grips my jaw and guides my attention back to him as I swallow thickly. "I'm sent here every day after class to try and get inside that godsforsaken city. Do you know what happens when I get inside?"

I nod grimly. *So this is where he's been...*

He keeps his expressionless face smooth and says, "Exactly. Skyfell, Void, whatever Heirahians are calling it. The fucking last city of Heirah will fall."

"I don't understand, Elias. Why did you bring *me* here?" I whisper as a handful of footsteps run by us, ignorant of our presence.

His eyes soften on me and he lets his shoulders fall.

Despair and regret mingle across his flexed jaw. "Because I think they're going to send you here with me after the exam. The Blood Crowns is an extermination, and they want the Novas to be broken and whole, ready to deploy. With the two of us here, I won't need to be in the city for the Void to reach the inhabitants inside. Our Shadows together will be enough to clear the entire city from this side of the wall."

The sounds of fighting and shooting fade away as I stare into Elias's gray eyes. "I don't understand, Elias." I shift to put distance between us, but he grabs my arm and stops me.

"I want you to be strong enough to stop me before they send us here."

My eyes widen. Another gust of wind berates us, and I can hardly keep my eyes open. "How would I be able to do that?" I bite the inside of my cheek to quell the trembling.

"How else? If it comes to that, I want you to kill me." The corner of his lip kicks up in a tired grin.

Bile crawls up the back of my throat and I shake my head. "I won't—"

"You'll have to or the world will perish. This is the last stand for humanity, Terra." Elias doesn't look the least bit scared for his life to end. In fact, he looks pretty at peace with it.

"What are the other options? What if I can't?" I grit my teeth and look away so he won't see my tears building.

He laughs sarcastically and says, "If you can overthrow the headmaster and empress of Fernestia, then that's a great start. Oh, and Dr. Cein, the master of the Shadows. Him too."

It all sounds so impossible when looking at the big picture, but what if we took a few steps back? An idea sparks to life in my head and I look up at Elias so quickly he flinches.

"What if I can get your heart back? You wouldn't have to obey them anymore." I hate how despairing and in denial I sound, but if there is hope for Raine, why can't there be a small flame for Elias too?

Elias scoffs, "It's not possible."

I shake my head. "Do you know that for certain?"

He stares into my eyes briefly and then firms his lips. "No—but Terra, the headmaster consumes our hearts. That's how he—"

"I don't think he does. Unless you've actually watched him devour your heart firsthand. His Shadow most likely has it hidden somewhere. We just need to find it," I say with more hope than I have.

Elias looks back toward the daunting wall of the city and grits his teeth. "Any idea where to start looking?"

29

Terra

Raine nudges me playfully as we head into our sex ed class.

At least since the first one we've focused on the very raw and eyebrow-raising things that can happen when two people with Shadows fuck. It's horrible all the same, but at least it doesn't involve Kallos bending me backward over a desk and Kai laughing his ass off about it.

The rumors spread like wildfire, but to my surprise, after I saved that Dvars student in Elias's class last week, those rumors ceased. It's nice to feel that most respect me because of a good deed, but others see it as a weakness of mine: the reluctance to let things be.

How can I go against everything that I care about

though? I still have my heart. I don't want to kill or let anyone die around me.

Finn grins at me as we take our seats and I shoot him a soft smile back. We both fucking hate this class. He leans over and whispers, "Have you heard more on the Blood Crowns exam?" I frown and shake my head.

I told him, Raine, Aervin, and Kai in secret. There are very few I can trust not to rat me out. We've been trying to figure out more about it, but late nights staked out in the library haven't proved fruitful. I think Arthur and Elias suspected I was listening in so they haven't returned.

Raine stretches out in his seat and yawns. His health has been relatively stable, which gives me a small reprieve from my impending doom. All we have left to search is Arthur's other study, the one he actually uses.

Kallos starts the class by discussing the last lecture's key takeaways.

I look out the windows and think about how we're going to get to Arthur's study at Za'Afiel. There has to be a portal that leads there, but Ash is the most guarded student here. When I asked him which nation he was from last week, he acted as if I were trying to use the bit of information against him in a trial.

The portal won't be too hard to find. It's more a matter of guessing which one will take us where we want to go, and so far, we haven't had any luck.

"Today we're going to pair up and practice restraining our Shadows," Kallos says as he flicks his hand and his Shadow wisps in the air, writing out today's lesson.

Restraint is sexy.

We all groan in unison and Kallos cracks a grin. "No complaining, get to it. Terra, unfortunately, your Shadow far outranks the others, so you're with me."

This is the only class I've been thankful for Edgar's absence. Though it makes me curious about how he's faring.

Kai swings his head to look straight at me and the way his mouth pinches into an evil grin almost gets me laughing. Finn elbows his friend as he gets up to find a partner.

The look Raine gives me makes me feel sorry for him, but I'm already irritated with the five girls who are fighting to be his partner. He just shrugs at me. "You can't be mad at me about it."

I roll my eyes as I walk to the front of the class, trying as hard as I can not to look at Kallos. But how can I not when his voice is low and crisp, his hair like gilded thread, and his eyes as bright as they come?

The three power brackets on each side of his mouth still look like stitches to me, but I've seen him so often now that's normal. Just like the six small earring bars through Finn's ears, they were hard to get used to at first but I hardly notice them anymore.

It's odd how quickly we adapt to change.

"Let's hope we don't have another mishap," Kallos says casually but I can hear the uncertainty in his voice. It seems like he might dislike this process as much as I do.

It's not that I hate being close to him or feeling the intensity between us. It's that we're in public and I have so many other men in my life at the moment. But what's one more? My Shadow doesn't seem to care.

I can't keep my eyes off Finn and Raine as they pair up.

Kai and Finn end up being partners because there are more men than women in the class, and their cheeks couldn't be brighter. Raine sits across from a gorgeous young woman. I've seen her in passing but have no clue what her name is. The different Shadow Houses don't interconnect much.

"All right, everyone has their partners. I want you to try your best to restrain your Shadows while being in close range to one another, like so." Kallos steps up to my chest, keeping less than an inch of space between us.

The pull in my veins is already reaching toward him; Amser's eager to get a touch of his Shadow once again.

"Now, some of your Shadows might resent others, pushing them away rather than drawing them in," Kallos says as a few student couplings step apart like repelling magnets. "Every Shadow has their counterpart, ones that they ward off cautiously. But most of you should be feeling that curious pull."

My body trembles with the effort to stay in place. Kallos looks just as strained, flexing his jaw before he continues with the lesson.

"Don't let them give in. Practice equal restraint together."

I glance over to Raine and his partner, but they are standing so far apart already, I can't help the relief that sinks into my chest. Finn and Kai, on the other hand, aren't so lucky. Their faces are pulled into tight frowns and Finn looks like he's about to have an aneurysm. His jaw is set and veins in his hands protrude as he fists them at his sides.

Kai's eyes flick to me and I burst into laughter with the

complete horror that falls over his features. His attention snaps and he and Finn collapse into one another. Their pull toward each other isn't surprising, they're practically inseparable.

As if in sync, more and more partners crash into each other, unable to resist the pull of the Shadows. It continues until Kallos and I are the only ones left standing.

A bead of sweat rolls down the professor's temple and he swallows hard, sucking in his bottom lip a bit before exhaling and turning toward the class, stepping away from me to lessen the draw.

"Good practice today, everyone. We will keep up this exercise in class until you can fully resist the urge and keep yourself in control. That's it for today," Kallos dismisses the class. "Hang back for a second, Terra," he whispers to me with a heated glance. Warmth spreads up my chest at the way his eyes trail down my throat.

I tell Finn and Raine not to wait up for me. Raine gives me a suspecting look but only smirks deviously before following the others out. Gods, I don't even want to know what he has in mind.

Once the room is empty, the air feels warmer across my cheeks. Kallos smiles at me and I awkwardly make my way to his desk. He sits with his legs spread wide, leaning back in relaxation while resting his jaw on his hand. He's like a fallen god, holy, unlike Elias.

Those golden eyes burn into my skin as I part my lips to mutter, "What did you want to discuss, professor?" I hate the rasp in my voice that exposes my nerves. I hope he wants to figure out this weird yearning between us.

His lips kick into a smile and those stitches on each side of his mouth elongate it. It's really fucking sexy—I shouldn't be as drawn to it as I am. My teeth sink into my lower lip as I try to quell the unwarranted lewd thoughts that dare breach my mind.

"Not so much discuss as just to let our Shadows figure out what they need to between each other. I'd rather have classes run smoother, so letting them get their aggression out is good. Or perhaps it's us egging them on? As long as you're open to it, of course." His voice is slick and calm, heavy with controlled desire.

Is he saying what I think he's saying? "How do you intend on finding out?" I ask as a shudder rolls languidly down my spine.

Kallos offers me his hand. I look from his palm to his eyes as he mutters, "By letting them mingle, how else?"

I hesitate before letting my hand slide into his. He wraps his fingers around my wrist and pulls me into his lap, turning me so my back is against his taut chest. A cold wave of lust spreads throughout my body as our Shadows tangle through every fiber of my being.

Kallos groans and wraps his hand around my waist as he arches his back, pushing the hard length beneath his pants into my ass. His fingers dig into my stomach enough that I exhale and sip in a quick breath before his lips are on my neck.

"Oh, little Nova, this was a bad idea," Kallos says in a dark, voluptuous voice. His other hand reaches forward and trails his index finger down my throat.

Chills spread over my skin and I can't think of

anything but how fucking wrong this is. And perhaps that's why I enjoy it so much. I desperately try not to think about the heat that's collecting between my thighs and Kallos's hot breath across my skin.

"Why?" I ask on an exhale, letting my head drop down to his shoulder.

"Because all I've ever known is control with my Shadow, and yours crumbles all that work in mere seconds. I cannot speak of the things I want to do to you." He slides his hand beneath my shirt. His restraint is evident in the way his veins push against his skin, trying to stop himself from letting this happen. His jaw tightens against my shoulder.

He bucks his hips lightly against me before cursing under his breath and pulling his hands back. I'm cold in all the spaces he was a moment ago. He stands, pushing the center of my back gently so I step away from him.

I turn to look at him and catch a feral darkness in his gaze. The parts of his eyes that are normally white have turned maroon.

"What's wrong?" I ask as I take a few steps back, not sure if I should turn and run or help him in some way.

He shakes his head and nods to the door. "Leave," he rasps painfully. It's so weak that I feel like I need to do something.

I step closer to him and reach my hand out to his shoulder for comfort, but he snaps his head up and snarls at me, his teeth sharp, those brackets that look like stitches stretching.

"I said leave," he grits out callously and I don't waste

another second. I grab my books from my desk and leave without looking back.

What the fuck was that? Is Professor Kallos a shifter like Frederick? He had that same splitting mouth. The thought of it curls my stomach. Was it my Shadow that made him change like that?

Amser answers, startling me because it has been quiet for days. *I wanted to play with his dark side. Why did you run away?*

I shake my head and try not to think about it anymore since Amser will just read my thoughts anyway. I'm in my mind prison still when I turn the corner and walk straight into a man's chest. The books in my arms nearly tumble from my grasp.

My eyes flick up and meet Elias's daunting stare.

He catches my books before they fall without even breaking our eye contact and the corner of his lip tilts up. "Hello, sweetheart. What are you doing up here past class hours?" His eyes drift behind me and land on something that makes darkness settle in his features. "Playing with Kallos, are we?"

My knees feel weak. But I don't find anger or jealousy in his eyes—only a morbid curiosity.

"Now *he* is someone I want to watch ruin you. Raine can join too and get some pointers from him," Elias says tightly. Desire lingers on his words and I have to swallow hard to move past the image he just painted in my head.

"Stop that!" I say sharply and he lifts one shoulder.

"I came to look for you when you weren't at the Nova House with Raine." He clutches my books in one arm and lets the other swing over my shoulders as he guides us down the corridor toward the south end of the castle.

My brow raises. "Where are we going exactly?"

He chuckles and lets his arm slacken around my neck. "Remember our talk of finding my heart? You were right. And I think I may have figured out where he keeps them."

30

Elias

Terra stills at the sight of the black gates.

"Where does this go?" she asks in a dreadful tone, sounding anything but excited to go on another outing with me. I guess taking her to the front lines of Whales of Tauh was probably a little too extreme, but I needed to get my point across.

"To Za'Afiel," I say as I stare at the familiar stone-framed doors. The last time I passed through the black gates was with my comrades.

She perks up at that and I level her a curious look. "Eager to go there for something?" I ask, not surprised when she lies and shakes her head. She and Raine are still looking for something to stop the blight. I hope they find it. The thought of not having someone to train with in the mornings and bullshit with casts a dark stone in my heart.

"You really think he hid them there?" she says incredulously, looking at the stonework like she doesn't entirely trust the craftsmanship.

I nod. "Velis did some snooping while Emerai visited the front lines. It's taken some time, but I think we may have found them all." Her eyes soften and a hopeful grin spreads across her face.

She's the only person I trust with this besides Arthur. He's been so distant as of late due to his lectures with Edgar. I don't know how he's found the time to oversee all his academics, but he's managed.

My expression grows grim. Since Kallos placed that cast on his Shadow, Edgar has fallen into a deep depression. Doom most certainly clouds his mind now. He's incapable of escaping his fate. Raine has avoided him at all costs—Edgar must have a twisted and cruel fate because Raine can't even look at him without turning pale.

Sometimes, I wish Raine could speak about his visions. I know his Shadow doesn't allow it, but I cannot fathom what wealth his dying mind holds.

"Shall we?" I motion for Terra to step through the black gates first and she glowers at me before stepping through. I wait another moment, staring at the black stones reminiscently before following.

Dark smoke pools around us like we've walked into a house fire. It's scentless and leaves cold tendrils of despair along my skin. I step out into the silent halls of Za'Afiel. The air is older here, the stones damp from the breeze off the ocean.

Terra leans over and peers out one of the windows overlooking the stone garden; from the third floor, you can even see the ocean. Moonlight drapes the snow-covered scenery with somber silence.

Many little mounds raise portions of the snow, reddened by what lies beneath. Terra notices and looks back at me with confusion and denial. Her brown hair has a light blue hue to it, the moon framing her in luminance.

"It's exactly what you think it is," I say in a monotone voice. There's a reason why the halls are so quiet.

"But Edgar described this place as peaceful... What happened?" she says sadly, as if she can imagine what this mansion was like filled with the laughter of many ignorant souls. Oblivious to the world filled with hatred beyond the island, thanks to Arthur's gift.

"The Empress of Fernestia wanted this faction shut down. They have all the Novas they've been searching for. Cein ordered the culling yesterday. I found out this afternoon when Arthur was sitting in his empty office in the Nova House for once instead of his study here."

Terra covers her mouth and leans over like she's going to vomit.

I shut my eyes as I think of the pain I saw in his. He didn't seem surprised about it; it was more like an old, dreadful wound, one he knew would eventually open. The circles beneath his eyes were dark. There were no traces of light in his eyes.

"They're ready to take Whales of Tauh by the end of next month. We have seven weeks... If we can find my heart and I can break free of Emerai's hold, humanity might still have a chance." I say it as if I'm giving a soldier orders. Emotionlessly.

"You keep saying that." Terra lowers her hand from her mouth and looks up at me. I raise a brow. "You keep saying *humanity* as if we aren't human anymore."

We aren't though, not really.

I ignore her comment. "Let's get to the cellar. I think that's where Emerai keeps them."

The halls are cold and the lack of life spills from every crevice of the stones. The silence is eerie. I wonder if there's a single soul left here. Perhaps the Darkflies have already left this place too.

"We're not going to run into Dr. Cein here, are we?" she asks barely above a whisper, like someone might hear.

I shake my head and hold the door for her as she steps through into the stairwell. "I'm trying to keep him away from you for as long as I can," I admit.

She looks up at me, flashing those emerald eyes. Oh, how I envy her light. "Why's that?"

"Because he's an evil man, Terra." She levels me a look that says, *But so are you,* and I chuckle. "Way more than me, sweetheart. Who do you think raised me?" I shove my hands into the pockets of my tactical vest and keep my gaze on the steps as we descend.

"That must have been terrible to go through," she says in a quiet voice after a few moments. There's sympathy in her tone. I'm not sure there's much more I hate in this world than pity, but oddly, when it's from her, I find that it's easier to accept.

I sigh. "Yes. It... was."

Stolen at a young age and being raised by a monster—it

makes you one in kind. I don't remember my real parents or the village I was born in. All I have are memories of torture and intense training.

The first Shadow. The start of all of this. Maybe that's why Cein keeps me so close. I'm his son in some ways.

My head hangs heavily upon my shoulders as I think of Cein. I've come to think of him as my father. How many times have I relished in the desire to rip that man's heart out? To watch him die slowly and let all his work come to an end?

But when all's said and done, I'm not sure I'll be able to kill him.

Terra pushes her hand into my vest pocket and wraps her warm hand around mine. A soft smile spreads over my lips.

She's still so human.

"I am in no need of comfort. The darkness holds me."

She doesn't retreat and only walks closer to my side. "Shut up. If I'm offering comfort, just accept it," she says with that cute attitude of hers. I want to shut my eyes and be in her presence for a while. Perhaps once the war has ended I'll have that little amount of peace. Should we be so lucky.

We reach the main floor and have to walk through the foyer and extravagant halls to get to the cellar stairs. Terra looks around in awe of Za'Afiel, her eyes shimmering with sadness. A place such as this should be filled with laughter and life, not the dark wail of a cold winter breeze.

She stops at the mess hall and releases my hand to explore. I guess we aren't pressed for time, so I follow her and watch her bright green eyes take in this haunted manor.

"Is this really where Arthur spends most of his time?" she asks sadly. There's so much longing in her voice for him—I envy that about the man. He pulls her heart in entirely.

"It is. Though he rarely walks through the manor. His study is on the third floor and that's where he stays most days," I say drily. She takes one last look at the massive windows that pillar the far wall of the mess hall. The view opens to the forest and the sea beyond, a cold and frozen world.

The cellar stairs are drab and covered with a fine layer of moss and dirt. A mildewy scent hangs in the air; Terra's nose crinkles at the smell of it.

"Why would Emerai hide the hearts down here?" She looks up at me with those green eyes and I stare for a second longer than I should.

"I thought the same thing at first. Velis led me down here and I was certain it was mistaken, but then I felt something strange in the room. I couldn't see anything, but I could feel it."

She raises a brow. "Is that why you brought me here? You think I'll be able to see them?" I nod and open the cellar door, the wood creaking on its hinges.

The cellar is a simple room built with discolored stones. Moisture hangs in the frigid air. A large furnace sits at the end of the room. It's the first time I've seen it unlit. Wooden crates line the walls, filled with palm-sized rocks.

I can't see anything that would suggest the hearts are here, but every nerve in my body is burning and screaming.

"They are here, I'm certain of it," I say as I let the shudder of the heavy air run down my spine.

Terra visibly shivers and wraps her arms around herself as she looks around carefully. Her eyes widen as she stares at the stack of rocks. She whirls to face me, eyes wide and filled with horror.

"You don't see all of the blood?"

31

Terra

Elias stares at me like I'm utterly insane. He looks at the crates filled with pulsing hearts, dripping blood and quivering, then shakes his head cluelessly.

"Are you talking about the rocks?"

My jaw drops and before I can reply Amser hums inside my head. *Only we can see the hearts. Emerai cannot hide anything from time. We see all the moments of a Shadow's past, what they've taken and tried to discard.*

I swallow thickly. How is this even possible? Then again, how is anything that's happened thus far possible?

"They may look like rocks to you... but they are hearts," I say with a knot curling in my stomach. They thump an off-beat tune, and as I watch them, a few stop moving, turning gray and cold before dulling into what truly resembles a stone.

My heart sinks. Those must be the people dying on the front lines... or at Alkrose. I wonder how many will be left by the end of all of this and how many have already been thrown away.

Elias's brows pull in. "Well fuck, how are we going to find mine then? They all look like fucking stones to me."

Amser whispers, *His heart is older, among the first to be stolen. It's tucked away with the others behind that wall.* I frown, not sure how my Shadow can sense all of this, but who am I to disagree with it?

"Amser says to look behind this wall." I press my hand against the cold stones and worry the entire room will cave in if we mess with it.

Elias's face is skeptical as black smoke pools at his feet and Velis emerges in its small feline form. Amser wisps from my veins and joins its mate. They stand side by side and let their tails tangle. My cheeks warm at the affection they so easily show for one another.

Elias's cold, gray eyes are staring at me.

"Will your eyes regain their color when you get your heart back?" I ask. I'm not sure I want them to change. The gray has grown on me—it's hard to picture his eyes any other way.

"I don't know," he says as he steps closer, pulling me into his arms as we stand to the side so the Shadows can dismantle the wall.

"Do you remember their color?"

"Nope."

The Shadows both place their paws on the stones.

Dark vines start to crawl up the wall and form into an arched door. The black veins look like spindles of poison, the definition of evil and rot. Velis sits on one end while Amser takes the other and they both look up at us expectantly.

"Has Velis ever done that before?"

Elias approaches the makeshift door and pushes the stone. It opens eerily. Dust and mold sting my nose. "Negative," he says curtly as he disappears into the shadows of the secret room.

I reluctantly trail behind him and wince at the dried blood that coats the stone floor. Enough light trickles in from the cellar to see shelves lined with stones and hearts. These ones are lined up like they're special, nothing like the piles in the crates.

Velis and Amser weave through my ankles and sit in the center of the room. Elias looks at my Shadow and asks kindly, "Which one is mine?"

Amser stretches like a cat that's just woken up from its nap and jumps to the middle shelf. It walks past a few stones and stops at a black heart. It looks straight at me and whispers in my mind, *Arthur*.

A breath escapes me and I rush to it, gently scooping the heart into my hands. It flutters, so much lighter than I could've ever imagined. So unlike a real heart. These, as I thought, are figurative ones. Phantoms of the real thing. But they hold the world inside them.

"This one is Arthur's," I say when Elias moves closer, his chest pressed along my back. He looks down at it and frowns.

"I wish I could see what you do." His voice is somber. I

wonder how many of the stones in here used to be the beating hearts of his comrades.

Amser jumps to the top shelf and walks along the edge diligently until it reaches the end and sits next to a white heart. It beats in slow, languid thumps. It's lost all color—each artery and vein that line the cardiac muscles are like ashen roots.

I move to stand beneath Amser and it nudges the heart off the shelf. I catch it with care and stare in awe at the two precious things in the palms of my hands.

"This one is yours," I whisper. I'm not sure why. It feels sacred to hold them and I don't want anyone else in the world to know that I have them.

Elias's eyes fill with what looks like fear but he swiftly blinks it away. I raise a brow when he doesn't take his heart from my hands.

"Now what?" I ask.

He shakes his head and gives me an uncertain, beautiful smile filled with hope. "I have no fucking idea. I didn't think we'd get this far."

I look back down at the hearts and smile. "We found them. We *really* found them."

Elias brushes my cheek with his hand as he mutters, "*You* found them. Now let's get out of here before anyone realizes we're gone." Velis vanishes back into him and Amser does the same with me. I shudder at the cold sensation that encases my bones as it settles back inside me.

"What are we going to do with them? Should we give Arthur his tonight?" I wrap my cloak around my front so no one can see the hearts when we get back to Alkrose.

Elias tilts his head in thought before muttering, "Let

me talk to him later about it. I'm not sure how he'll react to this. We're not supposed to be here, obviously. But of my comrades, Arthur is the most sensible."

I nod and follow Elias back through the manor and portal. He escorts me to my room, where I hide the hearts in the bottom drawer of my wardrobe.

"I have to leave for a few days, so don't do anything until I get back. Promise me you won't." Elias wraps a strand of my brown hair around his finger and holds my gaze until I close my eyes.

"I won't do anything... Are you going back to the front lines?"

He nods.

I wouldn't care what happened to him if he were the same hollow assassin I met in Navasik. But he's shown me that he's so much more than a shell of a man. He's still in there. He's still human, and I have his heart now.

I can fix him.

Arthur levels me a tired, unenthusiastic grin as I fail horribly again at the Shadow leeching technique. I can grapple his Shadow when he allows it, but when I'm attempting to take it from someone forcefully, that's where I'm running into problems.

"If you're going to use this in battle, it needs to be nimble and fast. Otherwise, your opponent will have no trouble killing you at point-blank range." Arthur steps across the lake's solid surface and resumes his stance.

Raine watches us as he and Finn chat idly. They throw spits of flame and ice long distances, trying to reach the shore on the other end. Raine's private lessons with Elias have been put on hold until he returns from the front lines in Whales of Tauh. It's easy to see that the training has been helping him immensely. His eyes, however, expose the pain of the blight wearing on him.

Raine winces with every wisp of power he sends out, molding his face into a firm, angry expression before anyone else can catch it.

"Focus, Terra." Arthur lunges at me and sweeps my legs out from beneath me.

I land on my ass and let out a low groan. "Really?" I glare at him and he raises a shoulder.

"We don't have time for games," he says with all seriousness and I try to match his mood, standing and refocusing. I stare into his gray eyes and swallow the dire need to tell him I found his heart. I promised Elias I wouldn't, but holding onto a secret this important feels like betrayal.

We practice until the sun dips below the mountains and the air stings our noses. I study with Finn, Kai, and Raine in the library until the sun sets, and by the time I'm back in my room, I collapse onto my bed. Raine will be here in an hour or two. Sometimes he makes it in here before I fall asleep and other times he just crawls into my bed long after I've dozed off. Either way, I enjoy his company.

I'm midway through the anatomy book when chatter arises in the hallway. My head perks up and I listen to the muffled voices. It sounds like Arthur and another male, but I'm not sure who.

The door is cold against my ear as I press close to listen. But the voices have stopped and the footsteps are leading away. I crack my door open and peek, seeing the top of Arthur's head as he descends the stairs.

Carefully, so as not to make a sound, I tiptoe to his door, trying the handle like I've been doing for weeks now with no luck, but to my surprise, it clicks open.

He forgot to lock it. Gods, this is stupid.

I quickly close my door across the hall before slipping into his room. My eyes widen as I take in his mystical room. It's unlike the others I've been in at Alkrose. His room is two stories tall, a full library against the walls above with wooden catwalks, rickety railing lining the edges.

No wonder he always smells like pages of old tomes. He's really made this place his own. I walk slowly through his impeccably clean room. Whereas Elias's room is black and filled with papers and books, Arthur's is a dusty shade of brown, scholarly and woodsy like a cozy cabin.

My fingers brush against the cream-colored sheets on his bed and I sit, looking around, but finding no notes or papers to compare to the one Raine and I found in the library.

I exhale and lie back on his bed for a moment. He's so meticulous and careful; maybe he really is hiding something. It seems like everyone here is in some way or another.

I must doze off at some point because when I wake, I'm staring into Arthur's gray eyes, the faded smears of green barely visible. My body seizes and I sip in a small breath as

I stare up at his face. His black hair tickles my forehead and cheek.

His lips are so close to mine, the warmth of them just out of reach. His arms are a solid force of muscle around my head, the weight of his body begging to fall upon me.

"I'm only a man, little shadow. What are you doing to me?" he whispers and his sullen gaze consumes my soul with thousands of emotions I could never articulate.

I want him to hold me—to touch me and ravish me.

He brings up his hand and lets his thumb gently coast over my bottom lip, drawing it open. His eyes flick down to my mouth, yearning and lust burning between us.

"Why are you here?" he asks, a hint of distrust and curiosity in his voice. It's unusual to catch Arthur off guard, so I relish in the sight of his bemused, handsome features.

Of its own volition, my hand reaches up and touches the smooth hollow of his cheek. His eyes are rimmed with red. He's so weary. I wish I could give him some relief. A person as kind as him deserves it.

"Another lesson?" I say softly, watching him as his eyes dip to my throat. He glides the pad of his finger down the tender skin and grins.

"What knowledge are you seeking?"

I daringly let my hand trail across his flexed neck and down to the opening of his shirt, tugging the fabric open with implication.

He chuckles softly and looks back at me with hooded eyes. "This is a lesson you'll have to see to the end. Are you sure you want to begin?" His eyes are feverish and dark. I want him to show me what he's hiding inside. I want to see all the darkest thoughts in this man's head.

I wrap my hand around the back of his neck and pull him down, his lips softly pressing down on mine. The groan that rolls out of his throat is filled with turmoil.

We're two Shadows burning out in a world filled with so much suffering. Arthur feels all of it, carries the weight for most of us who've already let go. I want to carry some of his burden.

He scoops me up and sets me in the center of his bed, keeping one hand at the back of my neck in a tight vice grip. My chin falls limply as he lets his teeth skate across my throat, sucking in my flesh and releasing it over and over again as he kneads my breast greedily.

He looks up at me and slowly draws my lower lip into his mouth, biting down on the plump part of it before sucking hard. I moan at the slight pain and he responds by shoving his hand beneath my pants, swirling my clit a few times before pushing two fingers inside of me.

My back arches at how much he fills me. Arthur devours the moans as he elicits them. He kisses me hard, our tongues hungrily sweeping and exploring one another. He pumps his fingers into me and angles them up, rubbing me relentlessly until my eyes are rolling to the back of my head and I'm on the verge of losing control.

Arthur breaks our kiss and leans back, pulling his black shirt off and tossing it on the floor. He shrugs his pants off and frees his dick. The length of it makes my throat dry and as he lines up his hips with mine, I'm certain there's no way it will fit.

It's always the quiet ones that are hung.

I fist the sheets as he slides this tip up and down my slit.

"You're soaking wet," Arthur teases and gives me a heated smile.

I look from his enormous dick to him. "I thought you said you were *just a man*?" He lets his head fall forward a bit before chuckling and slowly sliding the tip of his dick inside me.

Pleasure and pain race up through my core at the intrusion and I inhale sharply to keep from screaming. He throws his head back as he slowly thrusts just the tip of his dick inside me, easing his way in so as not to hurt me. My hands find his over my waist and our eyes connect briefly before he grits his teeth and grabs my flesh, pulling me in hard enough to bruise as he penetrates me.

This time there's no holding back the scream.

Arthur's hand flies down and covers my mouth, stilling with his pelvis pressed firmly against mine. We freeze, looking at one another with wide eyes. I've never seen him so flustered and the boyish look of worry that tugs at his eyes makes me laugh. He only looks surprised for another second before he cracks a smirk and chuckles with me.

Our laughter is short-lived as he starts to pump his hips into me again, slowly moving his hand before shoving a finger inside my mouth. I moan as I suck on him, eyes lolling as I try to focus on his lovely face.

His brows are pulled tightly together with pleasure, but he also looks so fucking anguished. I think I'm imagining it until tears start to brim in his eyes. I press my hand to his chest, but he drops himself onto me and hides his face in the sheets.

I tilt my chin up as he pumps into me slowly, letting out a quiet moan.

Why does fucking me make him sad? I thread my fingers through his black hair. It's so soft and smells entirely of him, torn pages and midnight candle wicks.

"What's wrong?" I whisper, pressing my mouth to the side of his head.

He leans up to his forearms and looks down at me. There's a wealth of sorrow in his gaze but the tears have dried. Arthur doesn't try responding, no, he lowers his mouth to mine. His kiss is so placid and soft. Like a lover would kiss another's shoulder, it's tender and light, filled with so much more than just the physical sentiment.

There's no doubt in my mind that he holds affection for me, but is that affection the cause of such anguish? Such torment?

Even our Shadows tenderly brush against one another, old friends, or perhaps lovers. Time and memory. Must we be apart?

I wish I could return his sentiment—how bruising and aching his heart is for me.

I'm pulled from the thoughts as my orgasm reaches the climax. My hands fist his hair and he lets out a low groan, moving his hips faster and harder until I'm unraveling completely beneath him. He sits back swiftly and wraps his hand around his cock, jerking it to finish himself off. I lie on his bed and stare at his ceiling, letting myself get lost in my thoughts again.

He feels so good and right.

So familiar, yet still unknown.

Arthur grunts as his come shoots over my stomach. I

smile as he collapses beside me on the bed, his raven hair falling over his forehead, a strand over his nose, partly hiding one of his eyes as he looks at me. He's not smiling.

We stare into each other's eyes with sullen expressions.

"That was the saddest, best sex I've ever had." I finally break the silence and he cracks a grin. I return it with a soft smile, pulling his face close and pressing a kiss to his swollen lips.

"I'm sorry, little shadow. I think too much," he says on a breathy whisper.

"That's broad—what could you have possibly been thinking about—" I remember Za'Afiel and all the children there who were *dealt with*. That was only a few days ago. Shit. How could I forget?

Arthur quirks a brow at my sudden silence so I shake my head.

"Never mind. We all have our secrets, don't we?" I caress his cheek and he does the same, brushing a strand of hair from my face and letting his hand rest on my jaw and neck.

Arthur's smile fades as he says, "No secrets are as terrible as the ones we cannot speak."

32

Terra

I stare dully out the arched stone windows as snow falls in clumps from the tall pines. The weather has finally been warming. It's beautiful, yet feels out of place in this castle of death—of rot. Birds have begun to chirp again, and the scent of wet moss and pine is heavy in the air.

Classes have slowly become more and more quiet. The students' eyes have mostly grayed. Only a few people, including myself, have held on to our hearts.

Raine slumps over his desk, napping. I watch him take long, slow breaths and pray to all the gods that he is dreaming of better things than Alkrose. He deserves so much more than this world has provided him. I wish I never met him. He'd live a long life if it weren't for me.

Kallos wraps up the afternoon lecture and draws my attention back to the present.

"There will be no class for the remainder of the week in preparation for the exam. The headmaster will address the agenda in the mess hall tonight, so be sure you don't skip dinner." Kallos's eyes linger over me and then flick to Raine.

Kai stands up and stretches as the other students leave. Finn turns in his seat, looking glum.

"I wonder what the Blood Crowns exam will entail," Kai says halfheartedly. His white hair is mussed this morning, evidence of his carelessness.

Though we don't necessarily know the nature of the exam, I know that it will be brutal. The Blood Crowns... I'm certain it will be as sinister as the name suggests.

Finn shrugs. "My guess is something with crowns." He shoots me a sarcastic grin and I shove his shoulder. Finn sobers and says more seriously, "As long as we stick together, though, we'll pull through."

Raine lifts his head and looks at me. I can hardly stand the sight of his diminished appearance. The blight is working its way into his soul. His pale skin and sunken eyes are enough to shatter a heart. He's still as beautiful as the day I met him though.

"I can handle the gory stuff since you guys are pussies. I've got nothing to lose," Raine says with a lift of his lips.

We share a dark silence and try to ignore the truth of his morbid humor.

The hallways are devoid of chatter. There's only the sound of feet shuffling across the tiles, making quick work to get to their next classes.

The four of us share Shadow riding, my favorite class. I'm glad the air is crisp and warm today. We exit the front doors and meet the fresh spring air. Kai nods at the Darkfly soldiers standing on either side of the doors while the rest of us ignore them as usual.

Kai eagerly meets Corvus at the edge of the half-melted lake. The dark waters lap at the ice shore in soft drawls like the sound of the sea in a shell. Finn sticks by my side, Raine on my other.

"He's always so happy," Raine complains and Finn barks out a laugh.

"That's exactly what I think constantly, but you know what I realized?" Finn looks from me to Raine. I raise a brow. "He's not happy at all. He just wants to cheer up everyone else. Does his contagious smile not reach into you and make you less sad?"

I watch Kai as he smiles brightly and hugs his comrade. Corvus's annoyed face softens considerably and the warmth Kai shows him reaches inside me too.

"Yeah, it does," I mumble.

Raine chuckles and adds: "Maybe that's why I can't stand the motherfucker."

Arthur starts the class by informing us that we'll be racing around the mountain range today. The teams that place first will have an advantage in the upcoming second exam.

I listen, but focus more on the bridge leading to the Nova House.

Edgar stands at its center; his lone figure looks bleak. It's much too far to see his facial features, but his white cloak waves in the northern wind. He hasn't come to class since the fight we had weeks ago. Arthur's been privately tutoring him. No amount of requests have brought Edgar from his room.

"Is he going to join us today?" I ask half-mindedly.

Finn follows my gaze and looks away abruptly as if merely looking at my brother makes him sick. "Gods, I fucking hope not."

Raine doesn't bother saying anything but the firm of his lips tells me he hopes not as well.

"Anyone who still can't produce a Shadow, I highly recommend learning to do so. You will die in the second exam without it," Arthur says loudly. The air is thick with fear. So many students have already been pulled from Alkrose, mainly Dvars and Tauri, for not being sufficient. Gods know where they were sent—to the frontlines, Fernestia, or to Dr. Cein.

I shudder at the thought of the unknown leader of the Shadows.

As we listen to Arthur drawl on about Shadows, another group of students come in through the valley, trudging wearily to the front doors. They've been coming in smaller groups each time, a bleak reminder of what the world outside of Alkrose holds for us. The five of us watch in silence, then flinch in unison as the destruction instructor opens the magnificent doors.

Elias stalks out past the tired new recruits. My stomach

instantly flutters at the sight of him. His cold eyes flick to me only for a second before he turns his attention back to Arthur. He takes his position next to him and nods.

Finn glances at me like I have any clue why he's here. I shrug.

"Elias will be observing today. Anyone he deems unfit for the second exam will proceed directly to the battle-front. Anyone who tries to escape will be exterminated." Arthur's brows pull together with disgust. I hate that he has to be a part of all this, that any of them do, but Arthur feels it so much more. It shows in every crevice of his face.

Elias remains emotionless and keeps his gaze on the Dvars students. Only a handful of them have managed to summon their Shadows at all, let alone ride them.

My jaw clenches tightly and I feel sick.

Raine threads his fingers through mine and looks down at me. "Fate has already decided for them. Don't hold onto it."

I bite into my lower lip, hating how everyone accepts this like sheep.

Our Shadows, all out of our bodies, make the front of Alkrose look like a black hole. Mist and threads of ebony smoke twirl around us as we prepare for the race.

Well, besides Finn's phoenix. Its flames are bright and burn red, orange, and magenta through the sky. I look up at him with so much awe, wishing for a moment that I could be as beautiful and different as he is.

Raine rolls his shoulders back and I watch intently. I've yet to see his Shadow's physical form, but from what Elias has been hinting, it's pretty damn impressive. A pool of black smoke sheds from Raine's back and shapes into wings as if they're his own. I let a gasp out and watch as he takes to the sky and ascends higher and higher. His Shadow engulfs him, shifting and solidifying in areas. White bones poke from the smoke mass, and in one hard beat of its wings, his Shadow lifts its head and reveals its huge skull.

"Fucking show-off," Kai complains beside me.

It looks like a dragon. The ribs shape its center and the knobby spine is similar to Amser's. Raine sits at the crook of the Shadow's neck, looking like a mere speck from down here. The Shadow has four long, crooked horns that shine with ivory points. He's a sight to behold.

Amser's form may be small in comparison to Raine's dragon and Finn's phoenix, but it is fast and nimble. I swallow hard as I look into the air. A few others can fly—Corvus with his monstrous raven and other winged beasts beside him.

This isn't a race, not really. It's a screening.

My eyes feel dry as I focus and level my breathing. Edgar steps out from behind us and startles me. Amser growls at him but he hardly pays me or my Shadow any mind. His emerald-green eyes flick up to me and send chills down my spine.

Arthur raises his hand and lowers it in one fell swoop. Everyone takes off with wicked speed, mud flinging into the air behind them and wind puffing from above as the wings of the Shadows beat.

But I remain where I am, staring at Edgar. Kai's ebony Shadow horse stops a few leagues ahead of me and he looks back at me. "Terra, let's go!" he shouts and his stallion resumes running.

Amser takes off, gripping the ground brutally and

thrusting us forward. We easily catch up to Kai, and once we do, I dare glance back at my brother.

He stands alone, the air turning black around him and whipping furiously. A long curl of spinal bones forms above him as the skull of a snake arches back like it's screaming. It pieces together in a matter of seconds.

My eyes burn. I watch unblinking as the monster inside Edgar's veins comes to life.

His Shadow is the image of true evil. Malice radiates from it. Sharp teeth arrow inwards—the sort of teeth made to trap things, never to escape.

Edgar sits atop its head. The coils of the snake's body curl to the left and right. I've never liked snakes. The way they move so fast without legs is disturbing, and Edgar's Shadow is the god of such wicked things.

"Move!" I scream at Kai and his jaw drops at Edgar's Shadow. It's comparable in size to Raine's airborne dragon, toppling trees as it slithers towards us.

"What the fuck!" Kai shouts as our Shadows bank right, throwing us into the thick of the forest. Branches snap and berate us as we keep up our speed.

Through gaps of broken trees, I catch sight of the snake veering just enough to avoid crushing a group of students. I have to stop and take a breath. I really thought he was going to smear them across the ground like insects.

33

Elias

Arthur's eyes follow Terra until she's hidden in the forest. He doesn't seem at all concerned about Edgar's Shadow decimating the trees as it blazes toward the mountains.

"Aren't you going to ensure no one tries to escape?" he says absently as he stares in the direction of the students.

I grin and nod. "Yeah, but I like to let them get a bit of a head start first. You know me. There's no fun in it if I can't hunt them a bit. Velis prefers it that way."

Arthur breaks his stare and gives me a frown. "You know, being barbaric won't hide your pain from me."

My jaw tightens and I fist my hands at my sides. "Shut up. You don't see anything when you look at me. No one sees anything."

His brows arch and a surprised grin pulls at his mouth. "How odd. Since when did you try so hard to mask it?" he murmurs, pulling out his notebook and scrawling something in it lazily. "By the way, we plan on casting Edgar's powers in two weeks. We need a bit of time to collect enough power. You should prepare for it as well." I level him an indifferent look. Since when did I agree to help? "You'd best be off then."

"You sure two weeks isn't too far off? Did you see his Shadow? Kallos's cast broke weeks ago." Arthur just lifts a shoulder and writes more down in his journal.

Whatever, it's not my problem. It's only my problem when it's time to put them down.

Velis pools from my skin and is at my side in a second. I mount it and I'm off hunting the stragglers. There are always a few that try to escape. I get it, this seems like it'd be the best time to try, but that's sort of the point.

Velis picks up on a Polaris student ten meters out of the boundaries like a hunting hound, veering to the left and increasing its speed until a dark green cloak becomes visible. The student turns and catches sight of me, his eyes rounding with fear.

I don't enjoy this.

Not at all. I'd prefer hunting Darkflies.

I raise my hand over the figure and close my fist over him. His head flies off cleanly, blood spiraling in the chilly spring air. A soft toppling sound thuds in the distance. I don't look as Velis redirects its attention to the next rule-breaking student, leagues away in a different direction.

All I can think about are Arthur's words. *Since when did you try so hard to mask it?* Haven't I always? Does it show more now? I shut my eyes and let the lull of Velis's steps take my mind elsewhere.

The second exam is near and I'd rather be anywhere else.

34

Terra

"I hate this fucking place," Kai says on a low breath. He shudders and shakes his head to try and stop his bodily reaction to the snake.

"Do you really hate serpents that much?" I tease with a meek smile.

Kai throws me a scowl. His face is pale and he looks like he might vomit. "They are vile, Terra."

I flinch as a scream echoes through the forest ahead. It could be Frederick torturing or killing someone. He's the only one of us who seems so eager to do so. "I thought this was my favorite class, but I take it back," I murmur.

For the better part of thirty minutes, we ride in silence to listen to our surroundings. I have no doubt in my mind that we're going to finish last, but I'm finding it hard to care. The only thoughts in my head at the moment revolve around Edgar. He won't speak with me or let me try to make amends, even though he's the one who attacked me. I miss him.

Kai's dark horse comes to a stop and he looks back at me. A faint smile coasts his lips as he mumbles, "They waited for us."

"Seriously?" I block out the sun with my hand and spot Raine and Finn at the bottom of the next ravine. They're perched on their Shadows and talking casually. How long have they been waiting?

As we draw closer, they notice and lift their heads. Finn's eyes shine with relief to see us, and Raine nods and grins at me.

Finn leans back like he's exasperated as he mutters, "We were really fucking worried about you guys. What took so long? We've been waiting for like—"

"Shut up, let's get going now that they're here," Raine cuts Finn off. I frown when he jerks his head for me to come to him. "Ride with me. We have to catch up."

I take one look at Raine's terrifying, black, bony dragon and shake my head.

He barks out a laugh and dismounts, walks up to Amser, and lifts me from its back by my waist. My eyes widen at the strength he still has. I press my hands on his shoulder as he lowers me.

"It's okay, you'll love it," Raine whispers against my ear. The warmth of his breath sends a shudder through me and all I can do is nod. "Just like the ziplines."

A bright sunset with birds flying toward the sun paints

itself in my head as I remember how he showed me his city's sky not so long ago.

"This isn't our last *zipline,* is it?" I murmur softly back, brushing a tuft of his black hair behind his ear and pressing a kiss to his neck.

He chuckles but doesn't answer my question, just looks down at me and tips my chin a bit with his fingers. "After you, my lady."

Raine's dragon has a low, vibrating energy around it as if it is constantly searching for fates to ruin. Its skull is enormous, with two icy pits for eyes that chill my blood. Black smoke rolls from beneath its bones. Only Raine's warm hand against my back keeps me walking toward it.

He smooths his hand over the muzzle and his Shadow lets out a low hum. Amser responds in kind as it fades back inside my bones. It clearly seems to trust the beast. At least one of us does.

We sit at the base of the dragon's neck, Raine behind me with his arms wrapped tightly around my waist. Finn has Kai on his phoenix and has to continuously bat Kai's hands away from the flames.

"All right, ready?" Raine says loud enough for Finn and Kai to hear. They give him a nod, and within seconds the dragon is lifting its wings, curtains of smoke and bones. One vicious beat later, we're taking to the sky.

The air is cold against my cheeks and the only sound I can hear is Kai screaming from a couple hundred feet to our right.

"Holy shit!" I shout, clinging to a spinal bone. This isn't like zip-lining at all. No harness or rope or line. Just one big bone to keep you in place.

Raine laughs behind me and grabs my hands, prying them away from the bone.

"Raine, stop it!" I laugh-scream and that only gives him more amusement. He burrows his lips into my skin where my shoulder meets my neck.

"I want you to feel everything up here. The wind between your fingers—the way your heart will rush when you're here with me." Raine slides his hands out behind mine and the wind threads through our fingers.

"Why are you talking like this?"

He waits a moment to respond. The seconds feel like an eternity.

"I want you to remember me this way. As a nice guy, the one who wanted you to be safe and warm. Not the cold, cruel man you met in Barkovah. When you think of me I can only hope you'll imagine the sky, the rush that I sent through your soul. That will be enough for me."

Tears stream down my cheeks and I let my head fall back on his shoulder. His hands slide away from mine and trail back to my torso, sculpting my form. He sends chills up my spine as he grabs my waist firmly, digging his fingers into my hips and pulling me close against him.

"You're more than the sky, Raine. You are the wind, the earth, the blood in my veins. I will never forget you." I choke out the words. He responds with tears that wet my skin.

Our sentimental moment ends abruptly as a black shard pierces Finn's phoenix, severing its head clean from the body. We don't scream, not even Kai—the shock and fear are still too tangible for us to react properly.

Finn's mouth opens in a silent gasp. It's Raine who

responds first, cursing under his breath. The dragon dips and swoops beneath Finn and Kai to catch them as the tendrils of Finn's Shadow return to his veins.

Kai lands awkwardly on the spinal bones and coughs violently. Finn uses momentum and lands perfectly on his toes, crouching to absorb the shock from the fall.

"Who the fuck attacked us?" Kai hisses behind us.

Raine grits his teeth and says in a lethal tone, "I'd bet a thousand coin it was Frederick." His grasp around me tightens and I scream as his dragon head dives straight toward the ground.

The wind throws my hair back violently and the approaching trees make my blood turn to ice. "Raine!" I shout but he doesn't let up.

Finn calls out from behind him, "There!"

I frantically search the approaching ground, eyes locking on five racing Shadows, one much larger than the rest, riding a snake similar to Edgar's but significantly smaller.

"That asshole can't go one day without trying to kill someone," Kai grumbles as the dragon spreads its wings and stops the descent. My entire body feels like jelly and my stomach curls. I'm never letting him convince me to do this again.

Kai hurls off the side of Raine's Shadow, and a few seconds later, we hear the men below shouting.

"Did you seriously vomit on them?" Finn laughs and Kai only groans with distress.

"Oh, we'll do more than that. If they want to fight, we'll give them a fight," Raine says in a low tone that makes me happy to be up here and not down there. I'd hate to find out what this Shadow can do to its opponents.

Kai protests, "Oh gods, please don't make it nosedive again."

The only reply is the dragon's immense screech piercing the sky. It's so loud that my hands abandon the safety of the bone and shield my ears. Then comes the blinding light. It's bright blue, like ice on a frozen lake. A ball of pure power begins to form in the skull's gaping jaw, growing bigger and increasingly daunting until all the sound in the world vanishes in an instant. A thin line of blue splits the sky and then the mass of power blasts from the dragon's mouth, wicked and horrible, scorching the trees. The pine needles shrivel and vanish like they've been hit with a bomb.

"You'll kill them!" I shriek, hardly able to hear my own voice over the roar of power crashing into the earth.

I turn to look back at the three men; their faces are shocked, horrified, and nervous. I don't think Raine knew the extent of his own strength, based on the sweat that rolls down his temples.

We don't speak, mainly because none of us can fucking hear, until the lake is back in view. The sun is already dipping behind the west mountain.

Finn and Kai are back on his phoenix—it's bright in the sky like a beacon. For some reason, even though our lives are filled with nothing but bleak and morbid things, I feel hope when I look at him.

Finn must feel my eyes on him because he turns and looks back at me, his black strands of hair blowing in the wind and amber glinting in his flashing eyes.

"There's Edgar." Raine points to the lake. I narrow my eyes at the depths of the blue water. Every inch of it is filled with the enormous snake, coiled tightly beneath the water's surface. Edgar stands on the shore with Arthur—the first to finish. Corvus's raven is just landing; he waves at us.

We land in unison and await the arrival of the remaining students. They come trickling in slowly. Still no sign of Frederick and his goons.

The longer we wait, the more dreadful the air becomes. I elbow Raine and he gives me a knowing look. "I think you killed them," I whisper.

Finn and Kai's faces visibly pale but Raine only smirks. "If I did, then they wouldn't have lasted in the second exam anyway."

We fall back into silence.

I keep eyeing the lake, knowing what lies beneath the tepid surface. It's disturbing because, from land, you wouldn't be able to tell his Shadow is there, coiling and festering beneath the dark water.

Finally, the remaining portion of our class arrives, Frederick and his comrades included. Their eyes are locked on Edgar and distrust dances behind their gazes. Frederick shoots Raine a glare but my companion only stands straighter.

Arthur waits a few more minutes, his arms crossed and eyes expectant. Elias is still out there. Did students actually try to escape? My heart sinks at the thought of Elias hunting them down.

"Do you think students tried to leave Alkrose?" I

whisper to Finn. He looks at me thoughtfully and eventually nods.

"Yeah, I'd be lying if I said it hadn't crossed my mind," he replies and Arthur glances back at us.

"I'm glad you didn't. He might've been lax with Terra, but Finn, you'd have lost your head," the professor says indifferently. He looks at me for a moment too long before returning to watching for Elias. The urge to brush my hand against his and feel that longing between us is almost impossible to resist. I clench my fists at my sides to keep control.

Finn frowns and Raine nudges his side. "See? Aren't you glad I talked you out of it?" I level them both with a stern look.

Before I can say anything to them, snow crunches ahead and I turn to find Elias slowly making his way toward the group. His breath curls in the cold air, his white hair catching the last remnants of the sunset.

Arthur looks him up and down, probably noticing the same thing I am: for once, Elias is not covered from head to toe in blood. "How many strayed?" Arthur asks as Velis disappears into dust.

Elias cracks his neck and stretches. "Eleven."

Arthur looks down grimly while Elias's face is as impassive as stone. "Edgar and Corvus were the first to arrive. You both will have immunity for the first stage of the exam, the name of which will be announced tonight in the mess hall," Arthur says before dismissing us to our Shadow Houses.

The five of us start to make our way back inside when

Elias grabs my arm. "I need to speak with you," he says in a hushed voice.

Raine and Finn glance back at me but I shake my head at them. Finn hesitates but follows Raine back inside.

"What is it?" I pull my cloak around my arms to edge out the cold. The sun is setting and the spring air has a bite to it.

He grabs my hand and leads me to the west side of the castle so we're out of earshot of anyone. His hands are freezing. Eleven students, that's how many he killed today. A shiver runs down my spine.

I don't want to care about someone like him, vile and sinister. But how do you carve out a cancer that has already grown? I should've stopped his roots before they spread.

Elias leans me back against the cool stones of Alkrose and lowers his head so he's looking straight into my eyes. I take a deep breath at his closeness and swallow hard.

"Two things: the headmaster knows the hearts are gone and the professors are going to place additional casts on your brother."

35

Terra

"What do you mean additional casts? He won't be able to protect himself if that's allowed." I shove Elias back and he glares at me.

"I wanted to be the one to tell you." His gray eyes soften but his brows remain pulled tightly together. "The others don't think he can control his Nova, like last time."

I stalk toward Elias and try shoving him back again. This time, he's ready for me and he doesn't budge an inch.

"Push me again, *sweetheart*, and I'm going to have to punish you," Elias whispers dangerously, grabbing my wrist and baring his teeth at me.

"Who's going to place those casts on him? *You*?" I throw back at him. When his jaw sets and he doesn't respond, my heart drops. "Elias, you *can't*. He'll be helpless in the exam." I try tearing my wrist from his grip but he won't let go.

"I don't have a choice. The others have outvoted me. I wanted him dead. Now let's talk about the more important issue at hand. The hearts—"

"I fucking *hate* you!" I scream in his face and bury my teeth into his hand. He finally releases me, eyes wide with rage, and he curses. I open my mouth to scream more, when—

"I DON'T HAVE A FUCKING CHOICE!" His voice is louder than I've ever heard it, unhinged and wild—cracking and filled with agony.

My eyes are wide and tears threaten to escape. His hands are on either side of my head and his entire body is trembling with emotion. He takes a few labored breaths, staring into my soul as his shoulders heave and his breath mists into the air around us. Then he whispers, "I don't want to do these things, Terra, but I have to." He pauses, unblinking, as he takes another few deep breaths, regaining his composure. "I never wanted to be the villain, especially not yours, but what am I supposed to do? Do you know what happens if he gets out of control? I'll tell you. I get sent to kill him. Even if I take back my heart and disobey Cein and the headmaster, what do you think happens to me? I'm the Assassin of Fernestia. I'm the death bell, the reaper, the void. What could they possibly take from me? *Guess*. I'll fucking wait."

I stare at him, my lower lip trembling until I gnash my teeth into it.

"Me."

"*You*. And that's something I cannot risk. Not ever. So hate me if you must, but you'll be safe and you *will* be mine. I don't need your affection in order to be happy. All I need is for you to still exist," he rasps. His glare is anything but loving.

I grab his face and dig my fingers into his cheek so his teeth pierce them beneath. He growls but I speak over him. "You aren't even capable of affection. You're just an empty puppet. The only thing you want is to possess me." I press harder on his cheeks and he doesn't even flinch as blood starts to drip from his lips. "Fuck. You." I release his face and shove him back again.

He staggers for a few seconds, blood spilling down his chin and onto the muddy grass. Then he looks up at me like a predator watches their prey.

"I'm going to give you five seconds to apologize." A manic grin spreads across his lips. His normally pearly-white teeth are stained red with blood.

I'm paralyzed with fear.

"One." His eerie voice is all I need to snap back to reality. "Two."

I turn calmly toward the front of the castle. "I'm not a child."

"Three."

I don't hear him count the rest because I'm already inside Alkrose and walking through the foyer. I need to tell Edgar, even if he refuses to speak with me. I need to tell him.

The front door opens loudly. I glance back and find Elias running straight for me.

"Are you serious?" I say under my breath and charge

up the stairs. A few students move out of my way and watch with their books clutched tightly in their arms as Elias surges after me.

What's he going to do if he catches me?

I decide I'm not going to find out.

The corridors are packed as everyone heads to the mess hall. It's a mandatory gathering. If I can evade Elias long enough, he'll have to give up first. I'm sure he's expected to be in attendance more than I am.

I hook a few lefts and a right, then ascend two more flights of stairs. The fourth floor is pretty empty since most of the classrooms are on the third level.

My pace slows. I don't see or hear Elias behind me. I let out a triumphant breath and make for the sky garden in the center of the castle. It's open and devoid of anything a space like this should have besides benches and a fountain that is dry as bones. I take a seat on one of the stone benches and try to catch my breath.

The air is cold and stings my lungs, but the view of the stars that linger above is worth the chill. A nostalgic smile tugs at my lips. Edgar and I used to stare at these very stars. Two dumb kids. And now... A tear falls down my cheek and I swallow the lump in my throat. How did we end up here?

A heavy hand weighs down my shoulder and Elias's white hair and gray eyes enter my field of vision, covering the stars beyond. His anger has vanished but blood still lines his soft lips.

His brows twitch with uncertainty. I like him best when he tries to understand what emotions I'm feeling.

His jaw flexes as if he wants to speak but he keeps losing the words somewhere along the way.

"Please don't place more casts on him," I whisper, more to the stars than to the assassin before me.

His eyes narrow with anguish, warring with something beyond my knowledge. The black of his tactical vest looks almost blue beneath the universe, his white cloak seeming to glow with the moon's iridescent light.

He walks around the bench and kneels in front of me, his ashy and woodsy scent making this feel like a night camping in the woods. Stargazing. What I would give for it to be only that.

I don't look down from the stars, not until Elias carefully trails his fingers up along my neck and threads them into my hair. He presses his thumbs to the hollows of my cheeks and guides my jaw down until I'm looking into his eyes.

There's more pain in them than I thought he could ever show. I see a man who's lost so much more than he ever should have. A man who knows what it is to have everyone you love stolen from you. He's spent his entire life building these walls.

"Elias," I murmur, our lips so close that they brush as I speak.

He tilts his head forward until it's pressed against mine. The warmth of his skin spreads heat through my chest. Velis and Amser pull so desperately that my stomach tightens into knots.

"I'm sorry," he says curtly, like the two words hurt to say. My eyes widen and his brows arch with vulnerability in response. Pressed this close together, I can only see his eyes. "It is beyond me, but I promise it is better this way. You know not the creature you're trying to keep. It needs to be sealed away," he whispers again, this time pressing his lips against mine and pulling me into him. His hand slides down my neck, burning my skin where he touches me as our Shadows make each movement unbearable.

Elias deepens the kiss, pushing his tongue into my mouth, and the flavor of his blood blossoms on my tongue. I grunt at the taste, but he just pursues me more viciously, running his other hand down my chest and gripping my hip tightly.

"I hate the things you draw from me. The things you steal away," he says into our feverish kisses. "You drive me into utter madness."

I moan as he bites down on my lower lip. My own blood spills down my chin. Never in my life did I think painful, violent kisses could be so erotic. He sucks on my lip and groans as he devours me. If anyone saw us right now, they'd think we were consuming each other, eating one another like starved creatures.

Perhaps that's truly all that we are.

He releases my lip and pulls back, dragging me off the bench and laying me on the cold stone bricks of the sky garden. His mouth is smothered in our blood and I'm certain mine looks no different. This is how I imagine his true self is: feral and fucking hungry for humanity. I wonder if he sees the same creature staring back at him.

A pool of black smoke spills from him and cushions the ground beneath me. Elias lowers his head down to my neck and nips my skin gently as he unzips my jacket. His cold hands smooth over my breasts and make my nipples harden. Warmth pools in my core and I let out a moan as he lets his teeth glide across my collarbone.

"I told you I'd punish you if you pushed me again," he says with anything but the rage he met me with earlier. I want to be as angry at him as I was ten minutes ago, but I can see it in his eyes that he's up against a wall. Nothing I do or say will change that. I will still warn Edgar though; it's the least I can do.

"How are you going to punish me?" I goad him.

He chuckles darkly and leans up on his forearms, one on either side of my head. His smirk is chilling and yet I find myself squeezing my thighs together with anticipation. "Oddly, I can't find myself in the mood to punish you. Not when you look so small beneath me."

I raise a brow and find that same heartless smile taking form on my lips. "Small things can be as venomous as they come."

"I suppose they can," he says with a deep voice, letting his eyes slowly move down to my lips.

"You said that the headmaster found out about the hearts?" I ask, my eyes darkening with the idea of Emerai finding out it was us.

"Yes, we have to keep them hidden until the end of the second exam. We cannot tell Arthur yet either."

My brows pull together with hesitation. It's been difficult not to hand him his heart and pray that he knows what to do with it already. How am I supposed to keep this a secret longer? "You said we'd give it to him when you returned. He deserves to know and I think he may be able to help—"

Elias's expression dulls. "No. You will keep it

between us until I say so or else you risk everything falling apart. Whales of Tauh, remember? Or do you need to see the wall again?" he growls against the shell of my ear and pulls away. The cold air rushes in everywhere he just was and leaves me empty. I follow him up and sit beside him, our arms touching, and that small connection keeps my heart fluttering wildly inside my chest.

He doesn't look at me as he wipes the blood from his mouth with his sleeve. A smear still remains on his jaw, making him look very much like the feral wolf I thought him when we first met.

Elias stands and offers me his hand. "We don't want to be late for the exam announcement." He's calm now, but lust still stirs in his gray eyes. I take his hand and he guides me back through the fourth floor. Dread forms deep in my stomach. I'm not sure how long I can keep my lips sealed.

After cleaning the blood from my face and neck, I quickly make my way to the mess hall. I take a seat next to Raine at the Nova table. The mess hall is boisterous with chatter and nervous energy imbues the air.

Lucina looks up at me as I reach for a roll. A full dinner won't sit well with my nerves. Her white hair is pulled back into a ponytail, and her bangs brush her brows. "Ready for the announcement?" she asks meekly.

I've spoken to Edgar's friends here and there, but

Lucina has been evasive. I quirk a brow but reply, "I don't think any of us are."

Her expression sullens and she takes a bite of her meal, chewing for a few moments. She mutters, "Yeah, that's how I feel too." Rowan leans over her as he reaches for a scone. His auburn hair is mid-length and wavy, much longer than it was when we first arrived. Vinnie flips lazily through the pages of his tome, studying diligently as always. They've become a calming presence for meal times. Well, besides Tamaris and Alani, who never can seem to get along.

"What did you place in the race this morning?" Alani asks Tamaris through a mouthful of food. The bow atop her head today is white, matching her cloak.

Tamaris and Alani share the morning Shadow riding class. I wonder how many tried to escape during that one.

"Fifth." Tamaris glowers and pulls her long, dark hair back into a ponytail.

Rowan laughs. "I was fucking last."

"We know," they all say in unison. Rowan seems a bit offended.

Ash sits off on his own, away from the group. I'm not surprised Edgar isn't here; he never is.

"Where's Edgar?" I ask, looking over at the instructor's table at the head of the room. Elias watches me silently, his gray eyes boring holes into my skin. I swiftly look away and swallow the dread.

I need to warn Edgar.

Lucina opens her mouth to reply but her eyes flick to the doors. I follow her gaze and see Edgar walking in alone. His ebony tactical gear is pristine, not worn like most of ours after daily practice. He plops down next to Lucina and gives me a brief, unsettling look.

Raine lets out a hard breath to let me know he still hates Edgar's guts.

"Edgar, I need to talk to you," I whisper. He looks up at me—his green eyes are filled with weary thoughts. His head jerks a bit to the side as if he's trying to silence the Shadow in his head.

I pause.

The casts would suppress his Shadow... It would make it quiet and less of a threat to his mind, wouldn't it? Maybe I shouldn't—

"What do you want to say?" Edgar asks coldly. I look at him, his pale skin, hollowed cheeks, and tormented eyes. I don't know if I can live with this decision.

Amser coils in my chest and whispers in my mind, *Sully is better if it sleeps. Let them try to make it rest.*

I swallow hard and go against my heart, shaking my head and giving Edgar a false smile. "I was just hoping we could make up after our fight?" His fractured gaze takes me in for a few moments before he looks back to his plate of food, ignoring my words. Pain flutters throughout me, but I swallow it down. Guilt takes its place.

"Attention, students," Headmaster Emerai calls out over the loud room and everyone silences, staring at the headmaster in his golden cloak. His black hair is longer than Finn's, reaching down to the bottom of his ears, but not quite as long as Arthur's. "The second exam has been decided and I'm pleased to let you know that it will be the only exam for the remainder of the academic year. We're anticipating an impressive team to come out of this exam."

He motions to the professors to his right: Elias, Arthur, Kallos, and Nekane.

"These are the last of the Blood Crowns. The first Shadows to prevail and earn their places at the head of Fernestia. You too will sit where they do should you survive and prove yourself to the Shadow Master and Empress Raven. The Blood Crowns exam will take place in four weeks. At that time you will need to prove your worth to Fernestia."

Emerai raises his hand to the ceiling and his Shadow glows in the air like Kallos's does, bright and golden, filled with light, unlike so many others. I still think it's unfair.

"Prepare to slaughter your classmates. The details of the exam will not be released until the morning of, so I will leave you with this: don't show your best technique to anyone." He laughs cruelly and drops his hand, all the light and magic disappearing with it. "For even your closest comrade may end up taking your head."

36

Edgar

Lucina and Aervin walk ahead of me while Rowan and Vinnie keep pace at my sides. The second-floor corridor is bustling with students trying to get to the mess hall for breakfast. The laughter we once all shared has left us. They feared me before my outburst with Terra, but now, they're all but silent around me.

I can't say I blame them.

It's been a long month and a half since I attacked my sister. It's hard to explain what happened exactly—I was in control, but not, as if Sully was manipulating my heart and mind. The only thing I remember is the consuming anger and hatred.

"Are you going to class today?" Lucina says hopefully.

Aervin glances behind his shoulder at me, his blonde hair covering half his forehead.

I shake my head and look over the sea of heads as we enter the mess hall. The Nova table is sparsely occupied, only Ash, Tamaris, and Alani are in attendance.

Alani looks up and waves at us with her usual cheerfulness. She's the only one who doesn't seem afraid of me. I don't think there is anything she truly fears in this world. A disorder, surely.

We take a seat with the two women and silently start eating. Chatter roars around us.

Ash sits off on his own, though Aervin always tries to convince him to sit with us. The others aren't so forgiving, and though I understand their disdain toward him, having felt the same way myself, I have the discernment of someone whose Shadow has altered him. Like a disease, it spreads, and there is no stopping Sully from consuming what little of me remains.

The only good thing that came out of my fight with Terra was my realization that I will be fine in the exam. Kallos's cast broke so easily, and I've since learned how to do many awful things with my Shadow. Being able to keep my friends safe is perhaps the only ray of hope keeping my head above dark water.

Arthur enters the mess hall, which is odd for him. He hasn't attended breakfast since classes began in winter. He slowly makes his way over to our table instead of the front where the professors sit.

"Hello, students," Arthur mutters as he dips his head to the others. Then his eyes find me and my shoulders lower with dread. I can't stand his boring lectures he's been forcing me to attend, but it's either those or normal classes where everyone looks at me like a freak. I was hardly able to force myself to attend the Shadow riding class two weeks ago.

I'll take the boring lectures.

"Edgar, I hope you've eaten, because we are starting class early today." Arthur smiles placidly and waits as I reluctantly stand up.

"No, he hasn't even had his toast yet," Lucina rebuts, leveling the professor with an angry stare. Vinnie hands me a scone and gives me a weak smile. His glasses have a crack through them now, having fallen off his face during a training session.

"Thanks. I'll catch you guys later," I say and turn without waiting for their reply. Arthur doesn't speak until we get to the fourth story. Arthur likes to teach in the sky garden, I'm guessing because he doesn't get a lot of time outside. His pale skin is an indicator of that much.

"Today's class will be short. I don't like lying to my students, Edgar, and I don't plan on starting now. Elias, Kallos, and Nekane are waiting for us today. They've decided that, because of your lack of control, you need to be contained."

I stop in the middle of the empty corridor. My muscles twitch in my arm with the memory of how the first time went. There's no way it's possible to break four casts.

"No."

Arthur stops and turns only enough to look at me. His black hair is smoothed back, only a few strands falling out of place as he cocks his head. "Come now, Edgar. Don't make this harder than it needs to be." I can hear the grief in

Arthur's voice and that only reassures me that if I let them do this, they're basically killing me and my comrades.

"No... I won't be able to protect anyone if you repress my Shadow." I fist my hands at my sides and level him with a distrustful look. "I'll never forgive you if you do this. Please, Arthur."

He stares at me as if he only sees the monster within, not even bothering to utter a word as hands come down on my shoulders, startling me.

I whirl and find the three professors circling me. *No.*

"I'm sorry, Edgar, this is how it has to be," Kallos says grimly as all the lights fade from my vision and the only thing left in the dark ocean of my mind is me, left out for the world to devour.

37

Finn

Studying and honing our power under the immense pressure of the approaching exam is wearing us thin.

Kai's lost weight, even though he eats more than enough for two people. His eyes have sunken a bit with sleepless nights spent training relentlessly.

As I look at myself in the mirror, I realize I have the same circles beneath my eyes. *Shit.* And we're still not even close to Edgar's frightening display of power, though I'm not so sure he's an issue anymore. He's like a ghost at Alkrose. Most students only catch glimpses of him at best.

Corvus has still been spending time with him. I'm not sure if it's out of pity or to get intel from him, but he told me and Kai that the professors placed additional casts on

Edgar last week due to his outburst at the lake. Apparently, he broke the first cast Kallos placed on him.

If that was Edgar repressed, as Corvus said, we don't stand a chance against him at full strength. So I'm relieved at least that we don't need to worry about him as much anymore. There are others just as strong as he was that day, like Frederick.

Water drips from my forehead as I hang my head over the sink in the Cosmos communal bathroom.

The exam is in two weeks and I'm so fucking scared it disgusts me. If my father were here, he'd beat me senseless until I was more afraid of him than dying in some stupid exam.

I lift my head and stare into the mirror once more. My amber eyes are fading into a more subtle orange, graying at the bottom... *Fuck*. I pound my fist into the porcelain sink.

Class is dull today. I open my palm and create burning feathers over and over to stay awake.

Arthur delves deeply into the history of Fernestia, the cities and festivals that they celebrated before everything went to shit. One in particular that he spends a few extra minutes explaining is the Sporlis Festival. He details that it was a meeting of the nations in which all would gather in peace and eat together. It sounds like it was a nice thing of the past. The way he speaks about it sounds like it happened a hundred years ago, but Arthur's in his mid-twenties, so it really it's been a decade or less. How can so much go wrong in that short span of time?

And what was the point of such a festival if it didn't hold up the one thing it was meant to? Peace did not last. Look where we all ended up.

I flip through my tome and hear a small sound to my right. I don't even need to guess where the sound is coming from since Kai has been making outrageous sounds for weeks when he gets bored or just feels like pestering me.

I glance over with an annoyed look. "What?"

Kai sparkles at my acknowledgment. "Hey," Kai whispers, motioning for me to lean in closer. I glance to make sure Arthur is still writing on the board before leaning in. "Corvus wants us to meet him in the foyer after class."

I keep the annoyed expression on my face. "What for? We usually don't study until after dinner."

Kai shrugs dramatically and catches Arthur's attention. He looks up and raises a brow at the two of us. I feign an innocent smile and Kai looks away awkwardly. The instructor stalks over to our desks and everyone's eyes are on us like beacons. Even Terra gives us a curious look. A few desks over from her, Frederick frowns maliciously.

I can't stand how sinister Frederick is. How he so easily murders Dvars students in the late hours of the night. I hate him as much as I despise Fernestia.

"Anything interesting you'd like to share with me, Kaidel?" Arthur rests his calm gaze on Kai.

His body sinks into his desk. "Nope. Sorry about that."

The professor hovers there for a few more moments. "Don't cause too much trouble this afternoon, Kaidel. Finnick, make sure he doesn't," Arthur says as if I should know what trouble my friend is going to cause. (I could make a few guesses.)

We both sink further into our chairs as chuckles rise across the room. Arthur stops at his desk and flips through some notes before continuing with his lecture. His eyes flick to Terra briefly—as they do every five minutes, it seems.

I'm convinced they are up to more than training during their private *lessons*, but honest to gods, as long as she's happy I don't care. She must feel my gaze on her shoulder because she turns and looks at me, those green eyes shimmering with the warmth of afternoon light.

I miss her being only mine.

After the day's lessons Kai quickly pulls me with him to the hallway. Terra waves me off before I can ask her to join us. She, of course, is heading up to talk with Arthur. She and Raine are still trying to get his notes, but apparently they're proving difficult to find.

Terra has been guarded about her own room as well. I'm beginning to think everyone has a secret except me. What could she possibly be hiding in there?

In the hallway we pass Elias and Ash. The Nova student has been lying low to avoid anyone's eyes. The professors are usually with him too. It's not news that he's the portal Shadow and as such is heavily controlled. I draw my attention back to Kai and he shrugs, seeming to be on the same page as I am.

We've developed silent communication. I hate to say it's from sex ed, but hey, our Shadows are rather chummy with each other and it's been useful. If my Shadow picks up on something off, it signals to him immediately. Like radios in our skin.

He's my brother through and through. The one I wish I'd always had.

Corvus is waiting in the foyer for us. The windows stretch high—at least three stories—and the glimmering air above us holds remnants of the firebird that I created so long ago. It's odd how the dust of our power lingers, holding space as if transfixed in time. Are we all this way? My hands tingle with the itch to release Laphia once more. I enjoy its flames, and in a way, we truly are one.

I stare at my hands as we walk down the steps and approach Corvus.

Corvus smiles dully as we approach. He isn't alone; I look at his companion and have to bite my lip to stop myself from making a horrified expression.

What the fuck is Edgar doing with him?

He's been holed up in the Nova House since the incident at the lake, avoiding everyone except his buddies. He even turned Terra away when she tried to reconcile with him.

He's like a shell of himself. The very thing Corvus described his Shadow as.

"Edgar, what brings you here?" I say as neutrally as I can.

Edgar's light brown wisps of hair curl at the bottom of his ears and cover most of his brows. He looks me up and down with a blank expression. Those emerald eyes are far more sinister than they were before. His skin is pale and the darkness beneath his eyes is nearly maroon, as if he has makeup on. Just looking at him has my skin crawling with goosebumps.

I shudder under his fractured gaze—eyes filled with so much pain and anguish. He's no longer Terra's brother and I don't think he's ever coming back. I'm not sure he'd want to if he could see himself clearly.

His voice is raspy as he says, "We found something you need to see."

Okay, what the fuck?

I look at Corvus for clarity and he mutters, "We think we've found the second exam's portal and believe it leads to Fernestia."

Kai shifts on his feet uneasily. "I know we're trying to uncover things here, but I don't think we should go through it." Kai's voice trembles with apprehension.

Corvus and Edgar raise their brows as if they can't believe what he just said.

Kai goes on: "We have no idea what's behind it... That would be incredibly stupid." His voice is sullen and I perk my head up at the sound of it. Each time Kai becomes serious like this it makes my chest seize. I don't want to think of death and how imminent it is for all of us.

How unfair it is.

I remember a friend's last smile, but not their face. It still infects my mind like a drug. It's not fair. We can't even properly remember our lost friends. I've asked myself a thousand times why our Shadows devour their memories, their faces, but there are no answers. Laphia won't tell me why.

I don't want to forget any more of them.

Corvus and Edgar are right. We need to figure out what's really going on here so we can all live and possibly retake Heirah someday. The fun and whimsy of learning the magic of the Shadows is just a ruse—a stupid ploy to keep us all busy while the Fernestians raise us for the inevitable slaughter.

"Kai." I rest my hand on his shoulder. "Let's at least go

look." Corvus and Edgar nod in agreement. Kai gives me a painful stare filled with betrayal and something that seems a bit more sorrowful. He just lets his head drop and looks away from us all with a curt nod.

"Good. Now that we're all on the same page"—Corvus takes a few steps closer to the window—"let's go."

I frown. Why do I have a really bad feeling about this?

The four of us make our way through Alkrose to a part of the castle that I've never been to before. The walls draw closer together. They're older here, built in a different time, or perhaps Alkrose was built over the remains of an existing castle. The stones are covered in discolored blotches and the smell of mildew fills my senses. The natural light from the more familiar hallways fades and I create a small flame in my palm to light our way from this point on.

We follow Corvus down a maze of hallways and finally come upon an immense stairwell that spirals down into an abyss of darkness. The stone stairs cling to the circular skeleton of the tower around a hollow center. My flames can't even cast enough light to use the steps safely, the darkness cloaks the area so heavily.

"Gods, how did you find this place?" Kai shivers beside me. Goosebumps spread across my arms and I hesitantly swallow. It's disturbing and creepy in this part of the castle.

I make the flame in the center of my palm bigger so the four of us can see one another's faces. "I don't think we should go farther. This doesn't feel safe," I mutter, studying their expressions.

Corvus has a smirk plastered across his lips and

Edgar's looking down the abyss of stairs with this blank stare.

"It's fine, Edgar, show them." Corvus's dark eyes glint in the dim light and the ominous feeling sneaks back into my chest.

Edgar starts down the stairwell, reaching his hand to the curved wall on his right. My eyes widen with awe. As his fingers glide across the dark stones, a path of light spreads over them and flows out in every direction, as if the light itself is devouring the darkness. It peels the shadows from the space like dust lifting into the air. Kai gasps and I realize I do too.

Kai beats me to say it. "How the fuck are you doing that? What is Edgar's power? I haven't come across this in my studies," he mutters more to himself than to us. His voice is distrustful.

"Darkness itself," Edgar mutters from below. I flinch. *Darkness?* What the fuck does that mean? Looking back at the brightening stairwell, I realize it's not that the darkness is being lifted into the air, more that it's being consumed. Edgar's consuming the dark... For what purpose?

My stomach twists uncomfortably.

"I don't understand." I narrow my eyes at Corvus. "How can he do that? The casts—"

Kai crosses his arms beneath his white cloak to disguise his trembling.

"The casts can't stop everything. He still has some power, but he has to take it first—steal darkness to use darkness," Corvus says nonchalantly.

"I don't trust him," I snap back at him, moving down a

step closer toward Corvus. "You saw what he did at the lake that night as well as we did."

"I saw power that could change the tides of war." Corvus's voice is cold and accusatory.

Kai shoves past both of us and shakes his head. "Both of you shut up—let's go."

Corvus and I glare at one another as we follow behind Kai.

No one says another word the rest of the way down the spiral stairs. Edgar is a good floor ahead of us; he didn't wait while we argued. After what seems like at least ten minutes of descending, we finally reach the bottom. The mildew smell is stronger in the depths of this tower; something sinister exists down here.

"Guys, maybe we should leave—"

"Gods, what is that?" Kai cuts me off.

Corvus and Edgar face a ten-foot door covered in golden thorns and twisted statues etched into the ebony stone. It looks prickly and poisonous, with barbed edges surrounding it. It's clearly not something to fuck around with. That's obvious.

Corvus looks over his shoulder at us. "We believe this doorway leads to Fernestia. You two don't have to come if you don't want to."

I can hear Kai clenching his teeth, and a wild light flickers through his azure eyes as he finally breaks and shouts at our friend, "Corvus, what the fuck happened to you? Just take a look around you. This is *insanely* stupid. Even I wouldn't do anything as reckless as this." Kai grasps Corvus's wrist to stop him from getting closer to the door.

Corvus whirls and rips his arm out of Kai's grip.

"Watch yourself, Kai," Corvus says venomously. He closes his hand around a shadow blade that appears from thin air.

Kai laughs in disbelief and raises his hand into the air. "*Meskill.*" Kai whispers his Shadow's name, and steam hisses from his teeth. Two ebony spears form from his Shadow. Kai spins them like a well-trained assassin, aiming them at Corvus.

My heart beats rapidly and my blood thickens inside my veins. My Shadow anxiously coils inside, waiting to see what my friends will do next. "Stop it, both of you," I shout, but they ignore me.

What should I do?

Kai lurches forward. "Come to your senses, Corvus!"

Corvus dodges a little too late and gets his shoulder sliced clean with Kai's black spear. He lets out a pained grunt but shakes the assault off quickly.

Kai lands on the other side of Corvus and Edgar and shoves his spears into the portal frame, barring the door. The weapons glimmer and become one with the door, sealing it.

Edgar catches on just as I do and the air suddenly shifts, energized.

"Remove those *now.*" Edgar's eyes burn like green infernos and instill fear in me. The turquoise fractures glow brightly and I know he'll blight us if I don't act now.

"Guys, enough!" I snap, raising my hand and summoning a wall of fire that breaks between them. Edgar's fists are clenched tightly, but the fire distracts him and the turquoise in his gaze returns to its former dim glow.

I take a deep breath, shaking, but steady enough to say,

"Please—let's not turn on each other. This is exactly what Fernestia wants." Kai stares at me uncertainly, his eyes flicking back at the other two with distrust. "I don't care what you two do, but enough fighting." My brows pull together with rage.

I can sense it firsthand, Edgar's wrath, and I never want to feel it again. I've never felt anything so rotten and twisted. One thing is clear: no matter his ideation, Edgar is on a path that will only carry death.

For everyone, not just Fernestia.

I don't waste time waiting for either Corvus or Edgar to respond. I grab Kai's wrist and drag him back toward the stairs. Kai opens his mouth to say something but I shoot him a warning look. He shuts his mouth and doesn't say another word the rest of the way up the stairwell.

The maze of hallways is difficult to navigate but I keep up our pace. I'm not sure what Edgar and Corvus decided to do after we left, but I'm not about to let them catch up to us in case they're still looking to fight.

After we finally make our way out of the lower floors, we emerge back onto the familiar main level of Alkrose. Only then do I let a sigh loose. I felt like I couldn't breathe down there. My anxiety was about to set my Shadow into a killing frenzy.

Neither of us speaks until we enter the homeroom of the Cosmos House. Kai still has his arms crossed and an annoyed expression firmly in place. I plop onto one of the sofas and exhale loudly. My entire body is sore from all the godsforsaken stairs and the tension in that pit.

Kai sits next to me and deflates. His eyes are stormy and sullen.

"What came over you down there?" I ask. Kai's mouth stretches into a thin line. I can't get a read on him. "Come on, Kai. Tell me what's going on."

He pushes back his white hair and shuts his eyes. "I don't want to lose another friend, okay? I don't want Corvus to get hurt. Or you. Or me." He sets his hands on his knees and grips them tightly. "And Terra, Raine, Aervin. *All of us*, Finn. I can't lose any of you. I can't fucking remember the other guy that came here with us. Not a damn thing about him, how fucked is that? Just that he was with us, that's it."

I frown at him with understanding. The thought of forgetting Kai as I've forgotten the other friend we had... it's horrifying.

What's worse, I don't want them to forget me.

38

Edgar

It's not easy to convince my comrades to join me in going through the portal, but with Corvus's help, they eventually agree.

Our plan is to investigate the portal and where it leads—recon for the second assessment and what exactly they have in store for us.

We're going to gather as much information as we can on Fernestia's infrastructure while also trying to figure out what exactly we're up against for the second-semester exam.

Today is the day we'll enter.

We skip class and head directly to the tower beneath the academy.

Kai put a minor blip in my path yesterday. There's no

doubt in my heart that we'll be fine. It's just a recon mission. I'm a Nova, after all; I can protect them even with my abilities suppressed, though I doubt we'll run into any trouble. I never thought I'd be thankful for a Fernestian, but I'm grateful Arthur taught me how to harness my ability to steal darkness. Without it, I'd be useless.

"Edgar," Lucina mumbles from behind her cloak's cowl. Her blue eyes have lost so much of the shine they once held—the blight is slowly killing her. It's part of the reason I'm so keen to get information directly from the source.

There must be something...

"Hm?"

Our footsteps echo in the staircase as we descend into the underground tower. We're the first heading to the portal.

"Are we going to be okay? You know... No one will get hurt, right?" Her long white hair whips with each step she takes.

I turn and raise a brow at her. "You don't think I can protect us if anything goes awry?" I know they all witnessed my fight with Terra. How could they not have? The entire castle was shaking with the tremors of our Nova Shadows clashing.

She tightens her lips. "No, that's not what I mean... It's just, do we even know what awaits us on the other side?"

I stop and Lucina takes a few more steps down before coming to a halt as well. She looks back at me with so much uncertainty in her eyes. I hate it.

"Fernestia. That's what awaits us. Nothing worse than

we're currently facing here," I say through gritted teeth. Lucina's brows knit with worry.

I level her with an indifferent stare and continue down the steps. We remain silent for the remainder of the decline and sit on the last step, waiting quietly until the rest of the squad shows up.

Alani, Rowan, and Vinnie are the first to show. They seem uneasy, but keep better composed than Lucina. Her eyebrows are still pulled tightly together and her arms are crossed. She's had doubts about the plan from the start, but I can't just stop because of how she feels. This is so much more than her, or me, or our friends.

Humanity is on the line.

Vinnie pushes his glasses up his nose. "Do we have the bags to collect anything that we may come across?" His dark eyes scour the ground until he finds a small pile of satchels and smiles. "Ah, there." Rowan follows him over and picks one up.

It was Vinnie's plan to bring these—brilliant as ever, of course. He made a point that collecting anything that can be of use there would be beneficial. He learned as much in his survival classes with Nekane. Most of it was recon and information on the enemy. Alani shares that class with him and was just as adamant about it.

Rowan's auburn hair flickers in the low light as he says, "When we get back, we should go to the roof again. It's so glum down here. I'm going to need to get some sun to wash this mildew from my nose." He waves his hands around his face for emphasis.

Vinnie nods and mutters, "Yeah, we should celebrate when we get back."

"I wouldn't mind grabbing some rolls too. The dining hall is on the way back up, so let's get some on the way," Alani chirps happily. She's always thinking about food. She often sneaks snacks from the kitchens. The head chef even made an announcement a few weeks prior about a thief stealing from the vaults. "I can't wait for the second-semester exam. I just want to get it over with." She crosses her arms as if it doesn't scare her at all.

"I don't," Rowan retorts, leaning against a wall with his hands behind his head. "The instructors act like we're all going to die. It sounds pretty tough."

Vinnie lets out a huff. "It's not just an exam. Those who fail will either be sent to fight on the front lines at Whales of Tauh or get slaughtered here."

Rowan swallows hard. "It's happening so fast... What if some of us don't pass the second exam?" He sullens and I firm my jaw at the thought of any of them dying.

"You probably won't," Tamaris's raspy voice roars down the steps, announcing her arrival. We all glance up as she approaches. Tamaris brings a fight with her wherever she goes.

"Oh, *hey,* Tamaris." Rowan rolls his eyes.

Aervin and Corvus are a step behind her yet she is just as tall as they are.

"I've seen how lazily you train," she grumbles and Rowan crosses his arms.

"Not all of us are as strong as the others. Why even try? We know how it will end." Rowan's bleak words strike my chest.

I step up to him and clench his shirt tightly, lifting him nearly an inch off the ground. "None of you are going to die. We are *all* going to make it out of Alkrose together, Rowan. I don't want to hear you talk like this again."

Why are they already giving up without a fight? Hasn't this been what we've trained for all this time? Against all odds, against the casts placed over my power.

I release my grip on Rowan, letting him sink to the floor and catch his breath. "Damn... A warning next time," he wheezes as he stands back up.

Corvus ignores the others and looks at me. "Prepare yourselves. We will be entering the portal shortly." His raven hair contrasts his purple cloak, not long enough to reach his shoulders but enough to pull back. Corvus steps over to the portal and the others watch as he prepares the doorway.

After a few minutes of silence, he speaks again: "Aervin. Rowan. Are you ready?" Corvus asks, glancing over his shoulder at them. They share a nervous look and approach the barred door, one on each side as they practiced, and then they whisper the names of their Shadows.

"*Avantis*," Aervin whispers.

"*Broktium*," Rowan murmurs.

A cloud of Shadows as dark as night engulfs their hands, sending ebony fissures up Rowan's side of the embedded spear and veins of black splinters on Aervin's side. The spears of Kai's magic crumble into fine, ashy dust and they smile with relief.

"We did it," Aervin says more to himself than any of us. The corners of my lips turn up as I step toward the portal, brushing my hands over the grooves of the delicately sculpted stones. *Finally*. My blood thrums with the first steps toward our revenge. Who knows what wealth of knowledge we'll find on the other side.

Lucina steps up next to me and sighs. "Are you sure about this?" She speaks only loud enough for me to hear. I shoot her a look and when she doesn't look away, I give her a stern nod. She shuts her eyes. "Okay. We can do this."

Corvus reminds everyone of our order. Tamaris and Alani take the head of the group. Lucina and I walk behind them while Rowan, Vinnie, and Aervin guard the back. Corvus is to remain the gatekeeper in case a professor should stumble upon us.

"Be careful and return if anything goes wrong," Corvus says.

I tilt my chin up in acknowledgment. "Let's go," I say in a low voice. Alani and Tamaris open the doors to the portal. They swing heavily and a blinding light showers over us. My heart thrums.

Sully is muted deep inside me. If it has any warnings for me, I cannot hear them.

We walk through the portal.

A cooling sensation covers my cheeks. I can't see anything except the light—no sounds or smells either. My hand searches the space near me but I don't find Lucina. A flicker of fear washes over me. We've only just entered the portal. There's no way we've already been separated.

"Lucina?"

Nothing.

A bead of sweat rolls down my forehead but I keep my composure. *It's okay. Everything is fine.* I stop walking and focus. Without Sully in my head, I've learned to use the power without asking it specifically to do things. I let out some of the darkness I've been collecting and try to dull the blinding light surrounding me.

Power thrums through my body and jerks the muscles in my jaw. Dark wisps of sand-like grains twirl in the air around me and lash out into the light in every direction like a wave. The grains pull the light away with them, darkening the space around me to a level I can see in.

Trees sway in the distance as a chilly wind blows through. I find myself standing on a large boulder by the sea. The mist carries the scent of salt that stings my nose, reminding me very much of Za'Afiel.

None of my comrades are in sight. I look behind me and my eyes widen with disbelief. No portal; There's nothing.

"But... how?" I whisper, grabbing my arms to prevent the dreadful trembling that takes hold of my body. "No, this is all wrong. We were supposed to come in together and—" I cut off my train of thought as I stare at the forest before me. There's no doubt we are in the lands of Fernestia. The very trees look grimmer than any I've ever seen, with their long, spindly black branches, but it is the stench of blood in the air that taints the ground here.

I shudder. *I have to find them. I won't let this mission go awry.*

I clench my fists and stride into the dead forest ahead.

I walk for what feels like hours.

The sky feigns night here, but I have an inkling that it is truly daytime as it is at Alkrose. Is there magic in these lands keeping the sun away? I can't help but notice the underbrush reciprocating the bleak deadness of the trees. Sun-deprived.

It's not until I change direction that I hear a sharp snap in the brush ahead. I instinctively squat and ready myself.

"Hello?" a familiar voice whispers.

I diminish the darkness in my palm as I recognize Rowan's voice. I follow the sound and emerge from a black thicket of branches.

"Rowan? Where is everyone else?" I ask calmly so as not to spook him.

His auburn hair flashes as he whirls toward me and a grim frown crosses his lips. I swallow hard, hesitant to ask again as I'm not sure I want the answer.

"Edgar, we didn't enter the same places." His voice is panicked. "I... I was alone and there were people. I ran until everything became quiet. But I heard... I heard Lucina scream and I didn't do anything. I don't want to be here anymore. I want to go back to Alkrose." His eyes are wild and filled with raw, contagious fear.

I flinch at the mention of Lucina screaming and take a wide step toward Rowan. "Where did you hear her scream?" I ask sternly.

Rowan's eyes fill with horror. "That way." He raises a trembling finger. His clothes are dirty and drenched from dew.

I grasp both of his arms and squeeze tightly to reassure him. We can't lose our heads. We have to focus and remember why we're here. "Rowan, we're going to be okay." He nods slowly at my words, like he desperately needs to hear them. "We have to find Lucina and the others. We need to stay calm and collected, okay?" Another slow nod. I smile to show him that I'm not afraid, even though a pit has formed in the center of my stomach. An eerie feeling wells from deep within me.

Rowan takes a steadying breath. "You're right." His brown eyes brighten with more determination. "Come on —I'll lead the way." He strides off with his fists clenched at his sides. I walk beside him as we head in the direction of the scream.

We walk in silence for a long while. The darkness of this place makes time seem irrelevant. It's difficult to tell which direction we're heading in but Rowan is certain that he's leading us the right way.

The forest finally breaks and we arrive at a vast field that extends farther than the eye can see. I glance up to the sky and am met with a sea of dark, angry clouds. I frown. I was hoping to see the stars. Of all the things in the world that changed around me, they always remained the same, but even they don't dare shine here.

My attention returns to the field as Rowan wades through the tall wheat. Their golden ears transform the ground into a gilded ocean.

Then, there is a wave of light. A million fireflies rise as Rowan steps through the field. Suddenly, I'm six years old again, Terra beside me.

I gazed down into my palm at the lone glowing insect that hummed quietly in my hand.

"Terra, why do they fly?" I asked. The glow in my palm fluttered as if it could fade at any moment.

Terra narrowed her eyes in thought. After a few moments, she smiled as she gazed at the stars. "They fly because their time is limited. Because their light is too pure for just the ground. They need to share their joy with the world around them while they can."

I cupped my hands gently together as I watched the firefly flicker out into darkness. "And why do they have to die?" I whispered low enough that I wasn't sure she heard it.

Her lips smoothed into a thin line. "Because they gave all they had to show us their light. They must rest—as we all do."

I blink at the warm memory.

A crooked smile forms on my lips as I stare across the field. Their beauty only lasts moments before the insects find a new place to rest.

"You were wrong, Terra." My distant smile fades into a frown. "They die because they are fucking bugs."

39

Terra

The sun dips beneath the distant mountains as I mentally prepare to sneak into Za'Afiel. It was convenient that Elias revealed the doorway. Now we know exactly how to get there. It's not ideal that I had to wait this long to return, but I didn't have the chance given that Emerai noticed someone taking hearts and increased the guards. At least now it's calmed down enough that I don't think we'll face much trouble if we stick to the third floor.

I wish Edgar was coming with us since he knows that place pretty well, but we'll just have to take our chances alone. An ache throbs deep inside my chest for the lost kinship, but Raine's blight is more important at the moment.

I zip up my tactical vest and let my eyes linger on the bottom drawer of the wardrobe. The thrum of the two hearts still softly flutters inside, and my lips firm with guilt. I want to tell Arthur that I've found his heart—to hand it to him and see his face light up with hope. But Elias made it clear we can't speak of it until after the exam. Emerai is watching, listening everywhere.

Raine raises a brow at me as I shut my wardrobe.

"Having second thoughts?" he asks as he slowly moves up behind me, letting his hands glide smoothly over my waist. I shake my head and turn to face him. He grins at me and presses a soft kiss to my lips. "This has to be a match."

I want to believe that too—I desperately want to.

As we leave my room we bump into Ash passing my door.

"Where are you two headed?" he asks with a small raise of his brow. His silver hair is mussed with sleep and he looks just as reserved as he does daily. At least he's not filled with malice like Edgar is.

Raine looks at me with an expectant stare. *You're better with words than I am*, his eyes tell me with a flicker.

"Just to explore the south tower." I shove the note deep into my pocket and spare a quick glance down the hallway to make sure no one else is going to question us. The Nova House has been oddly quiet this evening. I wonder where everyone is.

Ash stares at me for a few moments before furrowing his brows. "I don't believe you."

Shit. I still can't tell if he's their little lapdog already or not. He's always with a professor or the headmaster—they like to keep Ash very close. If they consider him that precious, he must be special. The portal keeper. That gives me an unsettling thought: if he dies, do the portals close? That would almost certainly bring a huge advantage to Heirah.

I try to bury the disturbing idea of killing him just to find out.

Raine steps forward and backs Ash against the wall, bumping a few frames that tilt like they're about to fall. "What do you want, huh? Stay the fuck out of our business." Raine's voice is low and sharp.

Okay, so it looks like we are going straight for the rip cord then.

Ash keeps his face smooth and unfazed as he presses his palm against Raine's chest. "Now I'm *really* curious. What are you two hiding?"

I huff and level Raine with a disapproving look. He just flexes his jaw to let me know he doesn't care.

"Okay, listen." I tug on Raine's arm so he lets go of Ash and we can de-escalate this situation. "We're trying to find a way to break the blight curse," I say in a low whisper.

Ash's eyes widen and he considers me for a moment. His dark gray hair looks almost black in the hallway and he stands only a few inches taller than me. "There is no cure," he says firmly, but there's hope in his eyes. For his comrade Lucina, I'm sure.

I pull the note from my pocket and show him. "We found this in the library and think the handwriting belongs to Arthur. If he's the one that wrote it, I think he knows how to stop the blight."

Raine gives me a dirty look for giving our secret up so

easily, but I truly believe Ash can help us. He spent a lot of time at Za'Afiel too.

Ash looks over the note for a few moments, then looks back up to us, handing the piece of paper to me.

"Okay. Follow me," he mutters before turning and making his way down the stairs to the homeroom. Raine and I trail behind him.

Ash glances around the room swiftly as if he fears we're being watched and then draws a circle with his finger on the coffee table. A dark hole appears and I stare wildly at him.

"Is that—"

Ash cuts me off. "Go quickly. Only Terra—Arthur will sense Raine's blight if he goes with you. When you're ready to leave, just head to the gardens and you'll find a wall of greenery. Walk through it and you'll return here."

I don't want to go alone, but Raine's eyes are already so gray and I don't think he has much time left. I swallow hard and nod. "Okay, I'll be quick. Thank you, Ash." I hug him and he gives a surprised exhale. Raine grunts and rolls his eyes, but I kiss him on the cheek anyway.

"Be careful—I'll be waiting for you," Raine murmurs as he caresses the edge of my jaw. His black hair is side-swept with a few strands hanging over his forehead. I nod and slip into the dark hole before my anxiety and fear get the best of me.

It feels like falling slowly, suspended as if the air is thick like water. My feet land on solid ground after a few moments and the darkness lifts. I'm standing in the familiar long corridor with brilliant windows that allow the moonlight to illuminate the walls.

It's as silent as it was a few weeks ago. Not a soul stirs here.

I look to my right; the large ebony door is shut but moonlight shines dimly beneath the crack. This must be Arthur's study. Why else would Ash put the portal here? I send him a silent thanks as I reach for the handle and turn it. Darkness drifts from the study in wisps of dread around my feet.

But the scent that follows... I know this scent.

It's distinctive, old books and pages, long-burned candle wicks and pencil shavings. I'm certain I've been here before, even though I'm also sure I haven't.

I step through the doorway and stand in the center of the study. Arthur's long desk sits at the end of the room with a wall of books behind it. My feet guide me to the wall of tomes and I grab one from the shelf. Before I can crack it open, I turn, sensing I'm not alone.

On a single chair in the center of the room sits Arthur, leaned back casually with one leg over the other. His gray eyes are on mine, calm and observant.

The right side of his face is lit only by the moonlight, but I can see all those beautiful features all the same, his high cheekbones and angular jaw. He has a hand pressed up against his cheek in a bored fashion. His shoulder-length black hair blends into the darkness behind him effortlessly. My stomach sinks at the sight of his angelic features.

"Terra, might I help you find something?" he says with an almost eerie tone.

I lower the book to my side and stare at him. A shudder crawls up my spine. This feels like a trap; why was he waiting here like this? He watches me struggle to find any words and a slight smile spreads across his lips. My Shadow draws near to him, yearning to be close, but I want the opposite right now.

Arthur stands slowly. I almost forgot how tall he was. His slender figure is unfitting of the tactical gear he wears; he's fit for a crown and royal suits, not war clothing.

Of all the professors to catch me in their study, at least it's Arthur. If there's one I can trust, it's him. He lifts his hand and offers it to me, a silent request that I go to him. That calm, warm smile still lifts his lips.

I swallow hard but slowly walk toward him. Once I'm standing before him, he tilts his head a bit and chuckles softly.

"You act like a mouse caught stealing cheese," he says light-heartedly.

I look up at him with surprise and then back down to the book in my hands. "I'm hoping you can help me... and I'm sorry for breaking into your study," I apologize as I hand him the book. He looks down at it nostalgically and turns it in his hand to examine the back.

"You could've just asked. I'm not so scary, am I?" His smile grows and I find the same one spreading across my lips as well.

I reach into my pocket and pull out the note, opening it and handing it to him. "I really need to find the person who wrote this."

He takes the paper and reads it a few times, his eyes narrowing at the subject of the blight. "Terra, I know you want to help him—"

"I *have* to," I correct him and his eyes only soften more with pity, but he nods and takes a long breath.

"Well, I think I may know who wrote this. It wasn't me." He hands me back the note and sits on the edge of his desk, crossing his arms over his chest and looking out the window.

Arthur's eyes hold so much sorrow. Everything about him is imbued with it. Perhaps it's why I find his presence so comforting. I fight the urge in my chest to get closer to him—when we touch, everything else becomes blurry and it's only him I see.

"You know." His voice brings me back out of my thoughts. "Sometimes we try relentlessly to fight against the current, the waters cold and deadly, but often, it is for naught. We drown regardless." His eyes remain on the moonlit window.

I frown and step closer to him, reaching for his hand. His eyes flash to mine. For a moment I think he's going to pull away, but he doesn't.

"Raine will fight until he's gasping for breath, as will I," I mutter as I grab his hand and hold it, waiting for my Shadow to greet his as it always does. "Something tells me you're still fighting too. You've been struggling against this for a long time. Haven't you?"

His brows pinch together in a pained expression that says more than he ever could. Our Shadows mingle gently at our fingertips and I feel every sliver of that sadness. I stare into his eyes, trying to figure out what this feeling is. It's so starkly different compared to all the others. My Shadow has always been ravenous and hungry for Elias and Raine. But Arthur is different.

Our Shadows greet one another like lost lovers meeting after centuries spent apart. Their dance is soft and forlorn, so much so that I feel like weeping. Arthur raises his other hand and brushes it softly across my neck, sending a shudder through me.

"Yes, I have," he murmurs with a sad smile and pulls me closer, wrapping his arms around me. I instinctively do the same. His scent of burned candles and old pages is welcoming and tears fill my eyes for reasons I refuse to acknowledge.

"I don't understand our connection through the Shadows. Everything with you is familiar and lost all at once. Will you ever tell me who I am to you?" I ask in a hushed voice.

He remains quiet for a moment, breathing in my scent before pulling away and smiling at me. "Time and memory are old friends."

I quirk a brow, letting my body fall into his again. I close my eyes and try to focus on the warmth that exists between us. "It feels much more than that."

Arthur lets his dreary head fall to my shoulder as his hands wrap around me tightly. He holds me like he'll never let go.

"Perhaps it was."

40

Terra

Hearts are confusing things—Shadows more so, probably because I have no control over how mine guides me. I only know that I feel the emotions it stirs in me with raw conviction. Or is it my own heart? It's becoming too hard to differentiate.

"Can you tell me who wrote this? Please," I beg Arthur.

He gently pushes me back and stands, moving to place the book in the spot I pulled it from. Hundreds of tomes fill the bookshelves. He lingers there, so I approach him and watch in silence as he grabs another book. This one is older, near the top shelf.

The covers all look the same, the spines etched with

faint words here and there. It makes no organizational sense to me, but it does to Arthur, and I'm sure that's the point.

He takes his time flipping through the middle of the book and stops, pressing his forefinger to the left page.

"Here it is. I thought it sounded familiar. I think Kallos is the one who wrote that note," Arthur says under his breath as his eyes continue to scour the pages for information.

I bite my lower lip in frustration. "We already compared the handwriting to his and it wasn't a match."

Arthur glances up at me briefly, his gray eyes bright beneath the shadows of moonlight. "You might've grabbed someone else's notes from atop his desk. I'm positive it was Kallos." He closes the tome and sets it aside on his desk, perhaps for reevaluation once I leave.

"What makes you so sure?" I ask, hesitant to believe him on a whim even though he seems anything but a deceitful man.

He sits in the chair at his desk and catches me staring at him longingly. That warm and nostalgic feeling I get when we touch has an air of happiness and contentment around it that I know I will never experience with another. After our night together in his room, I've been reluctant to get too close to him. Everything feels too real and raw with Arthur.

A soft smile spreads across his lips and he opens his arms, offering for me to come to him. He pulls me in close and I tuck my head comfortably on his shoulder, fitting snugly in the crook of his neck. I know he has the same longing as I do. He wears the misery clearly on his sleeve.

"I'm sure because the person who wrote this note was desperate to save the one blighted." His voice is deep with memories, making my throat tighten with dread. "Elias blighted our comrades when he was still getting used to his Shadow. Some on purpose, most by accident. But a few of our friends were unfortunately among them, one of which Kallos was hellbent on saving. He's the only one who ever came close to finding a cure."

I don't need to ask if he saved them, I already know he didn't, but I ask anyway.

"They all died?"

Arthur brushes the pad of this thumb over my arm and leans his head on mine softly. "Yes, they all perished."

"What happens to the blighted when they die?" Another question I don't want to know the answer to, but my traitorous lips ask it regardless.

"First, they become lethargic. It's the initial sign that their time is ending. Second, an illness ravages their flesh, like radiation poisoning. Bleeding noses, eyes, gums. Then finally, they die from the pain of their suffering."

I lean over the armchair and dry heave. My stomach twists ferociously at the image of Raine enduring such a death. Arthur rubs my back soothingly.

"It's why we resort to killing them in the last throes of the first stage now. The suffering only hurts everyone in the end, the blighted, their friends, and the students overall," he says matter-of-factly. I know he's probably numb to it by now, but I'm not.

"That's disgusting," I snap and stand from the chair.

He remains seated and nods. "I do hope Kallos can

help you. He's someone you can trust." Arthur hands me the note and I take it, shoving it back in my pocket.

Amser is already rueful that I've separated from him, and the firm line his mouth is pressed in tells me he feels the same way.

I go to leave but turn once more to look at the beautiful man before me. "Arthur?"

"Yes, Terra?"

"Was Elias the only Nova in the beginning?" I don't know why I question it. I shouldn't, but I do. Elias wouldn't lie, would he?

Arthur's face hardens, his jaw tight and flexed. "Why would you ask me that?" he says as if I've cursed his name simply by asking.

"He knows Edgar's Shadow. And I think the rest of you do too, and that's only possible if there were other Novas in the past," I say steadily, watching his features soften as he exhales.

"He wasn't the only one. But he was the only surviving Nova after the first year. Let's leave the ghosts to rest, little shadow." He pauses before continuing: "There is one thing you should know before you go." He leans forward in his chair, face sobering into despair. "I could've mentioned it sooner but wasn't sure if it was time." His mouth twists like he's still deciding whether or not to say whatever secret lurks behind his lips.

My brows knit with worry. "What is it?"

When he speaks, his voice is strained, clearly taking no pleasure in saying the words. "Edgar crossed into his exam portal early. He and his friends tripped the reroute and have been sent to a place in Fernestia we call Noctili.

There, soldiers wait for the disloyal students and euthanize them on sight."

I'm too stunned to reply. My mouth opens a few times but words evade me.

Arthur's mouth firms and he shakes his head as he says, "You should tell Elias and go before it's too late."

My chest is hollow. I'm unsure how to feel about this. Edgar tried to kill me, but he's still my brother. "Why are you telling me this now?" I finally manage to ask.

Arthur stands and leads me through the hall. "He's a Nova," he says bluntly, and there's obviously another reason but he won't say. "Here, this door is faster than Ash's makeshift one." Arthur opens one of the doors near the end of the hallway. Darkness awaits inside it.

"You knew he was helping us?" My voice is muddled with stress.

Arthur just smiles and shoves me inside the doorway. The next second, I'm standing in Arthur's spare room in the Nova House.

I don't waste any time dwelling on Arthur's actions. The only thought traveling through my mind is that Edgar is in danger. I take the stairs two at a time until I'm standing before Elias's door.

The light beneath the door is on and I can hear papers shuffling. *Thank gods he's here.* I open the door and Elias turns to look at me from over his shoulder. His eyes are apathetic and instead of asking what I need, he only raises a brow.

"Edgar went to Noctili. *Please,* help me," I say between heavy breaths, adrenaline pulsing wildly through my veins.

His eyes widen at that and he turns to face me. His

white hair is slicked to the side but a few strands fall over his forehead. "Where did you hear that name?"

"Elias, we need to—"

He stands briskly, shouting, "*Where*, Terra?"

My skin pebbles with goosebumps at his enraged tone. My Shadow distorts anxiously inside my chest.

"Arthur," I say quietly.

Elias's eyes narrow at me before his jaw tightens and he shakes his head and curses. "I won't go there."

A knot forms in my throat. It's becoming increasingly difficult to swallow. "He'll die," I beg.

Elias gives me a cold, uninterested look. "I don't care."

My bottom lip quivers without my permission. "I'll save him myself then," I shout back at him and turn hard on my heels, sprinting down the stairs.

"Terra, don't fucking go there," Elias growls after me but I don't stop until I'm in the homeroom, Raine and Ash blinking up at me with shocked expressions.

Elias catches up to me and sets a heavy hand on my shoulder. "I'll go," my assassin says with trepidation, though his eyes are heavy and distant.

Raine's eyes flare. "Go where? What happened, Terra? Are you okay?" He approaches, ignoring Elias and inspecting my body for any harm.

"We need to hurry. I'll tell you on the way," I say quickly.

Ash stays at the Nova House while the three of us make our way out, Elias leading the way. Finn and Kai are walking across the bridge toward us—I told them to meet in the Nova House after midnight so I could tell them if the notes matched or not.

"What's going on?" Finn's amber eyes shift to Elias distrustfully, then back to me with concern. My lower lip will bruise at this rate from my anxious biting.

"Edgar's in trouble," Raine mutters on my behalf and I blink my appreciation at him. Elias doesn't stop walking so we hurry to catch up, Finn and Kai in tow now too.

Kai looks at Finn with horror as he mumbles, "You don't think he and Corvus went through that basement portal do you?"

Finn's face pales and we all fall silent with dread.

41

Edgar

The fields carry on for miles in every direction. After a few minutes, a warm glow illuminates the sky from beneath a canopy of trees. Not a glow from the fireflies. No, this light is man-made.

Fire.

"There, that's where I heard her scream." Rowan's throat bobs as he swallows his guilt for fleeing. Fear rises in his eyes once more and I wonder if he'll flee again.

I place my hand on his shoulder. "Let's get closer. We need to be quiet and stealthy. Use your Shadow if you have to, okay?" I calmly instruct him. Rowan nods and clenches his trembling hands.

Tents and fires spread throughout the valley below. My nerves are welling within me but I push them down. I can't let myself feel anxious right now. We have to ensure Lucina's safety and we need to keep level heads. Feelings only make us lose control—I learned that much from the blight classes. Fear, anger, hate. I cannot allow myself to feel those while fighting, or I'll blight all my friends.

We sneak down to the camp, keeping low in the ears of barley. The bushes rustle just a few yards ahead of us. I raise my hand to signal Rowan to stop. Silently, I narrow my eyes against the dim light. I can just make out the tips of four heads. I catch the glare of a pair of glasses and the glint of blonde hair.

"Oh, thank gods." I breathe a sigh of relief. Rowan eagerly creeps ahead. At least we're all back together now.

As we approach, our friends hear us and turn around. Their eyes are wide with fear and readiness to fight.

I quickly whisper, "*It's us.*" A few release their held breaths and they move forward to meet us. Tamaris, Alani, Vinnie, Aervin. Lucina is the only one that may have been captured. We can save her—we *have* to.

Aervin lets the tension in his shoulders ease. "What the hell happened?" They all stare at me expectantly as if I know the answers. I should know... I'm the one that sent them here so carelessly.

"I don't know. I didn't think portals could transport us to separate locations. Unless this was intentional..." I trail off. Could this have been a trap? I'm certain that this is the portal selected for the exams. So why... Shame rises up inside my chest. I should've listened to Kai and Finn.

"How will we return to Alkrose?" Tamaris growls. Her long black ponytail rests over her shoulder. She has a good point.

I clench my teeth together tightly. "I don't know."

"Excuse me—*what*?" Vinnie snaps. His usual collected composure has fractured.

I shake my head and desperately look to Aervin for help. He only returns my panicked gaze and lowers his head. "I don't know either," Aervin admits.

Alani covers her mouth as if to keep in her breakfast. Rowan shares the same horrified expression.

The pit sinks deeper inside my chest. "We're going to be okay. After we find Lucina, we'll locate the portal home." I force myself to say the words with unequivocal surety.

I'm about to say more when a scream fills the air. Lucina's scream.

Her voice is imbued with pain. The sound of it makes my blood thicken with despair.

"We need to move, *now*."

We hastily make a shabby plan, one that I'm not sure will work, but we have no other choice. It's already been far longer than I expected us to stay in Fernestia and nothing has gone as expected. Now my only goal is to save Lucina and get all of us back to the castle.

We split up.

Aervin is to retrieve Lucina and get her out. The rest of us will fight.

I have the task of taking out most of the Darkflies since my powers are the strongest. Even with the casts, the darkness I wield is powerful. The others are to serve as support and decoys.

This will work. It *has* to.

I rise straight up from our hiding spot in the brush. I

manipulate the darkness I've stored and create projections of black serpents that slither through the grass stalks. I can control around ten at a time, and that will have to do. The tents in the camp are ten feet apart and figures become visible as I near them. Many soldiers, men and women, sit close to the flames and drink what must be mead. The air swarms with the bitter scent of it. I take a deep breath and shout, "Hey!"

The air stills around me and in the corners of my eyes, I see my comrades tensing in their hiding positions.

The enemy soldiers whirl and reach for their weapons in a heartbeat. Some charge straight for me with no guns or knives at all and I know instantly that they are the most lethal—the ones with powerful Shadows. The Darkflies start to raise their hands up, the grim sky booming with licks of lightning as rain starts to pelt down on us. Dark magic pulses from each of them, plumes of smoky ebony dust.

Darkness is falling—it's descending around me like blood spreading in water, clouding around me and starving for my blood.

One of them shouts, breaking the sworn silence from both sides. "Kill them all!"

My teeth burn hot at the soldier's words. Sully twists inside my chest, desperately trying to break the casts placed on it to no avail. It pushes inside my skull. Its indistinguishable whispers are eerie. My arm hairs rise with goosebumps and I close my eyes, raising my deadly fingers into the air. It feels as though I'm about to play a song of death on the clouds themselves. When my eyes reopen, darkness swells in the space before me.

"I'm going to eradicate all of you," I mutter, my lips twitching into a crooked smile.

Threads of my rage manifest from the black mist around me. Gasps spread through the enemy troops and power explodes from them as they try to hit me first. The cloud of black surrounding me disperses as I close my fists and pull them to my chest, absorbing their Shadows in the blink of an eye. The field clears and their horrified faces are all that remain.

Their efforts are in vain.

My heart fills with wrath, a hate so dreadful and deep that I can hardly grasp my emotions. A wicked smile stretches across my face as I refocus my attacks and blood begins to spray. A song of destruction that I've been desperately waiting to hear for far too long is finally thrumming through my ears.

A female soldier casts her Shadow out toward me. It shapes into a fierce wolf creature, its face is a shroud of black—unlike Arthur's, which bears a skull—and it tears through the wheat field at an impressive speed. I'm quicker though.

I wave my hand over the wolf a mere inch from my face and the Shadow beast implodes into dust. Sully lashes out closer to the surface beneath my skin, cracking through a few of the power casts, and sends a surge of lethal smoke to surround the female soldier with black, shifting sand. Her screams are short-lived as her bones shatter inside the cocoon of my power. Her blood mixes with the rain that drums down from the sky. I extend my hand and let the liquid pool in my palm.

Vinnie and Rowan are in the thick of battle to my left.

They let loose a display of impressive techniques, fending off a few soldiers but remaining tight in battle with them. I search for Alani and Tamaris. They are cutting down soldiers on their end as well. Triumph floods me. These Fernestians are weak. I expected much more from them.

I knew we were ready for this. This changes everything. Hope and adrenaline fill my chest. Sully tears at the casts savagely inside me, completely breaking two and leaving two in place. I roll my shoulders back and crack my neck with the surplus of dread and power that my Shadow feeds through my bones.

I obliterate a few more soldiers as I proceed toward the camp—their blood sprays across the wheat like burst paint cans.

I thought killing would be difficult, but I don't feel anything.

Not a fucking thing.

A second wave of Fernestian soldiers spills from the tents farther back. These ones look different. Their tactical gear is gray, unlike the black of the ones we've just slaughtered. One of them in particular is especially menacing. His body is at least double the size of mine. His ebony helmet is spiked down the center. He holds a large crescent sword of fire with two hands. He's like a mythical god of war.

I narrow my eyes on this soldier. He must be the commander. His flames grow hotter with each step he takes, transitioning from red to blue. He's the image of brutality.

I can handle him. I can do this.

A smaller Darkfly steps from behind the ominous

knight. He's dressed in a simple dark brown leather coat and pants—clearly not suited for war. He stares at me briefly with the eyes of a goat. His appearance sends shivers up my spine. The small soldier looks away and speaks to the large one—no doubt giving him information that perhaps only his odd eyes can learn about me.

I flex my fingers. My only choice is to attack before they do. The commander lifts his head toward me as if newfound knowledge had been bestowed on him.

Clashing Shadows and weapons sound from behind me, gunfire and screams too. I'm keenly aware of everything around us. I raise my arm into the air and let it fall straight forward—aiming at the commander. Power licks at my fingertips as my black sand frenzies out with wicked speed. I dare lift the corner of my lips. No one can avoid such an attack.

The commander swings his blade and blocks my attack like it's nothing more than an insect to be swatted. The black magic counters and lands just a few feet in front of Alani and Tamaris, exploding upon impact and throwing my female comrades back.

"No!" I shout.

I flash my eyes back at the commander and try to hit him with a close-range attack. His hand cuts straight through it and grabs hold of my jaw. He cackles as his fingers dig into my face and he throws me with irrefutable force, tearing the flesh clean off my jaw. My body tumbles and rolls. My forearms snap as I attempt to keep them up.

Tamaris and Alani scream once more as the commander trudges toward them.

I struggle to my feet, blood spilling down my throat.

But before I can run over to them, the commander brings his blade down with a force I cannot escape. My eyes widen with horror as his dark helmet reflects the image of him slashing my feeble body. He's so close that I can hear the hiss of his breath as he straightens and tries to pull his blade from my body. He tugs over and over, shaking my limp, broken body like a rag until the sharp hook of the crescent blade unlatches from my bones. Black fire burns my face, chest, and arm.

My chest is burning. I'm on fire.

My breaths shorten and I let out a sharp cry. Blood gushes from my chest and soaks my tactical gear. Cold spreads where the liquid cools on me. My throat itches something awful, like ants are eating me from the inside out. I try to lift my head to see where the commander is. How did he move so fast?

Dying... Am I dying? My mind races and fear is all know. I trace the commander with my eyes as he heads toward my comrades.

"No... No!" I cry out desperately, the gurgling of my blood drowning out the words.

"Edgar!" Vinnie shouts, his eyes flashing with horror. He and Rowan charge toward the commander, unaware of his power. They won't be able to handle his strength. They need to run away. They have to get away.

"R-run," I choke out, but it's so quiet it doesn't reach them.

This is my fault. I don't want to watch. Please. I can't force myself to look away no matter how much I try. Darkness creeps in the corners of my vision.

A sharp cut slices through every other sound in the

night. The crackling fire, the rain, the gunshots, and screams—it all ends with a disturbing gurgle bubbling from my comrade's throats.

It stops all of my thoughts. All my dreams.

Everything.

My eyes meet Vinnie's, then Rowan's. The commander's flaming crescent sword hit them both at once. Their blood sprays into the night air like the wings of fireflies—they seem to glow with the heat from the Darkfly's fire.

I watch their lights flicker out. Their short lives spent.

I tremble as my veins start to chill. Cold seeps in and I can't tell if it's from death reaching for me or parts of my soul being ripped to shreds.

Vinnie's glasses project off his face and land against my forehead, the glass already shattered. Shards pierce my eye but I don't feel the pain. I just blink through the blood, unable to stop watching.

Half. They were cut in half. My friends are, they're—

I watch the two of them fall soundlessly, their innards tumbling out and surrounding their vacant bodies. Steam rolls off from their centers and I gag. Vinnie's eyes are bulged and wide, cheeks smeared with dirt and debris. Rowan's eyes are narrowed, twitching and distant as his lips mumble something before going still.

My stomach curls but vomit won't rise. Then I hear a wrenching scream from Alani. She's fallen to her knees at what became of Vinnie and Rowan. Her body shakes with terror and Tamaris stands in front of her in a sad attempt to protect her from the approaching commander. He stalks slowly toward them, lazily even, as if this is all so meaningless to him.

How many times have Alani and Tamaris fought with each other? How many times had they sworn hate for one another? Yet here Tamaris is protecting Alani. Selflessly. Foolishly.

I take another short, wheezy breath, my lungs losing their strength to take in air. I want to close my eyes. Desperately wish to look away to save myself from witnessing it. But I can't.

Tamaris lets her Shadow whirl around the two of them in an attempt to escape, but the commander cuts through it easily, his flames burning nearly white.

Tamaris holds strong, still standing above Alani as if she can actually do anything against the fucking monster. Her gaze flicks to mine in her last moments.

I see fear in its rawest form. I see the grief that she feels already from all the death that's come tonight. But more than that, I see the question in her eyes: *Why*? Why did we come here? The look of betrayal burns into my soul.

Why did *I* bring them here?

My heart twists and cracks. I want to fucking scream and scream until I cannot bear it any longer.

Tamaris closes her eyes and Alani braces against her leg. The commander brings down his blade with a single swing of Shadow hellfire. He strikes it straight through Tamaris's heart, piercing all the way through her torso and Alani's neck behind her.

There is no crying—no pain or blood.

Their bodies ignite into abnormal black flames, evaporating all but their bones in a matter of seconds. Their skeletons hold the positions they were in just moments ago.

Their jaws open in the silent wails they weren't able to let out.

Tears spill from my eyes. The pain inside me cannot be described. It's vicious and rotting.

I've lost everything. *Everything.* In a matter of moments. And the worst part is that it's all my fault.

It's my fault my friends are dead.

Pain crackles across my eyes, forcing them shut. I let out an anguished wail. Not for my own agony, the bleeding of my heart and soul, but for my mistakes that others paid for in blood.

Footsteps crunch on the gravel near my head and I know the commander has returned to finish me off. My eyes open enough to see a large boot crush Vinnie's glasses.

Four fireflies take to the sky from the barley around the boot, drawing in my weakening consciousness.

Fireflies. We were fireflies. Terra's words soak into my soul. *"Because they gave all they had to show us their light. They must rest—as we all do."*

I cry and the taste of death blooms across my tongue.

You were right, Terra.

42

Elias

I fucking hate Noctili.

Velis crawls up my spine and I have to enforce my inner shields for the turmoil we're about to face. There are too many memories there for me to handle on my own and I simply can't afford to shut myself off. Velis is too destructive and probably won't spare Edgar's friends, if they're even still alive.

My skin is damp with sweat and I look down at Terra to ensure she doesn't notice my distress. Her eyes are watery and focused solely on the portal.

Does Edgar really mean that much to her? Even after he tried to kill her?

An Ekko student stands at the entrance of the portal,

looking at us with a bewildered expression. Corvus, I think. Finn and Kai walk ahead of us to confront him, whisper-shouting about Edgar. It's too muffled for me to make out.

Terra's fingers fidget as her nerves get the better of her.

I lean down so my lips coast the edge of her ear. "Maybe you should stay here. I'm not sure what we'll find on the other side." Raine, for once, nods in agreement with me. He looks ready to accept the worst. At least I feel comfortable bringing him with me after our one-on-one lessons. As much as I hate to admit it, he's a fucking tank.

She raises her eyes and meets my gaze. "No. I'm going."

I reluctantly shrug. "Fine."

Finn looks back at us. "We need to hurry. They've been gone for a few hours already." Terra deflates, her shoulders trembling. Raine consoles her and I stiffen my jaw to prepare for the bloodbath ahead.

I approach the portal and raise my hand to it, resetting the alternate path so we don't all get separated. Stupid fucking kids—they have no idea what they sentenced themselves to.

"All right, we'd better be quick about this," I say through gritted teeth. "Ten minutes, that's all we get before the headmaster will notice my Shadow's absence from Alkrose. Leave the fighting to me, the rest of you get everyone who's still alive out. Got it? Ten. Minutes." I make my voice stern and they all nod uneasily. "Then let's go."

I enter first.

Fernestia brings a deep chill into my bones and unsettles my stomach. I don't think there will ever be a day that this place doesn't haunt me in some way.

I give Terra a concerned glance to assess her state of mind; she's expressionless. I sigh and look ahead. Darkness shrouds the sky and small pockets of clouds gather ominously in the distance—orange light warms the bottom of them.

The air is thick with blood. Velis hums inside my veins, starved for the metallic sting of death.

"What the fuck is that smell?" Kai pinches his nose and squints as if the smell is burning his eyes.

"Probably Darkflies and Edgar's comrades," I say with no regard. Finn's and Kai's faces grow pale. Terra swallows hard. Raine stares at me with a knowing look. He knows the scent of carnage just as well as I do. I respect that.

I give Raine a look and he picks up on my intentions immediately.

"You guys are with me. Let's get anyone we can out. Ten minutes," he says resolutely.

We race through fields of gold in silence. They're well-versed in stealth thanks to all the classes. I'm impressed they can keep their heads in moments like this. I focus my eyes on the crest of the field ahead where a warm light invades the darkness—clashes of Shadows, guns, and metal echo through the sky.

I flick one last look at the group of students before I sprint far ahead of them. I tear through the field and leave them to find survivors as I enter the camp solely to kill off any attackers. The tents are empty and blood is sprayed everywhere.

Novas are rare. So even if Emerai and Empress Raven

catch wind of what I do here, I'll have a solid explanation, I tell myself as I scour the area for movement.

My heart thumps inside my chest. The sight of blood instills me with excitement—Velis itches up along my spine. A blinding light bolts down from the sky and I dart in that direction.

My legs halt, muscles still quivering with adrenaline as I find what I'm searching for.

Edgar.

His body is gravely damaged.

Shit. I clench my teeth. I don't care about him, but he means something to Terra. And *that* means something to me.

I study his body to calculate the damage. A slash from his neck to his navel curls and sinks at least two inches into his core. Blood and singed black tissue have sealed some wounds as swiftly as they were inflicted. His guts are spilled beside him and steam rolls off them, curling into the chilled night air.

Edgar's face has been half torn away from below his nose down, stripped of all flesh. His teeth are bare. I observe carefully until I see a faint breath pull at his chest.

All reason tells me there's no fucking way he's still alive. But he is, and I find that more tragic.

I turn to look for the rest of them and my gaze lands on Edgar's fallen comrades. Something odd pulls inside my chest. It reminds me painfully of my own comrades who died just as terribly.

These students are maybe a year older than Edgar, and yet they fought so bravely. Their bodies lie still in the dim light. I don't need to approach them to find out if they are dead. Two are cut cleanly in half, while the others... They are mere skeletons, dark, burned flesh still clinging to the bones.

The crisping sounds of burning flesh and bubbling blood ceases as I shut them out. I let Velis take more control before my emotions break loose. Then I let my gaze fall on the shoulders of the monster responsible for this.

A commander dressed head to toe in tactical gear stands steadily by the skeletons. His small army of soldiers behind him. His black mask is shrouded in crimson blood and he wields a crescent sword of black fire borne from his Shadow. He is undoubtedly the commander of Noctili. He lets out a loud, crass laugh that echoes from beneath his mask.

I keep my face expressionless.

I'll end this before Terra sees what I'm going to do to him. I won't be kind, because although I don't like Edgar, I despise watching helpless students fighting for one another and dying like they never mattered.

The commander stalks forward and swings his blade in an obtrusive slash, creating a wall of bright white fire around him. The light shines through his mask, revealing his gray eyes.

When I don't move, the commander stops, perhaps not seeing me worthy of his flames. He tilts his head to the side and waves for his spare soldiers to take me on instead.

I crack a smile. I was hoping for as much—Velis is fucking starving.

I walk toward the first line of unfortunate soldiers.

They raise their arms to strike me but they're so slow. I step between them and tap their foreheads with just my fingertips, one on each side of me, not once breaking eye contact with the commander behind them. The soldiers' heads tilt back, stunned for a moment, before their blood ejects from the back of their skulls like bullets piercing straight through their brains. Their blood coats their fellow comrades, who abandon their magic and pull up their guns, carelessly opening fire at me.

I shudder as Velis slips from my body and creates a wall of shadow, absorbing their bullets. Velis lets out an angry growl that reverberates through the air and the soldiers gasp in horror. I let out a cackling laugh at their fear and think of a fitting end for them. Smiling, I raise my hand and pull down. Thumps sound in unison and their eyes roll to the backs of their skulls. Each falls limply, their spines torn clean from their vessels and stuck in the ground like poles.

A satisfying grin spreads across my lips.

Oh, how I've missed this.

The second wave is more hesitant and keeps a wider circle around me. I crack a knuckle on each hand, throwing my head back as if a tender ballad is playing. And it is. The crunching and slurping of their corpses sing a melody that shudders straight through me.

When my eyes open, the soldiers are nothing but nerves leading out from spinal cords. I once saw a similar display in a museum as a child. Dr. Cein took me to inspire my imagination.

Am I the artist he hoped for? Something wicked inside me hopes he'll see this display and be proud.

I release them, letting the nerves shrivel to the bodies below.

I smirk as I walk toward the commander, who's now trembling, his eyes wide with fear. His flame sword dwindles at his side.

"E-Elias? No, this was a misunderstanding, please—" the commander shrieks as he stumbles backward.

My smile widens. I love it when the Darkflies realize who I am. That look that flickers over their eyes is satisfying to watch. They are fully at my mercy and mine alone. I walk slowly until I'm standing directly in front of him. His sword has all but withered out.

He doesn't budge. At least he didn't run away screaming. There's something a bit respectable to be said about that. To face death so boldly.

"Goodbye, commander of nothing," I say bluntly. My smile lowers as my eyes widen with hunger for blood and vengeance. For the recreation of an awful memory.

I press my hand on his armor and nudge the commander backward. He falls so slowly. As he falls, his blood rises into the sky from his mouth and eyes. He screams for the tender bite of death that I withhold.

Until I finally flick my hand up and break each joint in his body apart. Each connection of his vertebrae along his spine and the deep sockets of his hips. The pops crackle in my ears, bringing a satisfied smile back to my lips.

The commander hits the ground in pieces. The entrails steam in coils along the remnants of his torso.

I stretch my arms out and sigh.

I should've limbered up first. I think I pulled something.

I walk back to Edgar and kneel at his side. Small, short breaths still rise from his lips.

Footsteps splash through the puddles of blood I've created and stop above me.

"For all that is fucking holy," Kai mutters with a breathless gasp.

43

Terra

For a moment, we all stand paralyzed by what Elias made of the Darkflies. I've never witnessed such gore and complete disrespect for life. It's harrowing and triggering, bringing me back to the night he killed the soldiers in the field. But before I can fall into ruin, I see my brother lying on the ground.

My hands shake violently above Edgar's torn body. His chest and face are completely ruined. His organs, beneath the thin layer of charred skin, flutter weakly, moving the tissue with each pulse of blood his heart can manage.

Tears stream from my eyes, dripping onto Edgar's pale face. He's unconscious, thank gods. I can only pray he didn't witness his friends being torn to pieces. My stomach curls; my intuition tells me he probably did.

None of what's happening to us is fair or just, so why would that change now?

"It's okay, Edgar." I bite my bottom lip.

I'm not entirely sure how long ago this wound was inflicted, but I try to heal it, stretching my trembling hands over his chest and closing my eyes. I'm able to reverse time on wounds, but I can only go so far back. My skill is improving with training, but it's still not perfect. I clench my fists and force myself to look back at his body.

Elias's bloodied hands clasp around mine. I flinch at the cold wetness of them but meet his gaze. "I don't think —" He cuts himself off and shakes his head. His gray eyes glimmer in the dark with remorse.

"I have to try," I say with less determination than I was going for.

I let my hands fall to Edgar's gaping chest, calling upon Amser. The Shadow's energy swells around my brother's chest. I seal his entrails back inside, but only with a thin wall of flesh. My Shadow whispers, *Any more is beyond our ability. He's been down for too long.*

Elias leans by my side and firms his mouth. Then he mutters, "Eight minutes. Time to go." Raine bends down and helps him lift Edgar's limp body, dripping blood as they return to the portal.

Finn and Kai approach with two survivors: Lucina and Aervin. I can't find the will to be happy about it, but a weight does lift a bit.

None of us speak as we cross the bloodied field of carcasses. We don't speak when Corvus berates us with questions and panic as we cross back to Alkrose. We just continue steadily toward the infirmary with heavy heads and somber hearts.

I stumble into the corridor leading to the infirmary behind Raine and Elias as they deliver Edgar to the medical personnel. My vision is blurry and Finn's hushed, comforting words don't quite reach me.

"Huh?" I say, looking up at Finn's sunken eyes.

He slows down, holding my hand softly so I stay behind with him while the others trudge into the infirmary. Aervin and Lucina were hurt, but they're not anywhere near death. I'm sure Elias is going to question them after he gets Edgar sorted. My thoughts are scattered and all I keep coming back to is the awful image of Edgar's disfigured face.

"Terra... I don't know what to say." Finn brushes dirt from my cheek. The worry in his eyes matches his voice. "You should get some rest. I can take you back to your room." He gently guides me down the hall but I stop with both feet firmly planted.

Finn stares at me, looking defeated and tired, but despite that, he pulls me into a tight, gentle embrace. His cloak smells of blood and fire, but his pine scent still lingers somewhere beneath.

My lower lip trembles as I mutter into his chest, "Finn, I can't lose him too. I've already lost everything else."

He grips me tighter and rests his head on mine. "He's

going to be okay," he says in a tight, uncertain tone. "It's going to be okay."

I pull away from him and look up at his somber face. His eyes are sad and weary, but his amber light hasn't faded too much into the horrible gray. There's hurt in his gaze and guilt tugs at my heart.

"I haven't lost everything... I still have you," I whisper as tears brim in my eyes.

His breath deepens and a weak smile spreads across his lips. "That's one thing that will never change. I'll always be by your side, Terra. I'll catch you a thousand times if I have to."

We sit on the floor of the hallway with our backs pressed to the wall. Medical personnel move in and out of the infirmary, sparing us timid looks here and there. It's hard to say when our friends will be out. Raine and Elias have yet to emerge and the night is already waning into dawn.

My eyes burn with sleep deprivation. I lower my heavy head to Finn's shoulder and he holds my hand, his Shadow circling mine warmly beneath his palm. I long to stay with him like this for a while.

"Terra."

"Hm?"

"I wish I would've left with you that day. I regret so many things in my life, but none as much as that day. I should've taken your hand and ran blindly into the unknown. Love would've been all we needed." Finn's voice cracks.

Words evade me, and I'm not sure there are any that

would suffice for the topic. So I settle on squeezing his hand tighter and leaning into him more.

The sun is rising above the mountain tops by the time Raine steps out of the infirmary.

Dark purple rings color the skin beneath his eyes. He looks at us in silence, his eyes landing on Finn's sleeping hand clutching mine.

Raine offers me his hand, his once royal-blue eyes now a dark gray-blue. I slowly untangle my arm from Finn's and take Raine's hand. We walk down the hall silently. I only glance back to see if Finn is still sleeping. His head is leaned forward, arms resting in his lap. Alone, he looks like a grieving man who's fallen asleep against a gravestone.

Once around the corner, Raine stops and looks at me like he has terrible news. I ready myself to hear the words that Edgar has passed.

"He's going to live," Raine mutters and pauses. The dread only grows as I wait for him to say more. "But his face... and his friends—" He cuts himself off and shakes his head slowly, not meeting my gaze.

I saw his face before he went in there... It looked like he was wearing a half-skull mask, his teeth bare and skin torn at the edges. *So* much blood. I swallow and nod slowly. "I know. How many of his friends died?" This is going to ruin Edgar.

"Tamaris, Alani, Rowan, and Vinnie. Four in total," Raine says in a hushed tone.

My stomach curls. All faces that I've grown used to seeing in the Nova House over the past few months. "He's already so lost in the darkness... This is going to destroy him."

Raine firms his lower lip and looks away, unable to meet my gaze.

"We should get some rest. The second exam is only a week away and we'll need all our strength," Raine says as he combs a hand gently through my tangled hair.

I shake my head. "I'm going to see Edgar first. You head back. We can start training after we sleep."

He seems hesitant but dips his head before pressing a kiss to my forehead and leaving. I make my way back to Finn and lean down, threading my fingers through his soft black hair and brushing it to the side. His amber eyes slowly open as if he was having a nice dream. I'm jealous of the small reprieve he's had.

"Did someone come out?" he says in a groggy voice, rubbing the dreariness from his eyes.

"Yeah, Raine did. I'm going to head in and see Edgar now." I don't want to ask him to join me, but I'd be lying if I said I wasn't hoping he'd come anyway.

Finn stands, pressing his back against the wall to slide up. "Let's head in then." His fingers find mine and he gives me a weary, reassuring smile that bleeds into me.

"Thank you, Finn."

He squeezes my hand and we walk through the infirmary doors.

Only three beds are filled: Edgar, Lucina, and Aervin.

Lucina and Aervin have smaller wounds, not life-threatening, but they're bandaged nonetheless. They're sleeping heavily, I suspect with the help of a potion.

Elias stands at the foot of Edgar's bed and glances up at us as we approach. He doesn't look bothered one bit, though his emotions have always been hard to read. His black tactical gear is drowned in red and his skin is sticky with blood. "If you look at him, you're going to be upset," Elias says without sparing us a glance.

I grip Finn's hand and step forward anyway.

Edgar's sheets are smeared with mud and blood. His arms are hooked up to tubes and bags of liquid. My throat is tight as I stare down at his fleshless jaw.

"Why won't it heal?" I ask as metallic flavors bloom across my tongue. Shadows usually heal non-mortal wounds quickly.

Elias's eyes drift up to me and Finn, resting on where our hands are clasped. "The black fire that Darkfly wielded was laced with his Shadow's ability to stave off healing. We can recover from daggers and wounds from other Shadows, but wounds that are embedded with malice are different. A sort of poison for other Shadow vessels. Haven't you been paying attention in Nekane's class?"

I don't respond—I only stare at my brother with a pit in my chest.

Edgar's dark brown lashes are pressed tightly to his cheeks, fluttering with dreams.

I hope they are good ones. When he wakes up, I'm not sure what will be left of his heart.

44

Edgar

A cold breeze sweeps across my skin, beckoning my eyes to open. It's blurry at first, but I recognize the stones above me as the ones in the infirmary. How did I get here? My mind takes a few minutes to catch up and once it does I sit up abruptly, wincing at the pain in my abdomen as I look to either side of me.

I'm alone and it's dark.

I glance down at my hands, eyes widening as the gap in my memory fills in.

My left hand is wrapped in bandages, but it appears thinner than the other. What happened back at the portal? I look to the other beds but I'm the only one here. My chest sinks.

The others didn't make it.

My knees curl up to my chest and I wrap my arms around them tightly. This isn't real. It can't be. It's not true.

We never should have entered the basement portal. I fist my hair tightly, pulling the strands violently between my fingers. Hot tears stream from my eyes and burn my cheeks until the sensation vanishes just below my cheekbones.

I flinch. *What?*

I loosen my grip on my hair and let my fingers glide down my face. Now that I think about it, I can't feel anything past my cheekbones.

Am I numb? No—that isn't it.

My eyes widen further as my fingertips trace the hard, bony surface where my lips are supposed to be. No longer are they soft and fleshy. I spread my hands over the front of my face and a strangled sound escapes from my throat as I realize my entire jaw and upper row of teeth are nothing but cold bone.

I freeze and hesitate, letting my eyes fall back to my left hand.

"No," I murmur in a pained, ghastly voice that's not my own. I don't recognize anything about myself anymore. I stay focused on my hand, knowing what I'll find beneath the gauze and bandages.

I work the wrapping off and raise my hand to the dim moonlight.

Bone, dry underlying muscles, and tendons. A shudder runs through me, deep and rotten. A lump swells in my throat and I toss the blanket from my legs and inspect the rest of my body.

My legs are unscathed but my entire chest is wrapped, dry blood staining the fabric.

"This must be punishment. I'm the reason they're dead." I try speaking again and wince at the sound of my new voice. It's raspy and eerie, just like Sully's voice—like a Shadow's.

I glance at my hand once more, closing and opening it. The fleshless arm still moves like normal. How is beyond me, but I can't find the strength to think about my own circumstances while the deaths of my friends are still so raw.

A creaking sound wails through the infirmary and someone stalks across the stone floors. I glance over to my side reluctantly, not wishing for anyone to see me this way.

I meet Terra's sullen eyes.

My expression softens. The last memory I have is of her kneeling by my side on Fernestian soil. She saved my life. She came to find me even after everything I've done to her.

"Edgar, you're finally awake." Her voice quivers. "I'm so sorry." She wraps her arms around me and cries into my shoulder. I'm stunned for a moment because we left off on such bad terms. Tears pool in my eyes once more and I embrace her.

"Don't be sorry. Thank you for coming for me." I try to make my voice less eerie, to no avail. Terra flinches and pulls away to look at my face. It takes everything inside of me to not turn and hide. I know what she must think of me.

I'm a monster. Inside and out.

Her hands press against my cheek and she smiles weakly.

I'm shocked by her reaction, but then again, perhaps she's seen my face many times already. I have no idea how much time has passed. "I'm so happy you can speak. I was so worried that you wouldn't be able to," she admits. A small breath of relief slips past her lips and I can't help but wonder if I will ever smile again. If I will ever feel a sigh of relief escape my lips. I'm not sure what expression I can even wear anymore. I only have my eyes left. What do they reveal? I wonder.

"Did any of us survive—" I pause and clarify, "Besides me?"

Terra's eyes warm only a fraction. "Yes. Aervin and Lucina are safe. They've been visiting you for the last few days."

If I could gasp, I would. But only a grunt escapes my throat. "Thank gods."

She nods and knits her brows. "We weren't able to bring the others back... Elias wouldn't let us return for their bodies."

I stare at the floor and nod absently. It makes sense that they couldn't, and from what I recall happening to them, there isn't anything worth returning for.

Rowan's fearful eyes swim in my memories and I clench my teeth. Without flesh to muffle it, the bone-clacking sound is chilling.

"It's my fault they're dead." The guilt burns inside my chest, so painful and hot. It churns like a knife. Sully seems to thrive in the madness inside me.

Terra frowns, looking as if she's contemplating something. She grabs my hand softly. "Elias didn't want me to tell you this... but you can turn it off, Edgar."

I stare at her dully, raising my brow just a bit.

"You can turn off your pain, the emotions that are eating away at you... It's what I had to do to survive for a while. You can too, should you need it." She presses a kiss on what's left of my cheek and walks toward the door. "The second exam is in a few days. I think they expect you to participate in some way, but if I don't see you before it starts—good luck."

"Thanks, Terra. You too," I say grimly, only thinking of what she said.

Corvus stops by early the next morning. I couldn't sleep at all. Each time I closed my eyes, I was visited by my deceased friends, begging me to save them and bring them back. I woke in a cold sweat.

Corvus can't bring himself to look at me. He's the first person to treat me like a monster. He stands sideways, looking at the foot of my bed rather than anywhere in my general direction.

The act wounds my already defeated heart. I actually considered him a friend.

He only came to say one thing to me—something that carves a gaping hole in my soul. "You were supposed to protect them. I never would have agreed if I knew you couldn't," Corvus says, the words empty of emotion. I think it would hurt less if he was angry, but he says it just to salt my wounds. And then he leaves.

And it festers.

My bones wrench and twist as I fist my hand tightly on my lap.

I thought I could.

45

Elias

Terra's been quiet since we brought Edgar back.

It bothers me, like a needle pressing into your skin over and over. I want to know what's ailing her and causing her so much pain. Her brother, obviously, has gone off the deep end. But I think it's more than that. I think she's hurting from the loss of humanity she feels in the world around her.

I thread my fingers through her soft brown hair and she gives me a dull look in her standing mirror.

"What's going on inside here?" I tap the side of her head and she sullens, pulling away. It's been a few days since we brought Edgar back to Alkrose and she's still like a walking corpse. The second exam is closing in and all the other students have been focused on training for the Blood

Crowns exam. I take a long breath and sigh. "You know, you could just—"

"I'm not turning off my emotions again," she snaps, crossing her arms and sitting on the edge of her bed.

I raise a brow and sit next to her. "And why is that?"

She glowers at me and I laugh.

"If you want to suffer, then suffer," I say with a shrug. Terra studies my features for a moment. She's the only person I've ever let get this close to me before, and I can't say I don't admire the way she takes me in like I'm so amusing. There's a distinctive trust in her eyes that makes me feel cold-hearted.

"How many times have you turned off your emotions completely?" she asks meekly.

I glance down at the floor. It's not something I need to even think about because I know the answer. "Only once."

Terra perks up and she leans closer to me. "Really?"

I nod. "I can understand why you don't want to turn it off again. It's hard to come back to your own mind after being numb to it all, isn't it?" A forlorn smile spreads across my lips. Her hand reaches up and smooths across my chin. The feeling warms my chest.

"I wasn't going to say anything, but after talking to Arthur, I think it's okay. I've been helping Raine find a cure for his blight," she admits. Terra's gaze grows distant but she shakes her intrusive thoughts. "I'm going to speak with Kallos. He knows how to get rid of it."

I flinch. I wasn't aware she was helping Raine research a cure for the blight. Didn't I tell him not to mention it to her? I lower my shoulders and groan internally. Good thing they didn't run off telling everyone.

"Then go speak with him," I mutter indifferently.

She shoves me and I play along, falling back on her bed. Terra stands and looks down at me with that serious look she gets when she studies. I've grown fond of it.

"Come with me," she begs and I can't help but laugh.

"No. I won't be doing that. You seem reliant on Arthur though, have him go with you. He's chummy with Kallos."

Her brow raises. "Do you not get along with Kallos?"

I stare emptily at her ceiling, the stars and novas colliding and burning into the universe. Of course we get along. He's one of the first Shadows, like I am, but I'll always be the outcast. Always the burden. If he truly has the cure, it's only because I blighted our comrades. It's my fault and I don't feel like facing those demons today.

I settle for shutting my eyes and muttering, "Don't press me on this, sweetheart."

She huffs but goes back to her desk to continue her studies.

I get up and leave after staring at her ceiling for the better part of thirty minutes. The homeroom has been empty since Edgar's incident. It's almost as if no Novas are here at all. Just like it was before.

My study is cold. I leave the fireplace off and sit in the dark for a while, thinking of long-dead ghosts and how I wasn't there for Kallos after it all went down. I fist my hands through my hair and lower my head.

Don't think about it. Don't let them in, I chide myself.

I'll never be able to make up for those sins. Not ever.

46

Finn

Kai and Corvus leave for dinner. I wave them off and stay behind, lying back on the homeroom sofa and trying to decide whether I want to visit Edgar in the infirmary. Kallos told me that Edgar will be there until the exam. I've known him since we were children, yet I don't think it'd be right for me to go. Fuck, what would I even say to him? *"Sorry, you got all your friends butchered?"*

The more we try to fix things, the worse it gets.

The door clicks and I lift my head to see who's already back from dinner. Terra stands there, looking at me with the familiar kind eyes I remember from our time before the Skyfell. I smile at her and she walks over to me, sitting down on the sofa and hugging me tightly. I lower my arm around her and breathe in her pine scent.

"I thought we weren't meeting until tonight?" I ask in a hushed voice. She nuzzles into my arms more and my smile stretches. "I'm not complaining."

"Tell me everything is going to be okay." She buries her face into my shoulder as I lean back more, letting our bodies rest comfortably on the couch.

I hesitate, squeezing my arms around her tighter. "You know I can't lie to you. I wish more than anything that I could, but after Edgar—" I whisper painfully, letting the sentence die out because she knows as well as I do how it ends.

She lets a few sad half laughs out and pulls away slowly. Her eyes are rimmed with red, not from crying but from exhaustion. The love of my life looks so fucking tired.

"I know," she murmurs and draws circles on my arm, resting her head. We cuddle for a while and discuss Shadows and what we're expecting to come from the second exam.

"I wonder how many of us are going to be sent to Whales of Tauh," Terra whispers. It's morbid, but it's very likely we'll be sent there. "I don't want to kill people, Finn."

Her heart has always been her weakness. Aren't morals what keeps us human and sane, though? I hope she never gives in to the darkness.

I think for a moment, rubbing my thumb across her shoulder. "I'll kill if I have to. Even in the exam, we probably won't have a choice."

She stills beside me. "What if you get sent to Whales?

Will you kill our own people in cold blood?" Her question is cruel but she doesn't say it unkindly. She's honestly asking.

My stomach turns sour. "That won't happen."

"Why?"

"Because Whales of Tauh is a fortress stronger than any other in the world. It would take an insane amount of power to get through their walls. And the fact that even Elias can't get into the city speaks volumes. Even if Fernestia somehow breaks in, I wouldn't fight."

She sits up and her lips form a thin line. I raise a brow. Does she know something?

"What?" I ask.

"Elias is the one who summons the Skyfell; he's like their beacon. So as long as he can't get inside the walls to the city—" She pauses, taking in my horrified expression and swallowing hard.

"He's the one who... caused the Skyfell?" My chest constricts. I know Terra didn't do any of this and isn't responsible, yet it still feels like she's betrayed me. How can she even still speak to him? He's a monster.

"Finn, I—"

"Stop," I warn her and she deflates a little. "Do you realize how many people he alone has killed?" I stand and walk across the room to look at her from a distance. Sweat is building along my temples and I feel like I'm going to vomit.

Her expression sullens with guilt as she says, "Anyone with gray eyes is being controlled by the headmaster. Even if he doesn't want to, he has no choice but to obey."

My eyes widen and I pace, thinking of all the times

Nekane tried to coerce us into letting the Shadows sink in further until our eyes grayed. *Is that why?* It's yet another secret she's kept from me, and it stings.

"But only Nekane and Kallos have colored eyes still," I mutter.

She nods. "The headmaster has all of their hearts except them. They managed to keep theirs somehow. Kallos has the answers. All of them, I'm certain of it." She stands and meets my anguished gaze. "He knows how to reverse the blight and maybe even how to stop all of this. Something tells me he's been trying to hatch a plan all this time. Maybe he's just been waiting for students like us to help. Ones he can trust."

If that's true, then... there might still be hope for us.

My fists clench at my sides and I look over at the door to his study.

"How could you keep this from me, Terra? What else do you know that you're hiding from me?" I cross my arms and clench my fists where she can't see. My jaw hurts from being flexed with rage. "I can't believe you chose him over me. That's really fucking low, even for you."

Her brows pinch with regret and she lowers her chin. "Finn, I'm not trying to keep things from you. I promise I'll tell you everything when you've calmed down, okay?" She looks over at Kallos's study. I know she wants to skip past this so she can save her precious Raine.

"Fine."

Terra blinks at me with gratitude. "We're not letting him out of there without answers," she says with determination. "The blight ends tonight."

47

Terra

Finn keeps his arms firmly crossed over his chest; he's pissed that I didn't tell him about Elias sooner. I sink further in the seat next to him and try to avoid Kallos's haughty gaze from across his messy desk.

"Where is Raine?" The professor breaks the silence and my throat tightens at the sound of his name.

He's slowly dying, as Arthur said they do in the first stages—his energy is depleted and his lethargy has worsened. The blight is taking over rapidly.

I open my eyes slowly, taking a long, weary breath. "Raine hasn't been feeling well. I'm worried the blight will take him soon... so please—" I pause and look Kallos directly in the eyes, devoid of any gray. "*Please.* Give me the cure for the blight."

Finn turns to look at me, his pity visible, but I keep my gaze on Kallos.

The professor holds my eyes for a few long moments before deflating in his red, throne-like chair. Long strands of blonde hair lie over his shoulders, and a few fall over his forehead. He leans into his palm, cupping his jaw with his elbow perched on the armrest.

"The cure. Do you truly believe there is one, Miss Eldridge?" He laughs coldly as his eyes trail down to the note I found in the library. It sits squarely in the center of his massive desk. Kallos's eyes grow distant with memories, perhaps of his younger self who wrote it.

"Kallos?" Finn says hesitantly.

Kallos lets out a long breath and shuts his eyes. "No such thing exists. I wrote that note when I was filled with hope and defiance like you two are." His voice is pained and my heart starts to crack. *No.* "I'm sorry, Terra. You've been chasing mere wishes. This world is cruel. Starved. Relentless to the people we care the most for." He reaches down and touches the note dearly before handing it back to me. "Best say your goodbyes while you still can."

No.

"You're lying," I snap, standing abruptly and slamming my hands on Kallos's desk.

Finn stands just as quickly, setting his hand on my shoulder as he whispers, "Terra."

I know all the things he wants to say because he's said them so many times before. Finn has a kind heart as deep as the ocean itself. Yet nothing he can say will change the way my soul is eroding at this moment.

Shut it off. It's okay, Amser whispers inside me.

No.

No, Raine doesn't deserve this. And I'm the one responsible. I blighted him. I did this. ME.

"Terra," Raine's voice rasps behind me. Finn and I snap our heads to him, shock widening our eyes. My precious Raine, damaged and tired, stands there like this is all fine. "We did our best," he says sadly.

I run to him, throwing my arms around his torso and crying the second my face hits his chest. I can feel his ribs beneath his shirt. I clutch onto him, and Amser does the same with his Shadow, pulling it to his surface and longing for his fate to be different.

Raine pulls me back far enough to look down at me. His eyes are fully gray now. He leans down and presses a bittersweet kiss to my lips. I yearn to stay connected to him forever.

"Your eyes." I let my fingertips glide across his temples and he looks at me like a defeated, tired man. He's given up; I can see. I'll dig his heart out of Za'Afiel with my bare hands. I'll find it and give it back to him after I fix the blight. I *will* fix it.

The sound of Kallos's chair sliding across the tiles draws our attention. I turn as the professor slowly makes his way around his desk and to a photo on the wall—him and his comrades.

Kallos stands before the picture and stares at it with nostalgic eyes. He brings his hand up and caresses one of the girl's faces. At this moment, I realize she was the one he was trying to save six years ago. He's too young to wear this heartache, but it shines in his eyes undeniably.

Finn stands next to Kallos and mutters, "I'm sorry you couldn't save them."

Kallos looks over at Finn and nods thoughtfully. "I told you not to make any friends," the professor breathes out. He looks back at me and Raine, golden eyes filled with regret. "It brings nothing but pain... *But*, there is something you can try that may remove the blight."

My lungs seize and Raine stills beside me, his hand engulfing mine and squeezing.

Kallos looks horrified that he's even considering telling us but he goes on: "You have to place the blight in someone else. Transfer the curse to another... I made a mistake when I tried it on—" His voice cracks and he clears his throat. "I think I know now what went wrong, but either way, you'll have to place the blight on another soul. You have to take another's life."

A horrible smile crests my lips.

I realize now how evil a heart can truly be, how greedy it can become if the circumstances permit. Because I don't care as long as Raine gets to live and breathe and be by my side. I will become that which I despise the most if it means he gets to live.

"I'll do it," I say without a shadow of a doubt.

Finn's eyes widen at me, surely seeing me clearly for the monster I've become.

"No, you won't," Raine grits out. His eyes are anguished; he desperately wants to live. "I'll die and you'll forget me, babe. This is how our fates are meant to be. No amount of playing with other's lives will save me. Look at *him,* for gods' sakes. He lost everything. He couldn't save any of them." Raine's voice is shaky, his grip on my shoulders trembling.

"Raine, stop—" I cry.

"*No.* This is the end, Terra. This is how I go," he says definitively. No arguing or trying to get around it. "I've seen my death a million times. Over and over inside my head. This is the end of the line; this is where we must say goodbye."

Tears spill over my eyes. For some twisted reason, I start fucking laughing at all our wasted efforts.

"So what was all of this for then, Raine?!" I shout in his face.

His lips only pull up in a sad smile, and that tears my heart out more. He brushes the pad of his thumb across my cheek and presses a kiss to my forehead. "It was fun, wasn't it? Pretending we could find another way? I wanted to have one actual adventure with you. It was selfish of me to give you such hope. I even made myself believe a little."

My breath hitches and I fist his shirt tightly. "You knew all along? Raine... Raine." His name stings like fire in my throat. "I can't go on without you."

He laughs and pulls me in. "You can and you will."

Finn comes up behind me and wraps his arms around me too. I don't know how I'll carry this weight.

My eyes lift to Kallos. He watches the three of us cry and hold each other, and I see in his eyes the undying sadness of losing those he loved so dearly.

Someday soon, I'll have that look too.

Unless...

Kallos watches the darkness take hold in my eyes and his frown deepens. He knows what I've decided to do, and he nods grimly.

But who do I dare place this curse upon?

48

Edgar

Arthur stops by to inform me that I am still expected to participate in the Blood Crowns exam. I am to achieve the same goals as the others, alone, as punishment for trying to pass through my portal early.

I'm so tired and hollow that his words barely reach me. I move through the motions of leaving the infirmary and heading back to the Nova House to get dressed.

I zone out the terrified gasps and the way the other students give me a wide berth.

A monster. I am a monster.

Sully lingers ever so close in the back of my consciousness, scratching a long nail across my brain and waiting for me to let him in. It's all but broken the casts. It claws relentlessly through them, and the more despair I have, the stronger Sully becomes. The two casts that remain are brittle, and I know I can make it disappear without much effort.

The homeroom is empty and I'm grateful for it. Ash, Raine, and Terra are probably preparing for the exam. I slip into my room and avoid the mirror as I pull off my ragged pants and bandages. Surely my reflection will be even worse than what I've already seen of myself.

Slowly, I glance up, bracing myself for my new identity.

It takes everything I have not to look away.

I *am* a monster. I look undead. A walking and breathing corpse. A permanent reminder of what I've done.

My bones glisten in the warm glow of the room. Everything below my nose and cheeks consists of bone, teeth, and tendon. It's as if I'm wearing a mask.

My eyes trail down to my ribs. The center of my chest is flayed with a deep cut, charred black and maroon. A thin veil of sinew holds my organs; that veil flutters with my heartbeats and each breath I take.

Vomit lingers in the back of my throat but I swallow it down, turning sharply away from the mirror and toward the wardrobe. I carefully get into my tactical gear. Though my wounds appear painful, they aren't. It's impossible, yet here I am.

"Did you keep me alive?" I ask Sully. My voice isn't as eerie sounding as it was when I first awoke, but it's still hushed and damaged. I'm not sure someone with wounds like mine can ever talk properly again.

Sully snakes through my body. With major parts of myself missing, I find that I can feel it more vividly on the bare bones.

Sully responds, sounding like a voice behind a shut door, *Of course, I've learned hard lessons since losing the last one. If not for the cast that was placed on you, we could have saved all your friends. Now you're alone. As monstrous as me. It's their fault.* Its voice is as vile as the words it speaks.

I lower my eyes to my body again. With the tactical vest and gloves, it's hard to tell anything is wrong with my body. But my face is a different story.

"I have my sister," I say, though I don't sound so sure. I don't even know why I'm speaking with Sully. I know it has nothing but dreadful things to say and yet—

And yet she didn't tell you that the professors were planning on placing the casts, Sully says with a curt laugh. Its claws scratch the figurative door in my head and the sound gives me goosebumps.

She knew? My body stiffens and my stomach curls as tears sting my eyes.

Sully laughs again. It's annoying that it can read my thoughts so clearly. *If you let me sink fully into your heart, I'll help you destroy them. All of them.*

I look around the room for my boots and shove them on, tying them while I think about what it said.

"Everyone?" I murmur absently.

Everyone, Sully says vehemently. As if all humans are meant to perish. *Don't you want to see your friends again? Merge with me completely and you'll never be alone again.*

I was filled with so much rage before we stepped

through that portal, but now I only have despair and pain. Self-loathing.

As I walk across the bridge I notice students splitting into different groups in the courtyard below.

Arthur is sitting casually in one of the windowsills when I reach the bottom of the stairs. He looks unbothered and holds a dark notebook in his hand. He lowers it as he notices me.

"I'm sure you feel much better in a clean set of clothes," he says with a small smile. "I was waiting to escort you to your exam portal."

He leads me into the underground tower and I follow slowly behind. My punishment is to clear this exam alone. It seems fitting. I half hope I don't come out alive.

Arthur doesn't speak until we reach the doorway at the bottom.

"I'll be accompanying you," he says meagerly. I finally meet his gray eyes and raise a brow. He shrugs. "There's something I want to show you."

That draws a laugh from my chest. I hate the way it sounds leaving my mouth. "What could you possibly show me that would matter right now?"

He smiles. He seems a bit on edge compared to his normal placid behavior. "You'll see," he says as he opens the portal.

49

Finn

I don't sleep at all the night before the Blood Crowns exam. I haven't slept well since we retrieved Edgar. *Fuck*. I rub my eyes and sit up in the top bunk as sunlight peeks through the drapes.

Kai mumbles, "Couldn't sleep either?"

He swings his legs over the side of the bed and stands, stretching and groaning as I hop down from my bunk. Kai has dark rings beneath his eyes but smiles at me anyway.

"Yeah, I'm too anxious for today," I admit and start stretching too. Gods know what the day will bring. I really don't want to kill other students, but my hands may very well be red by the end of this.

"Me too, but hey, we'll be okay," he says with uncertainty, but there's hope in his eyes.

I pat him on the shoulder and bring him in for a tight hug. "We'll keep each other safe. No matter what."

The homeroom is quiet. Even Frederick doesn't bother stirring up the others; worry pulls on his frown. His gray eyes shift and he stares at me with a silent, lethal promise. Kallos doesn't bother pepping us up with a speech or explaining. His shoulders are heavy as he leads us down to the courtyard where the other Houses are waiting.

The sorting begins.

I had a feeling they'd be grouping us into teams, but as students move to different sides of the courtyard and intermix with other Shadow Houses, I'm not sure there is much reason behind it. Fifteen groups in total, each with around fifty students.

Kai gets put in a group with Terra and Corvus and a mix of other House students. Knowing they're together helps calm my nerves a little, but after seeing what happened to Edgar's friends, I haven't been able to shake the fear of what this exam will bring.

How strong the world really is compared to us.

Raine gets sorted over to my group and I let out an audible breath of relief. He walks over to me and crosses his arms like he's bored and has better things to be doing with his dwindling time. A strong facade that I see right through. Last night he was on the brink of breaking along with Terra.

Don't get me wrong, I want the guy to live, but Terra would destroy herself if she killed someone else for it.

I doubt I'm Raine's favorite person, based on how he looks at me when I talk to Terra, but as long as he's going to watch my back, I'll watch his.

"Any idea what the Blood Crowns will entail?" I ask as I watch the sorting continue.

Raine looks at me silently for a moment, as if considering whether I'm worth speaking to. I don't bother meeting his gaze; I'd rather see where Frederick is going. Somehow I'm not surprised when Kallos points him in our direction.

Revenge is a dark and resentful thing. Everyone says it's never worth it, but I disagree. My scowl deepens as I watch Frederick shove a few Dvars students to the side. I fucking hate him.

"I don't think we're allowed to kill our own teammates, so keep it together," Raine mumbles dully at me.

I take a long breath and finally look at him. He's a good inch taller than me but our features are oddly similar. His dark hair and broody demeanor always make me believe he saw dark days long before Fernestia came into the picture.

"We don't know that until the headmaster gives us our tasks," I reply sharply.

Raine quirks a brow. "You're right. Killing the people *in* our groups might be the task." There's no sign of doubt in his eyes and that's quite unsettling. I'm not sure Raine would spare my life should it come down to it.

The sorting finishes quickly and Headmaster Emerai finally stands before us on the hillside. His power is so immense that just his mere presence is enough to prickle your skin. He wears a different, thicker cloak today: black fabric with golden antlers that protrude from the top of his hood. It's difficult to believe that he's the headmaster since he's so young. All the professors are.

Headmaster Emerai smiles broadly and lets his eyes

flick over our heads like we're no more than lowly sheep. His eyes only falter when he stares at the Nova House students.

"Welcome to the Blood Crowns exam. I hope you have all prepared for today and are ready to get your hands dirty." Emerai raises his hand and lets his golden Shadow dust spill into the air. The dust weaves through the students in slow vines, like ribbons being led beneath water. I'm mystified each time he does this without fail, especially because his magic is so similar to Kallos's. "Each team will have a king or queen that they must protect from the other groups. Your goal as a group is to take out a rival monarch in order to pass. Once your team has slaughtered a royal, your team's exam will end and all of you will pass."

There's not a single gasp or uncomfortable shuffle of feet, but everyone's breaths have grown heavy and loud around me. The golden dust ribbons pass me before jerking oddly and returning to circle my legs.

The students in my group take a few generous steps away from me and even Raine's eyes glisten with concern.

You've got to be fucking kidding me.

Emerai's gaze finds me, and his smile grows more intriguing. "If your group executes another royal before your own dies, then your monarch is safe and will pass along with your team. This exam extends over a period of twenty-four hours. If your team fails to slay a royal *or* protect your own, then your group will proceed to the front lines in Whales of Tauh."

I trust Raine to remember all the rules because the headmaster's words are in one ear and out the other as the dust forms a gilded crown above my head. It's bright as fuck and is like a beacon in this cold, gray forest. My eyes shift to the others. Several other crowns are glowing brightly. The faces of each of the students beneath them are as pale as mine feels.

"You will bring me the head of a royal and place it in the bowl at the center of the arena. Once you've deposited the head, a Darkfly will come to collect you." The remainder of Emerai's power forms a sizable golden bowl at his feet. My stomach sinks and every single face on my team looks at me slowly, expressing dread for me and relief that they weren't selected.

My eyes naturally linger over Terra and I let out a long sigh of gratitude that she doesn't have a crown. But that relief is short-lived.

Kai stares at me with a long frown. The golden crown sits above his head like that of a king, but horror written all over his wide blue eyes.

"Fuck," I mutter under my breath, gritting my teeth.

There's no way everyone on our team is going to work together. My eyes shift to Frederick and I recoil at the way he stares at Kai with malice. *Like fucking hell I'm letting you cut my friend's head off.*

Raine nudges me and brings me out of my stupor. "We'll figure it out."

I groan, nodding and listening the best I can as Emerai continues: "You are not permitted to decapitate your own monarch and you will receive no assistance of any sort until your team has a head. Understood?"

No one speaks—we only look around anxiously at each other.

"Good. You will proceed to your portals now. May your Shadows be ferocious and guide you to victory."

Frederick wades through the moving students as we follow the Dvars House professor, Flik, back toward Alkrose's main tower. Raine stiffens beside me but says nothing as Frederick approaches us.

"Well, look who I'm stuck protecting today. You'd better pray to your dead mother tonight to thank her for this outcome. I was going to kill you just for shits and giggles, but now I can't. So I guess your other friend will have to do, yeah? How many of those do you have left anyway? I can't even remember what the first one looked like," Frederick says cruelly.

Neither can I. And that's his fault.

I swing at his face, my knuckles crashing into his jaw like a sledgehammer. Frederick loses his footing for a moment but jerks his head back toward me as if I merely slapped him.

He's a freak of nature. My palms become clammy as the edges of Frederick's lips start to fissure and split and his jaw lengthens like a snake.

"Hey, knock it off. Settle your drama after the exam. I actually *want* to win this," Raine says sternly, like a captain giving orders. My eyes widen at the sharpness in his voice but Frederick's mouth sews back together slowly as he huffs, giving me one final resentful look before turning to follow our group.

"So it's true," I mutter as we trail out of earshot of Frederick.

"What's true?"

"That you were the Captain of Barkovah after everyone left."

Raine shoves his hands into his pant pockets and sighs. "You're just now finding out?"

I shake my head. "No, but it's the first time I've believed it. There are others from Barkovah who arrived after you, and they talk about you like you're an idol. You were a hero to them and your leadership shows." One question has been bothering me for a while now, needling at my brain. "Did you ever see the previous captain?"

He tilts his head back in thought before shaking his head. "Can't say I ever saw the man. The people hated him though." My eyes widen and I look over at him. "He was hardly ever around and he was violent with anyone who crossed his path. There were rumors he'd even beat his own son."

I stare coldly at the tiles as we walk through the main floor of Alkrose. How did those rumors start? I thought we were perfectly hidden away in Navasik where that awful man could break his family one bruise at a time.

Thoughts of my father only make my throat dry.

The conversation dwindles as we come to a halt. Professor Flik smiles ominously at a large door, arched at the top and made of a fine wood. His light brown hair is curly and freckles are sprinkled across his nose. "Best of luck," the instructor says lightly. He doesn't care one bit if we'll return or not.

Flik opens the door and we step through single file. When the blinding lights fade, we're standing in the shade beneath a canopy of trees. They aren't pines and the air is considerably warmer here. Leaves flutter on the branches and the scent of pollen on a spring wind tickles my nose.

We've been sent to another faraway location.

Before I can even fully survey our surroundings, a serpent the size of a building tunnels around us and creates a black wall of smoke. Its head rests above the coils and looks around our team for predators.

"While I keep us safe, someone with high marks make a plan," Frederick says with a smug grin, ordering us around already. *That didn't take long.*

I swallow at the sheer size of Frederick's Shadow. I thought he was dangerous before, but it's much worse than I could have imagined.

Kai better stay hidden. I pray that Terra and Corvus can keep him safe.

50

Terra

Kai is having a full-blown heart attack.

There isn't much to say to him. So much for going down fighting; he's already given up.

"There's no way you guys can protect me. Oh my *gods*. I'm going to fucking die," he says over and over until Corvus smacks the back of his head.

"Shut up. We'll keep you safe," he growls.

"Are you kidding? You didn't see what Shadow magic does to a human body... It's awful," Kai snaps back at him. I think back to Noctili and the absolute weight of magic and blood in the air there.

Corvus narrows his eyes at his friend. "I saw what was left of Edgar as clear as day."

"You didn't see everything else, including what Elias

did to the Fernestians." Kai visibly pales and my stomach churns at the memory as well. It was much worse than that day in the field when we were traveling to Barkovah. It was in Noctili that I realized how starkly different our powers are. He's a god.

The three of us are the last to step through the portal on the second floor. This one isn't nearly as intimidating as the one in the basement. We're plunged into darkness for a few seconds before blinking through narrowed eyes at the harsh light.

We're in a forest. The trees are an unfamiliar species and the growth on the brush makes me assume we are in Cyprin or Lamnah. Their springs yield plants faster because of the warmer southern temperatures.

Branches beneath our group's shifting feet is the only sound as everyone takes in their surroundings. They slowly turn their heads to Kai. My eyes linger there too. The awful gilded crown atop his head glows dreadfully. It might as well be shouting to all around that we're here and waiting for an ambush.

"Well, don't just fucking stare at me!" Kai snaps at us and a cold fire I haven't seen blaze in his eyes before ignites. "You three, run a two-mile perimeter to see who's near us. Terra and Corvus will stick with me. The rest of you figure out who among you will make a barrier to protect me," he orders boldly.

Everyone stares at him with wide eyes, the stench of fear heavy in the air.

"Now!" Corvus shouts to back him up and it breaks their shock; they all scatter to their roles.

I frown. The three patrolling students look like they

might fall over at the sound of a branch snapping. "I think I should go with the patrol. Corvus will protect you, just make sure to stay hidden," I mutter and start walking away to join them.

Kai sighs and whispers, "Fine, but hurry back. I have a really bad feeling about this whole thing." I hold his gaze and nod grimly.

The dense forest stretches out in every conceivable direction. Visibility is low with all the shade, brush, and tree trunks. The three other students in our patrol are from the Polaris and Tauri Houses, so I'm glad I tagged along. If they ran into Cosmos students, they'd die swiftly without someone stronger to protect them.

I ride on Amser's back with the Polaris girl sitting behind me. My Shadow is the spitting image of Velis—if it weren't connected to my soul, I'd get the two mixed up. The other two students ride on a tall stag-like Shadow. Its horns are spindly and dissipate at the ends in a constant shadowy wisp. As demented as the Shadows are, I'll admit they are beautiful in their own dark way.

We're about to turn west to check the last side when the trees finally break and a large meadow opens before us. I signal to stop and we dismount our Shadows to huddle behind a bush.

The clearing is vast and empty, a terrible place for any

group to congregate unless they're trying to bait others into attacking first.

"There's movement over there," the male student from Tauri whispers. His eyes are incredibly perceptive; I don't see anything. I glance over at him. His pupils have shifted into mere slits, like a cat's.

"Should we get closer?" the Polaris female asks.

"No. We should get back to the group and let them know what we found, then come up with a plan from there," I instruct. Nekane's survival class taught me something, at least. *Don't take risks.*

The three of them nod and we mount our Shadows.

A dreadful sensation crawls up my spine as we turn. Amser speaks calmly inside my head, *You'd better run quickly if you want to escape them.*

My head jerks up and my heart beats erratically. "Shit, they know we're here. We can't lead them back to the group!" I hiss as our Shadows dash into the forest with wicked speed.

The cat-eyed male shouts, "What do we do?!"

My mind whirls and the only thing I can think of is to run in the opposite direction of our camp and try to get behind the pursuers. But we aren't even granted that small chance.

A bolt of black electricity strikes the two males on the elk Shadow, hollowing out their chests in a second. Their blood hits our backs like a hot wave of sticky tar. I inhale sharply and push down the panic that's rising inside me.

The Polaris girl behind me screams as they fall. The elk creature dances chaotically around their bodies for a moment before vanishing into dust. "Wait!" she shouts in my ear.

"They're already dead!" I growl. We shouldn't be out here killing each other like fucking animals. Fear is driving everyone fucking mad.

The Polaris girl trembles behind me and then a sharp pain pierces my ribs like ten daggers in my flesh. When I glance down, I see her sharp fingers, black at the edges, plunged into my torso.

Amser hisses inside my veins viciously and I feel that hatred in my soul grow.

I elbow the Polaris female in the face and Amser twists violently to throw her off. Her body hits the ground hard and she rolls like a ragdoll until her spine hits a tree. She throws her head back in an eerie scream filled with despair.

My stomach curls and I swallow the bile in my throat. Amser doesn't give me another second to think before it takes off sprinting again. The female screams and cries until a sharp snap reverberates through the canopy. Then it's awfully quiet besides the sound of Amser's rushing paw steps.

Shit. "Why did she do that?" I grit my teeth and hold my sides. I'm healing, but slower than usual. She must've had poison in her claws.

Her Shadow longed for one of those males, Amser replies, even though I wasn't necessarily asking it directly.

"So she tried to kill me over it?" I grip Amser's spine harder and glance back to see if we're still being followed. The silence suggests that I've lost them. "We need to get back to the group. Quickly!" I hiss under my breath.

Kai's crown is visible from over a hundred feet away. Panic races alongside me as I dismount and push him low to the ground.

"Gods, what happened?" Kai breathes. Corvus doesn't need an explanation. He already knows based on the fact that I've returned alone.

"They're coming," Corvus says, almost to himself. He lifts his head to speak to the others. "Get ready, they're coming. Search for their crowned student so we can finish this!"

Kai curses and shuts his eyes, releasing his Shadow from his veins, and I feel a bit of relief as it pools around him and forms a protective cloak of sorts. "Thanks, Nekane, for your object-forming tangents," he mutters. I'm a bit remiss that I didn't take those tangents as seriously as Kai clearly did.

A silence falls over us as we wait, hiding beneath bushes and in the trees high above, some standing out front bravely, their Shadows apart from their bodies and giving our clearing an inky appearance. The wind dies down and sends an unsettling dread through my body.

A shard of black pierces one of the students standing before us. They fall to the ground without so much as a cry. The shard protrudes horribly from their skull.

Then utter chaos unfolds.

Thirty-some people rush from the front. Our teammates fall from the trees like hunted birds falling to their fates. Shadows of all shapes and sizes clash into one another and the scent of blood invades my senses.

"Do you see the crown?!" Corvus shouts over the screams. Growls from Shadows erupt from all around us. Dirt smears his usually impeccably clean face.

Kai blocks his eyes with his forearm as a wave of dust and blood blows across us. My lungs squeeze with the assault and I cough until the dust clears. Metallic flavors bloom across my tongue and I have no choice but to try and ignore the taste of death.

I search through squinted eyes across what now is a battlefield. Falling trees shake the ground beneath our feet, but I don't see any crowns—

My heart stops and I swallow hard.

A gilded crown shines through the crimson smog, and a familiar deathly flame flickers around the person walking towards us. I don't need to wait to see his face. I know it's Finn.

"He doesn't know it's our group he's attacking!" I shout at Kai and Corvus before bolting blindly toward Finn, dodging warring creatures and humans alike along the way.

The blood smog breaks as I get within a few feet of Finn, and the world seems to slow. Our eyes catch as he unleashes his phoenix, the beautiful creature encasing us in a whirlwind of fire that steals the air from my lungs in the blink of an eye.

Finn's amber gaze softens on me and a weary smile grows across his lips. I reach my hands up to his shoulders and he catches me. Our noses press together and I take a deep breath as death parades around us.

"You're attacking us," I mutter because I'm not sure what else to say.

"I see that." Finn chuckles softly. "I didn't know it was you."

His phoenix keeps us safe in its vortex. If I stare at him long enough, I'm certain I could stay trapped here in his embrace forever. Finn's dark hair lashes with the wind but his sharp jaw remains steadfast, orange flickering flames illuminating every smooth and hollow part of his lovely face.

He fists the back of my cloak against my skin and pulls me in tightly as he murmurs, "I was so worried about you, Terra. There's no world I can live in without you." He pulls back and presses his forehead to mine, staring into my eyes as the flames dance around us. He leans in and kisses me, a short brush of our lips imbued with so much affection. "Let's get Corvus and Kai and figure out what we're going to do."

I snap out of my momentary trance of Finn and his dancing fire.

"Yeah, where's Raine? He's in your group, isn't he?"

Finn nods and as he does, his Shadow takes to the sky, leaving us behind. The cold air around us is unwelcome now. The fighting has slowed as so many of our comrades are dead—for literally nothing. Guilt throbs through me but I don't have time to be sad.

Raine kicks a man on my team square in the chest, not even trying to follow through with a killing strike. He glances my way and his eyes light up. I run to him and he opens his arms wide to hug me. Finn follows slowly behind and frowns at our connection.

"We didn't know it was your—"

Finn cuts him off. "Yeah, we already established that. Let's stop the fighting."

Raine releases me and frowns, nodding toward Frederick, whose massive snake Shadow is flattening trees and people alike to create a wide-open space.

"Good luck stopping him. He wants Kai's crown," Raine says grudgingly. His jaw flexes and an irritated pinch pulls his brows.

Of course, Frederick is after Kai. Such a malevolent man pursuing frivolous greed.

"Finn!" Kai spots us through the clearing smog and runs to us with Corvus at his side. Their eyes are wide and alert, and I'm relieved only to see a few scuffs and cuts on them.

Raine looks at the four of us and his eyes darken. "Let's just go before Frederick sees us. We can pass this stupid exam just by keeping our kings safe for twenty-four hours."

That's the method I prefer as well.

However, I wonder if this entire exam was based on that idea. *Like an experiment.* Dr. Cein looms in my mind, that faceless man. If each team refused to kill another crowned individual, there would be no death. There's nothing in the rules about refraining completely, only keeping your own king or queen safe. All this bloodshed was spurred on by fear.

"I agree," I say sternly. Finn looks at me as if considering his options, but nods.

"All right, let's get the fuck out of here then," Kai says

easily and darts toward the cover of the forest. We follow in silence, only speaking freely once we're out of earshot of Frederick.

The cries and sobs grow distant. We make a temporary campsite once the sun begins to set. My legs tremble—we opted for traveling by foot to keep our cover; Shadows aren't exactly a quiet way to make it through the forest. Their sheer size doesn't help either. Raine's dragon is too noticeable, same with Finn's phoenix.

Raine finds a hollowed-out tree base that forms a sort of cave. It's the largest tree I've ever seen, the trunk at least eight full arm-lengths around. The red-hued wood has an earthy, ancient scent.

We sit comfortably inside. It's an enormous space, uninhabited by animals, and we're lucky for it. Corvus takes up watch at the mouth of the trunk while we circle up and try to figure out our next move.

"I think we should stay here until the clock runs out," Kai mutters brazenly.

Finn's lips flatten and he shakes his head. "We'd be sitting ducks. We have to wait until daylight to do anything because our crowns will light up the entire forest at night, but we honestly might not even make it that long."

Corvus glances back at us and adds: "I know there are a few really good tracking Shadows in some of the other factions. They'll find us in hours if we're anywhere near them."

"I don't want to kill anyone. They're just students like us," I say hollowly, thinking of Elias's murderous ways and how empty he is. I don't want to become like him. But a worse thought crosses my mind as I remember what Kallos said last night.

This would be the perfect opportunity to pass on the blight. I squeeze my knees as I wrestle with my intrusive thoughts.

Finn leans closer to me and wraps his arm around my waist, pulling me close until our heads are resting against one another. "I don't either. We can get by with knocking people out if it comes down to it," he says with less certainty than I needed to hear.

Raine doesn't seem convinced, but he keeps his silence.

We remain quiet as the night darkens. Cries and screams pick up again after a few hours.

I fall asleep and dream of class in Alkrose. How normal and sane it all felt until Edgar took his friends to Noctili. When my eyes open, Raine's shaking me by the shoulders, his gray eyes burning with terror.

"Run and don't look back."

51

Edgar

A cavern surrounds me, walls dripping with moisture. The roof of the cave is at least one hundred feet up and the rocks that form it are an odd dark blue hue. This place is damp and depressing.

I step forward and glance down at a substantial puddle. Drops from above ripple through it, making my reflection nothing more than a blurry ghost. But even that's enough for me to shiver at what I've become.

Arthur walks past me, his steps echoing throughout the cave. "This is the cave where all my comrades and I made oaths to one another," he murmurs nostalgically. I lift my head and watch him as he bends down, picking up a flat rock that fits in the palm of his hand. "We all had to make decisions, Edgar. Ones that brought us where we are today." He slowly looks over at me, gray eyes somber and knowing.

I stand beside him, gazing down at the flat stone in his hand. "Is this part of my exam?" I ask harshly.

He grunts out a low laugh. "Always eager to get straight to the gist of things, aren't you? I wanted to stop here first to show you the promises that we couldn't keep. That it wasn't our fault what we ended up doing. Sometimes one must consume the lesser poison, but it is poison all the same."

My brows pinch together. What is he trying to get at? "I'm sorry about your comrades, professor. It's easy to forget that you've gone through the same things I did."

Arthur smiles wearily. "Your heart is good, Edgar. Whatever comes to pass out there, don't forget that." I stare at him with confusion pulling on my expression. "To pass this exam, you must retrieve crowns from two of the groups. The headmaster has required you achieve this task alone since you went to Noctili, and you will need two instead of one like the rest of the groups."

My heart clenches tightly. "And how do I retrieve a crown?"

Arthur's smile fades. His skin looks almost gray in this dark, gloomy cavern. "You must behead the person who wears it."

My shoulders feel so fucking heavy. I just want to sleep. "I have to cut two heads off?" I mutter distantly, thinking of the ease I feel about doing so and how disturbing that thought is.

"Yes. I'm sorry, Edgar, but if you don't get the two crowns, Headmaster Emerai will have you and your friends euthanized for disloyalty to Fernestia. If you cannot be controlled, you're no good to them." Arthur's voice is pained. He takes no pleasure in any of this.

But I still hate him.

My fingers curl, the bones of my fleshless hand cracking as I fist them tightly. Aervin and Lucina are all I have left—I won't lose them too.

Arthur frowns grimly at me and places the flat stone in my palm before walking toward the portal. "Good luck, Edgar," he says grimly as he vanishes. The door goes with him.

I look down at the plain stone and flip it over. There are words carved onto the surface. I grit my teeth at them.

A hollow laugh sounds from my skeletal mouth—giving in to my demons. Sully sinks deep into my chest and the last two casts shatter like they were nothing but glass. Undiluted power burrows into my bones, and when I open my eyes, I feel so much fucking better.

"All right, Sully. Let's ruin the world."

I drop the rock to the floor of the cave, the words facing up. I walk away from the promise they couldn't keep.

We will be the last of the Blood Crowns. We'll stop Fernestia and save the world.

52

Terra

The five of us bolt through the decaying forest. Screams of terror fill the night air and my lungs burn viciously with each step I take.

"What's happening?!" I shout over my shoulder as I dare to look back. The trees are draining of their color, as if the dirt sucks the life away from the roots. They shrivel before falling and breaking the earth with their hollowed trunks.

Finn's hand is clasped tightly over mine, fear blazing through his eyes. Raine, a few steps ahead of me, yells above the crashing trees, "Someone is getting rid of the forest, so we're all out in the open. Stay on high alert!" A tree falls in our path as he says the latter and more screams bellow in the distance.

"*Fuck*," Finn growls before pulling me in another direction. Kai and Corvus curse under their breath as well.

"Should we take to the sky?!" Kai yells but Finn shuts that idea down quickly.

"And be an obvious target with *two* crowns up in the sky for all to see?" Finn shouts back. The roar of the falling trees is deafening. Kai curses again between breaths.

We finally reach an opening and burst out into a large meadow. Four other groups are already gathered here too, opposing one another with their crowned students hidden in the center of the groups. Everyone seems too stunned to do anything. We all just watch as the trees crash to the ground. The entire forest is leveled in a matter of minutes.

Dust and black smoke rise from the debris and one sole individual stands in the center of the destruction, clutching the long black hair of a severed head dangling at his side.

"Edgar?" I whisper his name.

The students recoil at his power and disperse in different directions, herding their crowned individuals to the backs of their groups.

The five of us remain still, stunned and shocked, not certain yet if we should be running as well.

Edgar's lifeless eyes lift to me and he starts walking slowly towards us, raising his hand in front of him just as he did when he attacked me on the bridge.

"Move, now!" Raine shoves me behind him as his Shadow falls over his shoulders as heavy black smoke. Finn doesn't waste a second, pulling me to run, but I can't unlock my eyes from my brother.

More than anything I don't want to give up on him, but he's not giving me a fucking choice anymore.

I plant my feet firmly and I tear my arm from Finn's grip. He looks back at me with surprise.

"We can't leave Raine to fight alone," I shout. Kai and Corvus stop running too and glance uncertainly at one another.

Finn's brows pull together in anguish but he nods. "Okay. Kai, keep going and keep your fucking head." It's not funny in the slightest but Kai bursts out laughing, maybe from the shock of it all.

"I'm staying," Kai says firmly.

I look back to Raine. Edgar approaches at the same slow pace, calm and forceful, the head in his hand bleeding profusely and making my stomach churn. It's one of the queens, her long black hair muddied from the ash of the trees and her own blood. It doesn't look cleanly cut; it looks like he ripped her head from her body.

Raine's Shadow grows to an enormous size, bones rising from the darkness around him and forming the ominous Shadow dragon I've only seen once before. The bones of wings rise into the sky, and an entire being made of nothing more than shadows and bones lets out a roar so deafening it shakes the ground.

"Are you sure he even needs our help?" Kai says in awe as the Shadow beast flies above us. Raine looks back at us. His eyes aren't as confident as his power suggests.

Amser calls from the back of my conscience. *Sully has broken all the casts. The Destiny Shadow cannot fight him alone.*

My stomach clenches and dread consumes me entirely. "Yes, he does need our help." I run back to Raine's side and ignore his angry shouts for me to flee.

Finn takes my other side and glares at Edgar. "We don't need to fight. You already have a crown," Finn says icily to my brother in an attempt to prevent any more bloodshed.

Edgar's soft brown hair is matted with crimson. His face is already horrifying with the missing flesh over his jaw and teeth, but there's something sinister in him now. More than just his Shadow's darkness. It's his own rage and malice too.

"I have to collect two," Edgar says eerily. His voice is a ghastly, broken sound. It shatters my heart because it makes him seem so inhuman.

"Two?" I say, eyes widening. How fucking terrible.

"It's nothing personal," Edgar mumbles as he raises both hands toward Finn and darkness whips out toward his neck. A flash of fire catches and lines Finn's neck like an iron neck guard. The darkness collides with Finn but he holds his footing.

For a moment, we stand in silence. It's too morbid to imagine how it came to this. How my sweet, pure-hearted brother became *this*.

I step forward, conjuring my power. Tick marks of time arch above my head like a clock. Edgar looks at me and a flicker of pain sears through him, but the emerald green that once lit his eyes is gone. An unsettling red has taken its place.

He looks like he's merged with Sully, but his eyes aren't gray. Amser speaks quietly in my mind. *The headmaster cannot control Sully. No other Shadow can.*

I grit my teeth and prepare to attack my own flesh and blood.

"Don't interfere, Terra." Edgar's eyes narrow on me.

It's too late for him. I'm not going to let him kill Kai or Finn.

I shut my eyes briefly, then imagine slicing his leg off. A second later, a flash of black cuts into Edgar's flesh and his legs sloshes to the ground. He throws his head back and laughs.

Kai vomits behind us. Raine doesn't wait to see if Edgar will retreat. His Shadow dragon sucks in air and a blinding light forms in its mouth. Not a fraction of a second passes before it unleashes its fury. It douses Edgar in a powerful assault, the strength of which causes the wind to lash around us violently.

I shield my eyes and sturdy my stance. My heart is wearing a hole through my chest.

The light vanishes, and Edgar is still standing. My chest sinks as I stare at his bleeding leg. He easily shielded the attack from Raine and dismissed the remnants of it with the flick of his fingers.

"No fucking way," Raine growls between gritted teeth.

My brother lifts his hands once more and aims for Finn. *It's now or never,* I tell myself as I instinctively pull Finn out of the way. Edgar's attack makes a snapping sound but is invisible to the naked eye. *Remember what Arthur taught you.*

I take a long, deep breath and link my fingers with Finn's. He looks at me, those amber eyes flashing with affection and fear.

"Do you trust me?" I ask as Raine's dragon collides with the ground and shakes the earth beneath us. Kai clings to Corvus as he unleashes his massive flying Shadow.

Finn looks at me steadily, unwavering. "Completely."

I siphon his Shadow into me. The space it takes burns like fire inside my flesh. Finn sucks in a breath and winces against the dust that surrounds us. His flames wisp around his body as if the phoenix is dancing at our power. My clock etched in the air in turquoise shines brightly with Finn's flames.

"Together," Finn says through gritted teeth.

The pain that burns inside me is agonizing but I smile weakly at him and nod. "Together." Then I shut my eyes and sever the Shadow perfectly, leeching Laphia from Finn.

The burning ceases and the dust clears as Edgar guts Raine's dragon. The Shadow cries out and withers away. Raine falls to his knee and looks a moment away from passing out. Sweat clings to his brow and his jaw clenches tightly.

"Edgar." I say his name not with rage, but with gentleness. His hate-filled eyes lift to me and I hold my hand up with resolve. The power inside me is strong enough to destroy him completely, but I hesitate.

He looks relieved when he sees the flames and time marks lingering above my head. He wants me to finish him.

But how can I?

He sees my hesitation and lunges for me, his Shadow emerging from his spine and crafting into a truly horrifying creature, a decrepit, bony person holding strings like a puppet master pulling at Edgar's limbs.

Amser roars inside me. *Now or never.*

That snaps me back. My jaw trembles but I crush the last remnants of our bond and let my Shadow loose. Amser erupts from my veins, cloaked in fire, bearing four tails and a vixen appearance as it descends on Edgar. It takes the strings of his Shadow between its teeth and severs them. Then it turns on my brother and ignites his entire body into an inferno.

The sight of his body going up in flames makes my knees give in and I fall to the dirt. Finn clutches me and helps me back to my feet, carrying me over to Raine. The three of us stand together, watching the flames in silence.

Amser looks at me for a moment and a flash of black strikes through its torso, sending it back into my vessel. I clutch my chest painfully and wince. Edgar lies on the ground with his arms spread out. He's burned badly, but his skin is already repairing itself. He slowly stands, lets a low chuckle out, and spits blood.

"Fine. I'll leave your precious friends alone, dear sister," he says coldly.

Edgar's skin completes its healing, leaving behind the cursed wounds that remain bony, and sways his gloved fingers over his leg. The blood vessels come to life on the detached portion of his limb and reach back up to his body in greeting, connecting with all the corresponding pieces. His bone aligns as he walks away from us without another word to find another crowned student.

We don't try to stop him.

"He's—" I trail off.

Finn bends down next to me, setting his hand on my shoulder and taking a deep breath.

"Let's just be grateful he took pity on us. I can't say I'll do the same for them," Raine says with disdain and I look up in time to see another group approaching us. They want our crowns.

"Raine, we—"

Corvus gives me a grim, understanding glance. "We have to, Terra. They aren't really giving us a choice and I want to get the fuck out of here in case Edgar has a change of heart."

There's always a choice, isn't there? To not be vile? What are we giving up if we concede to the dark? Perhaps this is what the exam was made to do: break our spirits. Loosen our hold on our humanity.

Two crowns glisten within the opposing group. The sun rises behind them, casting their faces in shadows. That shift in reality settles upon me.

I'll do it here. I will save Raine.

Silence ensues as I watch Finn's phoenix tear through the sky and rain down on them with flames too bright to look at. Kai and Corvus slice students across the chests with their Shadows extended on their arms like blades. And as the blood starts to tickle my nose, I shut my eyes slowly.

My Shadow shifts outside my body once more and attacks other Shadows approaching us. They bleed black liquid as the different creatures bite, stab, and tear at one another. It's all so volatile and raw. The heat of the massacre rolls into the dawn and I spot a male student reaching up and aiming an enormous ebony bow at Finn.

He will do.

I charge at him and place both hands on the male's

back, forcing all my focus into drawing the blight from Raine and funneling it into this vessel. I don't think of anything but the future I crave with Raine by my side. Amser thrums in my bones and a surge of energy passes through me and into the man's back.

The male cries out and falls to his knees, writhing and pulling himself into a ball as the blight takes hold of him. I stare at the man's face and horror falls over me as I realize what I've done. Who I've placed this curse upon.

Aervin.

Raine gasps behind me as he throws a lifeless body to his side. He looks from me to Aervin and back. His eyes are so much clearer than they've been and I think he might smile at me, but a forlorn frown pulls at his lips.

"Terra, *what have you done*?" he says in a low, disappointed voice.

My hands tremble and I look back down at Aervin. He was aiming right at Finn, wasn't he? His eyes are wide and he cries out in agony, clutching at his chest.

"I—I can't let you go, Raine," I cry and look up at him with desperation. He only gives me a sad, distant look before he lowers his head.

"I'll take care of the rest," Raine murmurs as he presses a weary kiss to the top of my head. I open my eyes and look at him, my lower lip quivering. He brushes his thumb over it, looking at me with great sorrow burning behind his eyes. "Don't watch."

But I do.

I watch as he walks past Finn and the others. He stops in the center of the battlefield, his dragon above roaring with fury that must resonate deep within Raine's own heart. I watch with a defeated frown and slumped shoulders as he reaches his hand up and fists the air. The students on the other teams still, their eyes wide with horror. Then Raine pulls his hand down quickly, and as he does, blood spurts from all of their noses. Brain matter mixes in the fluids that exit their skulls, drawing vomit to my throat. They fall one by one and then all at once.

Not a single person remains standing, and the stench of their deaths hangs heavily around us. My throat tightens and I want to scream. I want to leap into the depths of the sea and scream until I drown, taking all these horrible images with me.

I look down at Aervin, no longer squirming in pain. Blood leaks from his nose and his eyes stare far into the distance. His blonde hair is muddied from the ash.

A chill sets deep into my bones. I killed Edgar's friend after he spared mine.

I've become the one thing I hate most.

Raine wades through the bodies until he reaches the crowns. He bends down and severs their heads and then he stands in place and looks at what he's done. At least fifty bodies lie motionless around us. The ashy terrain provides a somber embrace for them.

Finn's phoenix dissipates into the air and Raine's dragon fades until it's nothing but black dust on the wind.

"We've become exactly what they wanted us to," I say in a hushed voice, staring at the bodies.

Finn falls to his knees and lets his head drop, but Kai starts to sob. His soft cries are all that I can hear as we gather ourselves enough to walk to the center of the arena.

Raine holds one head while Corvus holds the other. They cradle them gently, as if they can still feel. I guess it's better than the callous manner in which Edgar carried his.

"Raine," I mutter but he ignores me. I clench my hands at my sides. "Raine, I only did it to save you."

He finally looks back at me and grits his teeth. His lovely black hair is wind-blown and falls over his forehead messily. "I know," he says slowly and pauses. "But what did it cost you? What did it cost your brother?"

I flex my jaw to keep the tears from falling. "I didn't know it was Aervin."

"You can't trick fate. I wish you would've listened to me," Raine says sadly. The others look at us, not bothering to say anything. What *can* be said?

The gilded bowl glints in the distance and I let out a relieved breath. I want this to be over.

Edgar stands over the bowl, dropping two heads before we get close enough to draw his attention. He shoves his hands in his pockets and waits for Darkflies to arrive. He has his two crowns, so I guess now he doesn't want to hurt us.

We remain on guard as Raine and Corvus drop their heads into the gilded bowl. The six of us wear blood and silence alike.

I can't look at Edgar—because of my guilt and because he's no longer my brother.

After five minutes of waiting, someone else appears in the distance, a female, carrying a male comrade behind her. My heart falters as I catch sight of her white hair stained with blood.

Lucina has Aervin's limp body slung over her back, struggling to carry his weight, and she screams.

"Edgar—she killed Aervin!"

53

Terra

Edgar looks at Lucina with wide eyes, disbelief flickering across his gaze before he slowly trudges towards her. Lucina falls to the ground and Aervin's body topples off her shoulders.

His glazed-over eyes stare deep into my soul. I know his death is my fault. Finn and Kai make painful sounds no one should have to swallow. Aervin was their friend too, he trained with them, shared classes with them.

I did this.

Edgar falls to his knees beside Lucina and frantically searches her before trying to shake his friend awake. When Aervin remains very much dead, Edgar throws his head back and wails. The sound is twisted and eerie, his teeth bared, but his pain cuts into me all the same.

Finn shifts his feet with discomfort and that snaps Edgar's attention back at me.

There's a sea of betrayal in his red eyes. The white of them have gone black.

"I'm going to make you suffer until the very end. That's my promise to you, Terra," he says coldly as he stands.

Darkflies finally appear, but the second they do, Edgar's jaw ticks and the pure force of Edgar's Shadow smashes the soldiers apart. Their blood and entrails whip across my face and terror befalls me unlike any other.

I'm in shock and can't find the will to move at all. Raine sets his hand on my shoulder and I turn to look at him. His eyes are blue again and he doesn't look tired anymore. Just sad.

"This is goodbye, baby. I should have told you I loved you at least once—"

Edgar's at my side in the blink of an eye, his hand going straight through Raine's chest.

Time slows and the drops of blood that fly from the impact look like raindrops cascading around us. Raine doesn't react to the impact. Perhaps he's seen this fate a million times and has already felt what he does now. But my heart shatters in every conceivable way as he smirks at me one last time and slowly shuts those royal-blue eyes.

I raise my hands, calling on my time magic to reverse this clock. But Amser stays silent, letting Edgar take Raine to the ground and tear his heart straight out of his chest.

It may as well be my own heart.

Raine's neck arches and he lets out one pained groan

before his muscles relax and his body stills. Finn, Corvus, and Kai all watch, stunned.

I crumble to the ground and cradle Raine's head. His eyes are closed like he's only sleeping. Edgar tosses his heart into the gilded bowl carelessly.

Tears blind me as I retrieve his heart. It's still warm in my hands. I try to place it back into his chest. The others watch in silence, tears falling from their pained expressions. Edgar stands next to Lucina, who's still crying atop Aervin.

I force Amser harder this time. *Please, fix him.*

It responds, *Sully's will cannot be undone, little shadow. Destiny has come and gone.*

Veins protrude from my temples as I force power into my hands.

"Why?" I cry, speaking to Amser, but Edgar answers, eyes dull and void.

"You think I'm done? Finn's next."

Finn flinches, but Elias appears between Edgar and us. He looks at me for a split second before turning to Edgar.

"Killing Darkflies? That wasn't part of the exam," Elias says in a neutral tone. Kallos and Nekane show up a moment later and give us all grim looks.

My arms are wrapped around Raine. He's still warm and some part of me is holding onto hope that they can help.

"Go, *now*," Elias growls and Edgar levels me with one final glare before picking up his fallen comrade and following Nekane and Kallos through the portal. Lucina trails behind them. "You guys too."

Finn, Kai, and Corvus hesitate but Elias fists his hands and they reluctantly go, leaving me sitting in the ashes of the forest with my beautiful Raine sleeping upon my lap. His black hair is tangled with twigs, so I slowly start pulling them out. I rock myself as I whisper to him, "It's okay. I'm here, Raine."

Elias remains quiet for a few seconds before he kneels beside me, speaking softly now that we're alone. "He is gone, sweetheart." His voice is uneven. I look at him through blurry eyes. He swallows thickly and tears brim in his eyes.

"He can't be," I sob, pulling Raine closer and pressing my cheek against his. My eyes widen at the absence of warmth; his skin is quickly cooling.

The ruinous lump in my throat won't fade and my eyes burn with tears. I brush my thumb over his cheek and whisper, "I love you too, Raine. I should've told you."

Elias carries Raine's body back through the portal and I sway absently beside Finn's throughout the end of the exam ceremony.

Emerai is accompanied by the Empress of Fernestia, Raven. Her presence is formidable, but my mind and cares are elsewhere. They discuss what comes next for us here, what is expected as we prepare for the last stretch of war.

Finn holds me tightly and whispers reassuring things

into my ear. I wish I could hear him. I can only feel his kindness and the sorrow he sends me.

Once the ceremony ends, the surviving students retreat to their dorms.

But I can't go back to mine, not ever. Not to where Raine slept in my bed, not where his scent is still very much alive in my sheets. I want to die with him. It's my fault.

Arthur intervenes as I walk to the Cosmos dorm alongside Finn and Kai. Finn keeps his hand protectively over my shoulder. Kai looks so tired and worn down. His eyes are swollen from the tears shed today. I'm not sure he can even make it back to their room.

"Good evening. May I speak with you, Terra?" Arthur looks troubled and has a sympathetic look on his face like he already knows what happened during the exam.

I nod. "I'll be there in a second," I tell Finn.

Once he and Kai disappear down the hall, I look up at Arthur. The smooth planes of his cheekbones are hollow and his eyes carry so much dreariness.

"I'm sorry about Raine. He was always at your side, and there's something to be said for a companion so loyal." Arthur brushes a stray tear from my cheek. His soft gray eyes search mine.

"I don't want to forget him," I choke out, my voice wavering and choppy with my erratic breaths. It hurts so badly—I can't accept it.

Arthur pulls me in close. His black tactical gear and white cloak smell like torn pages and like... like Za'Afiel's empty hallways.

"I will remember him for all of you, don't worry—"

I cut Arthur short as I shove him away and turn, running as fast as I can down the corridor toward the southern tower. Arthur hurries behind me. "Terra, where are you going?" he calls out but I don't stop running.

I unclasp my white, bloodied cloak and let it fall to the tiles behind me. I take the path I remember from when Elias brought me to the manor before, finding the black door in an abandoned room. I don't wait for Arthur, throwing the ebony door open and jumping into the portal without a second thought.

The second my feet land on the other side I run through the cold, dark hallways. Silence and frost are all that stir here. Arthur's footsteps sound behind me.

"Terra, must we do this?" he says exasperatedly. "What are you looking for?"

I stop at the edge of the stairs and look back at him. His long, black hair is disheveled from the chase and he takes deep breaths.

"Raine's heart."

It's here. It has to be, that's why I couldn't heal him. His heart wasn't really there. It was a fake. It's here. *It is here.*

Arthur's face pales and he sucks in his lower lip before shaking his head slowly. "Oh, little shadow... no. It's not here." His voice trembles and my knees threaten to give out on me again.

"It's here. That's why it didn't work," I say shakily and start down the stairs. Arthur follows quickly after me. The dreary mansion is as cold as the water in the lake out front of Alkrose. My bones chill with each step I take and the lump in my throat becomes harder to swallow.

I trudge into the thick snow at the entrance to Za'Afiel. The snowstorm is raging and visibility is low. Arthur lets his hand fall heavily on my shoulder.

"Terra. There's nothing here but graves." His voice is strangled and I know he's thinking of all the children who were sent here to perish, buried beneath the snow in this awful fucking place.

Deep down, I know I'm in denial. I know it. But my body moves desperately all the same and my mind won't stop spinning.

I ignore him and walk to the cellar. The air is colder than before, the mildew scent distant from the frost. Arthur doesn't stop me as we walk down the steps slowly. I nudge the door open and step into the room at the bottom.

The piles of hearts that were once fluttering and alive are now mainly still and gray, a reflection of all the death the day brought. My lower lip trembles and Arthur lets out a low breath.

"Terra, I know this is hard, but there are no—"

"You can't see them," I shake my head and tears spill down my cheeks. "You can't see the hearts just like Elias couldn't, but they're here. They're all... dead." I hang my head and let out an agonized scream.

Arthur lets me scream until my lungs can't conjure the air any longer, standing still beside me with anguish burning his eyes.

My breaths are raspy and hurt so fucking bad.

He's really dead, isn't he?

"It's m-my fault," I croak and press my palms to my

eyes. "He's dead. And it's all my fault. I can't live with this, I can't."

Arthur steps closer to me and offers me his hand. I look up at him, my eyes stinging, but he simply smiles. His long, dark lashes kiss his cheeks as he shuts his eyes. "Take my hand. I want to show you something."

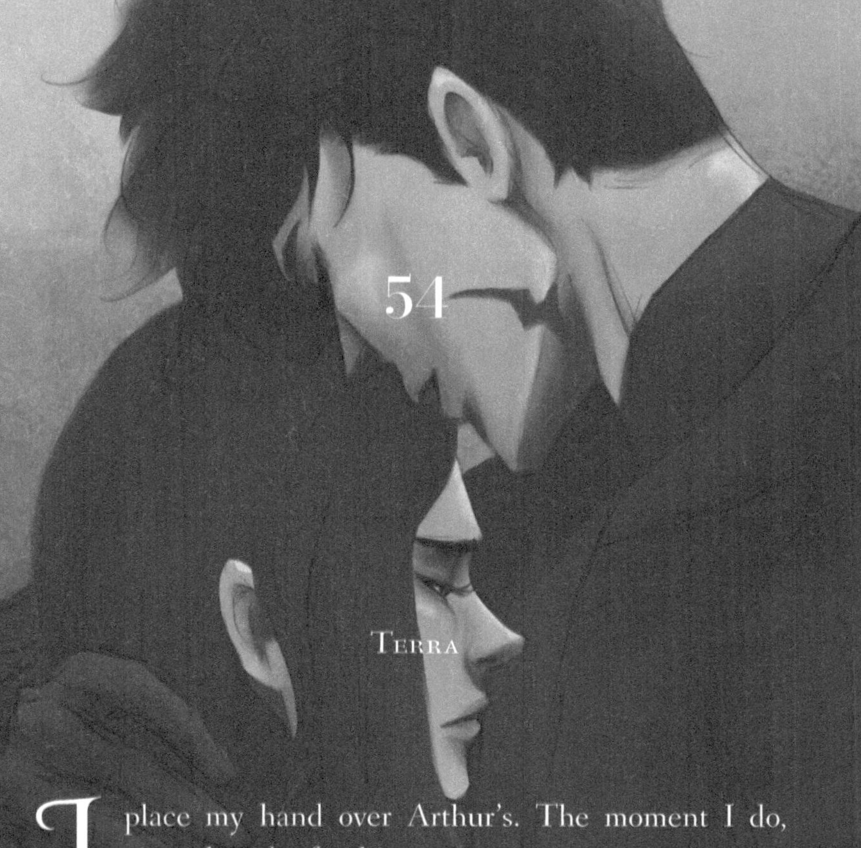

54

Terra

I place my hand over Arthur's. The moment I do, warmth and soft whispers swarm me.

It takes me a second, but Raine's presence engulfs me entirely, as if he's standing right next to me again and giving me looks or hugging me. I can't see anything, but I can hear him. Feel him. Smell his crisp scent. Tears spill from my eyes. I want nothing more than to be here forever.

When I open my eyes, a sense of both loss and acceptance overcome me. Arthur stares back at me, his mouth turned in a sympathetic smile, one that's not meant to be happy, but sad and reassuring.

"What was that just now?" I ask, still feeling Raine's

touch on my skin and his scent lingering around me. I wish I could wrap myself up in him and never wake up.

Arthur lowers his hand and lets go of me. The connection to Raine instantly ceases. "His memories," he says softly. "I will always have them. I'm the keeper of memories, after all. Anytime you find yourself losing pieces of him, I will show you. Again and again, if I need to."

"*Arthur*... thank you." I stare at his hand and feel more like myself again. The pain is still very much present, but there's something light about knowing I don't have to forget Raine like I've forgotten the others. There's a small amount of solace in that.

He nods and tilts his head. "Can we get back to Alkrose now? I'm afraid we'll freeze if we stay here much longer."

I decide I'm not going to wait for Elias to tell me when I can give Arthur his heart. The exam is done and I have to do it now.

"I have something I need to give you."

My room is dark, the only light my fireplace that never dies out. Arthur takes a seat at the edge of my bed as I rummage through the bottom drawer of my wardrobe.

I find his heart, still ebony and fluttering softly like a bird. My hands twitch as I recall how still and unmoving Raine's heart was. I take a deep breath and calm the war in my head. There aren't any tears left in me tonight.

Arthur raises a brow at me as I extend my hands to him, cupping his beating heart and wondering if he'll be able to break Emerai's hold on it.

"I know this looks like a stone, but trust me, this is your heart."

He raises both hands to accept it. His eyes widen the moment the stone touches his palms and the black heart pulses faster. My own quickens as Arthur's eyes narrow.

"Terra, how did you—"

"Why would you go and do that, sweetheart?"

Arthur and I flinch simultaneously and I turn to find Elias leaning against my doorframe, his arms crossed. The hallway is dark behind him. His eyes are impassive and a chill rolls down my neck at his demeanor.

"It's *his* heart, Elias. I wanted to return it to him." I look back to Arthur. His eyes are filled with turmoil. What's wrong? "Arthur?" I ask, leaning forward to touch his face.

Elias mutters behind me ominously, "You've just set the devil himself free."

My stomach sinks and Arthur looks at me, letting those tears fall onto his heart as he whispers, "I hate this part."

55

Edgar

Lucina sleeps by my side, her white hair spread over my sheets. Painful cries escape her lips.

I sit at the edge of the bed and glance down at her. My eyes are heavy but no rest will visit me. Sully hums in the back of my mind, *The girl is in pain.*

Yeah, and so is everyone else in this castle.

My gaze lingers around the hand I thrust through Raine's chest. The bones are stained red. I crack my neck and look away, not willing to see the horrible things I did today. For nothing, I might add.

Aervin is dead.

Lucina is dying.

Sully laughs darkly and scratches its long finger down my spine. *The girl is dying no matter what. I promised you'd see your friends again, didn't I? It's time for us to leave this place, Edgar. Time for us to make things better.*

I look down at Lucina once more. She winces in agony.

"What are you saying?" I ask Sully. My fingers twitch at my sides.

If you kill her, I'll bring them back. You've collected enough darkness to bring back three. She and that boy you're so upset about will be by your side forever. Sully plants the dark seed in my head, and the longer I think about it, the less I find wrong with the idea. She's dying no matter what I do.

Why shouldn't I make it painless for her?

I smile and let my hand glide across her cheek one last time. The warmth and softness of her lips will forever be a mystery to me. It will haunt my existence, but at least I can keep her here with me.

Her neck is weak. It takes only one swift jerk to snap it.

She never even woke up. What a pleasant thing I've done for her.

I brush her white strands from her face and press my bare teeth to her lips. A kiss she'll never know I gave her.

Sully shifts under my skin and whispers, *Good. Now wake them up. We are the Necromancer and play with the dead we shall.*

Power thrums through my bones and darkness crawls over Lucina's body, seeping into her skin and fading. I watch for a few moments as her eyes slowly open.

The whites of her eyes are black. The pain and fractures are gone. She sits up, swaying a bit before looking up at me absently.

Sully doesn't have to tell me that Lucina's soul isn't

here anymore, that much is evident. But she's breathing and moving and looking at me like I'm not a fucking monster.

Giddiness flows through me. I move through the castle quickly, Lucina trailing behind me in equal silence like a puppet. The professors left the pile of bodies from the exam in the courtyard to be burned at dawn.

And they think *I'm* the monster?

I find Aervin, his body covered in frost with the early morning spring air, but still very much intact. The darkness flows from my veins and into his, and when his eyes blink and open once more I start to cry. Holding my friend close, I say, "She took you from me. But you're okay now." I wipe my tears away. Aervin blinks at me and tilts his head. But when I smile, he reciprocates like a mirror and that's enough for me.

He and Lucina look at one another before returning their attention to me. I close my eyes and think of Vinnie, Rowan, Tamaris, and Alani, rueful that they couldn't be here with us.

Sully claws at the back of my mind. *You still have one more.*

That's right.

I look down and find Terra's beloved male. Raine.

He looks asleep and peaceful. How cruel it would be if she were to see him again, dead, a tool for my liking. I smile widely and let the darkness take him.

Raine's eyes open slowly and the world will suffer for it.

56

Finn

Terra should have been back by now.

I pace our room with dread. Kai passed out the second we got back but I can't rest until I know Terra is okay. Fuck, even my chest hurts with the loss of Raine. He wasn't very friendly, but I liked the guy.

My steps falter. I'm going to go look for her.

The Cosmos House is quiet. More of us survived than the other Shadow Houses, but everyone is worn out. I make my way through the homeroom and overhear Kallos in his study. His voice sounds unusually sharp and loud.

Curiosity gets the best of me and I press my ear against the door.

"What do you mean Arthur and Elias have their

hearts?" Kallos growls and—I assume—slams his fists against his desk.

A deep and familiar voice responds. "Exactly what I said. He has his heart. We'll be taking Whales of Tauh soon. Get your students ready."

There's a long pause and sweat drips down my nose.

"Yes, Dr. Cein."

I inhale a gasp and straighten. Dr. Cein? But why does he sound like...

The door swings open and Kallos gives me a disgruntled stare as he steps aside. The man behind him has gray hair streaked with dark strands of brown. His eyes are as evil as I remember, as auburn as my own. He wears Fernestia's black cloak, a sun emblem at the center. And the motherfucker smiles at me the same way he would when he'd beat me.

"Hello, son."

Acknowledgments

Wow. How is this the sixth book I've published!? I've met some pretty amazing people on this journey and guess what, all of them are readers!! That means YOU! Thank you to every single reader who takes a chance on my wild, dark stories. I wouldn't be able to publish as quickly and diligently without you!

I would also like to thank my beta readers, Kenzie and Jay. You are the real troopers. It's not easy to read a book in the first stages, the messy and raw stones that aren't yet polished. I'm so grateful for your insights and for all the support you give me. (Who else would tell me my beta draft isn't complete garbage?!)

Thank you to my proofreader, Cierra, for being so supportive and bright with ideas. You are so diligent and well versed in anything book related. You're my go to!!

Thank you to my husband for being a wonderful beta reader as well (he loves this series). Your constant support and feedback keeps my wheels turning!

About the Author

K. M. Moronova is a very dark-minded creature. She primarily writes dark romantasy books that are tragic and sad—often with mentally ill characters. She lives in the forests of Montana and craves adventure solely in her mind. She can be found most days drinking coffee and listening to sad songs as she dries flowers. Once the sun sets she brings out her laptop and writes all her woes away.

She also has a knack for drawing an outrageous amount of fan art of her characters.

instagram.com/K.M.Moronova

tiktok.com/@K.M.Moronova